"Mail, you two." Jubal tossed envelopes and small packages to us. Noelle caught hers with one hand. Mine landed in my lap. Something shifted, went sideways and down. I was sucked down with it, down, deep and fast. A spiral, a whirlpool. Blackness closed in. *Blood. So much blood. Pain. Pain.* I hurtled from the chair, scattering the mail. *"No!"*

I recoiled on the far side of the room. Bounced off the wall and cowered there. Scrunched against the corner. Slid down in a small heap of terror. Someone was screaming. Whimpering. Moaning. It was me. And I couldn't stop.

"Tyler?" Jubal's voice sliced through the agony.

I slapped a hand over my mouth to muffle the sound. And I stared at the packages. Three of them. *Blood and pain. Davie.*

"Get Evan. Get Bartlock," I whispered. "Close the store. Quick. Noe, go to the loft. Please. Keep Jane upstairs. Don't let her back down." With a sudden jab, the headache was there, just over my left eye. It rammed at me, a pickax of pain. I rocked back my head, eyes closed against the shrill ache and the sight of the boxes on the floor.

I didn't hear their responses, was aware only vaguely of movement. When I opened my eyes, all I could see was the packages, still scattered on the shop floor. I couldn't look away. I could only stare at the packets as tears ran down my face. *Davie. Oh, God. Davie.* Finally my moans went silent. And then I heard only the sound of my breathing.

I don't know how long it took Evan to get there, but he was huffing for breath when he arrived, coat lapels undone and flapping. He knelt in front of me, his hands cold on my face from an outside run. "What is it?" he asked me.

I focused on his eyes. Green, gentle. With odd-colored flecks in the irises, like the brown of old wood. "They cut Davie." I was whispering, tears a solid rain down my cheeks. "They sent me pieces of him."

GWEN
BLOODSTONE
HUNTER

MIRA®

ISBN 0-7783-2221-1

BLOODSTONE

Copyright © 2005 by Gwen Hunter.

www.MIRABooks.com

Printed in U.S.A.

ACKNOWLEDGMENTS

As always, this book could not have been written without
the knowledge and wisdom of those willing to help.
It was a labor of love, and for that I thank:

Daniel "Chip" Bailey—cop advice

Dawn Cook—writer advice

Pat Gentry—prayer

Jeff Gerecke—selling the novel

Norman Hege—advice about gold

Kathryn Hege—advice about jewelry

Mike Hege—advice about jewelry making, gold, and the odd
last-minute answer

Rod Hunter—great answers to odd questions and reading
Bloodstone repeatedly

Misty Massey—writer advice, and a last-minute reading that
saved my sanity

Sue Minix—writer advice

Benjamin Prater—tae kwon do information

Lynn Prater—pa information

Mike Prater—computer suggestions

Susan and Benson Prater—every weird question got an answer

Fran Riser—writer advice, and suggesting the town

Fazelle Scaggs—stone and rock and gem show advice

Miranda Stecyk—WOW! You are simply the best.
Long-distance hugs and kisses!

Larry Walker—the driveway, cows, fantastic view and being a
great host

Joyce Wright—my best reader, biggest fan

And many others who helped with this novel. Thank you all!

To my husband, Rod,
My Renaissance Man
In this our 20th year

1

Icy water dripped off my fingers as I turned the jagged stone into the light. I tilted the bucket that displayed uncut, unpolished rocks and lifted a block of greenish rough from its water bath. There were striations in the rough that might make it unstable. I flipped open my jeweler's loupe and studied the colors that swirled through the mottled bronzed petzite. It was lovely rough, but felt friable. It wasn't worth the risk to purchase it for cutting, carving and shaping, unless I could get it cheaper than the rock hound was asking. A lot cheaper. I named a rock-bottom price and when the owner was offended, I moved on.

Across the makeshift aisle in the old convention center, a man in a brown plaid shirt and khakis moved with me. He'd been in my area several times since I arrived at the rock-and-gem show, and I adjusted the backpack that was slung across my shoulder. Though there was little chance of a light-fingered theft in the crowded room, it paid to be cautious. And in such a crowded space, I couldn't draw on my natural gifts to read him. Too much emotional interference. The man in brown stopped at a display and lifted two uncut agate nodules.

Maybe I was being paranoid, but I was glad I'd left the

spring designs in the hotel safe. Security for the patterns was something new for all of us, but since the Oscars last year, we'd had to be more careful. Bloodstone Inc. became the hottest jewelry design company on the East Coast after Evelyn Crosby wore one of my ruby necklaces when she accepted her award. We were making money, and competitors weren't shy about trying to get advance notice of our concepts.

I smoothed down the Velcro closures on my pack and checked the strap hooking it to my belt. As if he knew he'd been seen, the brown man drifted away, but I got a good look at his face. Scruffy. Ordinary. Medium brown color scheme from hair to eyes to clothing to boots, as if he'd been designed for dull. He ducked his head as he moved into the aisle near the outer door.

In the next booth I caught a glimpse of something different. The fine hairs along my arms lifted in excitement. At the bottom of a white plastic bucket was a large lump of dark charcoal-tinted stone with one bluish nub where the owner had polished out a nickel-sized spot. When I pulled the double-fist-sized hunk of rock from its water bath into the light, I found I was holding a slab of labradorite. Its color was an unexpected deep shade of finely mottled blue, deeper than lapis, with pale blue swirls like water in the Mediterranean Sea. The color softened into water-green, wrapping around the blue like a lover's arms, hues soft and satiny.

I kept my face impassive, but put my canvas backpack on the display case and hefted the hunk of stone from hand to hand, turning it slowly. It was free of cracks and showed no evidence of damage from the elements. With a corner of a cloth attached to my jeans belt loop just for that purpose, I wiped the slab, scrubbing at its craggy surface. The blue swirled through and through.

"How much of this you got?" I asked before I even bothered to look at the booth proprietor.

"For you, Tyler, much as you want."

I looked up quickly. "How you doin', Rett?" I asked easily, hiding my disappointment. I figured the price had just gone up dramatically. That seemed to happen a lot now, as rock hounds followed the money to Bloodstone's successful door.

"Good 'nuff, I reckon. You can have that at a reasonable price, long as you give me a good deal back on a necklace and earrings set for the wife, cut from that bluest part right there." Everett Longworth nodded to the polished blue nub and scratched his belly with one hand while punching numbers into a nineteen-seventies adding machine with the other. "Emily Sue likes your work and I got me a twenty-five-year anniversary coming up in September. Lez you and me dicker some," he said with relish. Rett loved to dicker over stones. Any way he could get out of paying sales tax or reporting earnings to Uncle Sam was good by him. And Rett was enough of an emotional projector that I knew he liked me. That always helped.

We dickered. We settled on three lumps of rough labradorite for me and a good price—a really good price—for Longworth's sterling-silver-and-labradorite anniversary gift in a design that would be created just for Emily Sue, his long-suffering wife. Once we agreed on a price, Rett threw in several polished cabs of a lovely gray kyanite I could easily use and some freshwater blister pearls in the same shade as the cabochons. Two of the pearls were larger than the pad of my thumb and had a spectacular shape, flat and free-form. Noelle would flip over them. It was nice to know at least one of the rock hounds of my acquaintance wasn't trying to take me to the cleaners.

Deal concluded, a promissory note for an anniversary gift in Rett's hands, I pulled the backpack to me to add in the twenty pounds of well-wrapped rough and cabs, and unhooked the pack from its strap. I'd done well.

Pain slammed into me. In a single instant, time snapped and stretched. I lurched, hurled slowly forward across the labradorite. The world tilted. My breath left in a shocked spasm. I caught myself with both hands. Buckets of rough flew, stone and water in the air. A second blow made a one-two punch of pure agony. Piercing pain blossomed from both kidneys. Paralyzing. My knees collapsed. The display table smashed down beneath me. Air shot from my lungs. I had a glimpse of the brown man's face as I twisted in midair and landed on the concrete floor in a puddle of icy water, clattering stones, and a nearly electric misery. I saw a boot coming at me.

Everett shouted and surged forward. My backpack and canvas tote seemed to hang in midair for a single moment, then they whipped away. Bodies blurred by pain sped by. Time wrenched back as I curled up on the floor, tried to remember how to breathe and wondered whose blood was on my hands.

It was mine.

I was patched up in first aid, the big red cross painted on the wall next to the security sign. Spitting mad, I was left sitting on a stretcher in a sterile cubicle, my hand in a bowl of icky-looking brown cleanser, instead of being out on the convention-center floor looking for my assailant along with the security officers.

I was so mad I couldn't pick up anything from anyone around me, even the EMT guy only two feet away. It all was an emotional and mental haze. So much for the St. Claire family gift. Psychics-R-Us had failed me again. As usual, being a receptor for the mental and emotional feedback of others hadn't saved me from danger or prevented bad things from happening.

I'd cut my palm as I fell, most likely on a jagged piece of rough. I didn't tell the EMT that I'd been kidney-punched in addition to the flesh wound. He might have made me go to the hospital to pee in a cup, and I figured I could tell all by myself if my urine turned red and bloody.

The head of security, a pompous off-duty cop with the unlikely name of Tommy Thompson, stepped in from "reviewing the crime scene," as he'd called it when he slogged out the door ten minutes earlier. "You're lucky, little miss." He wiped his shiny forehead and huffed two quick breaths, winded by the thirty-yard walk. "He could have used a knife on you."

He could have used a bazooka, too, I thought, but I didn't say that.

"I've determined that the *in*cident took place in a location not covered by the *se*curity cameras. And further, that your backpack and canvas tote are both gone." He spoke as he pulled a form from his desk and started writing, detailing his startling observations for posterity I'd guess.

"Oh. Really?" I said.

"You could use a stitch or two," the paramedic on duty said, grinning into my face as if he had read my mind. *Now, wouldn't that be a change around.* "But if it was me, I'd just make do with the butterfly strips, ointment and a bandage, and take it easy."

"I'll take the latter."

"Your call." He gathered supplies and dried the icky-looking stuff off my hand prior to applying butterfly bandages. I hissed a breath when he pulled the first weird-looking adhesive strip across my flesh and closed the wound. It hurt like heck. The second strip wasn't any less painful.

"You had seen the man several times today, you said?" Tommy asked, dropping his bulk into a tired-looking chair and peering up at me from under his brows. When I nodded, he said, "And all you can tell me is he was medium height, medium weight and brown. Wonder why you didn't report him to the *se*curity department? That's what I'm wondering."

"I saw several people various times today. It's a pretty small crowd in an enclosed space." *You idiot.* "You want everyone here paranoid and reporting all the multiple sightings? It's a show, for pity's sa— Ow!"

"Sorry," the paramedic said, teeth showing in a grin. But he pulled a white elastic mesh tighter still as he wrapped my hand.

"How much you think he got?" Tommy asked.

"My money is in a wad in my jeans, along with my driver's license and credit card." I shrugged my shoulders to rearrange the wet shirt across them. It was cold in the room and the cloth was chilling. "But the value of the gems and rough exceeds seven thousand dollars."

Tommy whistled.

I agreed. It sucked an ostrich egg.

"If you'll let me see the tapes I'll be able to point him out. I'm sure," I said.

"This it?"

I looked up to see an elderly man in the doorway, the red cross bright on the wall behind him. His bald head seemed to rise out of a too-large collar, the security uniform making him look like a kid playing dress-up in his daddy's cop clothes. He was holding up my canvas backpack, the straps dangling.

"Yes!" I leaped down from the table, strawberry-blond braid flying, unsuccessfully trying to hide a grimace of pain. The paramedic sighed, a resigned sound that said he knew I was hurt worse than I had claimed. He finished wrapping my hand as the tiny security man dumped out my belongings on the stretcher.

"Good work, Lionel," Tommy T. said.

The tiny man grinned. "I fount 'em in the men's room in section D. In the back stall. I gathered 'em up and brung 'em here."

"Anything missing?" Tommy asked.

I plundered through the pile. The papers and notebook were still in the back pocket, which was surprising. The receipts for the precious metals I'd ordered from a rep I'd bumped into were still there. And the rough I had purchased earlier, and which would have been harder to replace than ID or mere money, was all tumbled in the backpack, including a hunk of green turquoise with vibrant colors I had paid way too much to obtain. The sizable hunk of rare African bloodstone rough was safe, still in its newsprint wrappings. More surprising, the small bag of ruby cabs and predrilled focal stones I had picked up for a paltry $5,000 was here, as well. Relief washed through me. Forgetting my discomfort, I counted the cabs. All fifteen were still in the pack. Either the thief had been chased off before he finished looking or he hadn't known what he had.

"What's missing? What's them?" Tommy T. asked, and poked the felt bag that held the rubies.

"Cabochons," I said, which was the truth as far as it went. I pocketed the bag and pawed through the pile again. "The card key for my room. It's gone." And why would anyone take only a room card key, unless they knew exactly what it was and where it should be used?

"Maybe I better call your *ho*tel and talk to *se*curity there to keep an eye out." Tommy T. picked up the old-fashioned phone. "What's your *ho*tel and room number?" I told him and he dialed out.

I looked at my watch. Over forty-five minutes had passed. I had deliberately chosen a hotel close to the old convention center so I could walk back and forth to the rock-and-gem show. If the thief had wanted into my room, he'd had plenty of time to be in and out by now.

Within minutes, Tommy discovered that my room door in the hotel was hanging open and the place had been tossed. "Spit and decay," I cursed as I listened to the conversation, cuss words from my youth.

"We'll bring the little miss right on over," Tommy said. "You'll meet us in the room with the *po*lice? We got an assault to report to them boys anyway. Yeah. Good 'nuff. Hang on and I'll step in the hallway a sec." Tommy T. carried the phone into the hallway and closed the door.

"Important cop business," the EMT said. "Not for the likes of us lesser creatures."

I grinned at the man and read his name tag. "I like you, Winston."

"Ditto, little miss."

I punched his arm and we both laughed, engaging in small talk as he secured the trailing end of the white elastic mesh wrapped around my hand.

Tommy T. reentered, hung up the phone and looked at me hard. "You wasn't by any chance carrying any drugs, was you, little miss?"

"No." *You caricature of a hillbilly cop,* I wanted to add.

"Contraband?"

"No. Not that I'd be stupid enough to tell you if I was, but no. I'm guessing he was after the spring designs. I'm Tyler St. Claire, of Bloodstone Inc. in Connersville. And there are certain competitors who might resort to theft if they thought they could get away with it."

"Uh-huh."

"The designs are in the hotel safe."

Tommy T. just looked at me hard, hands on his ample hips. I thanked the EMT, shook Lionel's hand for finding my bags and shouldered my belongings.

"My patrol unit is right outside the front entrance. I'll be taking you to the *ho*tel. Here, let me carry that for you." Tommy reached for the backpack.

I jerked it out of his way. The pack was staying on my person from now on. Tommy's face hardened and I mentally backpedaled at his expression. "I'd rather you run interference and, uh, keep your hands free to draw your gun if needed," I said. And found a sweet smile to go with the ridiculous words. It must have been the proper "little miss" thing to say because Tommy's face cleared. He nodded, adjusted his utility belt and secured the butt of his gun in response.

Well, goody. Big cop-man on the scene. "Okay if we stop by the booth where I was attacked and pick up the rough I had just bought?"

"I reckon I can keep a watch-out for you for a couple minutes. But you tell me if you see your brown man again. He might be back."

"Thank you, Captain," I said, padding his rank. I wanted to barf at my tone, but I had to use what worked. Feminine dependence and obsequious servility were the tickets to Tommy T.'s heart. And I didn't have time to be as sincerely irate as I wanted nor to give the man a lesson in behavior modification.

"Just a sergeant in the sheriff's department, little miss. But we aim to protect."

I smiled, bit my tongue and led the way to Rett's booth. I was cold, wet, starting to hurt, and an old-fashioned, redneck, chivalrous man could be useful. I happened to need a man with a gun and an entrée to the *po*lice for safety. A ride to the hotel was mighty handy, too, but I had a feeling that if he knew I considered him a free taxi, Tommy T. would have balked at the lift.

Back on the convention-center floor, it was short work to convince Everett that I was fine, collect my extra twenty pounds of rough and walk to Tommy's car. I settled into the rear of the cop car without demur and laid my head back for the short ride, thinking of a hot shower and clean, dry clothes. Rather than talking, Tommy T. whistled a breathy tune as we drove and it was almost pleasant.

The hotel room was another matter entirely.

* * *

My room had been ransacked. I dropped the heavy pack in the doorway and surveyed the mess. The hotel manager and a city cop were standing in the middle of the room and met my eyes with anger and suspicion. I just shook my head and closed my mouth. I'd be looking at me like that now, too, if I wasn't in my own shoes.

The tiny fridge had been left open, its contents on the carpet, the small unit turned on its side. The television set was pushed across the bureau, about to fall to the floor. The microwave was hanging open. The one comfortable chair had been upended, the bed had been stripped, the mattress half off, sheets in the corner. My clothes had been ripped from the suitcase and closet and thrown across the room. One of my favorite red cowboy boots was on the mattress, the other nowhere in sight.

The room safe had been ripped out of the closet and was split open. It looked like someone had attacked it with a log splitter and maul. It was in pieces of shattered plastic and hacked metal. I was glad I had put my good emerald earrings and my favorite necklace in the hotel safe along with the designs. The emerald pendant alone was insured for nearly five thousand bucks, but the replacement value would be much higher. I usually just stored them in the room. That would never happen again. As it was, the amethyst nuggets I had bought on the first day of the show and stored in the room safe were clearly goners.

A female officer with a dog on a leash entered and the manager went to stand in the doorway. The mutt was a black terrier mix with long legs and a tendency to quiver. It couldn't have weighed twenty pounds, and started to tour my room instantly. My eyes narrowed and I glared at Tommy T. who backed up a step. I had flown often enough to know a drug-sniffing dog when I saw one. "You have got to be kidding."

"Nobody took your valuable cabochons. Must a been looking for something," he defended himself.

"I told you—"

"I know what you tol' me. Won't take us but a few minutes to check out your story."

I rolled my eyes and moved into the room, righted the chair and sat. The cloth of my wet shirts and jeans stuck to the upholstery, a cold slime against my skin. This was ridiculous.

"Anything missing?" the manager asked.

I spotted my other red boot under the bedclothes and my other pair of jeans. Two sweaters, a jacket I hadn't worn to the show because the temps had risen overnight. Undies. I traveled light. Bending forward in the chair, I leaned over the safe to verify it was empty. I sighed. "Some amethyst I got yesterday. Maybe six hundred bucks' worth. I have a receipt somewhere."

"And why was they in the room safe and the other stuff in the hotel safe?" Tommy asked.

I scrubbed my face and counted to ten. Remembered to breathe past the irritation. "Convenience," I said. "Laziness," I added, and refused to say more.

Tommy made a snorting sound. "Might want to check out the backpack, too, while we got Omar here. Little miss was greatly interested in keeping it to herself. And she says nothing was stolen from it. Mighty strange, you ask me."

"You are a moron," I said distinctly. Tommy's face darkened, but the female dog-handler snickered, as if she might secretly agree. Omar just went on sniffing, showing no particular attention to anything.

After ten minutes, the deputy brought Omar to me. "Sorry, but would you let Omar sniff you?"

I sighed but slid to the floor by the chair and held out my arms for the small dog. The deputy appeared surprised by my action and maybe she hadn't intended for me to get on the floor, but it seemed the quickest way to get this nonsense over with. And besides, my back was really beginning to hurt. I propped against the chair and Omar sniffed all around me, paying particular attention to my shoes but not acting very excited about them. Which just proved that he was a male dog, because they were the latest sport wear by Lorenzo Banfi and any self-respecting female animal of any species would have been impressed.

"Nice shoes," the dog handler said.

I held up a foot and rotated my ankle to show off the lace-up. "Thanks."

When Omar was done, I asked permission, then ran a hand down his body and told him he was a good dog. And he was. A sweet-tempered mutt with happy black eyes that looked into mine with adoration. A dog who had never met a stranger or an enemy. I could put away my hope that he'd pee on Tommy T.'s leg for me. Omar went back to work.

"We'd like permission to see your belongings stored in the safe," Tommy said.

My temper shot into the royally PO'd stage in a single instant. My mouth took over before I could think. "And if I say no?"

Tommy T.'s face went permanently harsh, and I figured that meant he was tired of my glaring and immune to any womanly wiles I might have faked, had I not been so mad.

"I'd be forced to ask a judge to provide a warrant. And we'd likely find the need to hold you overnight for questioning."

"Let me get this right." I levered myself up from the floor. My back was stiffening and I was not exactly graceful, but anger gave me strength I might not have had otherwise. "I'm attacked in a public place and I'm the one being investigated?"

"Attacked. Hotel ransacked. Nothing taken. Or not much.

Mighty strange, you ask me." He hitched his utility belt for emphasis.

My mouth opened to argue. I wanted to tell Tommy T. he'd rue the day he took me on. I really wanted to slap him silly, but that would land me in jail. Instead, I blew out a hard breath. The cop was bigger than I was, both figuratively and literally. Fighting him would take time and resources I didn't have at the moment. And I had to face the fact that it did indeed look weird to have been attacked and so little taken. I reined in my temper, counting slowly to twenty with my eyes closed.

When I could speak without calling him a redneck, undereducated, inbred hillbilly, and getting myself into double trouble, I said, "Let's go." When he started to reply, I said, "You call me little miss again and I'll write a letter to the city or county board about your needing a course in social adjustment or whatever the heck they call it." The female cop laughed, a startled burst of sound. I figured she agreed that a moment of politically correct time-out would do the burly cop good. Tommy T. just glared.

2

I had been cleared of wrongdoing in everyone's eyes except Tommy T.'s and had returned to my room to clean up my belongings. The attack on the room's decor had worn out my welcome and I suddenly had no desire to return to the show for its last three hours. Most of the vendors would be packing up to leave and the best bargains of the entire weekend would take place on the leftover, picked-over items but I couldn't make myself care. My back was giving off little spasms of warning pain, my hand was throbbing, and I had a headache from the short and unprofitable spate of temper I had been forced to hold in. A temper hangover without the joy of a real row.

I took a hot shower, swallowed back two ibuprofen, layered on dry warm clothes and slid into the red boots. After checking out, I tossed my belongings into the back of the Geo Tracker and headed home early. I was nearly out of town when I had a sudden wild hair and did a U-turn at the bottom of a steep hill. I was in Asheville, there was a fabulous spa nearby. Why not indulge?

Lying in bed, just before midnight, I lifted a leg from my mattress and wiggled my toes. Polished nails caught the light.

I'd paid a small fortune for the leg waxing, massage, facial, manicure and spa pedicure but the afternoon of pampering had been worth every dime. My face was still tingling from the ginseng-and-pearl hydrating mask, and every muscle in my body felt loose and pliable from the hands and elbows of the masseuse. Even the bruised places on either side of my spine felt better. Noelle would have a fit that I took a spa day without her, but after being kidney-punched, I had deserved the indulgent hours preceding the drive home.

The dark, red-brown nail polish seemed to turn greenish in the candlelight, much like the hunk of greenish turquoise I had bartered over at the rock-and-gem show. The skin of the fist-sized turquoise rough was a vibrant burnished brown that seemed to bleed into the rich green nodules throughout. I had never seen such lovely turquoise. Pretty great-looking toes, too. Heat seeped into my bones, soothed the pain in my back.

The light flickered over the puckered scar on my left shoulder. I flexed my fist, twisting my head hard to the right. It was an old scar, an injury sustained when I fell on a pick as a young woman. I had nicked a tendon, leaving the shoulder occasionally stiff in winter. It had taught me a lesson most people learn as toddlers—never run with sharp objects.

I turned the page of the cheesy romance book I'd picked up at the spa and sipped the Blue Moon Blonde, its ice-crusted bottle catching the light of the full moon through my front window. Fragrant candlelight wavered beside my bed, haloing the wedding band on the bedside table where I had placed it when I took it off a year ago. Stan had wooed and won me and then dumped me for a bleached-blond bimbo. The bastard. I pushed the memory away.

I drank again and slipped lower against the pillows, the silk teddy shushing against the sheets, and finished off the bottle, twisted off the top of another. Despite the attack and the incident with Tommy T., the bruises and soreness, I had done better than expected at the show—I had done spectacularly well, in fact, selling almost all last year's remaining rough stock, trading for rough for the spring line and getting some polished cabs and focal stones I could use as is. And the rubies…. Just for the deal I'd scored on the rubies I deserved a moment of revelry, even if I had to carouse alone. One cab was of such vibrant red that I would recoup the entire seven grand from its sale alone.

With the exception of the stock stolen from the room safe, my losses had been few, and I hoped insurance would cover a portion of that. Yep, even with sore ribs and hand, a theft, a room ransacked, and a visit with a hillbilly cop, the show had been stellar. This year's rough stock I had picked out and brought home would cut and polish into exquisite pendants and focal stones. Picture agates from Arizona would marry perfectly to Jubal's asymmetrical silver and copper bezel settings and Noe's new line of dichroic glass beads.

Perhaps best of all, I had discovered the double-fist-sized hunk of African bloodstone rough that would work up into some of the shop's signature necklaces with bleeding-heart focal stones. Rich, vibrant bloodstone was increasingly rare in the world of lapidaries, and I counted myself lucky to have come across it. And Rett's simply sumptuous blue labradorite had stimulated an entire line of necklace designs. While getting my pedicure, I'd sketched out six fabulous new styles. All in all, a long, exhausting and delightfully successful event.

The cell phone rang and I jerked, focusing on the small gold unit, lights flashing all around its high-tech edge. It rang again, the sound crisp as breaking stone. I stared at the cell on the little table covered with candles, lotions, oils and unguents. The pleasure I'd been nursing drained away.

Again the tinny sound echoed into the cavern of the loft, and a slow-spreading dread twisted through me. Only bad things happened when the phone rang after midnight. I lifted the phone as it started its fourth ring, flicked my wrist to open it and said, "Tyler."

"There's a blood-aura on the moon tonight. I suggest you get out of the bed and get dressed. A policeman will be at your door momentarily."

"Aunt Matilda!" I started, as the line clicked dead. I tossed the cell to the table, threw off the covers and stood. "Blood-aura. There's no blood-aura. Crazy old woman." I pulled on a robe as the doorbell in the shop downstairs rang. Bending, I looked out the window, across the small porch I used in warmer seasons and up at the full moon, shining on a foot of fresh snow, brightening the entire world. A thin line of palest red circled the pure white orb. "Spit and decay!" I swore.

I slid my feet into slippers as the downstairs bell rang again, unrelenting. I tucked a three-pound sphere of polished bloodstone into a pocket as a weapon just in case Aunt Matilda was wrong about the occupation and intentions of my visitor.

Leaving the gas logs and candles burning, I raced down the steps, my heart in my throat. Not all blood-auras were evil, I told myself. Not all, but sometimes. When I was a kid, there was a blood-aura on a full moon. My mama had died. She had been killed less than an hour after Aunt Matilda had called to warn us all. The warning hadn't helped. Hadn't stopped the drunk driver from plowing into her car. Aunt Matilda's warnings never helped. The best I ever hoped from them was a single moment to catch my breath before I was pummeled by whatever she saw in her disastrous visions. But maybe this was one of the other times—a blood-aura that passed without incident. I could hope.

The stairway was cold and poorly lit, the treads creaking as I raced down. I found the keys to the shop on their ring at the foot of the stairs, turned off the security system, ran into the shop and unlocked the door. Without even looking through the window into the night, I heaved open the door. Icy air blasted in, chilling my bed-warm skin. Scent rose from my massaged flesh, a sweet, oiled aroma.

I looked up, into his face.

Cool eyes, green flecked with brown and blue, stared back at me, dark brown hair falling over his forehead, full lips against an austere expression, chin marked with a reddish haze of shadow. The breath hissed out of me. "What's happened?"

"Why do you think something's happened?" He looked interested. Professionally interested.

I stared into his face, feeling the tug of blood to blood. He felt it too; I could see his reaction in the narrowing of his eyes. *A St. Claire man. Had to be.* I shook my head to clear it. A strand of hair whipped my cheek. "A cop rings my bell after midnight and I'm not supposed to think something's happened?"

His eyes narrowed. "Who says I'm a cop?"

"My great-aunt." *Stupid.* Stupid, stupid, stupid thing to say—I saw it in his eyes. I looked around him. No cop car in the street. No uniform. Just a man in a well-cut suit. My shock at Aunt Matilda's call had turned me into a fool and a chatterbox. I shoved the lock of reddish-blond hair off my face.

He offered a black wallet, badge on one side, State Bureau of Investigation ID on the other. "SBI, Special Agent Evan Bartlock. Your great-aunt." It was neither question nor statement. It was a phrase weighted with mild disbelief.

A cop at my door. A *St. Claire* cop at my door. A sign from Aunt Matilda, stirring the pot as always, keeping a finger in my business? Or something worse? An icy draft swept up my robe and I shivered in reaction, clutching the lapels close. I should have put on jeans over the teddy. Something warmer than a robe. "Great-great-aunt, actually. She's psychic. Sort of."

Bartlock's eyes narrowed and grew thoughtful, as he considered me. Suddenly they started to twinkle. "And she sent you down to meet me. At midnight. In a bathrobe with a tiny bit of lace sticking out at the shoulder. Hope you don't mind if I find that just a bit implausible."

He was laughing at me, I could see it in the depths of his oddly colored eyes. My hackles rose. I tossed back my head and thrust out my chin. "She called just before you rang the bell the first time and told me you were here." I was talking too much. It sounded stupid. I sounded stupid.

Something was wrong. There was a St. Claire relative on my doorstep in Connersville, hundreds of miles from home, a man I'd never met as a child. Currents wafted between us, currents I hadn't felt with anyone except my brother. Currents that were part of the family gift. Sudden fear undulated through me. What had Aunt Matilda seen? I could almost hear the cop's heartbeat speed up. He knew something I didn't know. Did he think I was guilty of something? What did he think I'd done?

"Are you Tyler Walker?"

I stared into his eyes, shivers of trepidation running up my spine, weakening my limbs. My back, where knuckles had injured it, twinged beneath the robe. I nodded. I had been a Walker until I took back my maiden name, but I didn't say that. I'd found a bridle for my tongue in the fear of Aunt Matilda's portent and in the inexplicable presence of a man from back home.

"I'd like to ask you some questions. May I come in?"

I wanted to say no, but he was a cop. It would be smarter if I let him come in, rather than be stubborn and have him take me downtown to question me. Two cops in one day. Yep. Something was wrong. Confusion, traces of anger and fear warred within me.

I held the door open for him, keyed the lock shut, reset the alarm and led the way up the steps to the second-story loft. Heat wrapped around me like a warm hand as I entered my apartment. Evan Bartlock stopped just inside the door. I could feel him scanning the open area as I crossed the width of the vast space. On the way, I placed the bloodstone sphere back in the bowl of stone rounds. I felt more than saw him note the weapon he hadn't seen until now.

I stepped behind my dressing screen. "I need to change," I said, dropping the robe, pulling on jeans, a bulky sweater over the silk teddy. Fuzzy socks and navy suede slippers. I could feel his apprehension from across the room, his assessment. He didn't like that I was out of sight. I could almost feel his desire to pull his weapon.

The cell phone rang. I came from behind the screen, fished it from the bedside table where I had tossed it, knowing it was Aunt Matilda. Not assuming or guessing, as most people would have done, but *knowing. Knowing* in the way of my mother's people. And it made me want to scream.

The phone rang again in my hand. Nearly four hundred miles should have been far enough away to keep them out of my life. But there was a St. Claire man in my apartment, a St. Claire *cop,* and I *knew* Aunt Matilda was on the phone. *Spit and decay!* If not for the blood-aura, I'd think Aunt Matilda was meddling in my love life again, setting me up with a man she considered perfect. It wouldn't be the first time. But even Aunt Matilda couldn't manufacture a blood-aura. No, not matchmaking. Trouble.

The phone rang a third time.

"You going to answer that?"

I tossed the phone to him. "Why don't you answer?"

A strange look crossed his face as he caught it one-handed. He flipped open the phone and said, "Bartlock."

I curled up on the big cushy couch in front of the gas-log fireplace and pulled a lightweight throw over my feet. His cool green eyes flicked over me once, twice. Stared.

"Yes. *You're* her great-great-aunt? Why in hell didn't you tell me—sorry, Aunt Matilda. Why in heck didn't you tell me—"

Near the bed, candles twirled scented smoke up in lazy spirals. The small lamp cast a soft glow through the silk shade adorned with glass beads. To my left, over the tub, were four prints from a deck of eighteenth century Minchiate Tarot cards. The two at the top stood for my parents. The one on the bottom left was Fire, in honor of me. The bottom right print was the King of Cups, its gold foil catching the light just as the gold leaf in the original might have done. The King of Cups. A card I'd always associated with my brother, Davie.

Breath slowed and caught in my throat. There was trouble, and it involved Davie. I *knew* it. Great. Just great. What had Davie gotten into this time? Last time it was a woman who was already married. To two men. At the same time. And neither man wanted to lose her to a third, so they joined forces and came after him. I got to hold his hand as he recuperated from the broken arm and nose and various bruises.

"Aunt Matilda, I—"

Flames flickered from the gas logs, their heat suddenly offering no comfort. I pulled my attention from the prints, back to Evan's strange green eyes, listening.

Evan's face was a gathering storm. "Aunt Matilda, I—Thank you, ma'am. You are, of course, in charge."

Now what the heck did that mean?

A moment later he closed the phone. I wondered if he had hung up on Aunt Matilda or she on him. When he stared at the small gold phone I figured Aunt Matilda had broken the connection. She was notorious for abrupt endings. She hated technology of any kind. She claimed using the phone was physically painful, and only resorted to calling from deep in the South Carolina Low Country when there was an emergency.

The blood-aura portent was Davie. What had my brother done now?

Evan handed me the cell and our fingers brushed. A tingle curled up my arm and I flattened back into the couch. I wasn't looking for a man, and if I had been, he wouldn't have been a member of my estranged family, however distant, and a cop. Uh-uh. *No way, Aunt Matilda, you conniving old witch.* I had no intention of jumping this guy's bones, heading down a rose-strewn path to the altar, or presenting Aunt Matilda with a St. Claire baby fresh from my loins. And nothing my batty old aunt could do would change that.

I had a moment to wonder what kind of St. Claire the cop was, gifted or charlatan? The family boasted both kinds, from the ultrasensitive Aunt Matilda to my cousin Raynold, who was as head-blind as a dime-store mannequin. Bartlock was a cop, so I was betting on a little of both.

As he withdrew his hand, I noted his pinkie ring, a lapis cabochon in a handmade copper-and-silver setting, the band shaped like interlocking crosses. I pulled the coverlet closer to me, tossing the cell phone onto the table by the sofa arm.

"David St. Claire is your brother?"

I looked up at him towering over me, and recognized the big he-man ploy. "Oh, sit down. I know you're a huge tall brute and could snap me in two like a twig."

At my acerbic tone, he almost smiled before he pulled a side chair close and sat. The fireplace threw flickering shadows that darkened his five-o'clock shadow to the color of old mahogany.

"Aunt Matilda is your aunt, too?" I asked.

"David St. Claire is your brother?"

So, there wasn't going to be a give-and-take of information. *Cops.* I thought the word at him, imbuing it with all the derision I could muster. He didn't blink. Two questions answered. He was pretty much head-blind and he didn't rise to the bait of sarcasm. "Yeah." I looked at the wall clock shaped like a rooster and added, "And you do know it's after midnight, don't you?"

"Your brother owns several small businesses in town. Any problems with them? Financial? Personnel?"

He was going to be difficult. Two could play that game. I crossed my arms. "No."

He considered me for a moment, as if my body language had given me away. "You were raised by Dumont Lowe. You didn't take his name? There was never a formal adoption?"

"No," I said shortly. I saw no reason to go into the details of our choices.

"Are you aware that David's history nearly disappears off the map for over five years?"

"No."

"As far as we can tell, he didn't work, didn't draw unemployment, filed income taxes on an income of zero, paid no rent, had no driver's license, didn't vote. To all intents and purposes, he vanished. With the exception of the tax records, we can't find a single record of him anywhere. No bank records, no property-tax records, no arrests, traffic tickets, marriage license, nothing."

I hadn't known that. I thought only I had lost my brother during those years; now it seemed everyone had. *No marriage license?* I just looked at the cop.

"No reply?" he asked.

"You didn't ask a question."

Mild irritation flashed across Bartlock's features, quickly masked, and I settled in to a study of him. He was maybe mid to late thirties. As a cop he was an intensely focused man. On a personal level, he was distracted. He focused intently on me, seeing me as a cop would. I had an instant to notice that before he asked, "When is the last time you saw your brother?"

The question shot through me, an electric zinger that

singed every thought. Suddenly a state cop at my door took on sinister overtones. *The last time I saw my brother?* Why would he ask that, unless Davie…? Bartlock had told Aunt Matilda she was in charge. What in heck did that mean? Confusion whirled in my mind. *What had happened to Davie?* "What?"

He repeated his question as he flipped open a thin spiral notebook and clicked a pen, his fingers long with prominent knuckles. "When is the last time you saw David?" His clothes were of the best quality. Expensive duds for a cop. I noticed these things on one level, while on a deeper level my mind was trying to put strands of information together into a picture that made sense. It wasn't working.

"He dropped Jane off for a visit Friday morning, before school, before I left town."

"Where is Jane's mother?" he asked, a tone that was half statement, half clarification.

I figured he already had the family relationships all straight in his head. Now that he had gotten past my monosyllabic answers, he was establishing control with a series of questions. No surprise there; I'd seen cops do that on TV. But knowing did nothing to assuage my antagonism. "Jane's mother is dead. Why are you asking me this when you know the answer already."

A half smile touched his lips. "Just establishing the parameters, ma'am."

That was a half lie. I could feel it. "What's happened to David?"

"Why would you think something has happened to your brother?"

After Tommy T., I'd had more than my fill of cops today. I suddenly wanted to throw something at this one. A well-placed punch across his jaw would feel very satisfying— until the cuffs clicked in place. I closed my eyes. "What's your next question?"

"Are you and David close or was there the usual sibling tension?"

"Yes and yes. We talk often, mostly about Jane. She—" I stopped myself. "What's happened?" I opened my eyes and found him staring at the lit candles around my bed, which was turned down, the green floral comforter and peacock-patterned pillows mounded, dark green sheets looking rumpled.

"As a matter of fact—" he turned his gaze back, eyes implacable and piercing, like a scalpel in the hands of a skilled surgeon "—the police have a security video of him being attacked and dragged off."

The words were a fist, slammed into my chest. I opened my mouth in a small O, fingers curled into claws. All my bravado collapsed in a single moment of fear. "Is he hurt?"

"We don't know, ma'am."

And then I knew. This was no jealous-husband predicament. This was a true, baneful, blood-aura consequence. Evil. Just like the night my mama died. The words were a breath stuck in my throat, aching until I got them out. "He's missing? He's been kidnapped?"

"It appears so. But—"

"And Jane?" I interrupted. "Is she okay?"

"She's at home, so far as I know."

"When? When did it happen?"

"Today, just before ten in the morning."

I closed my eyes on the pain. I'd lost Davie for several years when I was a teen. He had packed his bags and left home and seemed to disappear off the face of the earth. Now I had found he really did disappear all those years ago. And he had done so again. I couldn't bear to lose my brother again. When I opened my eyes, Evan Bartlock wavered in my tears, the flames behind him dancing on water.

"Does Jane know?" I asked.

"I spoke to her and her bodyguard earlier this evening."

I should have been here for Jane. I looked over and spotted the little red light of my message machine, blinking, insistent. I dashed the tears from my eyes. "Is she okay?"

"As well as can be expected."

I shoved my fear deep down inside me. It was like swallowing a down-filled pillow, the panic expanding and choking as I tried to control it.

"Why does Jane have a bodyguard?" Bartlock asked.

I took a deep breath past the lump in my throat, fighting the dread. "Davie's rich. Rich people have security." When Bartlock looked skeptical, I added, "Quinn came to work for him not long after Davie came back to town. He's as much a gofer as a bodyguard. Why? Is he a suspect?"

The cop's eyes tightened and his words were as circumspect as his eyes. "Everyone is a suspect at this moment. Even you. As for suspects with an ax to grind, I would have expected there to be an awful lot of people in that category. Especially females. Your brother was free with his favors, which should make women angry with him, but oddly enough, he seems to leave behind a broad swath of happy conquests."

I chuckled, the sound faltering. "Oh, yeah. Women love Davie. The jealous husbands and boyfriends may be a dangerous possibility."

I looked at my phone system again, feeling the pull of my niece's misery. But I really didn't want to call Jane or check my messages while the cop was here. Unused energy coursed through me. I needed to be doing something, anything, but my usual strategy of springing into action and making things happen until the crisis was past wouldn't work right now. I didn't know enough to act.

I threw off the down coverlet and walked across the loft to the kitchen space, poured water into a copper kettle and turned on the gas stove. The blue flame made a whuffing sound as it lit. Jane must be going nuts. And Quinn would be no help. Anything more intellectually or emotionally demanding than shopping, working on the cars and motorcycles David collected, lifting heavy objects and stepping in front of a bullet from a would-be assassin was beyond him. Jane needed me. She would be heartbroken. "So where was Quinn when David was taken? What can you tell me?" I asked as I got out two mugs and added two scoops of herbal tea to the kettle. Chamomile and blackberry with rosehips to calm me.

When I turned around, Evan was right behind me, leaning casually against one of the round pillars that supported the roof, the pillar looking small next to his shoulders. The green faux marble column was two feet in diameter. The cop was much wider. One hand was in his pants' pocket, the suit coat pushed back, exposing the gold of a belt buckle and the curve of a leather gun holster. The other hand held the notebook and pen. He looked menacing, in a I-can-kick-anyone's-butt-'cause-I'm-a-cop kind of way.

"You want tea?"

"Sure. That'd be nice." His eyes were on my hair, which was still piled up on my head, untouched from my massage so many hours ago. Then his eyes clicked down over me, almost mechanically, in a meticulous scrutiny. There was nothing intimate in his expression, just curiosity, a professional preoccupation.

One little, two little, three little St. Claires... My brother's favorite ditty. Davie was in trouble. Real trouble. And he might need this skeptical St. Claire cop's help. Something deep inside me wanted to titter in fear. I turned back to the tea.

"Where have you been the last two days?"

"In Asheville. At a rock-and-gem show."

"Can anyone verify that?"

"You mean like witnesses? Sure. I was seen by people I

know. I have receipts for purchases I made. I had a spa day this afternoon—yesterday afternoon. I was never alone. You can check." I stopped, one hand arrested over the teakettle. Ten a.m... I clenched my hand, thinking.

"Can you give me names?" he asked.

I named three people I had bought from and offered the name of a man I had lunch with who had wanted to date me now that I was free. I had told the guy I wasn't ready. It was partially true. I would never be ready for a date with MacIntyre Ingram. There's one guy I wouldn't be attracted to if I went ten years without a man.

Though I didn't name Tommy Thompson and Lionel, not yet, I named several other people I had spoken with, barely hearing their names or their shops. I even offered to get Bartlock their addresses and phone numbers. He wanted them now, but they were still packed in my Tracker in the snow outside. He glanced out the nearest window at the snow-clogged, rooftop garden and agreed that morning was soon enough.

Finally I said, "Ten a.m." I crossed my arms over my chest and leaned back against the counter. "It might be connected, though I have no idea how. Ten was a little over two hours before I was attacked and robbed at the rock-and-gem show. Almost two hours before my room was ransacked. And it was weird—even in the robbery, almost nothing was taken." I felt a chill at my own words. "Are the two connected?"

Evan's eyes glowed a warm green as he considered the question. Maybe I should have felt uncomfortable under his unwavering look, his book-em-Danno-scrutiny; maybe he intended that I feel uncomfortable as some interrogation technique, but I didn't. Now that the shock had worn off, it was oddly soothing to have a St. Claire man in the room, even if he hadn't bothered to clarify exactly how we were related.

Bartlock jutted his chin toward my butterfly-stripped, bandaged hand. "That where you got hurt?"

"Yeah." I flexed my hand. It was throbbing, though I hadn't noticed until he drew my attention to it. "The security officer was Tommy Thompson, a sergeant in the county sheriff's department. A uniformed guy named Lionel found my bag. There was a city officer involved, too. He took the report about my room and the assault, but I don't remember his name. And a dog handler and her drug-sniffing dog named Omar."

"A drug dog?"

"Yeah. They called in the dog because hardly anything was taken. I guess Tommy T. thought it was weird, figured it was something I didn't want to mention to the cops, like drugs. It ticked me off at the time, but I have to admit that I couldn't blame him. It was all kinda creepy."

"I guess they didn't find anything. No pot, no crack, no meth."

"Good guess. Just aspirin and Midol."

Behind me, the kettle had started a warm sizzle. Using a metal strainer, I poured two mugs of hot tea. "Honey? Sweetener?" I asked, indicating the honey pot and the blue pottery container of yellow packets. He stood beside me, adding honey to his tea in a slow drizzle, then stirring.

"Was David hurt? You said you have a security video of him."

"Yeah. It looks like he might have been injured." There was a tone in his voice that sounded distinctly un-cop-like. As if aware of that, Evan cleared his throat and said, "It's probably too late to get the sergeant tonight, but I'll call and leave a message."

"Do you mind if I listen to mine?" I probably should have waited, but I couldn't. Worry for Jane was rising in me like a tide.

He sipped, eyes sliding down to mine. "Do you mind if I listen in or is that a polite way to ask me to leave?"

Rather than answer, I crossed the room and punched Play.

Seven were shop related and I skipped past them, saving them for business hours tomorrow. I listened for my personal messages, hitting the button until I heard the sound of Jane's voice. She was crying, asking why my cell phone was off, and begging me to call as the message clicked off. Knowing she would not be able to sleep after learning her father was missing, feeling guilty for turning off the cell while being pampered at the spa and not turning it back on until I got home, I wanted to dial her number right away. But the next message froze any thought of consoling my niece.

A mechanical voice said, "You have something of ours. We want it back or he'll die."

I stared at the message machine, red lights twinkling.

Evan was suddenly at my side. "Play it again."

Numb, I punched the play button and the voice said, "You have something of ours. We want it back or he'll die."

"Again."

I played the message again, fear quivering in my belly.

"What time did that come in?"

I looked at the readout and said, "Eight twenty-two this evening." Beside the time of the call should have been the caller's number. Instead I saw only a series of *x*'s. "Caller ID got nothing."

"I'll need that tape." When I removed a computer disc from the back of the machine, Evan's brows went up. "I don't think the local cops can access anything that sophisticated. I don't guess you could make a tape of it for me? And I'll still need the disc for evidence."

I popped the digital disc into the phone and found an old microcassette recorder in my electronics cabinet. I made two tapes of all the messages, gave Evan one tape and the disc, and popped a replacement disc back into the phone, saving one copy of the messages for myself, for later.

Evan placed his copy and the disc in a paper envelope, which he labeled with my name, the date and the model number of my answering machine. As he sealed the envelope, he said, "Pretty fancy electronics."

I shrugged. "Davie likes toys. He keeps me up-to-date electronically. Changes my hardware systems annually. He also writes computer programs and installs them on my systems. It can be a pain, but he likes to tinker." My brother was hurt.

"Now we have a ransom notice. Local cops will be around. And they'll likely want you to come to the station for an interview."

I jerked at the word *ransom. I had what they wanted. I had…*something *and they took Davie to get it back. What?*

"What do you have of David's?" Evan asked, echoing my thoughts.

"I don't…." A shiver shook me. *This was real.* I turned away from the phone, staring at the apartment as if it could tell me what they wanted, these hidden, amorphous people who had my brother. The apartment was one huge space, the roof held up by three pillars painted to look like green marble. The bathroom was in one corner shielded from the windows, the toilet concealed in its own little cubicle. No closets, just a row of mix-and-match art deco armoires along one wall, chests and trunks here and there. There was no place to hide anything. I had nothing of Davie's. Nothing at all. I shook my head.

"What about gifts he's given you? Letters? Notes? E-mails? Photographs—"

I held up a hand to stop him and went to the cedar-lined maple chest at the foot of the bed. It had been my mother's and her initials were carved into the front on a raised panel of darker wood. Lifting the lid, I fished out a thin packet of Christmas and birthday cards tied with twine. I handed them to the cop as the scent of cedar wafted into the room. "You can make copies, but I want the originals back as soon as possible."

I pushed aside old wedding notices and invitations and the personalized stationery I had designed for Stan and me when we were first married. Moved a tin box that held my mother's well-read Bible, her crucifix and her little-used Tarot cards. The Aquarius deck was still sealed in its cellophane, the Waite deck and the Minchiate deck favored by most St. Claires showed only faint wear. Mama had eschewed the tools of the family trade, as I had. Her journal was beneath the Tarot card tin, the pages curled and often read.

To the side, I found an old three-ring notebook filled with photographs and Mama's little notations describing each scene and person. The St. Claire album. Childhood photos of Mama and Davie and me at the mountain cabin where we'd lived after leaving the Low Country. Happy. Then, later photographs of Mama and Dumont Lowe, the only father I ever remembered. The four of us had made a family for a few years until Mama was killed.

I glanced up at the Tarot prints hanging over the tub. They had been my mother's prints. She had kept them even after fleeing the St. Claires and their way of life. The gold foil that gilded the Ace of Swords caught the light. My father's card. Beside it, my mother's card was in shadow. The Tarot touched everything tonight. A tremor of premonition raced through me, and I shoved it aside and away, deep into the dark.

I returned to Mama's album, flipped through and saw Christmas photos, Thanksgiving photos. Photos of us all at the beach. Then, the year I was ten, they stopped. There were no more childhood photographs in the book. Life with Dumont after Mama died hadn't been hard. He hadn't beaten us or let us go hungry. He'd simply not loved us. And had never taken a photograph of us at all.

Two blank pages separated my early life from my adult life. I pulled a photo of Davie and gave it to Bartlock. Evan took the old album, too, flipping through its pages, not commenting on the scarcity of childhood contents. He closed it and handed it back to me. "What's that?" he asked.

I glanced into the chest and saw the .38. "It's a gun." *Duh.* "Davie says a woman living alone needs protection." With two fingers, I lifted the gun to the cop. "I have registration papers here, too." I offered the papers, but Evan barely glanced at them.

He broke open the little gun and rotated the cylinder. "Smith and Wesson Airweight. It's not loaded. What good is a gun without bullets?"

"You sound like Davie. I don't like guns."

"You know how to use this one?"

"I could hit the broadside of a barn if I practiced for a week or two."

Evan laughed. The sound was breathy, a stuttering exhalation. He handed back the gun. "It's a good weapon, but it's pretty worthless at more than fifteen feet and it kicks like a son of a gun. So to speak. If you don't practice regularly and you don't keep it loaded, why do you keep it around?"

"Sisterly submission?"

Bartlock looked as if he thought submission wasn't a likely character trait for me but he let it go. "This is all you have of David's?"

"Yes." I looked at the cards in Evan Bartlock's hands. "You'll take care of them?"

"I will." It sounded like a promise. Maybe not a sacred promise, but a truthful one. He looked at the top card and a smile threatened. "He calls you Brat?" When I simply nodded, he said, "I'm sure I'll have more questions later. And the local cops will want to talk to you. You plan to stay in town?"

"Yes." I replaced the photo album and closed the lid. The

reality of Davie being in trouble—real trouble—was settling into me like an illness, the flu or leukemia, stealing my strength, my ability to think, to plan. I traced Mama's initials on the chest with a finger. The grain felt unreal, plastic, false. I was numb.

Evan set his mug on the chest and moved across the open space to the door. Not knowing what else to do, I rose and followed him down the stairs. I figured his walking away meant we were done. I was too drained to think about manners. For once, I wasn't thinking about anything.

At the door to the shop, Evan stepped back and waited while I once again turned off the security system and keyed the lock. Outside, he turned to me, his face a silhouette in the moonlight, and handed me a business card. "You should put bullets in that gun. It would be a lot more effective as a defensive weapon than that rock you carry around. Call me if you think of anything or need anything. Aunt Matilda told me to take care of you."

I was pretty sure I saw amusement in his eyes. I realized I hadn't made him explain the family relationship, but at the moment I didn't care. And I wasn't putting bullets in a gun as long as Jane came to visit. No way. But I wasn't going to argue with him, either. I shrugged.

"'Night." Evan Bartlock, cop, bearer of bad news, long-lost family member, walked down the ice-crusted walk with a careful gait. I watched him go, a lump in my throat.

Across the way something flitted. I caught it in the periphery of my vision, a shadow in the shadows, but it didn't reappear. Unsettled, worried, I closed the shop door and reset both lock and alarm system. Heart heavy, I climbed the stairs to call Jane.

Though it was late, she answered on the first ring, her voice muffled, terrified, hopeful. "Daddy?"

"No, Jane. It's me."

She sobbed, the sound broken. Across the phone lines I felt the jagged edges of her shattered hope. "They said someone took my daddy."

"I know. I know. But the police are working on it right now." My heart wrenched, twisted through with fear, a faint thread of anger, and an overriding worry for my brother and his child.

"Somebody has to help him." Her voice was hoarse from crying, and I knew she had pulled the covers over her head, huddling into the center of her mattress, her stuffed animals gathered around her, her cat sleeping under her chin. "Somebody has to bring him back."

"The police will get him back." It was a promise I couldn't prove or guarantee. A promise that was more hope than reality. "The police will get him back," I repeated more firmly, as if to convince myself as well as Jane. "Tell me all about it," I said, as I curled into my cold sheets and pulled the down comforter over me. With the lights still blazing, keeping away the shadows, I set myself to comforting and being comforted.

3

*M*ist swirled around me. Cold. White and crimson. Blood on snow. Steaming and hot with life and with dying. I struggled to wake. I knew what this was. The dream. The vision. But I was caught in it. Ensnared, as always. "No!" I shouted, struggling to turn away. Pain gripped me. A cold so intense it felt like burning. And I didn't know if this was part of the vision, the nightmare that trapped me, or if I fought something more real than illusion. Thunder sounded. Always the thunder.

My arms were bound in front of me. My hands below the rope were blue, dead. Useless. Fists like a club, I crawled up the drift, the cold spearing me, my flesh so frozen it shattered and fell from my hands.

In a hole on the ground was a body. The first body. Davie, face pale and blue, empty of blood, the blood that soaked into the snow all around me. The blood I knelt in. Beside him was Jane. A tiny bundle. Jane, the day I first saw her, dead. Blood. So much blood.

"No!" I woke. Ripped myself free of the vision, the ugly thing that chased me and sat up fast. I was in my bed. In the dark. My sheets were sweat soaked, my breath a bellows. Fists that still ached gripped the pillows and pulled them to me in the cold loft. It was fading, slipping away. The awful nightmare that wasn't a nightmare, never had been, not exactly.

I opened my eyes at the sound of the alarm—talk radio. Some right-wing pinko fascist blaring at me. Or maybe it was a left-wing pinko commie. They both sounded alike at eight in the morning. I was annoyed enough to want to throw the clock through the window, but I'd just have to buy another one and it would be equally irritating. One of these days I was going to get an alarm I could program myself so I could wake up to the sound of applause or a classical sonata or the sound of birds in the trees rather than a buzzer or radio voice.

The memory of the night before roared back into my mind. A rush of heat swept through me and froze instantly into glacial rivers of fear. I swiped off the strident voice of the DJ and rolled out of bed, reaching for the remote and clicking to local news.

I raced through a shower, keeping an eye on the TV for news of Davie. The program seemed much more interested in the snowstorm that had blown in last night than in human beings in trouble. Twice an announcer read a teaser about a local man kidnapped, but it seemed they were saving the good stuff for the last part of the show. *Uncaring fiends.* I shot a fierce glance at the faces on the screen with each teaser.

I could almost hear my calmer brother murmur, "Temper, temper." But I was entitled to some hostility. I had gotten too little sleep between too many bad dreams, leaving me feeling as if I were insulated in misery. Davie was missing, not here to see me throw things. *Missing.* And someone thought I had something that would get him back.

I didn't know how to do fear, but I could put a hurting on anger. I slammed down my soap so hard it bounced off the shower wall and skittered around the ceramic floor. I dried off fast and slathered up with moisturizer.

Naked, swathed in shea butter cream, I looked in the mirror. I had dark circles under my eyes, making me look sick or grieving. The only part of me that looked like a professional jewelry designer was the hair. I'd fallen asleep talking on the phone with Jane and my hair was still in an upsweep of shining red-gold curls. Good hair-day. Bad brother-day. I'd trade good hair for Davie in a heartbeat.

When the announcers turned to each other with somber faces, I hit the volume button.

"We have a missing citizen, Georgia."

"Sounds serious, Michael. What can you tell us about it?"

"Tom is in the field and he has an on-the-spot update for us. But first, this video has been released by the police department. It shows local businessman David St. Claire being attacked in a service alley. It's pretty horrific stuff, so we're warning our viewing audience, especially our young viewers, to beware."

Yeah, that was calculated to make a hormone-driven, adrenaline-pumped preteenager turn off the set.

The screen changed to a drab black-and-white film of a service alley, at an intersection of another alley, a grayed-out Dumpster to one side, piles of garbage and boxes visible. A man with a knapsack on his shoulder walked along, his motion the jerky result of poor-quality, slow-feed video. *Davie.* I tensed all over, cold chills running down my arms and legs. *"Spit and decay,"* I whispered.

From the side, two forms moved in fast. My heart seized and stuttered. The icy chills scraped my flesh into peaks so tight they ached.

Two men, both in jeans and hiking boots, flannel shirts, one in a dark, bulky vest, approached my brother at a run. They didn't pause or appear to speak to Davie. They rushed him, cupped hands flying, feet kicking. Davie went down fast beneath the hail of blows. His pack fell and opened, unidentified things scattering. When he lay still, the men pulled him off, one carrying his backpack and gathering the fallen items. It took only seconds.

Acid boiled up my throat.

They never once faced the camera. All I could tell was that they were white and medium build. Your average Caucasian American males, mountain-living, outdoorsy type guys. As innocuous as the medium brown man who had attacked me at the rock-and-gem show. There were a blue-million of them.

A dull pain started below my ribs and spread outward. Nausea sloshed in my belly. I raced to the toilet and reached it just as I heaved, but my stomach was empty. Dry heaves caught me, doubling me over until the horror passed. Afterward, my legs gave way and I slumped to the floor, a sour taste in my mouth. I could hear the news announcer's vapid comments about the attack and could tell they were running the video again. In other circumstances, I might call them buzzards for using the video to boost ratings. Now I just wanted them to play it all day. Maybe someone would recognize the men.

When I could stand, I washed out my mouth with orange-flavored mouthwash and turned off the television. The loft swam around me. I breathed in and it hurt my lungs to take in air. I shivered hard. I didn't do fear, I reminded myself. I didn't. But Davie was in trouble. "Ashes and spit." The words were bitter, the sound a roar in my ears. But there was nothing I could do. Not a blasted thing.

I looked across the narrow rooftop garden to Jubal and Isaac's loft. Their large apartment spanned two shops below, and for a moment I wanted to rush over and bang on the French doors, fall into the comfort my friends would offer. But the drapes were closed tight against the early hour and the cold, and no light leaked from the edges. They were still asleep.

Shaking, I finished dressing. I had laid out tan tones for

today, to show off a turquoise set I would wear in the shop as display, but I had to stop and think about which shoes I should wear. Had to concentrate to make the choice between navy and tan boots. Had to work hard to think about makeup. Davie was hurt. Davie was missing. And once more, just as when I was a teenager, I couldn't help, and I didn't know where he was.

Unable to stop myself, I turned on the television again and caught the tail end of a local interview. At first I thought it was a man-in-the-street interview about the attack, but when I looked closely, I recognized Gail Speeler, a girl Davie had dated. She was distraught, her face chapped and red from weather and tears, her lustrous black hair falling forward over her face. She looked into the camera and grabbed the reporter at the same time. "Please bring him back!" she said. "Please don't hurt him. Please don't hurt him."

A vision slammed into me. *Someone was hurting Davie. Right now. Someone was beating my brother.* I *knew* it. The world tilted and went still. I felt the blows fall. *Heard Davie scream.* And the image vanished.

I could hear an arrhythmic wheeze of sound, a soft moan. The rooster clock ticked steadily. Light coruscated against my slit eyelids. Slowly I opened my eyes.

I was on the floor, curled in a tight ball. I uncurled gradually, stretching on the rug. Blinked. Tried to breathe in. Some wounded part of me expected to feel the shocking pain of fresh blows, but I felt only the bruises from the rock-and-gem show. The family gift, as usual, offering only enough to drive me crazy. Not enough to help.

And this…this vision was so like my recurring dream. The one I first had when I came into my gift, alone and frightened. The vision that still haunted me from time to time, coming in the dark of night, a mocking enemy to prick my mind and flesh, to draw blood. The ancient scene of violence and death and the sound of thunder. Of the sight of Davie and Jane dead, their life force bled out on the snow, minds forever dark and empty.

Anger started a slow surge deep inside. Fierce tears gathered in my eyes. My breathing sped up. I could feel my neck splotching with furious red welts. "No!" I shouted to the rafters. "No-no-no-no-no-NO!"

They were hurting Davie. And I had what they wanted. If I knew what it was, I'd shove it down their throats and hope they choked on it.

On the screen Gail begged again as the station replayed her plea. Gail was a dimwit, but she had a point. Part of me echoed her plea—with a twist. *Don't hurt my brother,* I shouted in my mind. *You can have anything you want, if you'll bring him back safe. But if you hurt him, I'll...I'll....*

Something molten solidified deep inside me. Grew cold. Jagged. Something I hadn't known was even there. *I'll track you down and kill you,* I mentally shouted to the man who pummeled Davie in my vision. *I will!*

I thought of the gun in Mama's trunk. The gun that had no bullets. The gun I hated. I wondered where I could buy ammunition. I wondered where the closest shooting range was. This was the Appalachian Mountains. There was probably a gun range within thirty yards of me. I climbed to my feet and clicked off the TV with a snap. Picked up the gun and thumbed it open. No bullets. Davie and Evan were right. What good was a gun with no ammo? I stuck it into my pants at the waist.

I was halfway down to Bloodstone Inc. when the thought hit me. The alley had to be long, with lots of hiding places. Areas where there was no security camera. Why had the kidnappers chosen to attack Davie under the direct eye of a camera? Because they just got unlucky? Stupid criminal tricks? Or because they wanted the attack on film...

The anger that had grabbed me in the apartment started a

fast boil at the bottom of the stairs. Unless they were born idiots with the luck of Murphy, the kidnappers wanted the attack on film. Why? What purpose would it serve, except to establish that the kidnapping had taken place. To make sure that someone—*me?*—knew he was taken. They wanted something. They had said as much on the phone message. What did I have that they wanted?

I paused at the foot of the stairs as another thought settled softly in the bracken of my mind. What if they wanted something but someone else had it? Would Davie have pointed a finger at me to protect Jane? Yeah. Of course he would. So, if I didn't have what the kidnappers wanted, then Jane did. I cursed beneath my breath, stopping short as a second realization hit me broadside. Davie was a St. Claire. Why hadn't he seen the attack coming? Why hadn't he sensed the attackers long before he entered the alley? Had his thoughts been so taken up with other things that he had been wearing mental blinders?

I had a feeling I was going to have to learn how to shoot. And fast.

In the shop, I turned up the heat to combat the snow that was mounding up outside. I opened the safe and started pulling out the black velvet boxes of our more pricey items to be put in the display cases. Anger made me clumsy and I banged a tray, scattering the contents to the side. All I could see was the .38, the cylinder open, empty, in Evan Bartlock's hand. All I could feel was the weapon at my waist.

Sick at the stomach, but now from anger that churned restlessly in my gut, I straightened the stock items and placed them in the cases, arranging all the displays for early customers who would start arriving at our ten-o'clock opening. I even polished the smudge-free glass of the cases and door and windows. Busywork to control the anger that flamed just beneath my skin, to keep my mind occupied, trying to banish the sight of Davie going down under the blows. To keep the memory of his torture at bay.

When I heard my name called, I was bent over, hidden beneath the antique brass cash register. I stuck my head above the customer-display area to see Jubal standing in the open door at his entrance to Bloodstone, looking around the shop. He walked across the store toward me, taking in the filled display cabinets. My business partner was in full-fledged, outrageous, queen-bitch mode today, his dark brown hair swept back, his steps mincing. "Where *is* Tyler, and how *did* you get into her body?"

I took in a breath that quivered painfully against my ribs.

Jubal made a sympathetic face and held out his arms. "I heard, honeybunch. And I saw the news. Come here, sweetie."

I wasn't the "honeybunch" or "sweetie" type. Not even the huggy type. But I found myself pulled against him as his arms wrapped around me. Jubal was warm, his body heat a furnace, and a shiver of misery ran through me, my breath throbbing and harsh. I gripped him, hands in his shirt, my ear against his heart, hearing its steady rhythm.

I was, only then, aware how cold I was. And just how angry. Icy rage thrummed in my veins, brittle and frangible, breaking off in sharp slivers that pierced my soul. My heart hammered with fury. A red haze misted at the edges of my vision. I was plain *mad*.

"It's okay. David will be fine." Jubal's voice rumbled through his chest. "The police will find him."

I shuddered. I didn't want platitudes. I wanted to bash something. "A cop came to see me. Evan Bartlock, from the State Bureau of Investigsation," I said. "And I had a phone call from the kidnappers." Jubal's heart rate sped up. His arms enclosed me tighter as I spilled out the story, my face in his shirt, my throat so tight that I could hardly speak. When I finished, he nudged me away and looked into my eyes. The concern I saw there quickly vanished, morphing into something I couldn't identify before he shuttered it. He took a quick step back. And then two more.

"What is that?" He pointed at my waistband and I remembered the gun.

"It's a gun." I pulled out the .38 and held it pointed at the floor and away from us.

"Oh, my." Gingerly Jubal took the weapon and retreated back into his doorway, setting the .38 on the floor out of sight. "Your throat. You look like you have hives." His pale blue eyes narrowed. "I've only seen you get all red and blotchy once before and that was when Stan's girlfriend came to the shop to gloat."

At the expression on his face, I felt the rage recede a bit and a wash of something else shower over me—the beginnings of laughter. Crazy laughter, but at least it was some emotion other than anger.

"I had to pull you off that woman," he said. "You *scratched* me! Don't you dare laugh! I saved us from a lawsuit. I was heroic. And now you let me take my life in my hands and touch you when you have a *gun?* I am not that brave. Not with your temper. You should have warned me."

I laughed, the sound shaky.

Jubal inspected me as closely as he could from across the room. "Girl, I thought you would be crying. Worried. In need of tenderness and the attention of dear friends. But no. Not *even*. You are…are…spooky-nuts. A clear and present danger. You, my dear, are rabid. Let me get you some ice."

I laughed. *Spooky-nuts.* Yeah, that would describe a St. Claire at any time.

"Isaac," he shouted at the bottom of the stairs to their loft apartment on the other side of the narrow smithy shop that subleased space from Bloodstone and shared our entrance. "Throw an ice bag down. Tyler is ice-cold all over except her neck. It's fluorescing!" A voice answered, words muffled. Jubal shouted back, "No, she hasn't cussed and I can't see that she's thrown anything. But she had a gun in her pants. And she looks *hideous!*"

"Gee, thanks," I said. My voice quivered. "You can forget that stupid bet you two have. I don't cuss. And I'm not dangerous."

"Of course not," Jubal soothed. "You don't cuss, honey child. We know that. You use multisyllabic, insulting expressions. You make up phrases that sound vile but really aren't." Emanations wafted from him, but they weren't soothing. Beneath the concern he still felt for me and for Davie, Jubal was laughing at me. I was getting really tired of male amusement. "And occasionally, you throw things. You—are dangerous."

I glared at him, eyes spitting sparks. "I—am—not—dangerous. And I am not funny."

Jubal grinned at me and I balled my hands. My best friend was enjoying this entirely too much. In one hand, he caught an ice bag that flew from the top of the stairs; in the other hand, he caught a velour throw. He moved close to me again. Slowly. He was wearing a dark-as-night shirt that brought out the delicate pale blue of his eyes. I'd smeared his shirt with makeup. He'd be ticked. Which made me grin back at him. I was pretty sure it wasn't a sweet smile. The dark blue shirt meant he planned to wear turquoise today, like me. Odd thoughts to have in the middle of a crisis. Not a temper tantrum—a crisis, I told myself, though I could see where other people might not be able to judge the difference.

Jubal held out the ice bag from two feet away, like a lion tamer whose newest wildcat was hissing and spitting. "As usual, Isaac says to meditate on calming things. Did you hear? He shouted out flowers as a suggestion. I think you should contemplate wild sex instead." I closed my eyes, fighting down laughter. Okay. So I was mad. But I was laughing.

Which had been Jubal's intent, to drag me out of temper and fear into humor.

But I hadn't thrown anything. Had never in my life thrown anything in anger until last year. Of course, that had been a bad one. I had bitch-slapped Stan's cheap, redneck, blowsy… woman, the one he was sleeping with. Then I had thrown a porcelain display bust at her and missed. I had broken a glass case instead of her face. The woman hadn't sued, but replacing the display glass and bust had been costly and my divorce had been painful.

I took a deep breath, opened my eyes and took the ice bag. While Jubal draped the throw around me, I held it to my neck and tried to find a meditative breath pattern, a clear place in my mind for the breath to fill. Long seconds passed as I let the ice work on the ugly red blotches Jubal had described.

"This Evan Bartlock you mentioned," Jubal said gently. "State cops can do more than the local cops. Forensics and SWAT teams and superduper spy stuff. Batman and Robin in uniforms, instead of those really cool tights." I shook my head at his ploys. Jubal was pulling out all the stops to make me feel better. Tears pricked at his kindness. "Holy cops and robbers, Batman," he tried again. When I still didn't smile, he said, "They'll get him back, honeybunch."

"And if they don't?"

"They will. But…"

"But what?"

He sighed, unconsciously theatrical, and went to the complementary coffee bar, busying himself with the coffeemaker and freshly ground beans. His back was to me, and he didn't speak for a moment. Finally he said, "A city cop came to the shop yesterday before you got home and talked to Isaac and me. He told us about the video and the kidnapping. And he asked if it was possible that David might have…" He stopped cold.

"Spit it out, Jubal."

"He asked if David could have staged the kidnapping. To get money or attention or to further a business deal or something."

Rage was sucked out of me in a single breath. *Davie, staging his own kidnapping? Davie, needing money?* A tickle started in back of my throat and stuttered into the open. And I laughed. Really laughed, a hard, belly-slapping hee-haw. I fell into one of the deeply cushioned wing chairs where customers sat when waiting for sizing or minor repair work. "Thanks. I needed that."

Jubal looked pleased with himself. "I'm here to serve."

I have a temper. I know it. It comes with the reddish-gold hair and double Scorpio influences and the fact that Aunt Matilda says I was born under Fire, the Tarot card that claimed "boundless creative energy waiting to be unleashed, passion and vitality." According to my dear, batty aunt, I was "swift movement and decisive action." Whatever. It also meant I tended to lose my temper, though I don't get really mad very often. I could count on my fingers and toes the times when I'd really lost my temper. Well, nearly. I only needed a couple of extra digits. Some people are born with extra fingers for counting in just such circumstances. Somehow that thought made me laugh harder.

I finally got my hilarity under control. "Lascivious, libidinous lechery," I said, in my version of cursing. "Davie has more money than you and me and this entire town. He offered the town a loan last year, for pity's sake. Why would he stage a kidnapping? And how can someone make money staging their own abduction? Is he going to pay himself a ransom? That's ludicrous."

Jubal brought me a cup of hot herbal tea. Chamomile, unsweetened, for my anger. I chuckled again and drank back the thin brew in one swallow. "Davie planning this is not sensible or realistic."

"I happen to agree, but the cops think different."

"Which cops?" I asked, thinking of Evan Bartlock. He hadn't said anything about Davie doing this to himself.

Jubal looked slightly abashed but pushed on. "That corporal. Harry Boone."

My anger surged back a pace. "Harry Boone is a lick-spittle, butt-kissing, hunk of horse hockey," I said precisely. "He's a local cop who got promoted because he planted a piece of evidence at a scene."

"Lick-spittle? That's a new one," Jubal said with delight. "How very British of you. Just because Boone tried to date you doesn't mean he's not a good cop. And nothing was ever proved about the drugs."

"He's a bad cop. He planted marijuana on the Loobray kid to get a drug arrest. His last promotion required three drug busts. He's angling for bigger things and doesn't care who he has to hurt to get them."

"You don't know that."

Actually I did know it, but I couldn't admit that to Jubal. The family gift again. I hadn't told them about the St. Claires and their multimillion-dollar psychic empire. Except for Stan, my lecherous ex, I had never told another soul about my family, and even to him I'd made them all sound like fakes. Most weren't. Not entirely.

I'd picked the truth out of Boone's head one day while he was eating in the Red Bird Coffee Shoppe. He was broadcasting like a son of a gun and the image of him planting evidence punched me in the head. I couldn't ignore it, but I couldn't prove it either. I'd tried, by asking questions about the arrest and getting his boss to look at it again, and by feigning interest in the man himself, hoping to pick up something that would translate into a clue that might help Anton Loobray. I'd gotten nothing tangible.

Now, Harry Boone didn't like me much. Can't say I blamed him. I'd gone from apparently smitten to openly detesting the guy overnight. After our one single kiss. The mess I'd picked up from his brain while in such close contact had been so icky that I'd been unable to maintain the pretence of interest. And then his boss had let slip my questions and the investigation into his arrest of Anton.

Presto-chango, I had an enemy in the police department.

"Speaking of the devil," Jubal said, his voice trailing off.

I turned and looked at the closed shop door. On the other side stood Harry Boone, the lick-spittle, butt-kissing, lying, evidence-planting, hunk of horse hockey himself. Behind him stood Jane, her face tear streaked, chapped and red from crying.

4

I grabbed my keys and ran to the door. When I got it open, Jane jerked her hand out of the cop's and almost leaped into my arms. "Somebody hurt him," she snuffled into my blouse. "I saw it on TV. Somebody hurt my daddy." My niece was not yet twelve, and small for her age, like most with St. Claire blood. And she was a frozen block of ice. No coat, no sweater. I shot daggers at Boone, sorry that looks couldn't kill.

"I know, darlin'. I know," I said. "Where's her coat? She's freezing. And where's Quinn," I asked the cop, remembering my theory that Jane had whatever they wanted. "Where is her bodyguard?"

Boone looked at Jane in surprise. It was clear he hadn't noticed she was underdressed and cold. "Quinn's downtown answering questions."

"And her coat?" Jubal asked softly.

Boone's horse-hockey-brown eyes skittered sideways to Jubal. Fear and hate mingled in them, the guarded emotions of a man not secure in his own masculinity, suddenly in the presence of a gay man. "Quinn didn't get her one when we brought him downtown."

"Daddy's—"

"Shh," I said, my hand stroking Jane's back. "Later. Later." I stared at Boone. "And Jane is with you because…?"

"Because the captain made me bring her to you, and bring you back to the station for questioning." His hate beat at me, so strong it was palpable. I dropped my wall in place, closing my mind off from him.

"When Quinn's free and Jane is safe, I'll come."

The cop bristled. "Now."

"She's volunteered to help with the investigation into her brother's disappearance," a soft Texas voice said from the side of the shop. "Tyler is only asking for a little time to make certain that her niece is safe, which seems a reasonable request in light of the facts that her father is missing, and that the captain sent Jane here."

Isaac stood in the open doorway, a massive, second-generation Latino from Puerto Rico, six-two, two-hundred pounds of muscle and brains, bald head shining as if it had been polished. He was shirtless, arms crossed over his chest, shoulders like hillocks of brawn above, six-pack glistening below, jeans only half buttoned, feet bare. Isaac leaned against the frame, deceptively peaceful. But everyone in town knew he had won three national-level martial arts competitions, and had black belts in several different disciplines, Hapkido and judo among them, and was a master in tae kwon do. Isaac appeared dangerous even at rest, much like a napping grizzly. "Arrest her or get out." He smiled with perfect teeth, something vulpine in his eyes. He didn't like Boone, either, and didn't care who knew it.

The cop didn't back out the door at the expression in Isaac's eyes, but his hands did twitch once. Boone looked at me, not hiding his rancor. "I expect you at the police department in one hour."

I nodded. An hour and ten minutes, I thought. Maybe a little more. I turned away, Jane's face still hidden against my chest, and settled into the wing chair, cradling her against me. I tucked her icy hands beneath my armpits and cuddled her close. I didn't look up when the door opened and closed, letting in a blast of winter air.

"Where's your coat?" I asked, my mouth against the top of her head.

"I forgot it at school on Friday. Quinn was supposed to take me in the Land Rover so I wouldn't get cold. But they kidnapped Daddy and the stupid police took Quinn."

"He'll be back. Both of them will." I felt, more than saw, Isaac cross the room. His huge hand stroked Jane's head, lifting her hair out of her collar. From somewhere, the velour throw reappeared and was tucked around us, sealing in our warmth. I caught the scent of chocolate and knew Jubal was making instant hot cocoa with little marshmallows, just the way Jane liked it.

"I want to stay with you until Daddy comes home." She angled her head up and looked at Jubal and Isaac. "I want to stay with you guys, too. Quinn is boring. I'm lonely. And he can't cook nearly as good as Uncle Jubal."

I heard the men laugh and I smiled into her hair. "I think that can be arranged."

Jubal held out a huge mug of hot cocoa, and Jane pushed into a sitting position, pulling her cold hands away from my arms. "Thank you." She drank. Isaac knelt near us and twisted the top off a small plastic jar. Using the tip of one finger, he dabbed some ointment onto Jane's chapped face. Jubal brought her some cinnamon crisp cookies, her favorites. The total attention of the three adults calmed her and Jane almost managed a smile.

"Are you going to help them get Daddy back?" she asked us.

"Of course," "darn straight," and "yes" answered her.

Satisfied, Jane swiveled in my lap, dangling her legs across mine and sipped her drink.

After the cocoa and cookies, Isaac dressed and together we drove Jane to school, stopping at the principal's office to make sure that no one except we three, Quinn and David were allowed access to her. In his quiet, competent, Zen-like manner, Isaac impressed on Mrs. Godansky that Jane's safety was the school's primary concern. I couldn't care less that reading, writing, and 'rithmetic were being replaced as the school's chief goals of the day. I just needed to make certain my niece was safe.

Just before eleven o'clock, Noelle whirled into the shop, a snowstorm on her heels. "Sorry I'm late," she called out. "But there's a front blowing in and a pileup of fender benders on the bridge over Spring Creek. Freaking flatlanders. They should stay home or leave at the first sign of frost." She swept off her cloak and fluffed out her dark hair. Over the weekend, she'd had it streaked with sections of burgundy and bright blue, and had her nails painted to match. She looked festive, a color-coordinated wild child.

"Like your parents did?" Jubal asked, droll.

"No fair. I'm a second-generation mountain girl. My family arrived before the rush of the latest useless immigrants."

"They aren't immigrants. They are wealthy transplants," Jubal said. "They are our customers, remember? They bring lots of money from far-off places and buy our neat stuff. That is how we make a living and pay for food, clothes and health insurance. Uh-oh."

At the last two syllables, we followed Jubal's eyes to the door. Harry Boone once again stood on the outside staring in, his body wrapped in layers of padded clothes and yet somehow still appearing insubstantial. His eyes watched me through the glass.

Jubal looked at his watch. "One hour, the man said, and it's been nearly two. Not at all prompt." Noelle's eyes widened. She backed away to Isaac, who put a steadying hand on her arm. "I'll tell you later," he said, his eyes never leaving Boone.

The door opened and Harry stepped in. We locked eyes a moment. What I saw in his gaze didn't require the family gift to interpret as ugly. The man hated me. When he spoke, his tone was harsh, just on the edge of insulting. "You're late. The chief sent me to get you. Get your coat."

My first reaction was to refuse, argue and stomp my feet, but I restrained myself as a customer slipped in the door after Boone. I had no intention of giving in to my baser desires and getting myself arrested in front of the clientele. Besides, I still felt the body blows my brother had suffered. Davie needed help and I needed information. I grabbed snow boots and coat, gloves and scarf, and prepped for the winter weather. Dressed warmly, I followed Boone outside into the cold, got in the cruiser's front passenger seat, and allowed the silent, seething man to drive me to the law-enforcement center.

Though Harry didn't like it, his boss Jason Reasoner met me at the front door and took me to his office for questioning. Alone. Jason was an okay guy, even though he didn't really believe me about Boone planting evidence. At five-eleven, hairline receding, waist thickening, he was burly, the way former college athletes get in their late thirties, a bit of extra fat through the chest, shoulders and belly. Jason ushered me in and shut his office door in Harry's face. I saw a flicker of animosity in Jason's eyes, and knew he didn't really like his newest corporal. Which gave me a warm fuzzy feeling.

After the niceties were over and coffee had been poured, sipped and grimaced over, he sat at his desk and turned on a bulky tape recorder, stated the date, time and our names. Without warning, Jason said, "According to an SBI special investigator, you have something that someone wants. Wants badly enough to kidnap your brother to get. What is it?"

I sat up in the chair, suddenly cold, for once feeling small in the presence of a larger person. "I have no idea. If I knew, I'd give it to them in a heartbeat." I put the nasty coffee on the desk in front of me and curled my arms around my body, not liking where this was going. I noticed for the first time in this awful day that my injured hand hurt, a pulse of pain exacerbated by the cold. I tucked it under my armpit.

"They'll get back in touch. The technician is at your apartment right now fitting your phone with the tracing system. It's something new, developed to make use of existing technology but that will let us track not only traditional line-based and cell companies, but also calls rerouted through multiple systems."

"Thank you for asking." The words were out of my mouth before I could think.

"Harry didn't get your permission?"

"No. Harry didn't get my permission."

Jason's face went beet red. He punched the tape recorder off. Hit rewind.

Score one for me. "Your corporal has a Lilliputian, bellicose mind and a vengeful, rancorous spirit," I said, tasting the words as I spoke. "He plants evidence at crime scenes, and he intends to make my life miserable."

"You have the apologies of this department. And I'll speak to Boone." Jason was bent over a file drawer as he spoke, annoyance oozing from every pore. "Do we have your permission to set up equipment in your apartment and trace your calls? It's fully automated, run and maintained from here to provide you with a semblance of privacy." He tossed a consent form across his desk to me.

I caught it, picked up a pen from his desk, and signed it without reading. "Sure. But I get something in return. What alley was my brother attacked in? And why do you think he staged this himself? And why is Harry Boone working on any incident that involves me?"

Jason took the form and stashed it out of sight. "He was attacked in the service lane beside Merkle's Long Ashes."

Merkle's was an upscale tobacco and cigar store across the street from Bloodstone. Mentally I drew up the image of Davie being attacked, the direction he had been moving. My brother was moving away from my shop. "Where had he come from? And more important, where was he going?"

"We don't know."

Jason wasn't much of a projector, but I could tell that wasn't the complete truth. I rephrased. "Where do you think he came from?" The cop's eyes did a little twitch.

Gotcha.

"We think he was coming from your apartment."

And suddenly I knew two things. The cops had a warrant for my loft, and they were there now. "Someone is going through my apartment right now, aren't they? There's a warrant. And you didn't bother to tell me."

"It's all perfectly legal. We think he may have been in your apartment some time before he was taken." The words were genuine, but a sly satisfaction seeped from Jason's mind. He had made sure I was in the law-enforcement center when the warrant was served. "We got a warrant for your brother's house, as well."

"You little sneak." The words jumped out of my mouth all by themselves.

The interview went downhill after that. And I didn't learn anything.

Back at my loft, I inspected the little black box at the phone. It was attached with long black cords that snaked from the phone plug to the bedside table. The rest of the apartment had been gently tossed. My belongings were only slightly disarranged, not totally trashed as I had seen on television. No fingerprint powder marred any surface, so if they had made a mess, they had cleaned up after themselves. I had expected to feel violated, angry as was my natural inclination. Instead, I was numb. This was crazy. All of this was crazy.

I was tired and hungry and wanted to do something—anything—for Davie, but there was nothing I could do. Not a blasted thing. So I stripped off the tan shirt and pants I had started the day in, opting for jeans and two body-fitting tees for the rest of the day, chewing a granola bar as I dressed. The unexpected snowstorm had socked us in and downtown was deserted. The shop was empty, presenting us with a chance to work together on the spring line.

Bloodstone Inc. was divided into sections, with the front third of the hundred-year-old building totally restored for customers, from its burnished, copper-toned, pressed-tin ceiling, down the sponge-painted plaster walls to the stained, three-variety-wood wainscot and the wide boards of the hickory floor. The rear two-thirds were mostly unchanged since the fifties, taken up with the stockroom, the door to the service alley, two kilns and a huge work space cluttered with makeshift tables and work surfaces. The back work area was poorly heated, except when the kilns were cooking and the acetylene torches were fired up to blue cones and Jubal's braziers were giving off steady warmth. Today it was cold, so I turned on the workroom's gas logs and twisted the blower knob to high before I started unloading the stock I had bought at the show.

With my tools—a loupe, a small tapping hammer, a tiny chisel—and naked eye, I analyzed the kyanite, the huge hunk of green turquoise, the rubies, the labradorite I had bargained Rett for, and the pearls and slabs of picture agate that would be so easy to work with. The African bloodstone I inspected with special care. Its colors weren't as vibrant as some, but the mineral matrix looked strong and even, good for cutting and shaping. It should work well.

The mixed bag of polished stone cabs I had found weren't the highest gem quality, but several did have a luster I liked and would work up fast for the online stock offerings. There were eleven amethyst and three emerald stones, with the rest ametrine, citrine, tourmalines, two moonstones and an opal. A nice haul for the spring line of bracelets, necklaces and pins, over half of which would go in the online catalogue or be shipped to the two retailers who handled Bloodstone's wares, one in New York City, one on Rodeo Drive. The rough, the finer ruby cabochons and one spectacular dependant stone were set aside for something special, for shop-only stock, intricate and detailed items that all three of us could design together.

Having nothing else I could do, I started working the hunk of labradorite I had been sucker punched over. With a diamond-tipped blade and wet saw, I slowly excised twelve large beads in rectangles, massive squares, rough ovals and several free-form shapes, letting the careful tedious labor numb my mind and worries. If the rough matrix proved stable, each stone would be a pendant or focal bead for a necklace, the blue heart bleeding into the soft green outer area. It was fabulous material, and I already knew I'd be keeping one of the free-form pieces for myself. I could see it hanging from a lace of leather thongs strung with heavy nuggets and glass beads in dark green and blue swirled with gold. It would be exquisite with my coloring.

My head was filled with the acrid stink of the copper Jubal was heating, and the cleaner smell of his torch. Today he was working droplets of gold into heavy globes and fusing gold dust and swirls of gold wire to copper plate. It looked like an experimental piece intended as a cuff bracelet. I watched a moment as he heated a bit of metal in the blue of the torch flame, and then placed it, bubbling, onto a copper band waiting on the brazier. The torch flame scarcely flickered, its center clear, the fire coning around it, forming a pinpoint of blue flame at the tip. At the moment, Noe's smallest kiln was heating up, awaiting some combination of glass, metal and chemical that would fuse into her trademark flame-worked beads. Flame was everywhere. Fire as a tool.

As we bent over our tasks an old rock CD played, the music obscured sporadically by the sound of my saw. Matchbox Twenty blared overhead, Rob Thomas crooning in a smoky, hoarse voice. We had listened to Matchbox for several years; Rob's rough voice seemed tailor-made for the work we did, and was one of the few artists we could all agree on, even after he went solo. Noelle liked Celtic and Scottish music, and Jubal claimed to like musicals from the fifties, though sometimes I think he played them only to annoy me. I liked seventies rhythm and blues. Matchbox somehow satisfied us all.

Over two hours passed without conversation, each of us involved with our own thoughts and chores. When I had ten stones cut and ready for drilling and shaping with the grinding wheel, I turned off the saw, wiped the stone dust off my skin, got us colas from the fridge and took a break, wandering the shop, watching my partners at the artistic and skilled labor that had made Bloodstone Inc. a success. Ignoring the cola, which I placed beside one of the shop's fire extinguishers, Isaac snipped a design into stiff copper, following the contours of a pattern Jubal and I had designed.

Jubal doused an oval of mixed, fused metals in a heated pickle solution, twisted the top off his cola and took a long drink, wiping the icy can over his sweating forehead before returning to copperplate and gold casting grain. He had used duct tape to create a support for the cool end of the copper. Good old American ingenuity. Make a tool out of duct tape and clothes hangers, then build a shopping mall with it.

I went to the front of the building, down the narrow, low-ceilinged hallway between workroom and shop. Noelle had tired of working glass and taken a break before I had. Now she was in front, curled in a wing chair, weaving a complex pattern with a crochet needle, stringing on large dichroic beads and depending dangles of copper and red-gold beads. The piece looked both velvety soft and tribal, with tactile as well as visual appeal. A composition of wearable art in shades of lavender and green and gold—I'd have to remember that for the catalogue.

Noe paused in the work and stretched her shoulders and neck before drinking. No one thought to thank me, each too alone in their creative worlds to actually notice my gesture. It was always this way when the weather made customers unlikely and we all could work together, companionable without the need for speech. Though I would never use my gifts to pry, I loved the busy hum of the thoughts of my friends and business partners, so involved in their tasks that my own mind could remain silent and alone inside my head without effort.

I was tired, as much from the focused work of cutting stone as from the interview at Jason's office and the night's little sleep. Like Noe, I stretched, trying to relax muscles that wanted to freeze in the position I held when using the saw for extended periods of time. Back at my workstation, I set down the labradorite and pulled open a drawer to locate a handful of predrilled, soft green, translucent selenite beads that might blend well with Rett's lab. I needed to cut and chip some slightly larger stones to be shaped, drilled and polished for stringing, but that was tedious work. My attention wandered.

Taking my cola can with me, I sauntered into the front to check the weather—still terrible—and back into the workshop, where I set the cola can down before going into the storage room. Stacked in the center of the room were battered wooden crates, pasteboard shipping boxes and other deliveries.

Each partner in Bloodstone Inc. had specialized talents. Jubal's talent lay in metalworking and displays; Noelle's genius was with beads and keeping our books; Isaac, with a Zen-like ability, could do almost anything he might want to try; my talents in the shop were design, stonecutting and shaping, and the stockroom. And the stockroom was in need of some serious attention. I pulled a low stool to the pile and lifted three wooden boxes to the floor, gathered mallet and a crowbar, and opened each wooden shipping container. The first two crates contained scrap for Noelle—gold filings, broken jewelry pieces, old wine bottles. One box even held screws, nuts, bolts and rusted metal for her to fashion primitive pieces.

I stored the contents on the appropriate shelves and containers and listed them on the master sheet for easy locating. The next three crates were for me, filled with stock I had bought sight unseen on the Internet. There had been a photograph, but if I didn't get to handle stone and rough, I had no idea how brittle or friable it was and so the purchases were always a gamble. I stored some and put the rest aside for future deliberation. It was frigid in the unheated room, but I thought I could empty a few more cartons before the cold forced me out. I opened a package that had been shipped to Jubal from a refinery. It contained some lovely twenty-four-carat gold buttons and a small sack of casting grain that should have been placed in the store safe when it came. With me out of town, it had lain in the less secure storeroom while my business partners dealt with customers over the weekend. I put it to the side for proper storage.

I pulled three wooden shipping crates into the open floor space and stopped, surprised at the weight. *Stone...*

My chilled flesh was suddenly, instantly, heated with a surge of *knowing*. This was why—part of why—Davie was being hurt. *This* was what they wanted. I lifted other crates, sorting through the stacks, muscles straining as I worked.

When I was done, there were four wooden packing boxes. Each crate was addressed to Isaac. The return address was a post-office box in town. Davie's PO box. They were post-marked the Wednesday before he was attacked. Sweat broke out on my arms and tingled down my spine.

Why send these to Isaac? Why not to me? No flash of in-sight, intuition or knowing floated in, nothing on the subconscious matrix, the family gray-space of mind-reading gibberish. Aunt Matilda had once called me a reluctant empath. Of course, she had also called me an untrained, undisciplined, insecure, frightened psychic, a St. Claire wild card with spikes of feral talent. Whatever. Out of all that, I usually preferred reluctant empath. Not today. For the first time in my life, I wanted a full-blown, St. Claire-nutty-scary, feral talent to find my brother. And I didn't have it.

"Useless gift!" I socked a crate. Pain spiraled up from my injured hand. *"Spit and decay!"* I cradled the hand and raged at my deformed talent. "Why can't you just *once* give me something I can use." When the pain eased, I checked the butterfly bandages. They were still firmly stuck. I wondered if the EMT had applied them with superglue.

A moment of rational thought surfaced and I studied the crates scattered in front of me. Securing the hammer and crowbar under my arm, I hoisted up one crate. Slightly un-steady, I walked from the storage room into the workroom, kicking the door shut as I moved.

Isaac looked up as I entered, as if he immediately sensed my uneasiness. Or maybe my fear. My St. Claire gift was not projection, but sometimes in extremes, one of us would display some new trait. Isaac put down a set of metal-snips and nudged his partner. Jubal looked up and saw me. Perhaps it was the surge of emotions in the room, but Noelle stepped into the work area, paused and walked in.

"What?" she demanded.

"Deliveries came while I was at the show?" My voice sounded alien, a hollow tone.

Noelle nodded, sticking a threaded needle through her lapel to secure it. "Saturday. Why?"

"The delivery man stack the crates in the back?"

"Yes." Her tone was uncertain.

I turned to Isaac, one heel grating on the floor. "Davie sent you something. Several somethings. It's in four packing crates, each identical to this one."

He glanced at Jubal, who shrugged. Neither one of them knew the crates were back there. Neither one had expected a delivery from Davie. Noelle shook her head.

"I'm wagering it's stone," I said, striding to Jubal. "It's heavy." I lifted the crate higher and dropped it onto Jubal's workbench. It landed with a weighty thump that made the sturdy counter wobble.

He set down his handmade, duct-taped tool and turned off his torch and brazier. With everything that created fumes now shut down, Isaac turned off the ventilation fan and the CD player. Instant silence crushed in, marred only by the tap and ping of cooling metal.

"Can I open this for you?" With a shaking hand and crowbar, I gestured at the crate. *This would free Davie. I had the ransom.* At his nod, I thrust the sharp end of the crowbar into the seam between side and lid and whapped the blunt end with the hammer three times, three ringing chimes of steel against steel. Working the crowbar out, I inserted it a few inches to the side and struck again, three solid blows. Isaac spun the crate and I repeated the two steps on the other side, hearing the quiet groan of nails as they released from the tight-grained wood. Isaac ripped off the lid and Jubal took it, setting it aside before stepping back to allow Isaac access to the box my brother had sent.

My sense of *knowing* had abated only a bit with my attack

on the crate, and I put down the tools, watching as the men pulled out white packing peanuts and sawdust. The throbbing in my pulse demanded him to hurry, to get beneath the packing, get inside fast. Isaac reached in.

From the crate came a paper-wrapped bundle that Isaac placed on the workbench. The wrapping crunched and crinkled softly as he pulled it away revealing a dirty, fist-sized, white-and-gray quartz rock. The silence in the room was fraught with tension, punctuated by a ping of hot metal and the rough cadence of breathing. I reached out to touch the stone. Lifted it to the light.

Gold glimmered through the quartz and the layer of ingrained earth that still coated it. Raw gold wire, two to four millimeters thick and as much as six centimeters long, twined on and through the duller quartz.

"Is that…" Noelle's sentence faltered into silence.

"Yeah. It's gold," I said. Freshly mined gold in one of its natural states. Carefully I put the specimen back on the bench. I looked at the box, then back at the storeroom where three other boxes waited. Heavy boxes.

"I'm closing the store," Noelle said, and withdrew to the front.

"What else is in there?" I jutted my chin at the box on the worktable.

Isaac and Jubal reached in and each lifted out two more paper-wrapped bundles. Sawdust cascaded to the floor. When they unwrapped them, each bundle contained dirty grayish quartz wound throughout with gold wire. I picked up another block of quartz and gold, this one small enough to fit into my palm.

Raw gold has many forms. The most commonly recognized form of gold found in North America had been the nuggets and gold dust made famous in the Gold Rush of

1849. But there was also gold leaf, crystal gold in dozens of classifications and categories, alluvial gold, dendritic gold and sponge gold among other common varieties. Varieties like wire gold. Like the specimen in my hand. I lifted another, heavier piece.

I held the jagged stones to the lights overhead, letting the crystalline center of the rock capture the illumination and throw it back. This one was dirty on one side, smoother where it had lain buried, in contact with the ground for long ages. One small area was cracked and stained where it had been exposed to the elements. Several marks showed where a pickax had been used to mine the quartz. Other sides were crystal spires or cragged, irregular depressions, where the quartz had broken from a much larger stone.

A larger stone with this much gold was out there. Close to the surface. Somewhere. Where? And someone wanted it. Wanted it badly enough to hurt Davie. A shiver of heat threaded along my nerves below my flesh, into my marrow. *Where had Davie gotten this stone?* It was freshly dug from the earth, I knew that much. The stone hadn't been cleaned or washed. It was a new find.

"Tyler?"

I snapped back and blinked, surprised. I had been oblivious, turned inward, silent and preoccupied ever since I first saw the crates addressed from Davie. I was holding two fists of quartz rough, staring into their pale crystalline depths.

I set the hunks of stone on the table, comparing them to the others there. Each appeared to have been cleaved from the same mother rock, though the other two showed larger, darker shadings on one side, where the elements had reached them.

"That's what they wanted when they took Davie," Noelle said, her voice reverent in the presence of this much gold. "Isn't it?"

"Best guess," Isaac said, his voice rumbling. "Lotta people would kill for that much gold."

"Where did he get it?" Jubal asked.

"There are more boxes in the storeroom," I said softly.

Moments later, three more shipping crates were deposited on the workbench and I could hear the blow of hammer on crowbar as they were opened.

Feeling as if I were wrapped in heavy gauze, insulated from the world, I watched my friends as they opened the boxes. None of them spoke or looked up at me until all the crates had been emptied. Two of them held quartz and gold in massive chunks, fist sized and bigger, four and six per box, much like the one I had opened. The fourth crate held a single huge chunk of quartz rough and a padded manila envelope addressed to Isaac in my brother's neat boxy print.

Isaac looked at me, eyes intent. Whatever he saw in my face made him pause. He gestured me over to him, ripped open the envelope and fanned the contents. There were several dozen documents, some photocopies, and a letter-sized envelope, unsealed. He opened it, removed the contents and scanned the pages inside before placing the first page in my hands. It was a letter from Davie.

Isaac.
Hey, man, I got some troubles, from recently and from my past. If you're reading this, then I didn't make it back to retrieve the boxes. Which means I'm either dead or missing.

You have the quartz, hopefully all five boxes. Don't go to the local cops, man. One of them, maybe more than one, is part of the problems. Maybe tied in with some people who are after me or the quartz.

You know I've been buying up land around here for years, and purchasing the mineral rights to others. I found this on a mountain I bought. Just dumb luck. Literally stumbled on it. Anyway, some local people with more money than sense found out about it and they've been pressuring me for use of mineral rights. Which means strip mining, glory-hole mining, or open-pit mining, all which would ruin the ecosystem for decades. I won't sell. But if you're reading this, then they didn't take no for an answer or one of the earlier problems got out of hand. If that's the case, there isn't anything you can do to help me with that. If it's only the stuff in these boxes, I might have a chance.

Tell the Brat to try a scan for me. I'll try to reach her. And try to convince her to call in Aunt Matilda. She says she hates the old woman, but she's just scared of the family gifts and what Aunt Matilda represents. She'll be ticked off that I told you the truth about the St. Claires, but she'll get over it.

Help her keep Jane safe. Take them to the family if they'll go. Jane may need help soon. All indications are, her time is on her.

Attached is a check to cover your expenses. Consider yourself hired. Take care of them for me, man. That's the first thing. Second, ask around. See if you can find me. And here's a letter for the Brat. Hug her and Jane for me.

—*David*

It was typical Davie. Organic. Nonlinear, like a free-form tapestry of thoughts, feelings, concepts and information. Nothing clearly defined or spelled out, not a thing. That was the problem with Davie's gift. He was a strong receptor, and growing up receiving random thoughts from others tended to force the brain to grow in random patterns, to cause the recipient to think similarly. It made Davie's mental processes hard to follow. Half of what I read in the letter was senseless to me. But I got the fact that Davie had trouble with some local moneymen and with the local cops, and had told my friends the embarrassing history and truths about the St. Claires. *Spit and decay.* I didn't look up at them as I accepted the second letter, the one with the salutation to me.

Hi Brat.

I know you're already mad that I told your pals about the St. Claires. But I figured you might need them some-day. Today's the day. There's stuff I haven't told you about my past. You know. The missing years. And I didn't tell you about the gold. So sue me. Main thing is, I'm in trouble and chances are it will head your way.

Projection isn't my strong talent, but I'll try to send you info. Do a scan. It won't kill you. Listen to Isaac. He was in the military and he's lethal. I've hired him to watch over you two. I've been getting impressions that Jane is about to enter her time. Call Aunt Matilda. She'll help.

I love you, Brat.
—Davie

Out of the corner of my eye, I saw Jubal and Noe reading Isaac's letter. Isaac stood relaxed against the worktable, upper-body weight on one elbow, feet crossed. Without even look-ing, I knew he was watching me, waiting for a reaction. "How much did he pay you?" I asked. Stupid first question. Stupid, stupid, stupid. There were so many more important things to ask.

"Twenty thousand."

I winced. It was a lot of money. It meant Davie expected big trouble. I refolded the letter, feeling the texture of the paper. The good stuff, heavy twenty-four-pound bond. Davie liked rich textures, good art, delicate china and massive, imposing silver, the finer things. "When did he tell you guys about the St. Claires?" That was the next thing I wanted to know. Which was stupid question number two. I felt my face flame.

"A few years back. When we first were incorporated," Noelle said. "He wanted us to know what you could do. We don't know why. It never made much difference to us."

"That's Davie." Three years ago. They had known about the St. Claires for three years. My fingers made little circles on the paper, feeling the texture of the letter. But only the texture. I got nothing else from a surface scan. No trace of emotional emanations. No hint of Davie at all. "He has reasons for the things he does, but you may never learn them."

"So," Jubal said, a hint of amusement and a deeper curiosity in his voice. "Why didn't you want us to know your family's a bunch of crystal-ball-reading psychics."

I flinched.

"She hates that, Jubal." Noe slipped an arm around me.

"What did he tell you?" I asked, my voice lower.

"That the St. Claires run a successful hotline, Internet Tarot card site, Internet astrology site, some palm-reading businesses, and stuff like that," Noe said, trying to gauge my body language. "And that some of you have real gifts. Him and you included."

"That if there were tough business or customer negotiations we should leave them to you. You can read people better than most," Jubal said. "Course, we pretty much got that already from the first time you convinced that old couple, the Smythes, to buy the moonstone stock, back before we moved here. You've always been pretty mystical about making sales."

I remembered the moonstone situation. Our financial plight had been grim. We needed to make a sale—a big sale—or quit. We were tapped out, sleeping, all of us, in a decrepit,

1950s-style one-bedroom apartment with mattresses on the floors, little heat and no curtains on the windows. The rent on the shop was overdue. Business was slow. We were hungry. Desperate.

And then the vacationing couple from Ontario had parked in front of the shop and come inside. I had turned on the family gifts and for once they hadn't deserted me. I had learned that their daughter loved moonstones, and that they were loaded. Despite the headache it caused, I read them like open books. Before the hour was out, I had sold them every moonstone piece we had in stock at top-dollar prices. The couple, the Smythes, had been back two times since and cleaned us out of moonstone jewelry each trip, concentrating on the more fabulous pieces, spending a fortune. Now we created certain items with them in mind. Catered to them for saving us, even though they had never learned we needed saving.

"He told us that you and he were receptors, not that he explained that very well," Noe said.

"That's all?"

"Pretty much."

I looked up at them, reading their faces. Concern. Puzzlement. There was no ridicule there. A bit of the pressure that had landed on my shoulders began to lift. But I had one more question to ask. "How often have you been to the family sites?"

Jubal grinned. "I got my natal chart done and my financial horoscope plotted out through the year 2017. I sold my computer stock when the chart said to and made a triple return. Haven't lost anything much on the market since."

"I had a Tarot reading by a woman named Olympia, but wasn't too impressed," Noe said. Isaac said nothing, his dark face impassive. I got the impression that he didn't believe in psychics. For some reason that relaxed me even more.

The words dragged out of me. "Olympia isn't the most talented of the family. Next time, ask for Aunt Matilda."

Isaac's brow went up a fraction. Noe still seemed concerned about something. Jubal looked like a kid in a candy store. I resisted the urge to open and give them a read. I had a firm policy against scanning the people close to me. It wasn't fair if it worked. And when it didn't work, which was most of the time, I got really frustrated.

"So?" Jubal took a draw on his cola and jumped up to sit on the worktable, swinging his legs, long hair sweeping forward across his fair skin. "Tell us about the family gifts. David was vague."

I looked at Isaac again. A corner of his mouth quirked up in amusement at his partner. He picked up the stack of papers that had been in the manila folder with the letters and started paging through them.

"Psychic gifts are pretty common," I said, feeling my way through the explanation. "Cults and entire religions have grown up around them, including some modern-day ones. Some people think that those with the stronger gifts are actually people with angelic or alien DNA, or alien spirits stranded here, energy beings stuck here on earth. Which is dumb, but no dumber than any other explanation for psychic ability that I've heard.

"The St. Claires have a gift stronger than most and it's passed through the matrilineal line. The family started making money doing readings back before the Depression, just after we made a killing in the stock market based on a Tarot reading made by Aunt Matilda's grandmother."

I shrugged out from under Noe's arm and moved across the room, picking up my cola. It was warm, but I drank it anyway. The family history included stories of financial success and failures, the rare lynching and burning at the stake, and a lot of plain dumb luck. I picked my way through what I wanted them to know, told about Uncle Mabry, who got himself strung up under a railroad trestle for cheating at cards.

He won too many games at one table using his gift for reading his opponents' minds to read their cards. The men knew they were being cheated but never figured out how, so they strung him up as a sign to others. Play fair or die.

Grandpa Horace had died rich and happy by depending on his wife's gift for reading the stock market and for certain other unspecified gifts she used in the bedroom. A few others, cousin Otto and Aunt Isabel, were minor talents but bigwigs in the family industry, and I mentioned them and gave thumbnail sketches.

"Davie and I are receptors, meaning that we can receive impressions from others, but I can't project at all. Davie can project, but he's inconsistent, undependable." At Jubal's reaction, I clarified, "He can send impressions to other people sometimes. So can our aunt Matilda. She's the family matriarch. The strongest among us. And no, I won't be calling the old bat. She's a busybody and a meddler and an evil old woman who only sees bad stuff in her visions. She's got a tongue like a sword and doesn't mind slicing me up with it. I won't call her."

Then I remembered the vision of Davie being beaten. "Well, at least not until I don't have another choice."

"And why didn't you want to tell us about your gift all these years?" Isaac asked, stretching out his Texan drawl, which I had always loved. The undercurrent said, *even if you do believe in all this nonsense.*

"Honey child, we are your friends," Jubal added.

"You might have run away from it. From me." I frowned. "Others have, because they didn't want me to know too much about them. Didn't like the thought that I might pick up on something private, which I would never do. And then there's the fact that, as St. Claires go, my gift is majorly unreliable. If you had begun to depend on me using it, then you might have gotten ticked off when it didn't work. I get mad at it all the time. It's frustrating." Clenching my injured hand in irritation, I inspected it and found it swollen and puffy. "It gives me stuff, but in patches and bits and spurts. And when I depend on it, it always lets me down. Like now, with needing to find Davie, with thoughts from him."

"What? You're getting something on David?" Noelle's eyes sparkled like a believer-wannabe, fearfully looking for proof.

"Just once." I looked away, back to the letter in my hands, ashamed that I knew what was happening to my brother and was unable to help. Nausea rose up my throat. "He was being beaten."

The silence was sharp in the room. I read horror. Pity. Amused disinterest. Thank God for Isaac.

Isaac lifted the papers he had placed on the table and said, "These are offers on different tracts of land David owns. Some are for the land outright, some only for mineral rights. Three companies have asked for mineral rights on several tracts of land." He flipped back and forth between pages. "But they all look like different tracts of land. I don't see anything in common. ComPack, Julian Rakes Mining, and HFM, Inc., the Henderson Family Mines. ComPack and Rakes are both traded on the stock market. HFM is local, still family owned. You know Sue."

I remembered Sue Henderson. Blonde, petite, fun-loving. "She teaches clogging and beading. The one who kept out that nice amethyst rough for me a few years back."

"That's the one," he said. "So we have three companies to concentrate on. I'll have our investment broker take a look at all three and send us a report. But we need law backup and your brother said no local cops. That leaves your Evan Bartlock."

"A St. Claire." I scowled. "One I know nothing about, except he's tied in with Aunt Matilda and I don't know how or why. *Ashes and spit.*"

"This scan David mentions—"

"I don't know how," I interrupted. "Well, I mean I know how, sort of, but I've never been successful." Stress started in my belly, a heated mix of acid and fear and frustration. I fisted a hand into my stomach, trying to ease the knot forming. Of course, I'd been fourteen the last time I tried a scan. I was nearly thirty now. And Davie had sent that vision of him being beaten. It had been strong. Stronger than any impression I had ever received.

Maybe now…maybe this time…

5

Carrying Davie's letter, I climbed the stairs to my loft, dread in every step. This was not going to work. Not, not, not. It hadn't before. I wasn't smart enough or talented enough to make it work. Never had been.

Unlocking my door, I surveyed the apartment. It wasn't the warmest place on the planet, with ceilings at twelve feet, Mediterranean-blue tile I had laid, hardwood floors I'd refinished myself, and ancient plaster walls painted in soothing peacock-greens and soft teals. Snow billowed outside the tall, narrow, arched windows. Stan had paid a lot of money to have the windows double-glazed and the walls insulated with some foam stuff they pumped in, making tiny holes from the outside and resealing them afterward. It was still a chilly place. The slightly warmed apartment, the table and chairs on the private porch at the back, and the wedding ring I no longer wore, were the only things I had taken from the marriage except a broken heart and brittle temper.

Stop. Get on with it.

I flicked on the switch that started the ceiling fans, to circulate what heat there was, and turned on the gas logs in the fireplace in the center of the apartment. The blower came on a moment later and I shivered in the growing warmth. I opened the maple trunk at the foot of the bed and lifted out the tin box that held my mother's long-unused supplies. The smell of the cedar lining wafted into the room, instantly calming. My mother had loved the scent of that tree and the texture of the grain, the way its cinnamon-colored heart bled into the paler outer wood. I touched her initials carved into the chest as I closed it.

I lit a candle, grabbed the afghan off the couch and carried them, Davie's letter and the tin box with me.

Shoving back the table, I sat in the center of the kitchen floor on the cold, bright blue tile, arranging my legs in a half-lotus, and wrapped the afghan around me against the cold, tucking it under my thighs and backside. I opened the little box that held my mother's supplies. It was rusty around the edges, painted like a stained-glass window, tiny bits of unconnected color that depicted an angel with wings furled.

From the tin box I took her Bible, unwrapped the crucifix, touched the Tarot cards there. I couldn't think. Couldn't make fear settle and sleep. It prowled the corners of my mind, a restless black cat.

Mama hadn't been a goddess worshipper, a wiccan or a cultist. She had studied none of the practices the gifted had drifted into over the centuries to try to explain and use their gifts. None of the St. Claires practiced the occult religions. We didn't need the crutch. Mama had been a pious Catholic like Aunt Matilda, and had raised me in the church. But then God and Aunt Matilda let Mama die. And all I believed in had died with her.

My stepfather had taken Davie and me to his church, a sterile, cold place full of people who talked about rules and doctrine, judgment and law, and seemed to have forgotten that God was supposed to be a God of love. I had once seen a women beaten for the infraction of reading her horoscope.

Yet, I had found God in that lifeless church, in one single

sermon about the nature of the creator. The preacher, a little dried-up prune of a man, explained the Elohiym, the supreme God, and El, another word for the almighty. Sexless, ageless, never changing, a being of unimaginable power and glory. And mercy. And somewhere in El's vastness, love. And though I didn't pray often, I knew El was there, nearby, if needed. I thought about God now in the chaos of my thoughts and fears, wondering if El wanted me to find Davie. Wondering if El was going to take away another one I loved.

The dark image of fear padding through my mind latched onto that thought with claws that drew blood. *What if the Elohiym wanted to punish me?* I forced that notion away, concentrated on my ritual. Nausea tried to rise, a physical manifestation of the fear that rode me. A headache started high in the front of my brain. I pushed both down and away. And concentrated on the candle and on El.

Scanning was supposed to be easier if you had something that belonged to the person you were scanning for. I didn't have anything of Davie's except the small chunk of gold in my pocket, the smallest piece from the packing crates, and his letter. I pulled out the gold, suddenly wondering if he had touched this or not. Wondering if he had packaged the gold to send it, had ever handled it. Maybe someone else was involved with this, someone who packed the boxes and then betrayed him. *Stop it! Get on with it.*

I stretched my neck and shoulders, trying to relax. Two years ago, Isaac had taught me how to meditate, to breathe in calm and serenity, to find the center of myself and fill that hollow place with peace and light. Since that time, I had tried the St. Claire gift a few times, just out of curiosity, using meditation to focus my mind. I had managed some small successes. I might have had more if I had practiced, but using the gift always cost me, resulting in headaches, some so severe that I was nearly incapacitated.

Breathing easily now, I felt my fear, anger and misery begin to drain away. The nausea abated, floated to some distant point. The headache stabbed, but then I expected that. The St. Claire gift came with a price.

A thought intruded. Jubal had wanted to follow me upstairs and watch. Now wouldn't that have been a hoot. I pushed away the image of Jubal peeking around the door to spy on me and once again found my center, a place of rest and tranquility.

I placed the gold and quartz beside the lit candle and the letter in front of me, lifted out Mama's crucifix and slipped it around my neck and flowed deeper into the meditation. I didn't know what El might think about the St. Claire gifts, but the presence of the crucifix was a comfort. I felt settled, still, calm. That was all that really counted in the ritual of a scan.

A scan was a simple search, a reaching, a way to say "hi" to the person you were trying to contact, though few St. Claires exchanged actual words. What most got was more in the nature of emotions, impressions, like looking into the eyes of someone you loved and reading their feelings. It was supposed to be a simple act for even the least talented receptor. If the person they were trying to contact was also a projector, then a message could be passed, a real communication. I closed my eyes, ignoring the cold that seeped into my thighs and feet, blocking out the fans and the blower. Concentrated on my breathing.

The sense of calm that had fallen over me deepened, spread outward, down my spine, into my arms and legs. I relaxed into the sound of my breath, the feel of cool air moving into me and out, bringing in light, health and peace, taking out darkness, disease and fear.

When I was centered, so relaxed my skin felt alive and glowing, my muscles liquid, bones soft and pliable, I took up

Davie's letter. Instantly, I got a sense of Isaac, his amusement and something else, an underlying unmet need, a place of darkness I had never noted in my friend until now. Surprised, I set the letter aside and wiped my hand as if the darker emotions had clung to me, which was pretty silly.

Taking a deep breath, I recentered myself, the calm coming quickly now. And I took up the quartz. It was warm, and nestled into the palm of my hand as if alive. No other emotions clung to the stone, just a warm hint, almost a scent, of my brother. At the edges of my mind came the thought that this was working. How weird.

Davie? Davie, I'm here. Davie? I called with my mind, searching for my brother. *Davie? Where are you? Davie. Davie. Davie.* The cadence of the syllables slowed, matched themselves to my heartbeat. *Davie. Davie. Davie...*

An ache began in the back of my neck. Slid down my spine and into my shoulders, hips, stomach. Arms. Legs. Replacing the peace. Bringing with it darkness.

I was cold. So cold. Disoriented. *Fear.* Nausea roiled through me. My pain lifted and fell with each breath. *I hurt.*

Davie?

The pain and fear grew. *I blinked. Saw a dirty wall. Once white. Metal jingled on metal. The pain spread, a wildfire in my bones.*

Davie?

Brat?

The wall came into focus. It wasn't dirty. It was bloody. Splattered. Pain speared me as I/he moved.

Brat. I'm hurt.

I saw a wrist, handcuffed to a curve of iron. Pain whipped me and was gone. Taking Davie with it.

I jerked out of the meditation. *"No!"* Anger blasted through me, a heated rush of fury. Tears blurred my vision. Pain like a lance of forge-hot steel pierced my forehead over my left eye. I hurled the gold across the room. Instead of shattering against the far wall, it landed on the couch with a soft bounce and didn't break. I couldn't even do that right. I never could do it right!

I took in a gust of air so cold it scorched. The headache exploded, a stabbing pain that brought me to my hands and knees, retching. A sob escaped me. It was always this way. Just enough to hint and torment, to tease and lure, and never enough to do me any good. But how else could I help? I wasn't a cop, a private detective or anyone else with access to ways to track my brother. For once, all I had going for me was the St. Claire gift and the boxes of gold downstairs. "Spit and decay," I whispered.

I looked over at the phone machine. No blinking red light. No messages from the kidnappers. Just an ugly black cop box, promising little and so far delivering nothing. And once again, I had thrown something in anger. I wouldn't be telling Jubal about this one.

I retrieved the gold and tried again but got nothing. Not a blessed thing.

After long minutes of trying to center myself, of trying to reach for Davie, I gave up. Fighting tears, shaking with fatigue and frustration, I blew out the candle and stood, my leg muscles aching with the cold of the floor and Davie's remembered pain. And the sight of the wall, splattered with Davie's blood.

I carried the afghan back to the couch and replaced the candle and the tin box. Rearranged the furniture. I washed my face and freshened my lipstick, tucked up some curls that had come loose, and popped two extrastrength Tylenol. I was trembling and knew I needed calories, so I stuffed a Snickers bar in my mouth and chewed, swallowing it down with a glass of milk. But I wasn't myself. I was fighting anger and frustration and tears. Not a good combination.

The gold rough went into my pocket and I left Mama's crucifix around my neck for the comfort the items brought me. The cross banged against my chest as I retraced my steps to the shop.

Evan Bartlock was in Bloodstone Inc., sitting in my favorite wing chair and holding papers I recognized as Davie's. Isaac and Jubal were there also, Jubal in the other wing chair, Isaac at the silver samovar making hot tea. Jubal looked around at me, a question in his pale blue eyes. I shook my head but knew he could see something in my face, something he'd likely hound me about later. I glanced at the papers, worried that some with the mention of the gold were there, too, but Jubal gave a faint shake of his head to reassure me. Mind reading, I thought sourly, but the kind that best friends do as a matter of course. Nothing mystical about it all.

Noelle was gone for the day, her cloak and boots missing from the door. Outside, the storm still surged, sheets of snow waving in the wind. The store was closed due to the weather, as much as the gold.

Bartlock looked up, taking in everything about me in one glance. I had a feeling he could have stated what I wore, how my hair was styled and my emotional state without a second glance. Whatever his St. Claire gift was, it made him a good cop. I didn't want his bloodline to make me feel better, but it did. Which made me a conflicted, unsuccessful, meager-talent, mind-reading, crystal-ball queen. I almost smiled at my whimsy and pulled up a stool from behind a display counter.

Isaac glided across the floor with a tray in his left hand. Bending, he offered a cup of tea in the good china to Bartlock. With a saucer. And a napkin. Which was way weird. Isaac usually offered the good china only to little old ladies with lots of money.

A mug with a dancing penguin on it went to Jubal, and then

Isaac crossed the room to me. I took the last cup, a Christmas tree mug of tea with steam swirling from the dark liquid, and sipped, knowing the caffeine would help my headache. The tea was the new Darjeeling from the Puttabong Estate. Very smooth, very rich, with an elegant floral scent. Seriously expensive. Isaac was going all out. I watched him a moment, and his eyes were on the cop.

Bartlock, wearing a suit no one on a cop salary could afford, was sitting in the wing chair, papers on his lap, jacket unbuttoned, silk tie knotted just so. The cup and saucer balanced on one knee, napkin beneath. He lifted the tea by its elegant, curlicue handle and sipped, a look of appreciation crossing his face, though his eyes were still on the papers. Most men, especially men with hands the size of baseball mitts, would look silly holding the delicate teacup with its curlicue handle, but Evan managed it with ease. Practiced ease.

And then I understood. Devious Isaac. He had just proved that Bartlock came from money and breeding, unlike my poorer branch of the St. Claires. The cup returned to the saucer with a faint clink, never wavering or tottering or threatening to topple from his knee to the floor with a crash. Bartlock managed it all with effortless grace.

"You really should take this to the local police," he said, as if continuing a conversation already taking place. Davie's letter to Isaac was in his hand. "They need them as part of their search for David. But I understand his warning and your reluctance. If a local cop is involved in his disappearance, that complicates things."

"Can't you do something on the state level?" Jubal asked.

Some emotion flashed across Evan's face, under his skin, close to the bone, a passion quickly shuttered. "I'm here unofficially." He looked at me. "Aunt Matilda hired me to look into the disappearance of a friend while I'm on administrative leave. When I got here, I discovered that her *friend* is my fourth cousin. Or maybe third cousin once removed. I get confused about that stuff. I—"

"And why are you on leave?" Isaac asked, his smooth voice stopping the cop.

Bartlock froze, face expressionless except for the strange something that crawled beneath his skin. He turned empty eyes to Isaac. When he spoke, his voice was barren of emotion, a desert under a full moon. "I shot a man."

He closed his eyes as if seeing the event replay across his lids in triple time. "It was dark. He pulled something out of his pocket." Bartlock opened his eyes and looked at me, his gaze cold over tangled emotions, a web of feelings that I could almost touch. Beneath the unfeeling exterior he was raw, offering himself up for inquisition. His soul was abraded and torn, too stunned yet to be called suffering or desolate. I pulled back from my awareness of the man, hiding behind my wall. My headache pounded, an ice pick in my skull. "It looked like a gun. And I fired.

"The man was unarmed except for a length of pipe taped to a brickbat. There was a note addressed to his ex-wife in his pocket. And he's dead." The room was silent. Bartlock returned to the papers. "So I don't have access to the resources of the state lab or databanks, but I can call in favors and get friends to dig up information for me."

Suicide by cop. I had heard of it.

"And the local cops?" Isaac asked, voice gentle.

"They know I'm here." The emotional, soul-baring moment was over. Bartlock's voice was back to business as usual. "They aren't too happy about me nosing around. They'd be really unhappy if they knew I had information they've been denied. But I understand your reasoning, not letting them have this information at this point. And frankly, it won't hurt much, especially since they shared most of their conclusions with me and some facts about the crime scene that didn't make the papers or the news."

"Crime scene?" I perked up. "What about the crime scene?"

Evan relaxed in the chair, took his saucer in one palm, fragile cup in the other hand and sipped his tea as he spoke. "Law-enforcement investigators determined that David's attackers lay in wait for him for some time. There are positive and negative results from that wait. The positive is that the cops have DNA samples from both men, should they decide to test for unimpeachable ID. But they're moving toward the negative.

"Because the attack was well planned, in a location that can only be considered questionable, directly beneath one of only two security cameras in the area, both in plain sight and monitored, investigators are fast reaching the conclusion that David planned the attack himself and wanted it on film. There are dissenting opinions, but they are in the minority."

"We heard that theory from Harry Boone," Jubal said. "The little weasel."

Bartlock grinned, the smile lighting his face and banishing the darkness I had seen. "Good description."

"Especially his mouth," Jubal said, "with that little mustache that quivers when he talks. And those beady homophobic eyes that twitch whenever he looks at us, as if gayhood is contagious."

"Gayhood?" Isaac murmured.

"Boone does seem to be leading the majority opinion, though how David staged his own kidnapping for profit is beyond me." Bartlock tapped the papers in his lap. "His letter and papers might make a difference in that opinion if they were considered as evidence."

"Why so?" Isaac asked.

"Because these papers mention mineral rights to various tracts of land. And raw gold was found at the crime scene."

Isaac carefully did not look at me. I stared into my cup. Jubal looked back and forth between us. "Well?" he demanded, one hand on his hip. When neither of us replied, Jubal blew out an exasperated breath, stood and poured Bartlock more tea.

"Well, what?" the cop asked.

"They're thinking. Very methodical on Isaac's part. He looks at every alternative and weighs every variable before making a decision. Makes him a killer chess player but for his family, it's emotional torture. Takes him forever to make decisions. He's a Libra, you know. Tyler will go with her gut. It's that St. Claire thing, combined with a double Scorpio influence in her natal chart, though it would kill her to admit it."

I glared at him, putting every bit of accusation I could muster into the look. Jubal had been looking into the St. Claires way more than he had let on if he knew my natal chart. He had been talking to Aunt Matilda. The very thought sent a shiver of fear through me.

"Thinking about what?" Bartlock asked him.

"About—"

"Stop," Isaac said. "It's Tyler's decision."

His dark eyes were on me, and I saw approval in them. Isaac wanted me to tell about the gold. Davie had hired him to take care of us. Aunt Matilda had hired Evan. I should tell; I would tell. But I remembered my attempted scan for my brother. I wanted something first. Despite my headache, I opened myself to the cop and took a chance. "In the alley. At the crime scene. Was the gold they found resting in Davie's blood?" I asked.

Bartlock's eyes swept to me and he frowned at my question. He wasn't used to being thrown off course, redirected. Wasn't used to being questioned by a civilian. I got that clearly from him. As a cop, he was accustomed to being in charge. And right now Bartlock had no authorization to command, guide or require anything from anyone. It was a new experience for him, an unpleasant one that brought home to him the changes in his life since he was forced to take part in a man's suicide scheme. Evan Bartlock was fighting a natural instinct to take control. He was feeling helpless. He wanted to hit something. He was angry at life, at himself, at Aunt Matilda and family demands, and chiefly at the man who had forced him to kill.

"Yeah. How did you know that?"

I pulled myself away from his thoughts, closing my wall around me in protection. "Can you get me a bit of the gold from the scene? Some…" I closed my eyes, forced to stop at what I was asking. "Some that was in his blood."

"Why?" Suspicion was clear in his voice.

"So I can try a scan for my brother."

"Crap." The word and the thoughts behind it were like an emotional slap in the face. An insult. "You're one of the *weird* St. Claires, aren't you? Aunt Matty sent me to another one of the weird ones." He stood, broadcasting his frustration. "I should have known." Even with my mind closed off I could feel the annoyance seeping from him. *The St. Claires are all fakes, charlatans. I'm related to a whole clan of con men.*

I blinked. *Aunt Matty?* He called the old bat Aunt Matty? "Can you get some?" I persisted, putting aside for the moment that he was working for the weirdest of us all.

Uncertainty churned with the other unhappy emotions in his mind. "Yes. Maybe. I'll try."

I stifled a sigh of relief and closed my mind to him as I slid from stool to floor. Fishing in my pocket, I pulled out the nodule of quartz and gold wire and tossed it to him. The cop caught it without fumbling the teacup. His eyes grew wide as he turned the raw gold and quartz to the light.

"Come on. You need to see this," I said. "But it's off the

record until we figure out who's responsible for the attack on Davie."

"I can't promise that. Not if it pertains to this case," Bartlock said, putting the teacup and saucer to the side, napkin neatly folded.

I stopped and turned, feeling heat rise to my face. "You're not here as a cop. Didn't Aunt Matilda pay you to come here? To help Davie?"

"I'm an officer of the court. That responsibility has my first allegiance. Aunt Matty knows that. And you need to remember that."

"You're willing to let those papers stay out of the investigation for now. Why not other things?" I asked.

"It depends on what the other things are. My point is that I can't promise anything until I know what it is." He held up the gold rough, waiting.

I crossed my arms and turned a foot out, into the aisle, blocking all progress with my body. "Uh-oh," Jubal said. Isaac just grinned.

"Okay. So if you see something that looks suspicious, in your opinion—you, who know no one in this town, know nothing about the political situation or the men and women in local law enforcement—you, an out-of-town cop working off duty for the aunt of the missing man, will take it upon yourself to decide what to do. *Unilaterally?* With no discussion, no input from us. Or from Aunt *Matty.*"

My foot started tapping. "And if you give what we have to the cops, and one or more of them are part of this and you get my brother killed, you'll just say what? Oops? So sorry?"

I advanced on the cop, dropping my arms, sending the cross flying back and forth against my chest. Bartlock's eyes fixed on the movement a moment before returning to my face. He reddened. "No way, Bartlock. We agree right now, that you'll give us five days with this information before you turn it over. Agree or get out. And I'll call *Aunt Matty* and tell her you think she's a charlatan. I'll tell her what you call her behind her back."

Aunt Matilda was a big stick. His blush faded in a slight pallor.

I caught a jumble of emotions from Bartlock in that single instant. A memory of Aunt Matilda appearing at his side when he was child. He'd hurt himself and though he hadn't cried out, Aunt Matilda was there just as if he'd screamed. An image of my own chest as he thought it might look if I had somehow forgotten to dress. A worry that Aunt Matty had sent him here, to me. A trace of thought that perhaps Aunt Matilda wasn't a con. *Maybe she's the real thing....*

Knowing that he hadn't been looking at the crucifix but my chest, I stuck it out a bit more, using what leverage I had. "Agree," I demanded.

The images from his mind faded. Bartlock sighed and glanced back at Isaac. "She always this way?"

"Serene and tranquil? Modest and unassuming? Doubtful, vague, almost shy? Yep. That's our Tyler. She thinks she's as big as we are. And she never bluffs."

Bartlock turned back to me, his eyes firmly on my face. But I could sense he was fighting looking down. Having opened my mind to him once, I was now reading him too easily. "Great. Okay, five days. Unless we get indications that suggest the cops need to see it, whatever it is, sooner."

"And you clear it with us first. No surprises or behind-the-scenes info-sharing," I said, tying down loose ends.

"What's the big deal? You got boxes of gold back there?" His eyes widened at our reactions. "You do? Boxes of gold?"

"Agree."

"Okay. Done. Whatever you say."

I led the way to the work area where the boxes were still

sitting, the gold-and-quartz rough, the white paper, sawdust and white foam peanuts scattered.

"Holy…" Bartlock lifted the largest quartz-and-gold rock into the air and turned it, brushing off dried soil and detritus to see it better. "This is from David?" At my nod he shook his head. "How much of this stuff do you have?"

"All that you see," Isaac said. "Four boxes. David's letter stated that there should be five boxes. But we only have four."

The cop in Bartlock took over and he reluctantly put down the chunk of mineral and stone. He lifted a box and checked the label, compared it to the other packing crates. "If there's this much gold in this room, how much is in the ground?"

"Enough to make a lot of men very rich for a very long time," Isaac said.

"And the fifth box?"

I shrugged. No one else answered. A cell phone rang, a simple ring, not a concerto or a synthesized series of pop music notes. Bartlock pulled his phone and glanced at the readout. It was a cute unit, a tiny acrylic thing in basic black with bright blue lights that pulsed as it rang again. His eyes darted to me. Then to the other two.

Aunt Matilda. No doubt about it. I was just glad I'd left my cell upstairs.

"Bartlock." He grimaced. "Yes, ma'am. Yes, ma'am. Yes, ma'am. I will. Yes, ma'am." When Bartlock hung up from Aunt Matilda's tongue-lashing, I expected to pick up a greater sense of frustration and anger from him. Instead the cop seemed calmer and, if not satisfied, at least resigned.

"Portents?" I asked.

"You know about the blood-aura?"

"Oh, yeah."

"Now there's a raven outside her window. And she read some cards and got the Ace of Swords reversed?"

"Tarot. She probably did a one-card reading. It means a

challenge met with the invocation of force, disastrous results and dangerous implications."

"You read these cards?"

"No." Mama had made me promise to never touch the cards, insisting that Tarot was a medium for the devil. I could still remember the fear in her eyes when she talked about the cards and her St. Claire gift. I didn't tell Bartlock that, however. It was none of his business.

"But you believe this stuff. This occult junk. Mind reading, palm reading, tea leaves, bumps on people's heads." Scorn dripped in his tone.

In spite of myself, my hackles rose. "Intuition? Gut reaction? Instincts?" I hated defending the St. Claires, really hated it, but Bartlock was pushing my buttons. "Insight? Perception? You never solved a crime by those? By making an intuitive leap that left your co-workers in the dust scratching their heads, asking how you figured it out?" He reddened again. I got the impression Bartlock didn't flush easily but something about me threw him off. Could be St. Claire weirdness or it could be the boobs. I wasn't wearing a bra and it was quite cool in the shop. I was betting on the boobs. Even with Davie in trouble, I liked that. I'm competitive. So sue me.

"That's not the same."

"Why not?" I grinned happily, knowing I was winning. "It's something other than logic. Go ahead. Explain using gut instinct and intuition to solve crimes. Tell me you use only reason and deduction. You can't, can you. No."

"You—" Bartlock rubbed his temples with one hand. Took several deep breaths.

I was betting he'd taken some anger-management or stress-reduction courses. Meditation. Yoga. Self-hypnosis. But now I was pushing his St. Claire buttons. Hard.

"You've still got your five days. Or forewarning, should I need to break that."

Knocks came from the front door of the shop. Not delicate knocks a customer might make, but the hard, resounding whams of a fist. Without thinking, I raced into the shop. Quinn and Jane were framed in the glass door. And something was wrong.

Quinn was upset but trying to hide it. For Jane's sake I masked my reaction, smiled and hugged her before sending her off with her uncles for a snack and homework. The moment she was out of sight, I turned to the bodyguard and demanded, "What happened."

"What's he doing here?" Quinn asked of Bartlock.

"He's a cop."

"I know he's a cop." Quinn tossed off his winter coat revealing a holstered gun and too many chest muscles, biceps bigger than my thighs. "He's been to the house, asking all kinda questions he's got no business asking, him off duty and all. I checked. He's got a reputation in the state. And some of it's not good." Quinn flexed steroid-bulked muscles, drawing attention to his oversize chest and the leather holster strapped around it. "Now, what's he doing here?"

The cop smiled; I could feel it through the back of my head, and the smile was ugly. "Our aunt hired me to find David," he said. "And since we've been checking into one another's backgrounds, let's discuss your little problem—your arrest for controlled substances. A small thing you didn't disclose on my last visit."

Something clutched at my heart. "Quinn?"

The bodyguard glowered and speared me with a stare. "David knows all about me. He didn't tell you?"

I shook my head.

"We can talk about it later. Right now, I—"

"We'll talk about it now," I said, taking refuge in a spurt of anger, my familiar companion when I was worried or frightened. The anger cleared away the last of my headache.

Quinn looked at the cop and back at me, dark things crawling behind his eyes at being forced to speak in front of the other man. "We knew each other from the gym. David was working out the day the frigging cops showed up and I got arrested and fired. I was eighteen and stupid and thought I had the world by the tail. And the cops didn't cut me any slack, which they coulda because of my age and no priors."

I knew enough about David's missing years to understand why he had helped a young impressionable, mixed-up kid. Davie had once battled his own addiction, to high-stakes gambling. And with his gift, his ability to win at any game of chance, it hadn't been easy. But that was a far cry from using drugs. "And the controlled substance?" I pressed.

Quinn had the grace to look uncomfortable, the bluster and the macho pose wilting a bit. "I was dealing juice out of the back of my trunk to pay for my own use."

"What's juice?" I questioned.

"Steroids," Evan said, censure in his tone.

"I had dreams of being the next Schwarzenegger." His voice claimed that dream had died hard. "David paid for my defense, got my record cleaned up, paid for my training and gave me a job."

That sounded like my brother. He braked for animals, even squirrels, rabbits and possums crossing the road. I'd seen him stop and help a turtle off the pavement and out of harm's way. I had once accused Davie of putting the local vet on retainer to take care of injured and sick wildlife he found and rescued. He hadn't denied the charge. Davie was a seriously nice man.

"Now, what is that cop doing here?" Quinn asked, the bluster creeping back. "I get back in town to find David's gone. Kidnapped. I don't like a stranger hanging around while David's in trouble and people are trying to get Jane. It's weirding me out, man."

"Trying to get Jane?" The bottom dropped out of my world.

"Yeah. Someone tried to take her out of school. Some guy. They caught him on the security camera at the front door, but he had his face turned away. The principal, Mrs. Godansky, told him to wait and called me and the cops but he bugged before we got there. Description I got could be anybody. And when I asked the cops about *this* guy—" Quinn nodded to Bartlock "—they tell me he's not on the case officially. But he's hanging around, conveniently at the same time my boss goes missing? Something ain't right."

"Davie's aunt Matilda hired him. He's our cousin," I said as Bartlock maneuvered closer, within range of my vision.

Quinn relaxed marginally, scrutinizing the tall cop. "David trusts his aunt Matilda. Told me she's okay people. But he never said anything about this guy. He ain't on the list."

The list was exactly that, a short list Davie had given Quinn a long time ago, cataloging the people approved for access to his daughter. "We have hundreds of cousins we don't know well. He's okay."

"Yeah, well, I don't have to like it. I got my eyes on you."

That seemed to amuse the cop. One corner of his lips quirked up, which made Quinn bristle. Men. Like a couple of junkyard dogs.

"You were out of town when David was taken?" Bartlock asked, which I had somehow missed in the previous conversation. "You didn't mention that to me, either. There seem to be fairly significant discrepancies in your stories."

"I was visiting my…mother," he said with a quick glance at me. I could almost smell the lie and got a quick impression of white thighs and rumpled sheets. Quinn reddened and I hid a small smile.

"I'll need your mother's name," Bartlock said, emphasizing the word *mother* slightly. "And her address."

"I gave them to the cops. I got nothing to say to you."

Bartlock shrugged infinitesimally. "Fine. So who was watching Jane?"

"A friend of mine. Part-time guy David hired last time I took vacation. The cops have that information, too."

I remembered the medium brown man from the rock-and-gem show. "Can I see the security photos?"

"Why?" both men answered at once.

I looked at the cop. "Gut instinct," I said deliberately, which seemed to fuel his amusement. I told them both about the attack at the show, adding details I hadn't mentioned to Bartlock when we first met.

"Cops'll want you to see the school images," Bartlock said. "And I've got a call into Asheville law enforcement about security film from the rock-and-gem show. Even without his face exposed on the school film, it may be possible to compare all the footage and see if it's the same man."

"Without a face?" Quinn sounded skeptical, slightly insulting.

"Physical traits, kinetic recognition programs, all sorts of things can be used." Bartlock's tone said it was all too technically sophisticated for us mere civilians. I wanted to shake both men. The "mine is bigger than yours" game was getting us nowhere.

"You're gonna help find Daddy, right?" We all turned to see Jane standing in the doorway, her face drawn, eyes large and fearful. "Right?"

"Right," I said. "All of us."

"No. You," she said to me. "Daddy said you can do things, if you would only try. He said you were like him but you were scared."

"Like him how?" Quinn asked.

"I'm his sister," I said quickly. Davie had told no one but family about his gift. Not friends. Certainly not bodyguards even if they were on the payroll. The fact that he had told Isaac and Jubal was indicative of his trust in my friends and his worry for me. "You know I'll help, Jane."

"No. I mean *help*."

I swallowed, remembering the bloodstained wall, the feel of body blows, aware of eyes on me, one set confused, one amused, Jane's desperate. I held out my hand to her. She was so tiny I often forgot she was nearly a teenager. Forgot that Davie told her things most adults wouldn't have, like there was no Santa Claus, no Easter Bunny and psychics really do exist, in the form of the St. Claires. "Yes. I'll help." Saying the words seemed to lift a burden from me I hadn't known I carried. "Come on. I'll tell you about it." As my niece took my hand and we started toward the stairs, I looked up at the cop. "When you get security video, let me know." To Quinn I said, "Jane will be staying with me until Davie is found."

"That's not in my instructions," Quinn said, his tone belligerent.

My little beacon of omnipresent anger flared. "I'm not asking. Jane is my legal responsibility should something happen to Davie. I think this qualifies." Quinn's face fell, as if he hadn't thought about how his life would change if something permanent happened to his employer. Not the brightest bulb in the Mr. Universe pageant lights. "Come on, sweetheart," I said to Jane. "We need to talk."

It was after dark, snow still blowing, when Jane and I finished our discussion. The girl was gloomy, angry and looking for something to kick by then, all feelings I understood. Jane had seen Davie's gift up close for too many years to think it was unusual, and though she had never seen me demonstrate mine, she believed all St. Claires were as strong as her father. She didn't want to accept that I had only a fraction of my brother's gift, and had been unable to pinpoint his location, inform the cops and rush in with guns blasting to save him. Just as her whole world was falling apart, her aunt Tyler was showing signs of being only human.

Suddenly Jane was too big to cry and seek solace with the one who had failed her. When she realized I wasn't the all-powerful being she needed, Jane stopped speaking to me. Instead, she pouted, her finger on the remote and gaze locked on the TV. Great. She was becoming a teenager just when I needed her to be a little girl again. My niece wasn't her usual gentle, kind self, but I couldn't blame her.

The ringing phone and a request to return to the LEC to view the school's security tapes saved me from groveling to get her attention, and I kissed the top of her head for apology. I left Isaac watching over her as Jubal and I dressed for the trip to the law-enforcement center. Bundled against the frigid cold, we stepped out the door to the service alley and slogged through twelve inches of fresh powder to Jubal's car parked near the street.

Winter nights come early in the North Carolina mountains, and though it was not yet six o'clock, it was dark, temperatures well below freezing. Breath billowed, pale clouds in the night. All sound was muted, even our footsteps in heavy winter boots, the world buried and still. Overhead, clouds were clearing and patches of black sky were visible, stars brightly massed.

I reached for the door handle of Jubal's SUV. Blurred shapes shifted in the corner of my eye. Silent. Not broadcasting an intent at all. I started to turn. They took form against the dark in a single instant. Men. One held a stick, swept up high, the other held something…a gun? Two men. Darting in from the night. I sucked in a breath to scream, a sharp hiss of warning. I shrieked and ducked beneath the first blow. Understanding came as I flexed down. We were being attacked.

Jubal dove against his assailant. Kicked high. Missed, twisted awkwardly. Fell to one knee with a soft grunt.

The man with the stick compensated for my dodge.

Whirled, the pole whistling with the motion. A six-foot pole with leather hand grips. A *bowstaff*. Martial arts weapon.

I lunged at him, bobbed beneath the whirling pole. Reacting. Not thinking. Hoping to hit his legs with my body and bring him down. Hoping it would give Jubal time to dispatch his attacker. And help me. The stick brushed over my scalp, along my body. Impacted my left elbow with a dull thunk. Pain crackled through me, electric heat. My arm went useless. I crashed into him.

Touch brought it all clear. His thoughts blasted. *Get her. Get her. Don't injure her.* He grabbed my good arm roughly, translating my momentum into a weapon against me. I fell toward the deep snow, a high drift beside a Dumpster, unable to catch myself.

A single breath sighed on the night. Another blur of movement. Blows landed. My attacker vanished. I rolled into the fluffy deeps. Snow buried me.

Shouts. The sound of flesh being beaten, a rapid staccato of thumps and grunts.

A gun fired. "No!" I shouted into the snow. Fighting to get my good arm beneath me, fighting to regain my feet. When I finally stood, Isaac was poised in the darkness, hands in attack posture, our utility vehicles and the falling dusk his only backdrop. Footsteps sounded as the men ran away.

"Jubal?" Fear laced Isaac's voice.

"I'm okay." His voice was thin, pained. "Sore and embarrassed, but uninjured." I spotted Jubal in the snow, on his side. He held an arm to his partner for a hand up. "Tyler?"

"I'm okay, I think." I massaged my arm and bent it slowly, testing its range of motion. It hurt like heck, but it wasn't broken. My mind skittered through the past few moments. Something was wrong with all this. I settled on the timing. Alarm blossomed through me. "Jane?" I asked Isaac.

"Locked in, security system enabled, with orders to open only to us."

Fear settled back, a crouched tiger ready to claw.

Jubal tried to put weight on his knee and sucked air between his teeth. "They were skilled in some form of martial arts. Don't know what kind," he said, his voice rough with exertion. He stretched his knee and winced. "Maybe just street fighting. Down and dirty. Did they know to expect us? Expect you?"

"Likely," Isaac said. He rubbed a bare lower arm in the icy air, wearing only indoor clothes, though he didn't look cold.

"They didn't even ask for our money. And why bring a gun and not use it first?" Jubal asked. "If they had stayed out of my reach and kept the weapon trained on Tyler, or just shot us—"

"They came to take me," I said.

The two men looked at me, standing in the night, snow covered, shivering. "They would have had to kill me to take you, honeybunch," Jubal assured me. Somehow the pledge wasn't comforting.

"A gunshot seldom kills like in the movies—bang, you're dead. They might have had to fire several times. Quiet little town like this, cops would have been all over it," Isaac said. "Maybe they weren't prepared for that."

"They were supposed to get me but not hurt me."

Isaac looked at me in the dim light, his eyes bright in the darkness.

"How did you know we were in trouble?" I asked, still putting pieces together.

"He heard you scream," Jubal said.

"No. Jane told me."

"What?" I said.

Isaac found my face in the dim light. "Jane told me there were two men waiting in the alley. She knew it. I was already in the alley when they attacked, just too far away to stop it."

"Not possible," I said. "Jane isn't from the matrilineal line of the St.—" I stopped. Lines from Davie's letter suddenly struck home, as painful as the whack with the bowstaff. And as disorienting. *Jane may need help soon. All indications are, her time is on her.*

"Well, scrofulous scabies," I spit. I socked the nearest thing, which happened to be the Dumpster. A dull tone resounded down the alley. Pain spiraled up my good hand. "Spit and decay." I cradled both arms across my middle, wanting to cry.

"What?" Isaac asked.

"Jane's mother. She was a St. Claire. Had to be. And Jane's about to come into her gift." Though my headache struck like a snake, sending fangs deep into my neck and skull, I reached out and touched Jane's mind. She was afraid. "Come on. She's alone." A siren sounded in the next block. "And she called 911."

"I'll stick around and talk to the cops," Jubal said. "They'll want a report."

"Okay. I can give them mine when we get to the law-enforcement center," I said. "Right now, Jane needs me."

We trudged back up the alley, me knocking snow off my clothes, Isaac taking up the rear, keeping an eye on possible return assault. Inside Jubal and Isaac's loft, Jane sat on the oversize leather sofa, dwarfed by the cushions, eyes huge in a pale face. She focused on us, her gaze sweeping from Isaac's knuckles to my elbow. Her breath was rapid, shallow. *She knew what we were thinking, what we were feeling.* Fear swirled through her, so intense it crowded out even tears. Confusion. Desperation. And I didn't know how to help.

My own coming of age had been simple, an easy transition. I had started my menses one morning, sensed my stepfather's muddy thoughts about breakfast, felt my brother's desire to get out of town, had seen through his eyes the suitcase already half packed at the foot of the bed. And I passed out. When I came to, the row between Dumont Lowe and Davie was over and Davie was gone. I had dimly felt a residue of anger, hurt, frustration and violence in the air. And an emptiness where my brother once lived.

"He left you?" Jane asked, a single huge tear pooling, falling from her right eye. "Did Daddy leave you because you started to bleed? 'Cause I'm bleeding and he's gone from me, too."

I raced across the room and gathered my niece in my arms, filling my mind with assurance and tenderness and memories of Davie's love for us both. Banishing my remembered fear and fury and ancient feelings of abandonment and worthlessness, I cuddled Jane in my lap, wrapping my arms and legs around her. "No, baby. You didn't cause your daddy to go away. He got taken. It's all different."

"But he left you." Her throat clogged with misery, both hers and mine.

"He didn't know that I needed him that morning," I whispered. "He never knew." And suddenly I realized the truth of that statement. Davie would never have run away from home had he known that my time of gifting was upon me. A time when no St. Claire was ever left alone. The certainty was almost shockingly painful, the way a bandage hurt when ripped off to reveal an almost healed wound. I hadn't been worthless, a sisterly pain, a nuisance. It wasn't me he was running from. Davie had loved me. Still did.

A joy I had denied myself for years welled up inside. Jane laughed through her tears, sensitive to my happiness. My niece and I rocked on the couch, sharing the certainty of Davie's love for us.

Deep in a hidden part of me, I knew I would have to be careful, oh so careful, of my thoughts and feelings from now on. *Forever.* And I wondered how Aunt Matilda did it, how she lived knowing so much about the others around her and hiding so much more.

With the exception of one recurring vision—the nightmare-prophecy—the long-ago trauma and grief of Davie's leaving had shut down my responses to others and helped me create my wall, the barrier I shut between my mind and the ones around me. How could I take that experience and help Jane with her coming of age? I had no idea. The wall was my constant companion, which had both benefits and drawbacks. I was more protected from the minds of people around me than most St. Claires. But the wall was also the reason my gifts had never developed strong and pure, like some of my line. Even if I could give Jane a wall like mine, did I have the right to deprive her of her heritage?

"Hot cocoa?" Jubal asked. The scent of chocolate was strong on the air. Jubal thought hot cocoa could heal the world, especially if it had miniature marshmallows floating on top. We sipped the sweet cocoa, warmth spreading through us.

When the chocolate was gone, I took Jane across our shared, narrow rooftop garden to my place and helped her with the other part of coming of age, offering supplies and demonstrating how they worked. Explaining how often she would experience the menses. We started her own calendar, to mark the expected evil day, with a code, so if a *boy* happened to see it he would not know what it meant.

For Jane's sake, I carefully, studiously, forced away the memory of my own first menses, with no one to help me but the lady working in the one-hour photo at the pharmacy down the street. My distress, annoyance, embarrassment at becoming a woman and having no one to share it with. No one to help me. Feeling Mrs. Langston's pity even through the wall I had already built.

Then, because it only happened once in a woman's lifetime, that coming of age, and because it should be a joyous experience that marked a wonderful change of life and not just the beginning of a forty-year curse, I invited everyone back to my place and opened a bottle of wine, allowing Jane a tiny sip, toasting her womanhood. Jubal and Isaac lifted my finest crystal with us. And if the wine helped Jane to finally rest, then that was all to the better.

An hour later than we planned, Jubal and I left again for the LEC. Isaac, the most capable among us, remained in my loft, watching over and defending my niece, who had nodded off, snuggled in the soft sheets and down pillows of my big bed.

6

Monday, 6:23 p.m.

As well as look at surveillance videos, I knew I would have to give a statement about the attack in the alley. It wasn't going to be the total truth. There were things best left out of any account, like Jane's involvement and Isaac's presence at the scene.

Jubal was a brown belt in tae kwon do, having taken up the sport when he met Isaac. But Isaac was a martial arts master, registered with the Kukkiwon in South Korea. He was a deadly weapon with his bare hands. If defending us in the alley resulted in injury to the attackers, it could lead to a criminal or civil lawsuit being leveled against Isaac, forcing him to prove he wasn't guilty of anything except defensive moves. That was much less likely if Jubal was my only defender.

On the way over, Jubal shared his version of the events in the alley, which omitted any mention of Isaac. I didn't like it, but I was going to corroborate his statement. I told myself it wasn't a total lie, as I hadn't actually seen Isaac touch anyone, being buried beneath a snowdrift at the time. But I refused to see misery come to anyone because of helping me. And there was no way on earth I was going to mention my niece's name to the cops.

Evan Bartlock met us in the airlock door in front of the LEC, wearing his overcoat, an unlit cigar between two fingers, as if he had been ready to light up. He tucked the cigar into a pocket and led us in without a word.

A cop I didn't know met us inside, skin sagging into folds at his jowls as if his flesh was melting from his bones or he had lost a hundred pounds overnight. A five-o'clock shadow darkened the drooped flesh, topped by a balding pate with a three-strand comb-over. His tie was spotted with grease stains. Overall, he looked unkempt and dead tired. Hound-dog eyes took us in with a glance and pointed for me to sit. "Tyler St. Claire?"

I nodded, suddenly aware of my clothes. Snowmelt had dampened my knees and gloves, and my boots were dark with melt and mud. My hair had come out of its piled bun and hung in untidy strands down my neck. I should have changed and combed my hair. Feeling disheveled myself, I took the seat he pointed to.

"Detective Jack Madison. The officers at the scene took a statement from…" He looked at Jubal and asked, "Jubal Bernard?" Jubal nodded. Madison sat down with a soft squeak of desk-chair wheels at the desk nearest me and moved his mouse, bringing up a screen on his boxy, worn-out PC. "Why don't you tell me what happened in the alley. Start with date and time, please, recount the event, and then describe the persons involved."

I gave my amended and altered story. When I finished, Jubal spoke and Madison typed, two-fingered and fast, asking questions as he did. At the end of the narrative, Jubal shrugged and said, "That's all." Madison looked at him a long moment before glancing at me. He stared at his computer screen, his mouth turned down. Both index fingers tapped the desk in front of his keyboard, a pensive rhythm. "And they just ran away?" Wary, I nodded. "After firing a gun at you? And they didn't try to rob you?"

"I don't know who they fired at. I was buried in a snow-drift at the time. I just heard a shot. They attacked, knocked me into a drift, fired a gun and ran off. And they didn't say anything. Not a word. Nothing. Not give me your wallet. Not your money or your life."

Bartlock gave a soft snort from somewhere behind me and I could feel his amusement at my use of the old robbery phrase. I didn't turn and look, but his humor warmed me. Madison wasn't amused by anything.

"Why do I get a feeling there's a whole lot more you're not telling me?"

"Because there was a whole lot more?" I wanted to add *you doofus* but thought it might not be politic. "But it was all so fast and I spent the last half of it blinded."

"And they attacked you with a bowstaff?"

I nodded.

"A martial-arts weapon, not just a stick?" Again my nod. "And you know that how?"

"Because Jubal uses one in karate practice. They hang on the wall in the do jang, just below the swords."

Madison's entire forehead wrinkled up with the last word.

Stupid. Stupid, stupid, stupid. Never tell a cop more than he asked for. *Swords.* How stupid can I get?

"Do jang?"

"It's a tae kwon do gym." I waited, but Madison decided not to pursue a train of thought that included edged weapons and fists of death and such.

"Uh-huh. You think the men were after you? That maybe they were the same men who took your brother?"

I hadn't said that. I had very carefully not said that. The men who attacked Davie on the security footage had used fists and feet, but it was a primitive beating, not skilled. There had been none of the balanced poetry of the trained martial-arts practitioner. But something in the original security footage had set my teeth on edge, something besides the violence. What if they were the same guys, pretending to be street hoods one time and revealing their true colors the next? Why bother? Was it because they hid who they were when filmed? Part of some plan? "It could be possible," I said slowly, "but I'm not sure it's logical."

"Why would you think that?" the detective asked just as carefully, his hound-dog eyes steady on me, his index fingers now quiescent.

Not sure I could put into words what caused my disquiet, I closed my eyes and thought back to the attack, separating each distinct moment into an individual memory, like a series of photographs I could view in overlay. Instantly I understood what I hadn't had time to process at the moment of the assault. "They were lying in wait. This wasn't a crime of opportunity. They had weapons that were suited to us specifically. They used more sophisticated attack modes than the men who attacked Davie, and they didn't try to rob us."

I fast-forwarded through the images of my impressions. "They separated the moment they reached us, one guy after Jubal, one after me. The guy after Jubal was fast. Vicious. Lots of quick strikes to the head, like this." I opened my eyes and demonstrated with a fist in the air that twisted on impact. "And kicks to the knees. They wanted to bring him down, knock him out, hurt him. These guys were trained, smooth. Not brawny rednecks like on the film of Davie."

I could feel the attention of the men behind me. Bartlock's interest, Jubal's fear that I would say too much. "The guy who came after me gave body blows with the bowstaff, which seemed intended to temporarily incapacitate me, not kill or maim. I think he hit my elbow by accident. The bowstaff is a deadly weapon in the hands of someone who knows how to use it. This guy did. He could have taken me down with two strikes, but he didn't knock me out or break a joint or bone."

"Let me see the elbow?" Madison asked.

I pulled off my down jacket and shoved up both sleeves, T-shirt and undershirt, to reveal the small purple spot just above my elbow. The bruise was sharp at the edges, fresh. I bent my arm and winced slightly. "It hurts but it isn't broken. And he could have shattered the bone with a bowstaff."

"Why did your brother hire Quinn Baker?"

The question seemed to come out of left field. "My brother has money. A daughter. He needed a bodyguard."

"But why Quinn Baker?"

I explained the story of Quinn being arrested and Davie taking pity on him, helping with his legal problems and getting him trained to be a bodyguard. All the while I talked, Madison's eyes roved my face and back to his desk, where he now took notes with pen on paper. When I finished, his focus locked on me and he said, "Did he know that Quinn has ties to the Roman Trio?"

"What is a Roman Trio?" I asked, feeling his intense interest, like a razor cutting into the edges of my mind. "Sounds like an Italian restaurant run by a set of triplets."

"They're a small-time crime organization based in Atlanta, with a strong foothold in Asheville. The Trio has ties to larger organizations. They help move drugs through the mountains for New York and Miami operations, as part of an established path from the Florida Keys to New York City and all points between. But drugs aren't their main niche. They run illegal gambling in the western part of the state."

"Gambling?"

His interest sharpened. I looked down at my hands, not knowing what to say and what to keep silent. What if Davie hadn't told me the truth about his years away? I had always known he was keeping something back. What if he was keeping something dangerous back? Something illegal? Illegal gambling? *He had once admitted to a problem....* No. Not Davie.

"If you know anything, you should tell me. Your brother's life might depend on it."

I looked back up at the detective. He would have promised me the moon if it would have made me talk. But he was right, and that counted for more than vague threats or empty promises. "Davie disappeared when I was a kid. Left home, ran away. I was fourteen. When he came back a few years later, he told me he had made a fortune in gambling. Davie has money. I accepted what he told me as truth." But what if it wasn't and bad guys were after him because of connections to the Mob? What did that have to do with the gold in the storeroom? I rubbed my forehead. Madison's concentration was phenomenal, but he was projecting and I was having a hard time concentrating on my own thoughts and not his impressions of the moment. It gave me a headache.

"Where was he all the time he was gone after he ran away?"

"I don't know."

"He never said?"

"I never asked."

Madison sat back in his chair. He didn't believe me.

"Why not?" I asked.

Madison blinked. I had responded to a statement he hadn't made aloud.

I decided to go for broke. "Why don't you believe me? What good would it do for me to lie to you? My brother came home with a child and made a life for himself here. All I ever wanted was for him to be nearby. To be family. When he came home I accepted what few stories he was willing to tell. His heart was broken because his wife had died. I figured he'd tell me more when he was ready." Except Davie's readiness had never come around. And now maybe it was too late. Davie's letter suggested that his past had caught up with him, and because I didn't pry back then, I couldn't help now. Tears gathered in my eyes. I rubbed my head again. I needed aspirin.

"Is that all, Detective?" Bartlock asked from behind me. Huge paws landed gently on my shoulders. Instantly calm descended on me. The hands began to knead tight muscles in my neck and shoulders. Warmth curled through me, chasing the chill away. "My cousin has been shaken up, attacked. She needs rest and she still hasn't seen the video."

Madison sighed. "Yeah. We're done." He flicked a card into my lap and continued by rote, sounding both strained and bored. "Don't leave town without notifying us. Here's my card. If you remember anything else, give me a call." He nodded to the far hallway and looked up at Bartlock. "You're welcome to take care of the viewing. I'll check in with you in a bit."

I picked up that the detective intended to watch us through a one-way glass as we watched the video. Devious little snit. But I was good; I didn't say it. I just rose and followed my long-lost cousin several times removed and my best friend into a small interrogation room and sat down after rearranging the chairs, my back to the mirrored window out of spite. Jubal sat beside me and held my hand, lending me his strength. I gripped his fingers hard.

The video from the school was in black and white, and the man who had tried to pick Jane up from school never lifted his head for a straight-on shot. It was the man from the rock-and-gem show. The medium-brown man who had knocked me down and stolen my bag only to leave it where it could be found, with nothing taken. The same man who had ransacked my hotel room. Was he looking for the gold? Had to be. Should I tell the cops about the gold in my storeroom? Couldn't.

"It's him," I said softly. "The guy from the show."

"And he wasn't one of the guys in the alley tonight?" Bartlock asked.

"I don't think so."

"I don't think so, either," Jubal said. "This guy moves with a rough, homespun rhythm. The men who came after us were fluid when they moved. Dangerous. This guy looks like he has something stuck up his backside."

"We likely have multiple players in this thing," Bartlock said. "Two men who attacked you in the alley. This guy. And maybe two more, the men who attacked David, assuming they aren't the same ones from tonight. We've got a computer program running comparisons on kinetic recognition right now. We should know something by morning."

"Can I take Tyler home now? She's beat," Jubal said.

"Sure. I'll be by in the morning."

"Come for breakfast," Jubal said. "We'll be having something special since the kid's staying over."

"Pancakes or waffles," I said, offering a tired smile. "Isaac cooks a mean rasher of bacon."

"I'll be there. And the police will be making regular runs by the store and your lofts tonight. To keep an eye out."

"Thanks, man," Jubal said, rising and pulling me to my feet.

I turned to the mirror and said, "You can come, too, Detective Madison. There's always room for one more."

Bartlock laughed out loud. He seemed to think I was funny.

We were on the way home, Jubal's small four-by-four crawling along a shoveled, salted, iced-over roadway, when it occurred to me to ask Madison about the police tap on my phone. I had also forgotten to get Davie's cards back. Timing is everything. I'd have to wait and ask Bartlock in the morning. I sighed.

"I agree."

I looked up at Jubal. "With what?" I was pretty sure I hadn't spoken aloud.

"That she's either slutty or has short-term memory problems."

I followed Jubal's gaze to the front window of the Red Bird Coffee Shoppe. Gail Speeler sat at an intimate table in the almost empty restaurant, her head bowed close to a man. The man's back was to us, but he had high-swept, jet-black hair and was wearing a shirt with one of those standup, round collars people wear in the city. Neru collars, or something. My sigh had obviously led Jubal to think I had already seen the couple and was reacting.

As we glided past the coffee shop, Gail put her hand on the man's arm, one of those feminine gestures that says, *See me. I am the only woman in the world.* Then we were beyond the window and, though I swiveled in my seat and leaned back, I saw only brick and mortar and ice-frosted window glass.

I wasn't sure, but the man Gail was touching could have been Colin Hornsburn, a developer with interests in high-end growth projects. That's what they called it now. Not housing developments or retail-commercial expansion—high-end growth projects. PC for the building business.

Colin Hornsburn had spearheaded successful projects all across the Appalachians. At a county council meeting last year, Davie had called him a rapist to his face, in front of witnesses. Raping the land, raping the mountains of their timber and water runoff, raping the animals of their habitat. Hornsburn had not been happy with the epithet. Davie was a dedicated environmentalist. Development of any kind made him edgy.

If Gail was so in love with my brother while on TV, why was she tête-à-tête with the enemy? I felt a spike of temper, the first since we were attacked in the alley. I rotated to face front. "I'm going with slutty."

"Yeah, me, too. Breeders," he said with false contempt.

I socked Jubal's shoulder. "I'm a breeder. My brother is a breeder. Not everyone can be gay. The species would die out."

"Breeders are disgusting." He backhanded me, hitting me in the chest. "Men and women. Together. Doing it."

"Gays are warped deviants and damned to the fires of hell." I socked him again. We both grinned. The exchange of blows and words made us both feel better.

"Holy tights and codpieces, Batman!" he said, stealing the last word. "The good guys are queer!"

I laughed softly.

Life would have been far easier for him if Jubal had been straight, or at least faked it and lived as if he were. But it seemed to me people were attracted to fairly specific types of things. Long black hair, or blond hair and blue eyes, or hairy backs. It wasn't a choice what turned me on, I knew what I liked. And it wasn't anything with boobs. So I figured gay people were in the same situation. You like what you like. It was only how you lived with the preferences that mattered.

A recently converted Bible-thumper had called Jubal names and for weeks made life miserable for Jubal and Isaac not long after Isaac moved in. Because the preacher had quoted scripture from the top of his lungs, standing on a street corner across from the shop, spewing hate instead of love— God *was* supposed to be about love, wasn't he?—I had a pretty good idea what the Bible said about people like my friends. I always wondered if there wasn't a way to get God's point across without resorting to hate, but I had never seen it.

Back at the loft, Isaac met us at the door with sleepy eyes and a relaxed posture. It was clear without asking that no one had attacked the place in our absence. "She's been asleep since about ten minutes after you guys left. No calls, no messages," Isaac said, folding a martial-arts magazine beneath one arm. I tugged him down and kissed him on the cheek. The men locked up, slipped out the side door and walked across the narrow rooftop garden to their place.

The SUV ride had been too short for the heater to warm up and I was frozen. I quickly stripped off my boots, coat and jeans and climbed into my bed with Jane. Her small body had heated the mattress and sheets and I snuggled up next to her, falling into sleep instantly.

I forgot to wall my thoughts against outside impressions. I forgot about fear and the openings to the mind in the dark of night. I forgot about dreams.

I opened my eyes to a cold world, gray and dark and alone. The small window beyond my feet glowed with false dawn. My wrist ached where frozen metal encircled it. Shoulder muscles were so stiff they pulled and howled with pain when I rolled over on the thin mattress. Springs groaned below me.

On the far side of the wall, I heard a scrape of metal on wood, the movement of a chair on the hardwood floor. I had caught glimpses of it when they brought me here.

Fast glimpses of a desk piled high with papers, rolled scrolls, books, calculators, an outdated computer. Memory pictures.

The paper they made me sign, giving up all rights to all properties I owned. The sight of my own hand, a finger broken. Wrist inflamed, swollen.

The feel of my chest where they had broken my ribs. Behind me, a door opened, flooding the room with light. "Well, I see the little rich boy is awake."

Fear caught me. Pain spasmed across my back and chest. Misery and tenderness flooded through me. *"Oh, Davie."* Shock took me up. *"Brat?"*

My eyes opened, my heart pounding. A cold sweat sheathed my body and I shivered. A headache throbbing over my left eye. The dream-that-wasn't-a-dream was gone. Outside, the night had faded to early dawn. Jane slept at my back, her small body snuggled into me for warmth, her breathing regular and smooth. I slid from the bed and padded on stocking feet to the window.

"No," I whispered to myself. Holding my head with a palm to keep my brain from exploding, I moved around the apartment until I found a window that revealed the shade of gray in my dream. "East," I said, speaking the words aloud so I wouldn't forget. "Davie's window faces east. No stars showed in it." Ignoring the cold, I placed a hand on the window frame and leaned in, putting my aching forehead on the icy glass. "He's in a business of some kind or a house with an office in it. They've made him sign papers. He has a broken finger, broken ribs, chaffed wrist, is handcuffed to a metal-framed bed on a mattress with no sheets. He has no covers and no heat. He has a watchdog, male, with a local accent. A bully who likes to hurt him."

I shivered with cold and with Davie's remembered fear and pain. He was afraid for Jane and me, as much as for himself. He was mortally afraid he couldn't hold out much longer. Davie was hurt....

I remembered the gun Jubal had taken and placed out of sight. I had left it somewhere in the front of the shop. I promised myself to get the gun, buy ammunition and get some target practice. Frozen, I took two Tylenol, padded back to bed and snuggled against Jane. Deliberately I left my mind open to the night and closed my eyes. And slept.

7

Tuesday, after dawn

When I woke again, it was to a dawn-grayed apartment, an elbow in my ribs. "You snore," Jane said.

"Do not," I mumbled.

"Do too. Like a hog in mud." She smiled at me, her long brown hair in a swirl across her face. "Haurghff-haurghff," she grunted, very piglike.

"Do not, do not, do not." I was reminded of Madison's comb-over and brushed the silken tresses off her brow. My hand was still touching her when she spoke.

"He must be weird. Why do men do that, anyway?"

I froze, hand in contact with her skin. Jane stilled, feeling my reaction. "I got that out of your brain, didn't I?" she asked.

I nodded. "Uh-huh."

"Like Daddy?"

I nodded again, my ear scrubbing on the pillow.

"And you can get stuff out of my brain, too? Just like that?"

I nodded yet again. "Sometimes."

"This sucks a great big ostrich egg," she said, quoting one of my favorite phrases.

"Yeah. It does. I know it's scary for you."

"Daddy says you got a wall that stops you from getting stuff like that. Can you teach me how?"

Quickly I stuffed the fear her question created into a dark hole in my mind and slammed shut the door. "I can try. But I'm not trained like Davie was. Mom was still alive and Davie was sent to live with Aunt Matilda when he came into his gift. She was there to teach him. I was alone and never got trained. At all. So I'm not sure how to share all the tricks of the trade."

"So call Aunt Matilda."

"Yeah. That's the best option." I tried to keep silent my thought that Aunt Matilda might demand Jane come to the Low Country for training, but Jane was already powerful. She picked it up.

"No freaking way. I'm not going anywhere until my daddy can take me. Himself. Period. And that made you glad. Why don't you like Aunt Matilda?"

I couldn't keep my reaction walled off.

Jane's face grew incredulous. "You're scared of her?"

"Stop it," I said, taking away my hand with an uncomfortable laugh. "A girl is entitled to a few secrets. Read my thoughts now." I deliberately thought of a bright pink, lop-eared rabbit with a blue studded collar around his neck and a safety pin in one ear. Jane shook her head. I put my hand back to her face. "Now."

"Rabbit. Punk rabbit. Almost Goth, but the collar needs to be black."

"Good." I removed my hand and tucked the covers closer to my neck. The room was cold. I needed to turn on the fireplace and blower. "Yours is like mine, then, at least today, though that may change. Like you, I pretty much need touch to make it work." I shook myself more fully awake and realized that wasn't exactly true. I pursed my lips. "Except for last night when you knew about the guys in the alley. Tell me what you felt, what you saw."

Jane blew out a puff of air and pulled the silky down comforter over her chin. "I was sitting at the table waiting for hot cocoa. Isaac was in the kitchen with his back to me. I heard a sound, like a scuff, like a shoe on the mat at the door. Then I heard a guy say, 'Okay, okay. They're coming. Hit him hard and I'll take her. Blank it all. Trees and bushes. Go.' And I saw some trees. And then I saw blood, and somebody liked it. I screamed it all at Isaac and he hollered for me to lock up, set the alarm and not let anyone in until he got back. And he was gone." Her face crumpled.

"And," I prompted.

"And then I was seeing the men but they looked like stick people." Her voice roughened, her hand slid into mine beneath the covers. "Like haunted tree people moving around. And they were hitting you and Jubal," she said as tears gathered. "And Isaac was flying like a bird and clawing and I was in everybody's mind at once. And I got so scared." A tear rolled sideways across her right cheek, another pooled against the left side of her nose. "And then it stopped. And I thought you were dead."

"A really great big ostrich egg," I agreed.

She smiled wanly.

What had Davie told her about the gift? He had known it would come to her when she came of age, but had never told me she was a St. Claire. How far had he prepared her? How did I tell her that the St. Claire gift was always like that? Really helpful. And totally useless. Never there when you needed it and then giving only fuzzy images or impressions. "Tell me what your daddy told you about the St. Claires. And about the gift. Tell me about how he prepared you for it." When she looked at me blankly, I added, "Did he teach you meditation or yoga or anything? Anything that seemed weird?"

"My dad is a psychic. He's weird with everything," she said, her tone working at being teenage-girl-world-weary, with a dash of parents-are-such-a-pain thrown in. But the sadness and fear for her father were almost tangible beneath. "Real new-age weird, always testing himself with rocks and metal, and talking to plants. But yeah, he taught me meditation."

"Isaac and Jubal are fixing breakfast this morning. It's early, but they'll be up. Shall we go over?"

"Sure. But you get the first shower."

"Why's that?"

"Because that way you get to heat up this refrigerator you call an apartment some. It's cold as 'lasses in here."

I knew she was quoting Davie and touched the tip of her nose, sending her thoughts of love and tenderness. "Done." Her smile brightened. I rolled out of bed, hit the cold floor and started my morning routine. Which wouldn't be routine at all, not until Davie was found. While in the shower, I pondered the things my niece had plucked from the attackers' minds. Trees and bushes. They had been shielding their minds from someone. Ergo, they knew about my gift. Now, that really sucked a big ostrich egg. A car-sized ostrich egg. That changed everything.

Dressed in long johns, denim and flannel, Jane and I tramped through deep snow on the roof to the boys' apartment where they were outdoing themselves. In the loft across from mine, the table was set with Jubal's good crystal and china on starched linen. Candles were burning in cut-crystal holders, flickering off the apricot-painted dining-room walls. There were fresh flowers on the table. It must be a gay thing, to be able to find fresh flowers on a weekday morning before anything opened. If I'd been a froufrou kinda gal, I'd have been jealous of the talent.

While Jubal loaded the table with elegant pitchers, platters and bowls filled with blueberry syrup, strawberry syrup, maple syrup, cane syrup, whipped cream, fruit, bacon, coffee, tea, milk and juice, and while the waffles cooked under Isaac's watchful eye, we discussed whether Jane was going to school. There were safety issues and then there were issues of a St. Claire sort. How would Jane react when surrounded by hundreds of classmates and teachers? How open to sensation, emotions and mental pressure was she?

Before Evan Bartlock arrived and while the last waffles were browning, we decided to test her. I didn't have a clue how Aunt Matilda tested her clan, but I knew what worked on me, and so devised a method.

I sat Jane on a stool in the kitchen, her eyes closed. "Now, I want you to practice that meditation ritual Davie gave you to clear your mind."

"The candle burning, the quiet place, I know, I know." The words were bored, but it was obvious Jane was excited. For the moment, she was the center of her world.

Without her knowing what they were, I gave the men very specific thoughts, dissimilar to the Goth bunny but just as odd, then positioned each man ten feet from her. I stood at the far corner of the room, a cup of strong black tea in my hand.

"Okay, fix the images firmly in your minds and walk slowly toward her. Jane, the moment you sense anything or get an image, let us know." Jubal glanced at me and I nodded. The men started forward. As they approached, step by slow step, I watched Jane's face. And was secretly glad when she didn't react. My niece was unable to pick up a single image from the men until they actually touched her.

"That was good, right?" Jane asked. "It means I have a wall like you?"

I didn't know whether to be relieved or worried. "It sounds good to me. Part two."

The men moved back to the far side of the room and this time I told them to remember events that caused them strong emotion. Emotion that they could feel to this day. "Emotion that is appropriate to a little girl," I mock-warned. Again Jane had no clue what to expect as they crossed the room to her. Step by step, my friends moved closer, their faces intent. Jane sat with eyes closed, expression serene. And so far, nothing.

I had once wondered if autism in children was a sign that the entire human race was becoming psychic. What if an un-suspecting child were suddenly bombarded with thousands of impressions, emotions, images from every side, from every person, with no hidden truths or protection from fleeting thoughts, hopes, fears, petty angers. What if the only way to survive was to shut down totally?

"Okay. I got something. Two somethings."

The men stopped. They were eight feet from her. Which was not good.

"I got a little puppy, squashed by a car. Oh...." Her voice changed, developed a soft Texan accent. "That was so sad. I loved that pup. He used to follow me around all the time." Jane's face scrunched up tightly. "And my daddy hit me." It was Jubal's speech pattern. "He thought I stole some gum from the store. But I didn't. Sissy did. And Daddy doesn't be-lieve me. He always loved her best."

Fear zinged through me, a whip-crack of horror. Jane's eyes snapped open, her face mirroring mine.

"Stop it, guys," I said, quickly envisioning a lit candle. I held the image as I crossed the room to my niece and touched her shoulder, pulling her attention to me alone. I thought happy thoughts as I analyzed her reaction, concentrating on visions of angels and fairies and roller-coaster rides. Each image held a reflection of a lit candle behind it. Jane slumped as my meditative thoughts stimulated her own. She relaxed and watched my face. I schooled myself to calm. Jane had personalized the impressions. Become one with the moment. And that scared the pee out of me. A thought I kept way back in the deeps of my mind.

When I received an impression, it was almost always at a distance, an event that I was seeing, not feeling, except with strong emotion or violence, like when Davie was being beaten. Unlike me, Jane had lost herself instantly, falling into the mind-thoughts-feelings of her friends. If her own personality was not strong enough to filter out the people around her, would she lose herself in the personalities of the others?

I remembered the only visit I had made to the St. Claire stronghold in the Low Country before my gift came upon me. Everything had been so strange, including the whispers that stopped instantly when I entered a room. I learned later that the secrets had been about cousin Imogene, who had lost herself, lost her mind, within a year after she found her gift. Was that a possibility for Jane?

I put a smile on my face and patted her shoulder. "Waffles are ready. You did good, Jane. Hungry?"

"Way hungry!" She hopped down from the stool and raced to her seat at the big dining-room table. Jubal and Isaac watched me for a moment, but I didn't meet their eyes. With a swift glance at each other, they turned to host duties and served the meal. My thoughts carefully kept to myself, I ate, the food like dust and ashes in my mouth.

Jane insisted she could go to school, contending that being surrounded by her friends would be a great place to practice building a wall against their thoughts. I didn't agree, but also had no firm defense against her attending except a sense of foreboding. She might take months to come fully into her gift. How long could I keep her isolated? Was I even supposed to? How in blue blazes was a St. Claire trained?

I was going to have to call Aunt Matilda.

Sick at the thought, I caved in and allowed Isaac to drive Jane to school.

In the storeroom an hour later, I realized that Evan Bartlock hadn't shown up for breakfast. I wondered what incident might have affected his plans. Surely something about Davie. I recalled my dream, impressions of Davie, his pain, his location. But there was so little to go on. A window that faced east and showed only sky, not a nearby mountain that could give me a landmark. A bloody wall. Broken bones. An office. Somewhere.

I couldn't help my brother. All my life I had hated the times when I was helpless, out of control, useless. It was probably why I became a lapidary. Working stone gave me control over the most fundamental of all things, the earth. If I could reshape a stone, cut it away from the mother rough, give it a shape that combined its inner self, which is trapped in the rock, and an image of my choosing, if I could polish it and make it a thing of beauty, then nothing was beyond me. There was nothing I couldn't do. And I was no longer helpless, at the mercy of the world.

Aunt Matilda, if she were here and saw my current indecision, would read the cards, probably laying out a Shadow Path spread. And then she would tell me all about my inner uncertainties, the fears I refused to face. Like I didn't know them already.

Outside, another storm was blowing in, this one sleet and freezing rain, which would, at first, melt yesterday's snow, then create a hard shell of ice on top. Town was deserted. No one would move around much and I didn't expect customers, yet someone had to stay in the front just in case. Noe wasn't coming in, preferring to work at home updating the Web site offerings, preparing invoices for shipping the sold items, and coming up with advertising blurbs for the spring line. Isaac had a class to teach at his do jang and Jubal had work to do in back. I had the display area of Bloodstone Inc. to myself.

Needing to do something, I pulled the wooden crate full of Davie's papers to me and carried it to the front of the shop.

Settling into a wing chair, I slid an afghan over my feet and began going through the files.

The morning passed slowly as I dug through financial papers, property deeds, county and state property-tax notices, letters and printouts of e-mails. I hadn't the faintest idea what I was looking for. I could only hope I'd know it when I saw it.

And maybe I did. I was on my third cup of black tea, the Christmas mug resting on an electric warming plate, when I found correspondence between Davie and some guy in the governor's office. Charlie Stunhold, assistant to the governor herself. The letters were photocopies in a folder marked WLS. The letter on top was a proposal from Davie to the state of North Carolina, that they work together in a joint venture to create a new kind of wildlife sanctuary, a place that allowed wildlife of all kinds to roam safely within the existing framework of the town of Connersville and its surrounding county land.

It was to be a test project, an experiment to show that modern man, who spent less time farming and living off the land and more time indoors, could cohabit the earth in relative safety with unfenced wild animals who could roam freely. He wanted wolves, black bears, elk, bison and even cougars to be reintroduced to the mountainous regions of the state. And he wanted to donate most of the land to the state for the experimental wildlife sanctuary. It was pure Davie, a vision only he could see, impractical and nigh impossible. A dream world.

The second letter laid out the bones of the entire plan, five pages of proposals Davie had put together with a lawyer, a team of wildlife and environmental experts from across the region, and a team at Clemson University. I paged through the letters, recognizing names and titles of important people in the state. People with ideas and the money to carry them out. A senator, three county commissioners and six big muck-ety-mucks in the state parks department were among the names. And he had secured promises from three other land-holders in the region to give, set aside, or otherwise make available large tracts of land for the project.

"Holy moly," I said, paging through e-mails and papers in the file folder. This wasn't just a dream. Davie was making it a reality.

I discovered that Davie had bought or optioned nearly ten thousand mountain acres over the past ten years. Ten thousand...

I stared at the letters and the amount of acreage. It was staggering. It represented more money than I could have believed. And Davie wanted to donate almost all of it for the project. Where had my brother gotten that kind of money?

I flipped through the rest of the papers for financial records that might explain what was going on, how Davie had secured rights and ownership to that much land. Even if he only optioned most of the land at pennies on the dollar, it was a disturbing sum.

And if the gold was on one of the hills he owned and Davie was refusing to sell, if he was holding the land with the intent that he would *never* sell, then it made an awful kind of sense that someone would kidnap him and keep him until they got the land and the gold.

I remembered the vision from my scan. Davie's keeper had forced him to sign some papers. Mineral rights? Land-use rights? How did they think they could use the papers without giving away that they were the ones behind the kidnapping? It was insane.

In the back of the folder I found two heavy beige envelopes, four inches square. Inside one was a beige card with columns of numbers printed in my brother's neat hand, green ink on the thick paper. I rotated the card over and over. Its edges were raised and shiny with fancy embossing; it looked like the card had originally been intended as a blank thank-you card or invitation card to a formal event. Heavy stock, like that used for weddings. I had no idea what the numbers might mean. Bank account numbers? Phone numbers?

Inside the other small envelope was a long, narrow, baroque, brass key with the number 123 engraved on it. It was shaped like an ornate safe-deposit key, except that it was embellished with curlicues and fleur-de-lis and it was old. Very old. The tarnish was decades' dark, the metal a rich deep brown. An old safe key? A key to open some religious reliquary? I turned it over and over, my fingers tracing its worn surface, hoping for an image, a vision. Getting nothing, of course, I closed it back in its envelope.

When the phone rang just before lunch, I was startled to realize the phone had not rung since the police had begun to monitor the line. It was really abnormal for Bloodstone to go so long without a call. Had the cops screwed up and rerouted our calls? Or was it just the weather? I heard Jubal pick up the receiver and speak. A moment later, he stepped into the front of the store and handed me the cordless phone. His face was tight with worry.

"Tyler St. Claire," I said, my eyes on Jubal's blue ones.

"Your brother won't last much longer." Dread pooled within me, seeping into my bones. It sounded the same as before, a computer-generated tone, devoid of clues as to its owner. "You have twenty-four hours before we start removing body parts as an inducement for you to cooperate. Forty-eight hours to get us what we want. Then he's dead."

I pointed to the ceiling and mouthed the words, *Check the caller ID upstairs.* Jubal nodded and raced for the stairs to my loft. Into the phone I said, "If I knew what you wanted, you could have it in a heartbeat. Just tell me what you want and I'll bring it to you."

"Coordinates. We'll call you. Twenty-four hours." The phone went dead.

I stared at the small cordless phone, clicking off the connection on my end. Distantly I heard Jubal clattering down the stairs from my loft. "No number on the ID. Just a line of *x*'s. But that black box was humming. Maybe the cops got something."

I looked from the phone in my hand to my friend. "They want coordinates. For the gold, I'm sure. And I don't have them. I don't have anything." I knew I needed help. St. Claire help. The thought of calling Aunt Matilda made my spine grow weak and sent spikes of alarm through my middle. But I found my finger punching her number, a number I hadn't called in years.

Far away, in the Low Country, Aunt Matilda's phone rang. And rang. And rang. Black despair twisted through me, twining deep into my marrow. She wasn't there. *Aunt Matilda is always there.*

On the tenth ring a click sounded. A mechanical voice said, "Leave a message. We'll get back to you." A tone sounded. Stunned to hear a message machine when Aunt Matilda was so vehemently anti-electronic, anti-machine, I stuttered a moment before the words came, and then they were a torrent. "Davie's been kidnapped. The kidnappers think I have something they want—coordinates—but I don't have them. I got a vision of them beating him but I can't find him. They're going to start cutting on him if I don't have what they want by tomorrow. And Jane is a St. Claire and she's come into her gift and I don't know what to do. Aunt Matilda, call me. This is—" Another tone sounded, then a click, and the line went dead.

I looked up at Jubal, tears shimmering his form. "I don't know what to do, Jubal. I don't know what to do."

"We'll figure it out, honeybunch," he said as he knelt at my side and took me into his arms. "You may not have the wicked, clairvoyant, psychic St. Claires, but you have Isaac and Noe and me. And you have prayer. Don't forget that."

I smiled into his shoulder, feeling the calm of his acceptance steal over me. I might be a failed St. Claire, one who never accepted her gift or lived up to her potential, one who ran from the gift in fear, but I had my friends. And that counted for more than anything else. And Jubal was right. I had prayer, even if I had run from El, too. I hugged Jubal hard and wiped my face, saying a small prayer, hoping El would listen to me even if I hadn't listened much myself recently. Calmer, I went back to the papers, hoping that the cops, if they got anything from the phone call, would notify me soon.

I was sitting in the law-enforcement center, subsequent to a fast, slippery drive across town. Madison and Evan stood to the side, watching a technician of some sort operate a videotape machine.

"The Asheville cops isolated the time, and sent us portions of the films from the rock-and-gem show," Madison said. "If you can spot him, they'll look through the entire day, see if they discover anything that will let us ID him. But so far, they aren't willing to just give up the tapes. Not without making me jump through some hoops."

On the small TV screen was a poor-quality video, people taking a step, then in the next frame appearing further along, taking a different step. It was hard to follow at first. I bent closer to get a clearer view, but my position didn't help the condition of the filming. It pretty well sucked a robin's egg.

"We have fourteen camera angles for you to view. If you spot him, say something."

No kidding. I'd thought I'd just let you guess.

On the fifth snippet of film, I spotted not the man but my

backpack, and pointed. "That's me. And…" I bent closer and away again. "That's him, there. Watching me."

Madison made a disbelieving sound, as if he was surprised that I would find anything. As if he thought I might have made up a story like getting kidney-punched and robbed. And having nothing stolen, et cetera, et cetera, yada, yada. Okay, he had a point.

In the tenth snippet of film I saw the brown man again, this time carrying my backpack. I tapped the screen and sat back, crossing my arms, grinning up at the detective. I didn't even have to say it. My expression said it all.

"I think we have enough to ID the man," he said stiffly. "Thank you for coming down to the station."

"What? I don't get to look through the mug books or anything?"

"We have technology for that sort of thing. When we narrow it down, if there's any question, we'll call you."

I swiveled in my chair and looked up at Evan. "That's it?"

"That's it." He seemed amused by my reaction. Jack Madison merely removed the tape and left the room.

"That man is just brimming with personality."

8

The sleet and freezing rain had tapered off, lying in crusty gray piles against the window ledges. The streets were thick with ice, and nothing moved outside except a local man who shoveled walks for drinking money, and the town's snowplows, which pushed the dirty sludge into drifts almost four feet high. A warm front was expected tomorrow and it would all melt, but for now, it was a dangerous, muddy, salted mess.

A figure walked past the window, feet crunching ice, body hunched against the wind. He slipped and almost fell before he turned and entered Bloodstone Inc. with a blast of cold air that chilled the shop ten degrees in a single instant. He was wearing city clothes, inappropriate for the mountains and the weather—a suit, wingtip shoes, a long wool coat. All gray and black. No muffler, no ear protectors, no hat, and thin leather gloves that looked stylish but probably didn't offer much protection against the cold. I slid Davie's papers back into the crate, set the afghan on top, and stood. "Can I help you?"

He pulled off the gloves as he answered, "Are you Tyler St. Claire?"

"Yes."

"I'm Adam Wiccam, Treasury Department." With a pale hand, he opened a leather wallet and showed me a badge and

ID. Any good computer geek can generate IDs, but this looked realistic, with a hologram seal to one side. He didn't offer to shake hands and neither did I. There was something about the man that I didn't like on first meeting, and touching him wasn't something I wanted to do.

"What can you tell me about your brother, David Lowe."

"Nothing," I said, startled. Dave had never gone by the Lowe name; neither of us had. Why…? I reached out with my gift, and touched—nothing.

"We've been looking for him for the last ten years in connection with a theft of government property." Wiccam smiled, a twist of lips that didn't reach his eyes, and I knew instantly he was both lying to me and telling the truth.

Davie, a thief?

As the thought crossed my mind, Wiccam closed off from me behind a wall of nothingness much like my own. The absolute darkness of the space where his mind should be was a shock. Was that what Davie found when he searched my mind? That emptiness? Remembering the men who attacked me in the alley, the men who projected trees and shrubs, I shut down my own mind, hard.

"We traced him to Connersville, but he isn't answering his phone or his door. Have you seen your brother recently?"

I didn't know what to say. This man was a liar, a very good one. He blended truth and lies into a confusing concoction that he might even believe on some level. And he had a wall like I did, though I bet his wasn't a medieval stone wall. His was probably some high-tech electric fence. His eyes were hazel with bright yellow flecks. They gazed into mine, curious, waiting. And as I struggled to open my mouth, his eyes changed. A kind of *knowing* entered into them, a knowing I had only seen with St. Claires.

Into the awful silence after his question, the door opened and Evan Bartlock entered, stamping his feet and blowing billows of breath until the door closed. Wiccam's eyes shuttered and he spun, coattails flying. As he saw Evan, I thought I caught a trace of annoyance cross his features, quickly masked. What was going on here?

Bartlock paused, reading the tableau of two people and the tension that bound us. Then he smiled. "Ms. St. Claire. Is my watch ready?"

We didn't repair watches, at least not the timekeeping mechanism. I opened my mouth, not knowing what to reply.

"The silver bracelet was soldered last night," Jubal said from over my shoulder. I closed my mouth. "But as we discussed, the metals may not hold. Differing metallic compounds often won't hold a solder joint for very long. I'd like to work on it again, if you don't mind leaving it another day."

"Sure. Awful weather, isn't it?"

I looked back and forth between them. Puzzled.

"Bad. But it should improve soon. Can I show you that amethyst piece again while you're here? I know your sister would love it."

"Great. I'd love to see it." Following that artful dialogue, they moved to a display two feet from Wiccam. I knew for a fact that there was no amethyst in that display. They were protecting me, making a point to be in close proximity to Wiccam. If I hadn't been so confused, I would have smiled.

"Here's my card. If you hear from your brother, please call me. We can save him a lot of trouble later on, if he'll just come in now." Wiccam put his card in my hand without touching me, nodded, and glanced at the two leaning over the display case as he went back out into the weather. Standing in the cold air, he pulled up his collar and crunched off.

I followed the man to the door and leaned against the cold glass, watching Wiccam as he moved unsteadily down the street, sliding in his city-boy shoes. I had said exactly six words to Wiccam, yet I knew he had gleaned much more from me than the six words would have shared, just as I had taken much more from him. Fingers on the glass, I considered what we had garnered from each other.

Wiccam was not a cop. He worked for the government, but not in a law-enforcement capacity. He was a very good liar, but hadn't expected that I would be able to ferret that out. He was gifted in ways similar to the St. Claires. He might have suspected that I was gifted, too, but he hadn't been certain of it until he came into the shop. He called Davie by our step-father's name yet knew we were siblings. He knew Davie was gifted. Now he knew I was, too, though he might not know how spectacularly inefficient and clumsy I was.

I watched Wiccam as he turned down Main Street and dis-appeared. He had come to the shop to discover what I was. And he knew Davie was in trouble.

Isaac eased into the line of cars at the front of the school. I braced myself with a hand on the dash, craning my head in an attempt to spot Jane through the window of the principal's office. Due to the weather, the school board was ending classes early, letting out at two, but Mrs. Godansky felt that Jane couldn't wait that long. She had called while I watched Wiccam walk away, telling me that the stress of her father's kidnapping was too hard on the girl. My niece needed to come home.

From the street I saw the back of Jane's head in the bot-tom of the window. She was moving slowly, as if she talked to someone who was not in view. Isaac parked and I shoved the door open, racing across the slippery ice to the school. The SUV doors locked behind me with a beep and Isaac followed, his gait slow and steady.

The heat was stifling in the old school, the air so arid it made my skin burn and nostrils dry with my first breath. I en-tered the school office and saw Mrs. Godansky standing by the printer, a silver cross and chain glinting around her neck. I noticed the door to her office was closed. *Who was talking to Jane?*

Mrs. Godansky raised a hand to stop me and opened the office copier with the other. "I have Jane's assignments here for the next week."

Isaac entered behind me. "Why?" he asked when I didn't respond.

"Jane is…" She stopped and seemed lost for words. *Embarrassed?* Mrs. Godansky flushed beneath her mound of gray hair as she started over. "Jane is not well. I think the stress of her father's disappearance is more than she can stand. I've put in a request for her to be homeschooled until further notice."

"What's happened?" I asked. There was no sound from beyond the closed door. "Who's with my niece?"

The principal ushered us away from her office door, into a huddle at the end of the scarred desk separating the front office from parents, supplicants, solicitors and unruly students. Godansky inclined her head and lowered her voice to indicate this was between us three. "No one. And that is part of the problem. Jane has begun talking to herself. Some of her teachers think she may need to see a…mental-health professional."

"I'm not crazy."

I whirled and saw Jane standing in the crack of the open door. Her face was blotchy red and her eyes were swollen from crying.

"And I'm not stupid and I'm not weird and I am *not* possessed," she said, her voice rising with each phrase.

"Of course, you aren't," I said as I knelt beside her. Carefully, I put a hand on Jane's shoulder and opened myself to her. Inside, she was a whirlwind of emotions, anger, hurt, shame, guilt. "Ashes and spit," I whispered, understanding what was happening instantly. She hadn't been able to wall off or filter out the thoughts of her classmates or teachers. She had been inundated with impressions from them all for the past five hours.

When I had come into my gift it had been summer. I had hidden away in my room for weeks, through the heat of July and August. By the time school started, my mind was secured behind a nearly unbreachable wall. Jane had been thrown into the maelstrom of kids, kids at their worst, their most uncertain, their most cruel age.

"Yeah, it sucked a really big egg," she said, starting to cry again. "A dinosaur egg."

"We'll take you home, Jane," I said. "And you don't have to come back until you're ready."

"Good. I hope it's not until next year, 'cause Mrs. Godansky thinks I got a devil in me. She thinks I need to be exercised."

My mouth fell open. Isaac turned his full attention to the stern, gray-haired woman. Mrs. Godansky had the grace to blush. I wondered what else Jane had picked out from the woman's thoughts. I gathered my niece close and filled my mind with all the good things she liked—chocolate, bubble baths, marshmallows toasted over the fireplace, her cat, Dynomite.

Jane leaned into me, wrapped her arms around my neck and sighed the words, "I never had a chocolate bubble bath. And she wants to jump the janitor's bones."

"Well, I never!"

I stifled a laugh and picked Jane up in my arms. Isaac handed me the keys and I carried the little girl from the building, leaving a thoroughly ticked off black belt master of death to deal with the humiliated and disconcerted principal. The *black belt master of death* part was Jane's. She thought Isaac was way cool. She wanted to know what jump bones meant. I was never so glad of my wall as now.

* * *

It took me hours to get Jane calmed down, leaving me with both a splitting headache from opening myself to her and then shielding so hard after, and a mental picture of Jane taking a chocolate bubble bath, an image she kept sending me. If I had kept drugs in the house, I'd have been tempted to sedate the girl.

Instead, we talked for hours, discussing the thoughts of her classmates, teachers, and even the clinical meaning of jumping bones. The birds-and-bees was not a discussion I had wanted to have with my niece, but since she could, in all likelihood, pick up impressions from Jubal and Isaac and any other sexually mature adult she might meet, it was best handled by me, and quickly. I could imagine the images she might pick up if she asked about jumping bones at the dinner table. The thought made me shudder inside. After I popped two ibuprofen, Jane and I also spent an hour on my wall.

I had never tried to show anyone except Davie what my wall looked like. When he finally came back from wherever he had disappeared to for so many years, he had searched me out in the phone book and come directly to the shop. I carried with me, as if it had happened only this morning, the vision of him walking in the door, Jane, a toddler, riding on his hip, plaid dress flared out, black patent-leather shoes kicking.

The first thing he had wanted, once we got over a tearful reunion and introductions, was to see my wall. He had assumed I had no St. Claire talent at all. He had thought it skipped a generation in me, as the gift had been known to do, because when he touched me, hugged me, he saw only an empty space. A nothingness. I had tried to open to Davie over the years, and had successfully shown him the shaped-stone wall, but had never been able to show him beyond it into the place of stillness in my mind. He couldn't seem to envision it, and words to help him had failed. Maybe it was impossible to see nothingness? I was willing to try again with Jane.

After the frank sex talk, which left her in gales of laughter about Mrs. Godansky and the janitor, after we went over the record of her friends' thoughts and indulged in a serious counseling session about looking into a potential boyfriend's thoughts, we sat on the rug in front of the blazing fire, ready to attempt my wall.

A lit candle between us, our knees nearly touching, we slipped into a meditative breath pattern, both of us concentrating on the candle flame, breathing in a sense of peace and breathing out our negativity. When I felt we had each reached a calm state of mind, I opened to Jane, let her see my image of the flame, light that lifted upward, unwavering and pure. I spoke, my voice soft and slow.

"When I need to blank out other people, other thoughts, when I don't want to accidentally project something a St. Claire might pick up, I envision a wall." I formed it in my mind, a wall of curved, shaped stone with crenellations at the top. "Like this. Inside is a dark, empty place, like…like the inside of a stone." I eased the wall aside to reveal an emptiness, the emptiness of stone in my mind. "Hard. Solid emptiness. A carved and polished double-fist of onyx. And I am within it, safe.

"I see the stone, its grain pure and hard as diamond. I feel myself inside the stone, breathing stone. Calm, like a stone, fills me. I am the stone." My wall closed back over the stone. Perfect emptiness all around me, within me.

"Ahh," she sighed. "Yes." Jane's breathing slowed. Stuttered. My eyes flew open. Her breathing stopped.

I broke the image and reached across the candle, grabbing Jane's shoulders. I shook her. "Stop it! Come out of it!" I said. She slumped over. Without thinking, I slapped her. Hard.

The sound of her shocked inhalation was wet, harsh, as if her lungs had closed up, folded over, crushed together.

"Jane!"

Her eyes opened and she took another breath, this one less labored. She blinked and touched her face, stunned. "You slapped me."

"Spit and decay! I'll slap you harder if you ever do that to me again." I remembered to breathe myself. My own lungs ached with fright.

"I saw it. I saw your wall, inside and out." A grin covered her face, and her eyes sparkled. My handprint was a sharp red outline on her pale flesh. "I can do this!"

"You will not do this. You stopped breathing."

"Yeah, okay, I forgot it was a vision. You can't breathe inside stone, so I stopped. I won't do that again. Promise. But I can do it—I can make a wall and enter the stone."

"No!"

"I'll breathe this time. I promise."

"No." I closed my eyes, feeling the fear rush over me in a wave of pure terror. *I could have killed my niece.* Of course she couldn't breathe inside the stone. That's obvious. I should have considered that part of the image and warned her, prepared her for the strength and texture of the mental picture. But it hadn't occurred to me. What else might I screw up on if I tried to teach her?

"Aunt Tyler. Really. I can hold the breathing and the wall. I can do this. I was just surprised how solid it was. It's hard to breathe stone."

I opened my eyes, surprised. "Breathe stone?"

She shrugged. "That's what you do. You breathe stone. You aren't afraid of the dark or of stone. It doesn't suffocate you. You just breathe it and it fills you up and makes you hard as stone."

Was that what I did?

"So we'll try it again. Okay? Only this time you won't hit me."

I looked into her eyes, eyes so much like my brother's, deep and warm and full of life. I knew what she would suffer if she went back to school without a wall. I knew how long Davie had been gone when he came into his gift. Months. It had taken him months to learn to master his gift enough to reenter the normal world. Jane didn't have months. And Aunt Matilda hadn't called me back.

"If you stop breathing again, I'll beat you with a switch. With a hairbrush. With a belt. I'll slap you silly."

"No, you won't," Jane laughed, her eyes glittering with excitement. She looked down at the candle and frowned.

My gaze followed hers. The flame was out. Gone. No scent of smoke was on the air. "Oh, crap," I said. I knew I hadn't touched the flame. I knew Jane hadn't. That meant one of us had snuffed the flame some other way. "Chatoyant coprolite!" I swore.

"Shiny poop?" she asked.

I managed a wry smile. "Sorta."

"Cool. Did I blow out the candle?"

"Sorta." I shielded my reaction to that fact from her.

"Double cool. So, can we try again?"

My headache was worse even after taking medication. I massaged my temples, knowing she was going to try again alone if I didn't try with her. It was the nature of adolescents. *Hey, guys, watch this…. Look, Ma! No hands!* I wasn't sure whether to laugh or cry. "Sure. Let's try. But this is the last time tonight. No matter what, we stop as soon as I say so, and you promise not to try alone." Jane looked mutinous. "I can read you. Promise."

"Okay. One more try."

"And?"

"And I won't try it alone."

I relit the candle and settled my mind, pushing the head-ache away. We breathed together, slowly, found a centered place and I showed her my wall. Inside was the dark, the dark of safety. The dark of complete control. And this time Jane followed me as I found the polished onyx stone and melted within it. Like me, she kept on breathing, steady and slow, no hitches, no stutters, no panic for Aunt Tyler.

"Good. Great. You held the wall. You are perfectly safe in the darkness of the stone. Now, we're going to slide out of it. Slow and easy. Find the light. Envision the candle and the light and the room. See it?"

"Yeah. Cool." I could hear the smile in her voice.

Brat? Jane?

I recoiled at the intrusion.

Pain. Fear and terrible pain. My hands! Cold and blood.

Jane screamed, and the image shattered like brittle obsidian.

I opened my eyes. The pain faded. *Davie*. That was Davic.

"Daddy! They cut my daddy!"

I took two Tylenol and gave a children's dose to Jane, who now shared my headache and was in state of numbed panic for her father. There was no way to shield her from the image. The St. Claire gift was once again more curse than blessing.

But at least the shock of Davie's scan had paralyzed Jane's gift. She was head-blind for the moment, a benefit after the hard day. When the phone rang and Jubal and Isaac said they could bring dinner over, I agreed and opened the door to our rooftop garden, letting in the men, the smell of fresh-baked bread and the aroma of stew. Jubal carried a bottle of wine under his arm and the loaf in a basket. Isaac carried a tray with a stainless-steel pot of stew and an armload of linen. Behind them was Evan Bartlock, with a half gallon of ice cream and a jar of fudge. Last to enter, holding a satchel and a large box, was Quinn.

The food-bearing males went to the kitchen, but the body-guard went directly to Jane, who was sitting on the couch covered by an afghan. He set the luggage aside and placed the cardboard box on the floor. I watched as he opened the box and lifted out a bundle of fur. Jane's face softened from misery and terror to fragile happiness in a heartbeat.

"Dyno. Kitty." She pulled the sweet-tempered cat onto her lap and up beneath her chin for a hug that melted my heart. "Look, Aunt Tyler. Quinn brought my kitty." She held the small cat up close and breathed in the kitty-fur smell, her face relaxing by degrees. The cat swiveled her head, licked Jane across the nose and started to purr. When Quinn glanced to see my reaction, I could only smile. It was the perfect cure for Jane.

While I stood and did nothing except watch my niece, the other men covered the scarred table surface with the starched linen cloth and napkins that were draped over Isaac's arm. They knew better than to think I'd have anything so elegant as the old damask. They set my antique kitchen table with my heavy stoneware and plain-but-serviceable stainless cutlery and my best crystal.

We gathered around the table, pulling wooden folding chairs from the chair rack along the wall and sitting with the noisy scuffling of a family. Which was weird. Living with Dumont Lowe, I had never known the simple joy of being together for comfort and food. I didn't remember the noise made by so many people in one place.

I found myself at the head of the table, Jane and Dyno to my right, Jubal to my left, and the others scattered about. Too busy to stay and visit, Quinn excused himself and clattered down the stairs into the night.

Like the family I had compared us to, we shared the meal. We talked about nothing evil, nothing weird, nothing St. Claire nutty. We laughed, told stories about our first meetings, about our youth, about interesting situations in our lives. I told tales about David as a young boy, being chased by too many girls. Jubal told the story of the first time he sparred with Isaac in tae kwon do, Jubal thinking he had learned so much and wanting to show off. He carefully edited out the bloody parts in deference to the diners. Isaac told about a dinner of sushi consumed on a trip to South Korea, deliberately making Jane groan with tales of raw tuna and squid and other equally gross food options.

Evan watched us all as we ate, his eyes falling on me several times and lingering there. Though he was silent most of the meal, over dessert he said, "I've a got a story for you."

"Go," Jane said, licking a glob of fudge off her spoon. None of us told her she had chocolate on her nose. It was too cute.

"My first meeting with Aunt Matilda when I was about nine," Evan said. "First meeting, not counting her visit right after I was born. That one I don't remember, of course."

"Cool. Did she read your mind?" Jane asked around a mouthful of fudge.

"No. It was spring vacation. We were living in Manhattan at the time, and made a detour to la-la land on the way to Florida. I remember it was cold in New York, some kind of freak cold spell. We had driven all night and most of the day, and when we finally stopped and got out, the heat was like a steam bath. It just soaked right into my wool clothes."

"La-la land?" There was fudge on her chin now, and Jubal was trying hard not to laugh. Face bland, Isaac just upended the jar of heated fudge over her bowl, filling it.

"That's what my father called Aunt Matilda's house." He looked guiltily at me. As I happened to agree with his judgment, I said nothing. "Flowers were blooming like I had never seen before. When Central Park is your idea of nature and wildlife, it's a shock the first time you see a Low Country garden. There was lilac and bougainvillea growing out of control, roses already open, mosquitoes were swarming. Bees were everywhere from Uncle Will's bee boxes. I remember the bees. And this mockingbird." His eyes lit up.

"I remember that bird!" I said, sitting up straight. "Standing on the eave of the house? Calling over and over?"

"Never shut up," Evan laughed. "Drove me nuts. We spent the night and that da-a-ang," he amended the word on the fly, "bird sang the entire time I was there. Woke me up at like four in the morning. Must have been sitting on the windowsill outside my room."

I sat up even straighter. "Me, too. The guest room on the left of the front door? It had an old down mattress on the bed, homemade blue quilt with a blue heron in the center?"

Evan looked at me strangely. "Yeah. Bed was dark wood with a curved headboard and footboard."

"A sleigh bed."

"Yeah."

"Aunt Matilda told me she never let kids stay in that room—"

"But she made an exception because of the mockingbird," he finished, his eyes on mine. Jane looked back and forth between us, far too interested in our expressions, her chocolate-covered spoon in the air, forgotten.

"The mockingbird was an omen," I said, feeling as if the words were dragged out of me.

"So she said. Maybe it was something she said to all the kids who came to visit?" he asked.

Reluctant to speak, the pause was too long before I continued. "She never let Davie stay in that room. He had to use the kid's room down the hall. The one with the bunk beds and the old toys."

"Well, well, well," Isaac drawled, his Texan accent stronger than I'd ever heard it. "Ain't this cozy. Kissin' cousins and all."

"Coincidence," I said.

"Kissing?" Jane asked. "Are you two gonna jump bones?"

Jubal spluttered. Isaac laughed, enjoying the interrupted story far too much. Evan turned red again. I looked at Jane, hoping my complexion would stay pale, but feeling the red blotches break out all over my neck. "Kissing cousins is an expression, nothing more. And we talked about that phrase."

Jane shrugged in a *whatever* gesture, her eyes gleaming. "Sorry," she said, but I could tell she wasn't.

"Want more ice cream to go with the fudge?" I asked, letting the story stay interrupted.

Jane looked down at her bowl, the fudge swirled with vanilla. "Nope. I'm fine."

"Coffee anyone?" I stood and crossed to the cabinet holding Stan's coffeemaker. It hadn't been used since he left me, but now seemed like a good time. Keeping my back to the room, I busied myself pouring ground beans and water. Isaac took pity on me and started a story about a trip to Montana and wild mustangs, which kept Jane enthralled. I could feel Jubal's eyes on my back and Evan's discomfort as I worked. Studiously I ignored both of them and the moment passed, their interest claimed by the mustangs, but Jane's question stuck in my mind. *Are you two gonna jump bones?* Spit and decay…

Eventually, even that annoyance waned, my embarrassment unable to keep up with the fast-flowing conversation, and I rejoined the group, passing out cups of coffee. When dinner was over, Jane and I were restored. Long before eight o'clock, I tucked my niece into my bed, Dyno sharing her pillow, and both girl and cat were instantly asleep.

Jubal and Isaac left, loaded down with dirty linens and empty pots, crossing the snow-covered roof to their place and grousing about who was going to shovel the garden this time. When I closed the door, it was to find myself alone with Evan Bartlock.

An almost preternatural clarity of vision welled up in me, an awareness that sliced beneath the skin into unconscious thoughts and emotions, into the soul of the man before me. He almost glowed with a richness of light. And then he spoiled it.

"You're going all St. Claire nutty on me, aren't you?"

I blinked away my vision of him and went to the pile of clean dishes by the sink. "No," I said. For a moment there was only the clink of dishes as I dried and stacked them. Then Bartlock was standing at my side, a cloth in his hands. He dried a bowl, then a plate, and stacked them neatly with mine.

"Sorry."

I nodded, drying a handful of cutlery. Minutes went by. Finally he said, "So, what do you see when you go all wacky on me?"

Laughter burbled out of me. I couldn't help it. Grinning, I looked up at him, then down at his hands, drying a plate, and decided on humor and honesty. "You'll make a good wife someday for some woman. You look good in a kitchen, drying dishes. You look good in jeans. You have nice hands and a nice butt."

"Thanks, but that wasn't exactly what I was asking."

I sobered. "You're a good man, trying to do a good thing," I said, as I let the St. Claire part of me take over. "You carry the darkness of guilt on your soul. A black place just here." I touched the center of his chest, below his heart. My damp fingers made a wet mark on his white sweatshirt. His skin was warm through the cloth. I kept my fingers in place, between the hollow of his ribs and closed my eyes, opening myself to him fully.

"You loved a woman recently. She had red-blond hair, like mine, and a temper like mine. But when you got in trouble, she stepped back, away from you. She hasn't called, and that hurt at first." Warmth rose up toward me from Evan. The warmth of the skin, of the blood, of the heat between a man and a woman. "But she's starting to fade for you now, in the cold of the mountains. And you find yourself wanting to kiss me. To reach beneath my shirt and touch me."

Bartlock stepped back, away from my hand. I opened my eyes and met the cool ice of his gaze, a look that was banked fires, like a smoldering mountain beneath a cap of snow. He wanted me to stop.

I let the gift settle over me like a heavy shroud, I heard the deadened tone of my voice. The coolness of the earth filled me, the emptiness of stone without a wall to protect it.

"Her name was Snub." Bartlock jerked. I'd scored on something that was private, between the two of them. The gift took me deeper. "Because of her nose. And you had been sleeping together for months before the shooting. You haven't heard from her even once, since.

"She could have come forward for you at the initial hearing, and she didn't. And you're a proud man, too proud to call her and hear the sound in her voice that will tell you, surely and finally, that it's over between you.

"And if you kiss me, you're afraid that I'll know too much about you, even more than I learned just now." I closed my eyes, letting the gift fall away. I remembered to breathe, feeling the freshness of a single deep inhalation. Tears prickled my lids. Pain chiseled at my brain, a physical pain both like, and unlike the pain in Evan's soul.

"I learned that you're a good man. One of the best I've ever known. Honest, fiercely intelligent. And you have a gift of the St. Claires. You use it every day, half afraid of it but depending on it. You know it's necessary to help you bring in the bad guys. I can tell you that you don't have to be afraid of it, though. Your gift isn't dominant. It's recessive. It'll never take over and make you nutty-weird like Aunt Matilda." A single tear crawled down my cheek, a slow salt burn on winter-chapped skin.

"Your children will have the gift, if their mother is a St. Claire. Because of the omen of the mockingbird, you're afraid that Aunt Matilda sent you here to find me. To make something happen between us that wouldn't have happened on its own. And you're scared to death of me because of that."

Suddenly his mouth was on mine. Warm, searching, with a defiance not against me or the St. Claire gift he feared, but against himself. Against his own fear. I smiled into his mouth and his tongue touched my lips. Heat roared up between us.

He slammed me against the cabinet, hands cupping my bottom, and lifted me to the counter. I heard a sound from myself, a moan that wasn't soft at all, only far away. Needing. My legs opened, wrapped around him. His heat enveloped me, filled me.

Hands slipped into my hair, dislodging the braid that secured it. His body was hard, pushing against me, mouth plundering as if he would know my every secret.

The phone rang. A single ring, from his coat thrown over the couch. He laughed into my mouth, teeth bumping mine. I opened my eyes. "I intend to come back to this," he said, his lips moving over mine as he spoke. "Soon."

"Okay by me."

"If that mockingbird knew something about what I might feel if I ever got near you, then that's one mighty smart bird."

I laughed low.

"And she didn't have hair like yours, gold and copper, like something Jubal would make in a forge. No one does."

I was obscurely pleased, a joy welling up in me like tears.

He moved away to find his phone. I sat on the counter, feeling tousled and warm and thoroughly kissed. I was in trouble. Big trouble. I wanted a St. Claire man. One Aunt Matilda had sent my way.

Evan rummaged through his coat and answered his phone. "Bartlock." A moment later he began asking terse questions, followed by short pauses. "When? How bad?" His face grew hard, thoughtful. "You believe him? What? Hmm. Yeah, I agree. Thanks. I appreciate the call."

He flipped the little phone closed, his eyes on me across the room. "You look good sitting there." When I didn't answer, he said, "Quinn was accosted in a parking lot. It was recently shoveled, so we got no footprints, no evidence. Quinn's got a bloodied lip and some bruises. He was loading groceries, out of sight of any security cameras. Claims he pulled his gun and fired four shots. OS say they recovered four casings. No sign of blood."

"OS?"

"Officers at the Scene."

"They think he's lying, don't they?"

"Yeah. They do. But they don't know why he'd lie. And they say they can't trace the phone call you got today. It was rerouted. Through Washington, D.C."

My pleasure was gone in an instant. "The people who took Davie didn't wait for the deadline. My brother was cut this afternoon. Jane saw it. So did I."

Evan half smiled from across the room. "You really are one of the weird St. Claires, aren't you?"

I considered him, feeling safe having this conversation when he was far enough away that I couldn't touch him but close enough to see his expression. "I don't know what I am. I went through the onset of the gift alone. I wasn't trained. I was always afraid of it. I built a wall between the world and my mind and I built it fast. Aunt Matilda never even noticed that it had happened. Being a St. Claire isn't something I can talk about with people. They get weirded out."

"I'll bet."

"Jane is coming into her gift, and I don't know what to do. I called Aunt Matilda for advice. I called her three times today, and all I get is a machine."

"Aunt Matty doesn't use a machine. She doesn't use any machines."

"I know. And she never, ever leaves Durbinton. She should be there. It scares me. I don't know why she hasn't called me back. And I don't know what to do for Jane."

"Is David still alive?"

"Yes. I *know* he is." I swallowed, remembering all the things I had caught in the brief glimpse of Davie, before I had to close it down in order to protect Jane from the images. "But he's hurt bad." I slid from the counter to the floor, landing with a soft thud of slippered feet. "He needs medical help." Tears filled my eyes and I blinked them away, feeling the pain that built below my breastbone. "He's got an infection. Probably early-onset pneumonia. He's been beaten. He doesn't know where he is." I sucked in a breath. My lungs hurt as they moved, an ache deep inside me. "I saw a room with a window that faced just like that one does." I pointed to the loft window. "But there's nothing in the window, no frame of reference. Only sky. He could be high up or the window could face down a valley."

"Can you sketch the room for me, and what you know about the place he's being held?"

I nodded and located a pencil and a pad. Drawing the outline of the room, I noted the placement of the door, the window. "It feels like an office. Davie's being kept in back, in a small room. It's got an iron-framed single bed here, table here. He's been beaten and there are blood splatters on the wall." I shook my head to erase the thought.

"In the next room, there's a desk here—" I indicated it with a square "—and a chair that squeaks." I drew in a chair behind the desk, but it was a guess whether that was the one that squeaked. There might have been others. "There are papers all over, maybe building plans, dozens of them, all with curled edges like they've been rolled up. And there's a four-drawer filing cabinet here. Davie can hear a man talk at odd times. That's all I remember."

Evan bent over my drawing, his body close. I wanted to touch him but resisted. "Not much to go on," he said.

"Yeah. That's the way it is with the St. Claire gift. Gives you just enough to not help at all. I want an address, I get one numeral out of four. I want to read someone to make a sale, I get that they have indigestion. I want—"

Evan's lips pressed to the back of my neck, heated, gentle.

"Okay. That I get." I turned in his arms and kissed him back, a slow, lingering kiss.

"I guess wild passionate sex is out," he whispered against my mouth, "what with a kid not twenty feet away."

"Oh, yeah. And I never have sex before the first date. Not even before the first six months."

"There's that." He pulled me closer. "Six months? Bet that's one of your rules that I break."

I figured it might be, not that I was going to admit that to Evan Bartlock.

"So how about we curl up on the couch and go through the papers your brother sent," he suggested.

I sighed into his mouth. "I think that's the best idea I've heard all night."

"Liar."

"So sue me." I disentangled myself from his arms and nodded to the door. "Downstairs in the storeroom. Crate beside the door, on the right, on top."

"Back in a flash."

"Hope you don't do everything in a flash." The words were out of my mouth before I could stop them.

Evan chuckled, a low, masculine sound that irritated even as it sent waves of heat coursing through me. "Not even. You'll see."

* * *

"What's this?" Evan asked.

I took the purple folder from his hand and fanned the sheaf of papers inside. They were poor-quality photocopies, the kind one got when the toner was almost out or when making a copy from a copy of a copy. Across at the top of each was a header with a seal, a ring with the words Department of Defense, United States of America, and an inner picture of a bald eagle, wings outspread, a striped shield over its breast, all rendered in shades of gray. The dates, the names of the sender and recipient, and much of the content had all been blacked out. Large portions of each document were useless.

When I looked at Evan his face was hard, the same kind of expression I had noted when he talked on the phone to his contact at the police department about Quinn. I shook my head and shrugged all at once. I had no idea what the papers were, but I could tell he did.

"These are parts of declassified material from the DOD," he said. He flicked the pages with a nail. "But the paper is old and yellowed. I'd say David has had them a long time, maybe since they were first released under the Freedom of Information Act. They look like papers that might have come from Military Intelligence to an oversight group in Congress." He pointed to a series of numbers at the bottom corner.

It hit me what he was saying and I couldn't help my expression. "My brother is a spy? A Double-Oh-Seven?" I mimicked shooting a gun and blowing on the barrel. "Bond. James Bond."

"It's not funny."

"Sure it is. I know Davie. He can't be a spy. He doesn't have it in him."

"But he has money. A lot of money. And if he got it from some other side by selling secrets..."

I rolled my eyes.

"You said he disappeared for years."

I decided the best defense here was to ignore the accusation. It was too stupid to suffer to live, but that wasn't something I could actually say to a man without hurting his delicate ego. "What's the Quantum Corp?" I turned to another page. "Here it's called Q Corp. I mean, Q Core." I flipped back. "It's Quantum Core, not corp. Not a corporation. You ever heard of it?"

"No."

Guess I'd hurt him anyway. Rather than massage the injured male pride, I uncurled from the couch, where my feet rested in Evan's lap, and padded to the PC. It was my latest hand-built toy from Davie. Always on, it had a powerful backup battery, a twenty-one-inch flat screen, and more memory than the Library of Congress, the Smithsonian and Google put together, as well as nearly enough computing power to replace NASA's system on launch day. Its firewall could defeat any automated or human-guided invasion; its protective software could isolate and defeat any spider, worm, virus, Trojan Horse or other attack. If you believed Davie, it was faster than a speeding bullet, more powerful than a locomotive and could leap tall buildings in a single bound. For all I knew, it had X-ray vision, too.

I jiggled the mouse, typed in google.com, and went searching for Q Core. When that came up mostly empty, I tried Quantum Core. I got nothing with that, too. Google asked me if I had misspelled the phrase and offered me a computer company and a software company, among other sites. I clicked my way through several more screens of listings. I was about to stop when I spotted a note in the body of text under a search result. A government site. The text read only "Q Core…psychic emanations, visions…"

I clicked on the site and found myself in a Department of Defense site. My system's red warning icon—the Death card in the Waite Tarot, a skeleton knight on a white horse, wearing black armor and a carrying lance—appeared on the top right of the screen. It meant that someone had noted my interest in the site or the information on the page, and launched a probe to see who I was. As I watched, Death lowered its lance and started galloping. A moment later, Death looked at me and said, "I am unable to stop the incursion. I am removing you from the site. Sorry, Brat."

The screen went dark for an instant, then the screensaver came on. But it wasn't my usual golden fish swimming along a coral reef. It was Death, poised against a rich blue background, his black armor gleaming, his lance at the ready. With a kick, he sent the white horse galloping. As I watched, his lance speared something small and tossed it off the screen. Death grinned at us, his skull showing perfect teeth. To his side, other images appeared—ugly pit bulls with horns, saber teeth and tiny red wings. Davie was imaginative with his software. This was an automated visual of my firewall fighting off a probe.

"Wow. Talk about the blue screen of death," Evan said.

I propped my chin on one fist and laughed softly through my nose as the knight unleashed murder and mayhem on the vibrant screen.

"Let me guess. David is a compu-geek, too."

"Yeah. He's pretty good."

Death speared one dog. Two replaced it.

"You ever seen this before?" he asked. "Or anything like it?"

"No. My system is still under attack, even though we left the site. It means something followed us through the Internet and Death is still fighting it."

"Sounds like a computer game. Looks like one, too."

"Davie's written some game programs." But the battle on the screen had me worried. Fights like these never lasted long. Never. Death, which normally won with a single lance toss or two, wasn't winning hands-down like usual. Not even by half a hand down. The icon was suddenly equipped with a shield and a sword, the galloping horse encased in black armor like his rider. Spikes grew from the horse's hooves, and his nostrils blew steam in curling white clouds.

The dogs morphed into gargoyles, replete with black-scaled wings, snarling faces and claws that dripped blood. One gargoyle slipped in under Death's guard and tore through his armor, four long rips that drew blood. Evan put a hand on my shoulder as if to offer comfort.

Death's blood dripped onto the fighting field and seemed to sizzle. As we watched, the vapor from each drop of lost blood rose and coalesced into a hand. Seven of the transformed drops emerged and began attacking the gargoyles, beating and slashing with cupped hands. Very kung fu. Though it was only a representation of a computer fighting off some sort of invader, the battle made my skin crawl.

Suddenly, a shaped-stone, medieval castle wall appeared, growing with amazing speed, curving around the fight, isolating it. The wall met itself and closed. It looked remarkably like the wall in my mind when I shut myself away from the world.

The screen went black again. "I have disconnected you from the Internet, Brat. The incursion was more than I expected. I have isolated it, but can't maintain the quarantine. Please call David and inform him of this situation. Until he arrives, I am shutting down your system." The PC went through a fast shutdown and the screen went black a final time.

"Well," I said. "That sucks a great big ostrich egg."

At midnight, I closed the shop door, locking it and switching on the security system. Evan Bartlock loped up the street, a jerky, uneven gait over the melting-freezing ice. Before he made the left toward his hotel, he swiveled. I wasn't sure he could see me, as the lights were off, but he waved anyway. Just in case. I opened a hand and placed my palm on the glass.

Back in the loft, I showered fast and pulled on footsie pajamas, pink-and-white striped, the fabric stretchy, which showed every curve. They had a slit across the top of the butt, so I could pull the back down and go to the bathroom if needed, but otherwise, the pj's were one solid, very warm unit. I turned off the lights and slid into the bed beside Jane. I snuggled against her warm body, shivering slightly. My cell rang.

I almost ignored the untimely summons, but it could be Aunt Matilda, so I rolled over, found the unit in the dark and opened it. "Yeah."

"Love the jammies, honeybunch. And the kiss was perfectly sizzling."

"Good night, Jubal."

"Details in the morning. We'll cook again. Isaac and I were mesmerized."

"Stalker."

He just laughed and we hung up. I'd have to remember to start drawing the blinds.

9

Wednesday, 4:12 a.m.

Are you there?

Go away.

Listen to me, Brat.

My eyes opened on the night. Shuddering agony filled me. *Davie's pain.* My body clenched with reaction.

There's a negotiation taking place. Someone else wants me. And another party is looking for me, someone very dangerous. You have to stay out of this. Stop looking for me. You have to take Jane and go to Aunt Matilda.

I'll never stop looking for you, Davie. Besides, Aunt Matilda is missing. I can't—

Missing? No! I—

The contact stopped. He was gone. All I caught was a sense of Davie's utter pain and rising panic. Unable to sleep, I got up, wrapped myself in a blanket and curled on the couch with Davie's papers. The ones about the land he owned I stacked on one side, and the papers from the purple folder on the other. I was looking for patterns, indications of... I didn't know what I was looking for. At about five-thirty in the morning I fell asleep, my head on the purple folder.

* * *

"I think it's just a panic attack, Ms. St. Claire. It's not uncommon when young girls first enter their menses." Dr. Sharpton was in his early fifties, balding, with pudgy fingers and a spare tire that would fit around a tractor wheel. When he bent over his desk to write on a prescription pad, he huffed for breath. "I'll write a prescription for a mild sedative. Just keep her quiet, let her lie around the house for a few days since she's out of school already."

"I am not having a panic attack and I am not crazy," Jane said. Her tear-streaked face was red and swollen. Suddenly her expression changed, becoming ugly, furious as she looked at her pediatrician. "I want another doctor. This one thinks all women are weak and whiny. That we stink."

Dr. Sharpton's pen lurched once on the pad, but he didn't look up.

"Jane," I said, warning, wanting to stop her but knowing I wouldn't be able to.

Spitefully she added, "And he has a smoking problem, and he's addicted to Krispy Kreme doughnuts. The cream-filled ones." Wiping her face once, her eyes bored into the unfortunate man's back. He hunched as if he felt her eyes.

Sharpton quickly finished his prescription, stood and thrust it at me. "If she has more problems, we can send her to mental health."

"I'll go to mental health if you'll go to Weight Watchers."

I spluttered with laughter. "Jane. Really." And the doctor was gone. I had a feeling this was the last time Jane would see the physician who had attended her since she was a kid. "Oh, well. Maybe it's time we got a grown-up doctor for you. There's a homeopathic practitioner in Asheville we can use."

Jane slid from the examining table to the floor and pulled on her T-shirt, her movements jerky with anger. She zipped up her jeans, her face hidden by a cascade of uncombed hair. "You know what they did to my daddy."

I closed myself off behind my wall of stone, shutting myself away from the fearful little girl. Once again, we had shared an early-morning vision of her father. A moment of dream-clogged misery. Of Davie and his pain. His rattling breath. His crusty bandage. "Yes," I said, my voice low. "I know."

"When we find them, I'm going to kill them."

I didn't know what to say. I didn't know how to help Jane. Once again, I had called Aunt Matilda. The phone at her house just rang uselessly, followed by the stupid message. Dr Sharpton seemed incapable of helping my niece. If I took Jane to a mental-health person, they'd never believe she was empathetic until after she told them what they had for breakfast and what they hated most about themselves. Not a good way to build trust and get her help. And even if we did get over that hurdle, no shrink would have a way to treat her. How did you treat an emerging psychic? Drugs? I fingered the small sheet of paper. Drugs, or an outlet for Jane's fury and helplessness.

"You ever fired a gun?"

Jane's head lifted. Her red-rimmed eyes were fierce. "No. Daddy was going to teach me when I turned thirteen. Next month. Can you teach me?"

"Sure, if you want to miss your target." Jane almost smiled and I knew I had hit on a treatment that might work. "There's a shooting range not far from here. We could take lessons. *If* you agreed to the ground rules."

"I know, I know. Daddy told me. No touching the gun for any reason if you aren't around. No showing it to friends, not that I have any left. They're all pretty weird when you can see inside their heads."

"All people are weird when you can see inside their heads."

"Not you."

A spurt of pleasure shot through me and I grinned. Jane

didn't need to be a nutty St. Claire to know how happy her words made me. She grinned back at me and I stood and opened the door.

"Those rules will do for now. And after we practice shooting a bit, we'll work on your wall, see if we can sustain the image for longer periods and still keep you breathing. If all else fails we'll try the sedative, at least when you go to sleep at night. It might help you get through without the dreams."

"No drugs. Daddy can't scan for us if I get all loopy."

That was my hope, but I managed to keep the thought away from her perceptive mind.

Noe cocked her head to one side, a tuft of bright blue hair standing up through the strap that held her ear protectors in place. "Not bad. Better than your aunt." She looked at me. "You, my friend, stink. I wouldn't trust you with a gun if my life depended on it."

The gunpowder smell of the indoor shooting range was sharp in my nostrils. "If I practice some more—"

"You may be less life threatening to the people around you. Someday. After a few years of steady work. At least this time you didn't hit the target to the left."

I winced, and Jane giggled. *Great.* Now, I was providing comic relief. But at least my niece wasn't so miserable anymore. Maybe next time I'd wear clown makeup and juggle the bullets rather than waste them, hitting the wall at the back of the room.

I loaded the small revolver again, inserting each brass bullet—each *round,* pardon me—and repositioned my ear protectors. My hands and wrists were quite strong from years of working stone, but even I could feel the recoil. I remembered Evan saying that S&W Airweights kicked like a son of a gun. He was right. I had a dull ache in both wrists.

Ignoring the spasms through my shoulders and upper back,

I assumed the firing position, my feet apart and legs braced, knees not locked but firm, arms in front of me. Left hand cupping the butt of the Smith & Wesson Airweight .38, right hand steady in a two-handed grip, I pulled back the hammer. I heard a faint click and applied a hair of pressure on the trigger.

I took a breath and released it slowly. The act reminded me of my meditation ritual, and I took another breath, forcing my back and shoulders to relax. This time I found my wall, the place of stone and calm and utter aloneness. For several moments, I breathed in the emptiness of the stone and the stillness of the earth. My eyes on the target, I exhaled one last time and squeezed the trigger.

The gun exploded, then five more times in slow succession. The little six-shot emptied. I pulled off my ear protectors and squinted at the target.

"Well, blow me away with an Uzi," Noe said, shocked. She punched a big button on the right of the booth where I stood and the target raced toward me on its complicated pulley system. On my target were five holes, each one punched through the black man-shape.

"You hit it, Aunt Tyler."

Jane and Noe giggled and high-fived each other. I just stood there and stared at the target I had killed. I remembered my vision, the snow, the blood, Davie dead. The St. Claire nightmare that haunted me still. I shivered with cold though the room was heated.

Back at the shop, I sent Jane to the loft to put our leftovers from lunch in the fridge, and to watch an old DVD we had picked up on the way home. *Hidalgo*. She said it was her favorite movie of all time, and pounded up the stairs whooping with excitement.

Noe fell into a wing chair at the front of the store and

stretched, patting her stomach with obvious contentment. "Oh, my God, that was fun. And that waiter was wild. Did you see the big amber earplug?"

"Hard to miss," I said, collapsing into the chair beside hers. "A hunk of amber that big stuffed into a hole in the earlobe? Now that had to hurt."

"Nah." Noe crossed her legs, twisting her flounced granny skirt in the process. "They do it like the tribes in Africa. Start small, with a piercing, and when that heals, stuff in something a bit bigger, then gradually bigger and bigger. His was the biggest I've seen outside of *National Geographic*. Really cool."

"Really not," I said.

"Mail, you two." Jubal tossed envelopes and small packages to us. Noe caught hers with one hand. Mine landed in my lap. Something shifted, went sideways and down. I was sucked down with it, down, deep and fast. A spiral, a whirlpool. Blackness closed in. *Blood. So much blood. Pain. Pain.* I hurtled from the chair, scattering the mail. "Noooo!"

I recoiled on the far side of the room, bouncing off the wall, and cowered there, scrunched against the corner. I slid down in a small heap of terror. Someone was screaming. Whimpering. Moaning. It was me. And I couldn't stop.

"Tyler?" Jubal's voice sliced through the agony.

I slapped a hand over my mouth to muffle the sound. And I stared at the packages. Three of them. *Blood and pain. Davie.*

"Get Evan. Get Bartlock," I whispered. "Close the store. Quick. Noe, go to the loft. Please. Keep Jane upstairs. Don't let her back down." With a sudden jab, the headache was there, just over my left eye. It rammed at me, a pickax of pain. I rocked back my head, eyes closed against the shrill ache and the sight of the boxes on the floor.

I didn't hear their responses, was aware only vaguely of movement. When I opened my eyes, all I could see was the packages, still scattered on the shop floor. I couldn't look away. I could only stare at the packets as tears ran down my face. *Davie. Oh, God. Davie.* Finally my moans went silent. And then I heard only the sound of my breathing.

I don't know how long it took Evan to get there, but he was huffing for breath when he arrived, coat lapels undone and flapping. He knelt in front of me, his hands cold on my face from an outside run. "What is it?" he asked me.

I focused on his eyes. Green, gentle. With odd color flakes in the irises, like the brown of old wood. "They cut Davie." I was whispering, tears a solid rain down my cheeks. "They sent me pieces of him."

"How do you know?"

"In the boxes. Pieces of Davie."

Evan lifted me from my crouch on the floor in the corner of the shop, and carried me like a child to the chair I had vacated. He sat me in the seat and accepted a throw from Jubal. He covered me with it, tucking it around me.

From a pocket, he pulled clear vinyl gloves, a pen and a small index card, and gathered the boxes. There were four of them. "Which ones?" he asked.

I was glad, so very glad, he didn't tell me I was being stupid or silly. Just a simple *which ones?* "The three in brown paper."

He glanced at his watch. With the pen, he wrote something on the index card, then set both aside. Carefully he opened the first parcel, using a knife edge to pry off the tape and unwrap the packaging. He set the brown paper to his left and used the same knife to remove the tape from the white box.

I was suddenly aware that we were not alone. The shop was closed, with that quiet hush of after-hours, though it was still afternoon. Jubal and Isaac stood behind the counter, silent, still, watching. Jubal looked once at me, worry in his eyes. Isaac watched Evan. I suddenly knew what he was thinking, what he was feeling. I understood the conflict in Isaac's heart. He wanted desperately to believe in something. In anything. And so he wanted there to be something awful in the boxes. And equally strongly, he wanted the boxes to hold supplies for the shop. Beads purchased on the Internet. Pearls. Sterling-silver findings. Something innocuous. Something that would reaffirm his view that the world was a logical, rational, unspiritual place. Through his own contradictory emotions ran a strong river of concern for me. I caught a quick glimpse of me though his eyes. A small bundle curled in the big chair. Helpless. Tiny. To be protected. And then I was back in my own head. The switch left me breathless. The room swam around me. I shifted my attention to Evan, who turned the box in one hand, inspecting it. Tape curled up around the edges of the lid.

Carefully he eased open the box and set it on the glass counter. Jubal and Isaac moved closer. I closed my eyes, not wanting to see their faces. Not wanting see proof of what I knew to be true. I heard a collective release of breath. And I *knew*.

"What is it?"

No one answered. I understood. No one could. Shaky, I rose and walked the few feet to Evan. He closed the box, pushing down on the top. With icy fingers, I stopped him. I could feel his eyes on me.

"You don't have to see this."

"Yes. I do." I took the box. The top slowly came away. I looked inside, not knowing what it was. For a long moment, it was just a whitish, pinkish cone-shaped thing. And then it resolved itself into a shape I recognized. The tip of a human finger, the nail rimmed in blood. They had cut off Davie's finger.

Something happened to me in that instant, when I saw Davie's flesh in the box. Something twisted deep inside. I felt myself alter. I hardened, an adamantine core with wicked needle-sharp barbs solidified in the heart of me. My soul condensed and dimmed. The headache split me open. And the world went dark.

Cops swarmed the shop. They asked questions I couldn't answer, questions I was too sick to answer. Evan answered for me, crafting a story that made sense out of the mail delivery, the open box, his presence. Because of the headache, I was unable to erect my wall. Through the pulse of pain that beat against me, pounding out a rhythm of agony, I caught glimpses from people in the room.

From Evan, I saw the thought that he was glad I had touched the box, that his story made sense only if my fingerprints were on the box. The thought that he was helpless to protect me. Powerless to help in the investigation. Powerless to find Davie before they tortured him again.

From Isaac, an embarrassed wonder. He kept looking at me. As if I was a lab rat that had performed well. Or as if I was some exotic and dangerous animal in a zoo. He was horrified at his own happiness that there had been something in the box. Shamed.

From Jubal, there was only tenderness for the sister he never had. Love and compassion and impotent rage. A need to protect. Through the pain of the headache that using my gift always brought, I centered my mind on Jubal. He became the point around which my mind circled, like a May Day pole twisted with ribbons of blood. I kept him near, held his hand and cried on his shoulder when technicians finally opened the other two boxes and discovered additional joints from the same finger.

When the police had all they could get from us and from the boxes, and when they had carried away the pieces of my brother in little envelopes they labeled as evidence, it was

Jubal who carried me upstairs to his apartment and laid me on his own bed. It was Jubal who got me medicine and warm tea, and placed a cool wet rag over my eyes, and left me to rest. Jubal. My best friend.

"You're sure this is a good idea?"

"It's the only idea I have. That makes it a good idea," I said.

"That makes it a bad one, too," Noelle said.

"Pessimist. There's a spot." I pointed to an empty parking spot.

I checked our clothes and jewelry in the ambient streetlights. I was in bright aqua jeans and dark peach T-shirt and sweater under a bulky coat, while Noe was a vision of dark beauty in all black, head to toe. I sported last year's green-and-peach aventurine jewelry; Noe was wearing megabeads of quantum quattro silica and bright glass turned with copper. We looked the prosperous jewelry makers.

"Yeah. We rock," she said, agreeing with my silent assessment. "So, tell me about this kiss I heard so much about today." Noe eased her front-wheel-drive Taurus into the narrow parking space on South Main Street. The snow tires made harsh grinding noises through the turn.

It took a moment before I remembered. Anything that happened before the delivery of the mail was a blur and took a moment to come clear. That was today? No. Last night? I couldn't help my smile, though it felt small and strained. "It was a kiss. It was a really, really, really good kiss. Come on. We'll be late."

"Hmm," was all she said on that subject as we slid from the car into the sleet and she beeped it locked. "Here we are. County Council versus Tree Huggers Inc. I wish Jubal had never let you see the newspaper. I'd have hidden it from you myself, if I'd thought you would want to come here. And I still say it's a bad idea."

Sleet made a shushing sound around us as we stood in front of a nondescript, blocky building from the early sixties. It was totally without charm or character unless ugly counted as an architectural design style. We entered the front door to find a steaming gathering, the heat so high that the coat-and-shoe ice from the assembled had melted into the air.

Glazed doughnuts and a coffeemaker, along with napkins and small foam cups, were on the long back table. The stink of scorched coffee was strong. The room was at full capacity, all facing the front. Had one or more of these people taken Davie? Tortured him? Had one of these people cut off his finger, chopped it up and sent it to me?

We stripped off our outerwear and draped the heavy coats over chair backs. No one looked to see who had entered and taken seats at the back. They were too busy booing a man at the front of the room. Colin Hornsburn.

The developer was of average height, wearing a crisp white shirt and sport coat, no tie and black slacks. He had the kind of haircut that made each strand look as if it had trained for the job and his skin had that shiny smooth look that simply screamed spa treatment. A city boy out of Asheville, by way of Atlanta.

"Gorgeous, single and charming," Noe whispered in my ear. "He's the developer who wants to put a housing development on the cusp of Mount Hoskins."

I remembered an article I had read somewhere. It had described the project as "tasteful, mid-six-figure, high-end residences that would impact the ecosystem only minimally." Davie had been incensed, raging about the people who wanted to destroy the environment. I remembered Davie complaining that the man was connected and rich. Rich enough to find both legal and government backing for the project. And Gail Speeler had been with him in the Red Bird Coffee Shoppe the day after Davie had been taken.

Hornsburn left the stage. As he took his seat, someone tossed a crumpled cup at his head. It missed, but the action brought a round of muffled laughter from the crowd. They didn't like the man or his ideas. Hornsburn swiveled in his seat and looked daggers at the row behind him, which caused yet more laughter.

Yeah. This was the kind of place my brother would have gone. This was his kind of fight. Davie in his save-the-world mode would have fit in here like hand in glove. Having no interest in politics, I had never known that county council meetings involved so much passion, pathos and entertainment value. Of course, so many people in high mental states was bringing back my headache.

I tried to wall myself off mentally, but since opening the mail the wall was sluggish. I had been using my gift regularly and now found that I wasn't having a lot of luck *not* using it. Wasn't that a kicker? I rubbed my temple, hoping the pain would hold off enough for me to learn something about someone that would lead me to Davie.

Two other speakers stood to expound against the development, one a self-described green-logger, who harvested trees in narrow sections or rows to impact the environment and habitat as little as possible. The other was a scrawny, tough-as-leather woman with wispy gray hair. Not much taller than I, she stood at the front of the room, clad in jeans, boots and a leather coat, and speared the crowd with crystal-blue eyes.

"My family and I have lived in these mountains for over two hundred years," she said in a whisky-and-smoke voice that instantly pacified the most vocal. "We've seen the change of the years. The decades. The centuries." She smiled as she caught and held the attention of members of the crowd. The words were like poetry. They had a rhythm that rocked as a mother rocked her baby. Soothing.

The crowd settled as the woman spoke, growing still. Actually listening. "We've seen the trappers and the settlers come and go, killing or driving off the wildlife. Seen the miners come and go, leaving treacherous landscapes behind them. We've seen the loggers come and go, loggers who raped the land and left it to erode to the sea."

I leaned again to Noe. "Who is she?" She wore a simple gold chain, diamonds in her ears, and an emerald ring with a stone big enough for a paperweight.

"Abby Marshall. She's the biggest property owner around here. Pulls a lot of weight with the County Council," Noe whispered, "though she doesn't attend council meetings very often. Bit of a recluse." She glanced at me, surprised at a memory. "Seems like one time when she came, Davie was talking to her. They acted pretty close."

"We've seen the railroads and the road builders, the park builders and the farmers. And not one of them added a blessed thing to the land. They each took and took and took, and the land gave and gave and gave. It fought its way back from the loss of the chestnut trees—a man-made disaster—and the damage of the loggers, who left thousands of acres of bare earth exposed to the wind and the rain. From the strip miners. From the farmers who plowed up the land, let the topsoil wash away, then stuffed the earth full of nitrates."

Abby's voice dropped to a near whisper. The crowd strained forward to catch the soft words. I felt my own skin drawing into slow prickles.

"Now the mountains are making battle against the golf course designers with their lab-created grass and artificial landscapes. With the developers, who want to stud the hills with homes and cut back the trees to make a *great view* for a rich family with no ties to the land, no ties to the earth."

Her voice strengthened. "Sometime. Someday. We have to make a stand against development and for the environment, for the habitats of our wildlife. *Someday!* Before the mountains are lost to us forever, lost to our descendants and their descendants." Her voice began to rise, slowly through the cadence of her words. "We have to find a way to live *with* the land again, as the ancient people did, as the Cherokee did, as a part of it but not stealing from it. We must remember how to give back to our land."

The diminutive woman stood straight. "Colin Hornsburn and his moneyman, Orson Wylie, don't want to give back. They want to scrap the plan that David St. Claire was putting together, a plan that would bring the people of this county into harmony with nature. And they want to do it for *money*." She spit the word as if it tasted foul. "David St. Claire is missing," she shouted to the room, her words resounding from the walls. "Taken by hoodlums. *Kidnapped!* The police can't find him. No one can. And I say he was taken because he wanted only good for this land. Taken because too much *money* was at stake."

She turned to Colin, pointed a finger at him, eyes like twin cutting torches, voice like a prophet of doom. "If this council gives permission for development to this man—gives it while David St. Claire is missing—gives it instead of tabling this motion until David St. Claire is found or someone else picks up the alternative plan and takes a leadership role, then I say our elected officials are all guilty of malfeasance. Of base mischief. Of misuse of the sacred office which they, which you—" she turned the pointed finger to the council seated to the side on the dais "—hold. Guilty. And you will pay a price." She nodded her head once, dropped her arm and walked off the small stage. The place erupted with boisterous ovation and shouts of approval. A young woman stood and hugged Abby Marshall as if in delight. A man reached over her shoulder to shake Abby's hand.

"Very dramatic. Especially that finger-pointing thing," Noe half shouted over the raucous applause, her tongue stud catching the light. Noe's tone was jaded, but I could tell she was impressed with the speech and the woman. "Abby can drink any man here under the table, beat them all at poker or in any financial bid for development. She's rich, she's tough and she's canny. They say she was a beauty in her day, but that she refused to marry because she couldn't find a man who was worthy of her." Noe grinned, her expression fierce. "And since she owns the local newspaper and two radio stations, she can change the political climate in a heartbeat. My money is on tabling the development."

Which happened quickly. As Noe predicted, the motion was tabled until next month and a recess was called. My brother had four weeks to be found, healed and gotten back in the saddle to carry out his dreams. I owed Abby Marshall a hug. The girl who had hugged Abby turned and moved with her. She was a pretty thing, with winsome features and a soft smile.

Others in the crowd were less pleased with the ruling. Colin Hornsburn stood, trailing a short line of men. Noe identified them as they filed past. "Orson Wylie, the man with the money. Floyd Feaster, bills himself as a land-use consultant to developers in the area. He's a geologist with a background in building."

A geologist? I studied Feaster as he passed by, a frown hardening his face. There were too many people for me to get a feel for the man's mind, but his body language was distressed, angry, frustrated. I knew just how he felt. It had been a while since I'd punched anything, too.

"The last guy is the construction expert, the one responsible for cutting roads through vertical hillsides and hanging houses from shear cliffs, making them safe enough for people to travel on and live in. He's out of Tennessee. Raybuck Arbuckle. Honest to God, that's his name."

Raybuck Arbuckle should start a country band with

Tommy T. The names alone would draw a crowd. Arbuckle was the only one of the three men who seemed unconcerned by the events of the past few minutes. He looked like the happy-go-lucky type, a man who should be lifting a beer in the corner tavern rather than cutting roads into the sides of mountains, but looks were often more deceiving than dependable. What I really wanted was to see inside his mind. And the fact that I wanted a moment alone with the guy to try out my St. Claire gifts was really scary, in a "who the heck am I turning into?" kind of way.

In the crowd, as we stood to mingle, I spotted Gail Speeler—Davie's "affianced," according to her television interview, which I didn't believe for a second. They'd dated, but that was it. Gail Speeler wasn't the first woman to think there was more to his feelings than there really was. Davie attracted women like honey attracted flies, and he didn't like letting them down when a relationship cooled. But if there had been more between them, Davie would have told Jane and me right up-front. That had happened in the past, too, though it fizzled after a while.

Gail approached Hornsburn and tapped his shoulder. She looked angry, but then, I'd been seeing a lot of that lately. People mad. Maybe I was reading things wrong.

To the side, watching them was a soft, willowy blonde. Eloise Carter. The name popped into my mind from a year ago. Eloise had set her sights on, and her claws into, Davie, determined that she would marry him. Davie had stopped dating her after two weeks, but the damage had been done. The woman had latched onto him and refused to let go. Getting her to go away had not been pretty. And right now, she was staring at Gail Speeler as if she would rather see the other woman flayed, filleted and fricasseed than take another breath.

"If looks could kill," Noe whispered.

"Yeah." Even with the background mental noise, I could feel her hate. The only thing good about the woman was her jewelry. It was *reeaaal* nice. Diamonds in her ears, several understated gold bangles on her wrists, a necklace that flashed at least four carats, ring with rubies in a spray across the globed setting. I looked back to the Hornsburn contingent. "Let's get some doughnuts."

"You go ahead. I want to scope out that good-looking green-logger. He sounds like my kinda man."

"Keep your hands to yourself, Noelle Constance Macdonald."

"Never. He has a really great ass."

"Your grandpa will put a hex on you."

"Not if the guy has any Irish genes. Gramps just wants to make sure I marry a man with sufficient quantities of God's own blood running in his veins."

I lost sight of Noe in the forest of shoulders and waists and backs. Being short has major drawbacks, finding anything to wear being only the more obvious. I got elbowed in the boobs twice before I made it to the fringes of the crowd, close enough to listen to Colin Hornsburn. And close enough to see Adam Wiccam.

He approached Hornsburn and I thought they might shake hands, maybe engage in some polite introductions and small talk, an exchange of cards. Instead, the government man just passed behind the developer and touched his arm before moving on.

What was the Treasury Department employee doing, touching someone in that deliberate way? Touching a developer that Davie hated.

I remembered the sense of *knowing* I had experienced in Wiccam's presence. A St. Claire kind of knowing. But I hadn't gotten St. Claire vibes from him. Not exactly. He wasn't one of ours, but there were other types of mentally endowed out there. Was Wiccam gifted? Was he trying to take a read from Hornsburn? Was this weird or what?

Then Wiccam was stopped by Detective Jack Madison, the man involved in the search for Davie.

"Well, well, well." The voice came from the room at my back. "Man trawling, are we? Need a little tryst between the sheets, I'm your man."

"You couldn't satisfy a blow-up doll between the sheets." *Snot and decay!* That had actually come out of my mouth.

Harry Boone paled, flushed, balled the fingers of one hand and reached to his hip with the other. As if he couldn't decide if he wanted to hit me or shoot me. Rather than commit murder in front of the entire town, he pivoted on a heel and goose-stepped away.

"That was good, Tyler. Why don't you just kick the man in the nuts and get it over with?" Noe said from the side.

"Yeah. My mouth—"

"Is going to get you shot someday."

Just then Colin Hornsburn passed behind me. Even without any St. Claire gift, I knew he was one seriously ticked off man. In a flash, I turned and touched his arm exactly as Adam Wiccam had. I opened myself to him in a rush. His anger didn't so much flow into me as slam into me, a tsunami of destruction. I jerked back. And fell against Adam Wiccam.

Pain exploded in my head, a ricochet of agony that bounced from temple to temple and lit up my mind like fireworks. Over the roar of pain, I felt Wiccam. I *knew* Wiccam. He was cold. Violence flowed though him like a black river, menacing, deadly. He was death. He wanted death. Wanted to kill. There was crimson on his hands. Blood on his bones. He caught me as I stumbled and smiled.

Something ripped apart in my mind. With the sound of shredding steel echoing in the darkness, I fell.

* * *

Shaking from pain and the reaction to Wiccam's mind, I barely made it up the stairs to the loft, Noe's arm around my shoulders as she half carried me. I scarcely saw Isaac and Jubal when I entered my apartment, stumbling to the kitchen and the drawer I used as a medicine chest. All thumbs, sick to my stomach, dizzy, I wasn't able to open the bottles of pain relievers, so Noe took them from me and shook out two Tylenol and two ibuprofen. I drank them back with a hand-ful of tap water and fell onto the couch.

The headache that I always got when I tried to use my gift was much, much worse than usual. After touching Wiccam, the pain was a caustic, cutting agony boring through my brain. I could hear myself groan. The pain was so intense that the light from the lamp hurt my eyes, and I had a moment to feel sorrow for migraine sufferers, if this was what they felt each time a headache took them over.

"What happened?" Jubal asked, his voice far away and yet booming.

"Shh. I don't know. She was fine one minute and then she collapsed. My mom used to have migraines and this looks like what she did."

"Jane?" I whispered, each letter burning acid across my mind. Shivers gripped me. Nausea boiled up my throat.

"Jane's in bed. Asleep," Jubal said.

Water ran in the kitchen, a faint tink of ceramic against ceramic, then metal. Someone was making tea. I hoped it was one of Isaac's eastern medicinal teas, the awful brews he con-cocted from stuff like bark and leaves and mold from the un-derside of last year's leftover firewood. I hated the stuff, but I'd try anything right now and the bitter tea might even help.

Time drifted in a haze of pain. A warm cup was placed in my hand and lifted to my lips, a straw slipped between them, making me gag.

"Drink it, Tyler." Isaac. His inflexible tone, the one he used in the do jang when he forced a student to try some new movement that they feared.

Obediently I sipped. Warm liquid puckered my mouth. It was like sucking on a tree root. The nausea faded instantly. I drank it all. Warmth filled me, spreading out from my stomach, to my knotted abdomen, to my spine. Something deep inside eased. I might have slept. For a while, I floated in the darkness, becoming sluggishly aware that the pain was beginning to subside.

But my feet were aching. I was having foot cramps. I moved my legs. The cramping worsened. I fought back to the surface of the dark lake beneath which I swam. My feet...

Someone untied my boots and pulled them off. They fell to the floor, sounding like a bass drum falling over and over. A large hand lifted my sock-covered feet into the cold air and settled them into a lap. Warmth kneaded the cramps away, pressing against my toes. I pressed back and groaned my appreciation. The hands continued to work into the muscles of my ankles and calves and up my thighs. Across my buttocks and into my lower back, where the migraine had twisted my muscles into a snarl. I heard myself sigh. The hands moved up to my shoulder blades, the very center of my back, working out knots that felt like stones. The aventurine necklace was unclasped and slid away. My earrings and bracelets were removed. An ice-filled bag was draped gently over my head. Each act of kindness seemed to bring more ease.

Gradually the sound of voices came clear. Jubal, Noe and Isaac. And closer, the deeper tones of Evan Bartlock. It was his hands on my spine, spreading warmth and healing from the outside even as the tea and the meds worked from the inside. Time passed.

Isaac spoke, Texan accent mellow. "If they are coordinates, then what do we do?"

"Then we find out where they are and call the cops," Noe said.

"The state cops," Evan murmured as I rolled over. "She's awake."

I could feel my friends gather around me, Jubal at my head, his hands just touching my temples. Noe took my hand for a moment before she pulled a chair close and sat. Isaac bent over the couch. I found I could place them all without opening my eyes. Jubal started a gentle scalp massage and I sighed again, managing a smile. "A queen and her court," I said.

"Don't get used to it, honeybunch. I'm the only queen around here," Jubal said.

I could feel the love and worry in his mind. The fear in Noe's. The calm of Evan's. The cop exuded warmth and peace. From fourteen inches away, I could sense Isaac evaluating me, assessing us all. The wall I usually hid behind was gone for the moment, pulverized by the massive headache. *Or by whatever had happened when I touched Adam Wiccam?* Had we touched before? It was all fuzzy right now.

"How's the head?" Evan asked.

"Not good."

"You know she's sick. She didn't cuss. Not even her version of cussing."

I considered a moment, then said, "Like a dipsomaniac douroucouli on Drambuie."

Evan laughed. "A drunken monkey?"

I was pleased that he got the joke and smiled at the sound of his voice. "What coordinates?" When no one answered, I said, "I heard you talking about coordinates."

"For the gold. To get Davie back," Noe said. She kissed my forehead and I heard her rustle as she went to the door. "It's past my bedtime. Later, guys." The door shut. Her mental aura faded, her mind filled with worry and images of the gold in the crates.

Weird. I could actually feel her moving away.

"Let's get you to bed," Jubal said, his voice inches from my face.

"Yeah," I said on a breath and tried to sit up. Pain lanced through me again. "On second thought…" I started to lie back, but an arm slid between me and the couch. A second arm went under my legs and I was lifted. The motion threatened to bring back the pain and the nausea.

Evan stopped, just holding me against him. "It's okay. I won't move until you say to," he murmured, his mouth near my face.

Finally my stomach settled. "Okay. Now."

A moment later I was between cool sheets, the room went dim, and I drifted off.

Long before dawn, a soft ringing woke me, my brain blurry with sleep. Movement in the loft. A man's voice. I froze, shocked awake.

"Yeah. You're sure. Two voice patterns? Speech? Okay. Why do they think that? Never mind. Tell the techies thanks." Evan Bartlock was in my apartment. I put out a hand and encountered Jane. No male body. The voice was coming from the couch. Why was Evan Bartlock on my couch before dawn?

"Because I spent the night here when you passed out cold. How are you feeling now? Still like a dipsomaniac douroucouli?" He had answered my unasked question. Now that was freaky.

I remembered the night before, the meeting, Adam Wiccam, the pain, and relaxed into my pillow. "Not so much." I slid a hand down my side and discovered I was pretty much naked. T-shirt and undies. Socks. "So, who undressed me?"

"I offered, but the gay guys objected. I don't see why they got to have the honors. They didn't even enjoy it." He sounded disgruntled, his voice closer in the darkness.

"And you would have?" I burrowed my head into the down, oddly happy. "Even with me in pain and unconscious?"

"Oh, yeah. A guy can always enjoy looking."

"Pervert."

The mattress sagged beneath his weight. Evan slid onto the bed beside me, on top of the covers. "This is better. Your couch is too short."

"Not for me."

"Yeah. Just too short for ordinary-sized people." The cop pulled me closer, the comforter and sheets separating us, and we drifted off toward sleep.

Moments later a scream woke me. "Daddy! *Daddy!* No, no, no, nonononono!" Jane thrashed, hitting my side.

"Jane! Jane. It's all right. It's all right, baby."

I cuddled the distraught girl against me. Evan turned on a light.

"Daddy's in trouble." Her eyes were haunted, pupils wide and black. "They put him in the snow," she wailed. "They put him in the snow."

And suddenly I saw what Jane was seeing. The vision bloomed in my mind, a visual and textural image, sharp and crisp and with all the detail of sensory input.

Icy white in the black of night. I'm cold. So cold. And I'm heavy. I can't move. A hand lifts me. Rolls me over. I'm outside. In the snow.

"You stupid idiot. Just tell me!" Shocking pain. A fist drawing back again.

"Daddy!"

The vision shattered. And was gone. Jane rolled against me and cried into my shoulder, her body racked with misery. I held her, rocked her until she calmed. And Evan Bartlock held us both. Rocked us until Jane quieted.

There was no getting back to sleep. Giving up, we all three got up and dressed, ate a silent breakfast of hot oatmeal, the kind that had to be cooked, not that instant stuff with the texture of gruel. Old-fashioned oats served with lots of sugar and whole milk. Comfort food. And we sat close together at the old table, knees touching.

10

"**Y**ou sure you're up to this? You were pretty sick last night."

I slammed my kitchen table across the floor in front of me and pushed the two chairs to the side. "They stopped calling. They haven't contacted us. And Davie's been moved." I bent and put the candle on the tile. "I can't stand around and do nothing anymore." So wired I was unaware of the cold, I sat on the floor and lifted Mama's crucifix around my neck. I settled myself, legs crossed, and positioned the candle in front of me, equidistant between my knees.

I held up my hand for the small packet Evan had brought from the local cops. Reluctantly he gave it to me and I opened the packet and emptied it, tossing the envelope aside. I set Davie's letter on the floor beside me and placed the other thing, the small bit of gold, into the palm of my hand, closing my fingers around it.

"Hit the lights," I said. The loft went dark. I struck the match and the smell of sulfur burned my nostrils. Flame bright, I stopped, stared at my hands lit by the match, my body bent over, my breath tight against my ribs. "He's going to die. Soon. He was outside in the snow. They're killing him, Evan." I lit the wick and waved the match out. I looked up. "So either get out or shut up and sit down. I have to work. And if I get a headache, then I get a headache."

I concentrated on the flame and calmed my breathing. Evan sat, though I could feel his eyes on me. I breathed in and out, letting the peace of simply being alive fill me. I forced out the images of Davie, tamped down the feel of his pain, his cold, his spirit hovering, indecisive, almost ready to go. I found the center of myself, and breathed. Just breathed. Only when a sense of peace had filled me completely did I allow myself to go deeper.

I regulated my breathing to a slow, easy pace. I closed my eyes, ignoring the cold that seeped into my thighs and feet, blocking out the fans and the blower and the green eyes watching me. Concentrated on my breathing.

The sense of peace spread and I relaxed into the cadence of my breath, my heartbeat. Peace seeped down my spine, into my arms and legs, to my fingers and toes. My body softened with the sound of my breath, the feel of cool air moving into me and out, bringing in light, health and peace, taking out darkness, disease and misery.

When I was centered, so calm my skin felt alive and glowing, my muscles liquid, bones soft and pliable, I opened my eyes. Squeezed the bloody bit of gold wire the cops had found in the ally. Wire coated with Davie's blood. *Davie? Davie, I'm here. Davie?* I called with my mind, searching for my brother. *Davie? Where are you? Davie. Davie. Davie.* The cadence of the syllables slowed, matched themselves to my heartbeat. *Davie. Davie. Davie…*

An ache began in the back of my neck, just as the last time I tried this, but now it was strong, harsh, a stabbing, wrenching pain. Replacing the peace. Bringing with it darkness. Growing.

Nausea roiled through me. My pain lifted and fell with each breath. *I hurt.* This was my brother.

Davie?

The pain and fear grew. I blinked. I was in the dark. The agony spread, a wildfire in my bones.

Davie?

Brat?

Where are you?

I don't know, Brat. Something new has happened. Some new component to the problem that I can't place. They moved me. I'm hurt. He shifted in the dark. Coughed, a long, wretched sound. Pain wrapped around him in tight bands, pain everywhere. *I'm not going to make it.*

Yes, you are. I found the coordinates. I'm going to find the gold and get you back.

You can't. They already know the—

Stabbing, blinding needles of light slammed into me. Pain whipped through me. Taking Davie with it.

The vision released me. I fell to the right and skittered across the floor, away from the attacking pain. *Blind. I was blind.*

My eyes jerked open. Panting, I looked up and was surprised that I could see Evan, his eyes appearing greener than usual, cool in the morning light. At some level, I had feared being blind. Where had that thought come from? Oh, yeah. The light…the light that Davie saw. I laughed, a harsh burst of sound cut off short. I had found Davie.

Euphoria shot up through me, a gusher of fresh water from the bottom of an empty well. Joy, like a heartbeat restored, pounded into me. Aunt Matilda had been right. The old bat had claimed that I could learn to overcome my disgust of the St. Claire gift and use it with delight.

And then the euphoria plunged. I crab-crawled into the corner. Horror-tinged fear roared in, replacing the exhilaration. I struggled to gather my wildly pitching emotions, to calm the passions that came from the scan. I fought to catch my breath.

"Tyler?" I jerked to the sound. *Evan.* I closed my eyes.

Suddenly I understood. The last time I tried a scan, anger had overtaken me. This time it was euphoria. My St. Claire gift came with strong emotional reactions, most of them having nothing to do with the success or failure of the scan. I had found Davie in my mind, but not in the real world. Once again, the St. Claire gift had offered much and given little. I still didn't know where Davie was. I laughed, and the sound dripped with despair.

I looked at the clock. Forty-eight hours had passed since the bad guys had threatened Davie's life. But he was still alive. Something had put off the timetable. Some new element had been added to the equation, but I had no idea what the element was or how to find out.

I rolled to my knees and blew out the candle. Anger replaced the roiling emotions, my own anger, fresh and hot and full of energy. I stood, lifting the candle, still holding the bloody bit of gold wire. I smiled, showing all my teeth to the cop across the room.

"I'm going to all the coordinates on the card. And if that doesn't work, I'm going to touch every single man in this town until I find the one who hurt my brother. Then I'm going to bitch-slap him till his teeth fall out."

Evan grinned. "Can I watch? I've always been partial to catfights." His face fell. "It didn't work?"

"It worked. He's still alive, but he doesn't know where he is." I set the candle on the table and shoved it back in place, a rasping sound of wooden legs on the tile. "Tell me again about the voice patterns."

"Headache?"

I stopped, surprised. "No. Huh. How 'bout that." *Just a panic attack bad enough to make me eat my pillow in fear.* I pulled my boots to me and shoved in my feet. "Voice patterns?"

"Speech patterns, actually. They say two different people gave the two messages. One was a woman. But that doesn't tell us much."

"Not yet, it doesn't. It will when we find them." I stood and looked through the windows into the rooftop garden, the sun so bright on the snow it hurt my eyes. The weather had broken, the temps in the sixties, fleecy clouds in a bright blue sky. Jane was being worked to exhaustion shoveling melting snow from the roof. Isaac thought physical activity would ease her nightmares. He was going to make certain that Jane wore herself out, first clearing the snow away, then taking up karate at his do jang, then doing schoolwork. He promised to keep her active, her mind and body occupied all day.

I should have been working my buns off in the shop preparing the spring line. Instead I was taking the card covered with stupid numbers that meant nothing to me, the card from Davie's boxed papers, the fancy card of thick, rich paper, covered with weird-looking numbers that my friends thought might be coordinates, and I was heading into the hills. How freaking dumb can I be?

"We should go through Davie's house first."

I paused and looked at Evan.

"The local boys went through it, but they didn't find much physical evidence of anything," he said.

"You think we can find something they missed?" I asked, thinking of Davie's house and the likelihood that no one would ever get anything from it. And that meant no one at all. Even me.

"Don't you?"

I tied my boot laces with quick looping motions. I grabbed a lightweight coat and a walking stick and nodded to Evan. "What the heck. Let's go to Davie's. Then I'm heading into the hills. You don't have to tag along. You're a city boy. A hike in these hills will wear you out."

"I'll live."

I could tell he was amused that a little bitty woman thought she might have more stamina than he. I considered feeling sorry for him, then I just shrugged and picked up car keys and sunglasses. "Suit yourself."

Quinn wasn't at home when we got there, I could see that even as I punched in the code at the gate. Not random numbers chosen by Davie, not someone's birth date, or a code that made a pattern on the security-code plate, but a mathematical sequence containing one error. Davie's idea of a joke. I punched in the prime numbers, and the error, up through 13–1,2,3,4,5,7,11,13. I never knew why Davie thought it so funny. My brother had a weird sense of humor.

I parked my little Geo Tracker in front of the unprepossessing-looking house. It was situated on a bald knoll, bald not because Davie had cut down tress—heaven forbid—but because the knoll was solid granite. I opened the heavy front door, ignoring the squeal of the alarm warning, and punched a second sequence into the security panel, more prime numbers and a different error.

The inside of the house was far different from the outside, barely seeming to allow for the known laws of physics. Outside, the house looked like a small brick-and-stone dollhouse, arched windows, arched entry, four chimneys, peaked roofline with lots of sharp angles. Inside, one realized that only the expanded foyer with the black baby-grand piano, the library, a guest suite, and a wet bar were on the entry floor. Most of the entry level was a huge deck overlooking the bottom floor. All living space was on the lower floor, with the ceiling opening up three stories overhead and the public area of the living space laid out to view.

The back wall of the house was windows, revealing an extraordinary panorama of a cleft in the hills, with a narrow stream, a waterfall, tall trees and massive tumbled rocks. The view opened up and down, and no matter how many times I came, I was always struck by how Davie had made the mountains his own, bringing them inside without damaging the environment or habitats.

Through the windows, a lone hawk was poised in the top of a dead tree, searching the ground, the limbs, the rocks for his dinner.

"Holy…" Evan's voice trailed off.

I looked at him. "I thought you had been here. With the cops when they did the search."

"At night. I missed all this." He walked to the edge of the balcony and looked out. "All I saw was black windows and cops everywhere."

"Where do we start?"

"David's office. Local LEOs took his PCs and laptop, his Mac. Your brother had some serious hardware. But he also had some files that looked unrelated to finding him. The cops couldn't think of a legitimate reason to take them. Well, not with me standing there, watching." He flashed a quick grin. "Had I not been there, I'm sure they would have found justification for taking whatever they wanted."

Davie had decorated in shades of charcoal, taupe, forest-green, black, cloud-gray and moss, colors taken from the view outside, with lots of natural stone, bronze and old wood. The wood had been scavenged from existing local buildings that had fallen into ruin, treated and worked into the design of the house. Even the floors, which were local oak, hickory and pine, had been taken from barns Davie had purchased, torn down by hand, and transported to the knoll.

The office was on the bottom floor, in a nook off the master suite. His bedroom was understated, a king-size bed with wool and silk linens, the headboard crafted from found articles: two carved chair backs, two narrow columns, a peaked door frame from a barn and a carving of a swan, his long neck reaching back to ruffle his feathers, wings outspread. Things that wouldn't have gone together until Davie had made them fit. The floor was bare wood, even in winter when a rug would have warmed the room.

A black leather recliner and a bronze antique swan-shaped lamp he had rewired were the only other furniture. Everything else was in the huge walk-in closet. In the office nook, it was a different matter. The floor was covered with a silk rug in a swan pattern, the black swan rising from gray water in a rush of froth. The walls were faced with shelving and desktops purchased when the local pharmacy closed, and on them perched every conceivable form of electronic equipment, or spaces where they had been. The monitors, scanners, printers and the oversize plasma-screen TV were still there, but had all been moved around. There was red fingerprint powder on everything, papers were scattered, a faint buzz of white noise came from an antique radio left on, the dial between the stations.

I punched it off. Silence closed in. Davie would really hate this clutter when he got back. I sighed. Evan was watching me. "What?" I asked.

"You don't seem that upset at the mess. Or at the fact that the cops took all his data." Evan propped a hip on the nearest desk.

I shrugged. "No *cop* will ever get the data on the units they took."

"Something about that tone sounds insulting." Evan looked amused, as if he found my comment patently ludicrous. To him, cops could do anything that needed to be done. Superheroes in ugly shoes and dress blues.

"Everything is encrypted by a program he created himself. Even with really state-of-the-art equipment and software, they have no chance at all. And if they try to take the hard drive out and slave it to another unit, it'll send a spike and fry itself and whatever other units it can get to."

Now he looked interested. "They can do that? Computer programmers?"

"Davie can. He's a computer savant. He regularly uploads all his data into a node where a wireless transmitter sends it to another FTP location he created just for that purpose. His files bounce from node to node before they reach his home base. Wherever that is. He works on the Web itself, in a virtual world all his own. And, no, I have no idea what the password is or where his FTP location is. So the loss of his data is unimportant, and the loss of the hardware means he has an excuse to upgrade. But he'll really hate this mess."

"Yeah. I kinda get the impression that David is anal about his space and privacy."

I repressed a second sigh. "Paper files would probably be there," I pointed to a wood unit once used in a lawyer's office. "But Davie would never leave anything important in his house in a format that could be taken from him."

"I'll start here, then," Evan said. "Maybe we'll get lucky."

"I'll go through the closets and the library. But it's a waste of time."

We spent the next two hours going through all Davie's files, papers and books. We found nothing. Not a blessed thing. I was feeling gracious when we drove off, and didn't bother to say "told you so." But I knew we could both hear the words hanging in the air. Subtle, I can't do.

Evan Bartlock was breathing heavily behind me on the trail. I paused to let him catch up and consulted the little GPS device that hung from my belt loop on a strap. We had stopped at a backpackers' general store on the way out of town and purchased the hideously expensive gadget, taking time as well to outfit the city cop for the mountains.

Evan was now the proud owner of hiking boots, thick socks, new long underwear for later, a backpack, a walking stick and a down vest. He refused to buy the lined jeans and the flannel shirts I recommended, but as long as the weather stayed above freezing, that wasn't a problem.

Evan sat on a handy rock outcrop and once again unlaced his left boot. As the boot hit the earth, the cop grunted in pain, which made me grin. A grin I was careful to hide. Blisters were rising on his ankles and toes, and across the balls of his feet, the water blisters and raw welts which new hiking boots would create in a heartbeat, until the stiff leather shaped to an owner's feet. I simply handed him a slim packet of Band-Aids to use as needed. So far in the past hour, he'd pulled off his boots twice and applied antibiotic gel and the bandages.

A cold wind whipped across the snow, blowing along the ground up the western slope of the mountain. Melted snow trickled, a melodic sound like bells made of wood and silver. Overhead, a hawk called in warning, a sustained *skreak, skreak, skreak, skreak*. On his tail, a blue jay flew. Their shadows crossed over us and moved up the mountain, following the wind.

Leafless branches streaked the snow-covered earth with shadow, and black patches of bare ground spotted the earth. Everywhere, water flowed and soaked into the dirt. The smell of wood smoke came now and again on the crisp cold air. The world snapped and cracked and trickled. I loved the smells and the sights and the feel of the air. Like spring.

I tried to will some of this warmth into my brother. I wanted to believe that he felt something. Some radiant expectation that I would find him. Some bit of hope.

When Evan picked up his boot to pull it back on, I moved on up the slope to its crest, pulling myself along with my five-foot-long walking stick when the vertical rise was too sharp for my hands and feet alone. Minutes later, he caught up with me, saying nothing, leaning hard on his own stick with each step. Up ahead, I spotted a surveyor's property marker, an iron stob with a yellow plastic flag on top. I crawled over a boulder and around a tree to the iron. This was the western boundary of the property. I consulted the card and the GPS device. They matched.

I pulled my binoculars to me and looked south across the line of the mountain, following yellow flags tied to branches, to wooden stakes in the ground. I had figured out that the iron markers were permanent, the ones that would appear on a map or a property plat, and the wooden markers were temporary, where the surveyor had to make an adjustment or take another reading. By following the flags, I could pretty well deduce the shape of the parcel of land.

Because there was little chance that a surveyor had found the gold or that the gold was on a property line, I could eliminate the boundaries of each piece of land and concentrate on GPS coordinates in the middle. Once I figured out where the outer lines of the property were, then I could deduce if any of the coordinates were at a midpoint.

About an hour into our search, and just after the first application of bandages to his ankles, Evan had suggested that the county office could tell us where each coordinate was and had called them for help. But the county was still inputting GPS coordinates into the new computer system and they couldn't help us. Not until next year. So it was footwork and deduction.

With the binoculars, I followed the line of sight as far as the yellow markers went, then I pivoted and followed the distant line back down a ridge toward a ravine. My best guess was that all of the coordinates matched a boundary marker. "Okay. Let's head back," I said. "These are a no-go." I dropped the field glasses on their thong around my neck and turned back. Evan was draped across a branch, letting it hold his weight. His head was hanging down, wet hair slicked to his forehead. A bottle of water was in one hand, but it looked like he might be too tired to lift it. "You okay?"

He raised his head. His face was flushed and he was breathing through his mouth with an effort. "I run ten miles three times a week. I play full-court basketball with the boys every Saturday. I work out at the gym two times a week. I'm in pretty good shape. But you aren't even breathing hard. What are you? A superwoman?"

I shrugged. "I hike once or twice a year. Four-wheel-drive vehicles use a lot of gas, so I walk a lot instead of taking the Tracker. I don't exercise much. But then, I'm used to the altitude." I grinned at him. "Maybe you're just old."

"Thanks. I really appreciate that. How old are you?"

"What? You didn't do your research? Or are you just trying to keep us in one place for a while longer so you can catch your breath?"

"Twenty-eight. Red and green. Five feet even. The records left out cruel and competitive and has a great rack." He said it to see if he could get a rise out of me. That, and to hold me in one place arguing or defending myself while he rested.

Fat chance. I laughed and started back down the trail blazed by the surveyors. Evan pushed up from the branch and stood straight. Eventually he followed. At some point, Evan even got a second wind and was able to keep up with me, though he never got back enough breath to engage in conversation. But I didn't think his feet would heal for weeks. Over the course of the day he used two full packets of Band-Aids and developed a two-footed limp.

Except for short breaks and a longer rest at one o'clock for lunch, we climbed hills all day. And we found nothing. Finally, at dusk, foot-sore and exhausted, we were ready to call it quits. We had hiked a dozen pieces of property to no avail. They had nothing in common, nothing that marked them as being of interest to anyone. Some had been recently surveyed, some hadn't been walked in years. Some were relatively flat and had been homesteaded in the past.

Some were so sheer a mountain goat would have needed climbing gear to scale them. Some were close to Connersville, some were so far out they took an hour to reach. None showed any evidence of gold, not that I knew what to look for.

All in all, it was a totally wasted day. And I was afraid I was going to be forced into plan B, touching and then bitch-slapping the men in town. And didn't that sound like a wise course of action?

It was nearly dusk and we stood midway up a hill, in a shallow, tree-tangled gorge created by water runoff. I stood on a stump, and Evan in a depression filled with leaves. The shadows were long across the ground, the sun already dropping behind the western hills. The wind had risen and the temps had dropped fast.

"Time to head back," Evan said.

"We can make the top of the ridge."

"Yeah, but we won't make it back down before dark. Let's go home, Tyler."

I tried to read the card. It was too dark to see the numbers. "Spit and decay," I said. The cop was right. I sighed, exhaustion and failure in the sound.

Evan stepped to me and cupped my chilled chin in his hand. Our flesh was cold, rough against rough, chapped from the constant wind. He kissed the tip of my nose and wound my scarf around my lower face. "We'll try again tomorrow."

Zipping up my down vest, he handed me my leather gloves for the trek back to the Tracker. He froze. "What?" I asked.

Rather than answer, he lifted my binoculars and focused on the ridgetop. "Look at that. People."

"Here? This property hasn't seen a human in ages."

"Quite a coincidence, don't you think?" He handed me the glasses. "You know 'em?" He pointed as I lifted the glasses and positioned the eyepieces. "Near that huge spruce, the one to the right of the blasted stump."

I found the place he described and searched down. A man came into view. I felt my heart lighten and my mouth form a smile, the first real smile I'd allowed myself all day. "Gotcha."

"You're sure it was Floyd Feaster?" Isaac asked as he dished up a hearty stew.

"Oh, yeah. It was him. I saw him at the county council meeting, trailing along behind Colin Hornsburn like a love-sick calf. We marked exactly where we saw him so we can go back if we need, but there didn't seem to be anything important about the spot. More tea, please?" I held out my glass and Jubal filled it. Evan tore off a hunk of homemade bread and passed the loaf to me, taking a bite of his own bread as he did. I bit and we both groaned in pleasure.

Isaac looked at Jubal. "Moaners. Both of them."

Jubal rolled his eyes. "They'll be noisy if they ever get around to it."

I blushed hotly. Evan laughed around the mouthful of bread.

"Get around to what?" Jane asked.

"Shoveling snow," Isaac said with a look of warning he threw at Jubal. "Tell your aunt about your day."

Jane's eyes took on a manic glow. "I shoveled snow and I learned some cool moves at the do jang. I can do an Ap Koob Yi and a Deui Koob Yi, and a Mom Tong Jireugi and… and…and a bunch of other stuff, I forget the names, and I got a Do Bok! See?" She bounced from the table and whirled in a fast pirouette to show off her white pj's, tied smartly with a white belt. "And Isaac said if I practice a lot I can reach a black belt in just a couple of years. I think it would be so cool to be a black belt.

"Jubal taught me how to snip silver. Real, pure, sterling silver. I'm going to make a necklace to wear back to school. And Isaac taught me how to do some origami. The turtle is mine." Jane pointed at the table centerpiece as she sat again and chattered on to another subject, her agile mind full of her day rather than the thoughts and feelings around her. I shot Isaac and Jubal looks of appreciation between bites of stew. I was famished.

At eight o'clock Isaac and Jubal left, carting dirty pots back across the bare, narrow rooftop garden, and Evan started washing dishes. Who was I to stop a man from feeling useful? While he sudsed up the stoneware, I put Jane to bed, this time in a trundle bed Isaac and Jubal had rigged up during the day. It was a foam mattress on a lightweight frame that slid under my bed when not in use, and they had made it up with linens donated from their own closets. I didn't ask who had owned the purple satin comforter that Dyno claimed as her own. True to Isaac's promise, Jane climbed into the bed, gathered the cat to her and fell instantly asleep.

Carrying a bottle of wine and two glasses, Evan joined me on the couch, limping less in his sock feet. We both needed showers, which brought to mind all sorts of lascivious activities, but they weren't happening in my house with Jane asleep only ten feet away. We'd just have to remain stinky. I took a glass of the strong merlot, exchanging it for a sheaf of Davie's papers and we settled in, a single afghan covering us.

For an hour, we went through my brother's papers again, looking for anything that might point to a bad guy. If we didn't find anything in here, all in all, the day would have proved useless.

Luck wasn't with us. Besides the coordinates, the only things that still came up suspicious were the Q Core papers and the antique, ornate key. There was still nothing it could open. I was turning the key around and around in my fingers, watching the way the light hit the tarnished metal, thinking that a necklace designed with an elaborate key pendant might be a great Valentine's Day item for Bloodstone's Internet store when Evan's phone rang.

"Bartlock. Yeah. On the mountains, hiking." His brows went up and his gaze went to his sock-covered feet propped on a small table. His toes twitched in pain. "Sure. It was lots of fun. A real vacation." I grinned at him but he ignored me. After a moment he said, "How good is the source? Yeah? You got someone on him? Okay. Kid's with her aunt. Yeah. I will. Thanks for the heads-up." Frowning, he closed the phone.

I looked my question at him.

"You won't like it." When I didn't reply, he said, "Seems Quinn has a bit of a gambling problem. A source claims a small-time bookie took his marker, then sold it to a guy in Atlanta. If the source is right, Quinn owes some major bucks to him."

The cold from outside crept into my bones. Colin Hornsburn was from Atlanta originally. And hadn't someone told me that Roman Trio was out of Atlanta? Would a major criminal organization bother to torture Davie? Wouldn't they just kill him outright? "How much is major bucks?"

"Close to fifty grand. Local law seems to think the attack in the parking lot was either staged to throw the cops off his trail or was intended as a warning for him to pay up. It could be considered a motive for kidnapping his boss, except that no ransom demand has actually been issued."

We both looked at my phone, which had been suspiciously silent. I glanced over to make sure that Jane was still asleep. The cat was on her chest, curled into a ball that rose and fell with Jane's deep, even breaths. I felt Evan's eyes on me but didn't look his way. "That's not the only thing he just told you, is it?"

Evan's cool eyes seemed to measure me. "You were fingerprinted when you applied to work in a day care about nine years ago. The crime techs found your fingerprints on cabinets and dishes in David's kitchen."

"Okay," I nodded, trying to be agreeable. "Bloodstone was just a dream then. I worked several jobs to support myself after my stepfather died. The day care and thirty screaming tots in dirty diapers lasted a whole day." And though I seldom went to Davie's, when I did it was usually to eat supper. I didn't say this to Evan Bartlock, who seemed to be wavering from cop to family and back again as he watched me. After a short silence, he went on.

"They confiscated old tax records. David was employed by the government for over five years. After a bit of digging, they discovered that he may have worked for the Department of Defense under an assumed name—which, believe me, is impossible—in a bureau called Q Core." I felt the hairs on the backs of my arms lift in excitement. "We need to discover what the heck Q Core is or was, and what your brother did for all those years." I nodded. Evan's eyes sharpened. "Oh, and by the way. When he worked for Q Core? He went by the name David Lowe."

When I woke, dawn was streaking the heavens, long golden bands of light against a dark sky, black hills below. I stretched slowly, pulling on muscles I had used in the hike. I was stiff but not painfully so. We had slept through the night, without waking to Jane's nightmares. I rolled in the warm linens and peeked over the side to the trundle bed. It was empty.

In an instant, I threw the covers from me and landed with a thump on the cold floor. The bath was vacant. The locks were sealed on the doors. The window-doors to the garden were shut. "Jane?" I called softly.

The loft felt empty, the way space does when no one has moved in it for hours. "Jane?" I shouted. A rustle summoned me to the kitchen. Jane, unmoving, eyes wide, was curled in a ball on the floor in the corner, pressed into the cabinets. Dyno was in her arms, asleep. "Jane?" I whispered. She stared across the apartment, right through me.

I fell at her side, touched her. Ice. *Like Davie…* "Jane." I gathered her to me. The little girl was chilled through, her flesh so cold she might have spent the night outside. Dyno woke and mewled a protest as I lifted Jane, half crushing the cat between us, and carried them back to my warm bed. I bundled us all under the covers, but knew Jane needed warmth faster than my body heat could give. I crawled back out, found an electric blanket in the armoire and plugged it in, tucking it around Jane beneath the other covers, before I mounded them high over us and cradled her again.

Her body was so still, her eyes so vacant. What had she seen? Had she been with Davie? And what in the name of all that was holy was I going to do to help her?

The cell phone was on the bedside table and I dialed Aunt Matilda from memory. The stupid message and the stupid beeps answered me. I wanted to slam the cell against the wall. Instead, I closed it and cuddled my niece.

Having nothing else I could do, I started talking. I talked about Davie, telling her of her father when he was a boy, how he was such a loner, spending his time with books and writing, with long solitary hikes in the hills he so loved. And I told her how he went away for a time, then came back, bringing with him his beautiful daughter, and how I fell in love with her at first sight. I described her skirt and the shiny shoes she had worn the first time I saw her. Told her how bright her eyes had been, shining and shy.

The blanket began to warm, giving off little clicks of sound as it heated. As I talked, Jane slowly began to relax. A half hour later, Dyno leaped from the floor and wandered across us with smooth steps, sniffing and purring, sticking her nose into the covers, padding across our pillows, rubbing her face over Jane's head. Satisfied that she had marked ownership of her human, she bounded back to the floor and settled by her water bowl and kitty-litter box. Jane didn't react to anything, and I knew she was deeply asleep. But what was I going to do with her? How could I help her?

11

Jane was snoring softly when I pulled the drapes closed to create an ambience of night and safety and went down to help open Bloodstone. I had watched over her for two hours, and though she didn't move, or wake, she seemed to soften and loosen as she slept, her brow smoothed in true slumber.

As Jubal, Isaac and I opened the store safe and the locked cabinets, setting out the wares for display, I described Jane's condition to them and told them I would be staying close today. I babbled an apology about the spring line, jabbered promises to do twice the work once Davie was found, and knew I sounded demented. They were silent, letting me talk. When I ran down, Jubal came over to me, took a display rack from my hands and pulled me into his arms.

"We'll take care of the spring line and the store, honey-bunch. It's under control. You just take care of your family."

"You're going to have to quit calling me that," I said, and I burst into tears. He let me snivel into his shirt, leaning into him. He held me while I cried until my tears dried themselves. I rested against him and sighed with comfort.

"Better?"

"Yeah." I stood away, hands on his shoulders, and met his true blue eyes. "Thanks. I know you guys will handle the spring-line designs. That won't make me feel any less guilty, though. I'm going to get some things from the back and take them upstairs. I can do some work up there, which will make me feel better. When Evan comes, will you send him up?"

"Sure. If you want to work, take the polished bloodstone up and string some sets. A bit of advice?" Jubal didn't wait to see if I listened. "If you don't jump that cop's bones soon, your head will explode."

"Jubal's right," Noe said. I hadn't seen her come in. She was bent over a display and stood upright, a mischievous glint in her eyes. "He has a nice ass. You should jump him and get it over with."

I laughed shakily and squeezed Jubal's shoulders. "You guys are shameless." To Noe I said, "You say every man has a nice ass, and you're all but married to the green-logger."

"Smitten. Not married. Not dead. Do the guy and get it over with. You'll feel better."

I rolled my eyes and unlocked Bloodstone's front door before going to the workroom. Some comments were not worth a reply, and some would only make me blush, so I retreated. Better part of valor, and all that.

In the back, I pulled boxes marked in Jubal's strong block print, BLOODSTONE HEARTS, BLOODSTONE BEADS, and MISC. STONES—GREEN. I gathered a fourth box containing findings: clasps, various silver and gold spacers, leftover pearls and stones from other projects, things I would need. While I worked I heard the first customer come in, the bells over the door tinkling, and registered the sound of voices speaking, though I didn't catch the words. On top of my pile went a final box of jumbled jump rings, spacers and green glass beads, a tool kit with several kinds of pliers, stringing supplies, needles and thread, scissors and a few odds and ends. While I worked, my thoughts turned to the ornate key I had tucked into my pocket. To keep it safe, I strung it on a thin length of leather and hung it around my neck. If I ever found what it opened, I wanted to have it handy. Arms full, I was ready to go back to Jane.

Lugging the boxes up the stairs, I entered the loft. The first thing I saw was that the draperies had been thrown open. The logs blazed merrily in the fireplace, and the trundle bed had been put away. My bed was empty. I almost dropped the boxes as I whirled, taking in the apartment with a fast pirouette.

Sitting at the kitchen table was Jane, her head bent attentively forward. Across from my niece, her back to the tall windows, was Aunt Matilda.

My mouth fell open. Emotions tumbled across themselves as they raced through me. Shock, anger, relief, gladness, hatred. Jane nodded. "This is so cool," she said. "It's like a computer game."

Jealousy wrapped itself around me. A red haze tinged my vision.

Before them on the table was a tin box painted with a stained-glass rendition of an angel. Beside it were three boxes of Tarot cards, and a deck of Tarot cards laid out in the Hagall Spread. Seven cards in three vertical rows, two cards to the left, two to the right, and three down the middle, with three across the bottom as if the upper seven rested on them.

Fury bubbled up in me. Without looking, I found a place to set the boxes and moved toward the kitchen table.

Aunt Matilda's voice, melodic and soothing, said, "The Hagall Spread is a tool for revealing the path of spiritual growth in difficult situations. It is a favorite of mystics and those confronting a major life challenge."

Neither looked up at me as I approached. I focused on the open tin box to the side and fought the desire to grab it to me. It was *mine,* and my mother's before me! It had been in my trunk. Aunt Matilda had gone through my things. I gathered my growing anger about me like armor.

"The Knight of Swords is the *significator* card you have chosen. While it isn't seen, and is hidden beneath the center card, it influences and directs all the other cards and they must be interpreted by its strengths and weaknesses. The Knight is a fearless and skillful warrior, a tornado, unfettered by emotion or material concerns. A card of action, indicating one able to boldly take on challenges that others consider terrifying or insurmountable."

"Challenges? Like my gift?" Jane asked.

"Indeed. The Knight of Swords is a person who inspires fear and awe through the purity of his purpose and the intensity of his intellect." Aunt Matilda didn't look up from the cards, but her voice caressed, as if no one in the world existed for her in that moment but Jane.

"Does it have to be a guy?"

"Oh, no. A woman may be this Knight, for she is one who accepts quests, missions of great importance, fraught with danger. The desire to save David is such a quest as a Knight of Swords might accept. She is one who is outspoken, who speaks frankly. Your choice of this card represents your heart and your purpose. It may portend the swift initiation or conclusion of a conflict. A decisive invocation of force."

"You will not do this in my house," I said. Fury rose in me, a slow, steady swelling of power. "You will not."

"It's Aunt Tyler. She's the Knight of Swords."

I stopped, caught in the trap of Jane's pronouncement.

"Ah. Then you were not thinking of yourself when you chose the Knight?"

Jane shook her head.

"I see. This card, the Two of Wands, represents the core or central issue of your current situation. When reversed, like this, it is indicative of the erosion of power and influence. Not knowing what to do, being caught off guard, hamstrung because of past decisions. Loss of interest, clarity or faith in a venture."

"She'll never give up on Daddy!"

"But do you fear that she will?" Aunt Matilda asked.

Jane's eyes filled with tears. "Yes."

"Stop this. Stop it right now," I said.

As if I hadn't spoken, Aunt Matilda tapped a third card. "This card represents something you did, or fear you did, to bring the situation about. The Page of Coins, reversed. This is the dark essence of earth, such as a chasm. Unfavorable news from outside. Irrationality, failure to recognize obvious facts, coupled with a decision to do nothing in the face of great need. Wastefulness, lack of focus."

My hands curled into claws. That she would dare to go through my things, find my mother's Tarot, my mother's hated cards, and do a reading with them. That she would *dare!*

"There was that phone call," Jane said. "I heard the message. Daddy said it wasn't important, but I knew he was afraid. And I didn't do anything about it. I didn't make him tell me." Tears gathered in Jane's eyes.

"Stop this," I said.

"Could you have forced him to talk?" Aunt Matilda asked. "Even if you had known what was going to happen?"

A red haze grew, closing in from the edges of my vision. Jane sobbed once. Aunt Matilda went on, inexorable. "Stop this." I spoke so low my words were a hiss of sound.

"The card here represents your beliefs, impressions or expectations." Aunt Matilda almost smiled. "Ten of Swords. Ruin, crushing defeat. Sadness and desolation in the aftermath of catastrophic and total collapse. A decisive conclusion brought about through the swift and merciless application of overwhelming force working against you. Someone took your father. You believe it was your fault, but it wasn't. It would have happened no matter what you did."

"I should have stopped them."

"You couldn't."

"Stop this *now!*" I shouted, fighting the urge to fling the cards from the table.

Aunt Matilda didn't even look up, her voice still speaking in the cadence she fell into when she read the cards. "You wanted me to come, Tyler. You wanted me to help her. I am here."

"Not like this." I heard the fury in my voice and, beneath it, pleading. And I hated the sound of it.

"Why not like this?"

"It isn't right. The Tarot is evil."

"There is nothing evil in the Tarot except that the Holy Roman Church outlawed it centuries ago. Though I love the church, the pope and bishops made an error when they banned the Tarot. They feared it, they feared that God spoke through the gifted and the cards, and not through the church only. They feared loss of worldly power and authority, should God speak through any means but themselves. So, just as the ancient bishops outlawed scripture the common man could read, they banned the cards and crystal balls and silver cups and candle, the tools of the gifted and the charlatan alike. They dictated that scripture would be only in Latin, that men be the only priests, and made our use of our gifts a heresy."

Aunt Matilda raised soft gray eyes to me. There was kindness there, a kindness so deep and pervasive I felt it enter me and soothe, as if a candle had been lighted in the dark. As if a huge hand had stroked me once and settled my ire. "God does not speak through the cards, Tyler. Nor does the devil, though either could if the heart of the quester was open to them. Only the psychic speaks through the cards. Only the pope's fear made it heresy. And only your fear, and your mother's fear before you, makes you tremble."

She turned back to the Hagall Spread and tapped the next card. "This card at the upper left represents the spiritual history, the things you've learned, or in this case, the things in the spiritual world that are affecting this situation. Six of Coins represents success. But when reversed it indicates insolence and conceit with material things. Overconfidence, bad investments and imprudent handing of acquired wealth. Contempt for those less fortunate. Thievery has precipitated the current crisis."

"I am not afraid," I said.

Without looking up, she said, "Your mother was. She gifted you with her fear. I know. I often read the cards for you, and have seen you reading your mother's journal.

"Jane, the card at the upper right represents the metamorphosis of the spiritual situation, and how your knowledge will evolve. The Ace of Coins is fortuitous. The seed of prosperity and material gain, perhaps as yet unseen. A new foundation from which to turn your dreams into reality."

"I only want my daddy back," Jane said. "I want to help him."

"Then you must focus on the practical, understand the dynamics of the natural world. You must search for a gift, or document or inheritance, or an unexpected opportunity for physical achievement. That is what the Ace of Coins is trying to tell you."

Instantly I thought of the heavy key and the gold.

"The card at the left of the lower line represents the person or qualities that will sustain your spiritual journey. The Two of Cups signifies love, the perfect harmony of union, in romance, friendship—"

"Or my daddy?"

"Or your father. A deep and palpable connection radiating joy and contentment. A great concordance or pledge of fidelity."

"He'll come home then." Jane's face lit up from within. "He'll be safe."

Aunt Matilda didn't respond to Jane's plea. "The card in the middle of the lower line represents the qualities that you express in this circumstance. The Ace of Swords, reversed. So many reversed cards." She sounded pensive, anxious. "The seed of defeat—perhaps as yet unseen."

Jane's face plummeted. "I'm going to cause him to die!"

"Hush, child. Study the cards. Let your mind open and focus your gift. The cards are only a tool helping you to understand what you already know. This card may represent how you could be used to prevent disaster. Your Knight of Swords must be prepared to face a challenge, to meet it with the invocation of force. Ace of Swords suggests reason and intelligence misdirected or cast aside, an action that may result in injustice and falsehood. An excessive power abused. It may suggest new ideas or information with dangerous implications."

Aunt Matilda's mouth pulled down. "Your aunt is your protection, your Knight. Yet you are the one they want. You are the one they were waiting for. How did they know about you? And who are they?" She shook her head to clear it.

"The card at the right of the lower line represents the person or qualities that will reveal spiritual knowledge. Knight of Coins, when reversed, is your enemy. He is molten magma, slow to action even in the most urgent circumstances. A thinker, a planner, a force of nature that cannot be diverted from the wrong path. The voice of duty and honor utterly divorced from reality. He brings death."

Aunt Matilda gathered the cards and shuffled them with a whisping sound, three times as she always did. The image overlaid the one from childhood, from the one visit I had paid to the Low Country when I was a child. Aunt Matilda shuffling cards, then turning the deck to face her, paging through the deck one by one as she turned each card upright. The silence in the loft built as I tried to mesh all my feelings, weave my fears into something manageable. It all kept slipping, like silk yarn through my fingers. Jane finally looked up and watched my face.

"My mother thought the cards were evil," I said. That one thought out of all the others was paramount. Mama had hated the cards. Therefore I should hate them, too.

"Did she write in the journal why she feared them?" Aunt Matilda asked, her voice soft as cat's feet across my mind.

"No. There are whole years when she didn't write anything in it."

She almost smiled. "Your mother was young when she married. Sixteen. Giselle and your father seemed to be very happy at one time. Seeming to be in tune with each other in mind and heart and purpose. Then your father disappeared. He packed a bag, took the car and left. He went to New York with no warning. No word. No explanation. And your mother lost contact with him, that fine and wondrous mental touch they had shared.

"The police became involved. They found the hotel where he stayed the first night he was in the city. His things were in the room. The bed had not been slept in. He was gone. Vanished.

"Giselle read his cards, over and over. And each time, they said the same thing. He was lost to her. He never came home. We never heard from him again. He never contacted his parents, who died in heartbreak before they turned sixty." Aunt Matilda put the cards aside and folded her hands, staring at them. "She so feared the truth of the cards that she ran away from them. And because of her fear, you went through your time of gifting alone. I hold myself responsible for that, responsible for the impairment and degradation of your gift. It bloomed deformed because you were alone and afraid. Giselle passed her fear to you, and from you to Jane, had I not come."

I picked out the one thing I understood from the litany of words. "I would never hurt Jane. Never."

"Of course not. But you are now her Knight of Swords. Only you can bring her father home. And you are much less than you could have been."

Jane looked up at me with something odd in her gaze. I recognized it as sympathy. As pity. The look stung me to my core. "I don't need the damned St. Claire gift to bring Davie home," I said.

Aunt Matilda finally lifted her head. "Don't you?" She turned back to Jane. "I am here to help you with your gift. Your father asked me to come when it was your time. And I am here."

"Davie asked you? Davie asked you to come for Jane?"

When Aunt Matilda didn't answer, but simply handed Jane the deck of cards again, I turned and strode from the loft. On my way out, I grabbed coat and boots, gloves, scarf. I passed Evan Bartlock at the doorway. I didn't know how long he had been there. I didn't ask. I didn't care.

The red haze of anger was gone, but the specter of jealousy still danced within me.

Evan Bartlock was silent for the first few miles. I didn't look his way or speak, even after I turned off the tertiary road onto what was little more than a trail, concentrating on the serpentine, two-rut path that wound up the steep side of a hill. Gunning the motor and applying the brake, I ground the four-wheel-drive transmission, maneuvering the deeply grooved snow tires into the melting muck.

Near the midpoint of the hill, we dropped into a deep hole in the pseudoroad and Evan's head hit the Fiberglas hardtop with a dull thump. He sent a look that accused me of hitting the hole on purpose, so I hit another one. He laughed. "You like doing this to me, don't you? Showing me what a weak, wuss of a city boy I am and what a tough broad you are?"

"Tough broad? That's an out-of-date, derogatory term left over from the fifties." He laughed again and I felt some of the anger melt away like the snow beneath the tires. I couldn't help it. I stuck my nose in the air. "I'm more like a goddess, Diana perhaps. A huntress, a woman who can outdo any man." A grin pulled at my lips when he shook his head.

Evan knew I was taking out my temper on the Geo and he didn't feel the need to try and talk me down from the rage or calm the ruffled feathers of the distraught little female. He even let me drive while I was mad, which was something that even Jubal had never let me do. I relaxed my shoulders and neck and slowed the SUV's mad rush up the hill. "Yeah. Guess I do like showing you what a city boy you are." I pulled into a small clearing that was level, more or less, and pulled up the hand brake.

Evan dropped his hold from the support grip over the door. His knuckles were suspiciously white. "So. You want to hear my news while we walk or while we're still warm and comfy in this matchbox of a vehicle fit only for midgets and grade-schoolers."

I laughed then and felt the last of the rage slip away, as he had maybe intended. "Midget is not PC. Neither is broad. Tell me now."

He settled deeper in the worn seat, one knee against the door panel, one against the gear shift. "The cops took some papers when they searched David's house. Financial papers. A will and life-insurance policy, among other things. They both name Tyler St. Claire as beneficiary."

I looked at him, startled. "Davie bought a life-insurance policy? Not my brother. He hated those things. Said he had too much money to need life insurance. That was for poor folk like me. How much?"

"You didn't say anything about the will."

"I know about the will. I was there when it was drawn up.

In the event that something happens to him, I gain custody of Jane and, for a nice fat fee, act as executrix of his estate until she's old enough. Twenty-one, I think, or maybe it was twenty-four, I don't remember." I scrunched up my face, trying to remember, and tapped the steering wheel. A moment later, it all came together. "Spit and decay! The will and the policy are motives for me to do away with my brother. The estate money alone is a small fortune for me."

"The policy was signed one week prior to David's disappearance. You have motive. If you hired some thugs, you could buy both means and opportunity. You're the one who received the two phone calls about David, one likely made by a female, possibly you, calling your machine from Asheville. You have the most to gain by his death. Even if they never find his body, you may be arrested for his murder."

One fact blazed through the litany of my possible crimes, and it nearly made me founder. I put my head against the steering wheel, against the back of my hands. My voice so hostile it was lost beneath the breeze outside the Tracker, I said, "My brother is not dead." Quietly I sat back, unhooked my seat belt and slid from the car, emotions I couldn't even name simmering within me. "I'm Jane's Knight. I'm going to find my brother and bring him home." I grabbed my walking stick, slammed the door and started up the hill, GPS unit and Davie's card in one hand, my walking stick in the other. Evan followed.

It wasn't spring yet, nowhere near, but some of the trees were in early bud, with rounded, red leaf tips thrusting at the sky. In the day's warmer air, squirrels chittered and bobbled along branches and capered from tree to tree. A feral cat, black with one white ear, sat behind a root, watching for a mouse. It tilted its head our way and dismissed us as unworthy, tail twitching.

Following a hard, silent climb, we reached the corner stob

of the property, the iron almost buried in the loam. It matched the GPS coordinates on the scrap. Breathless, looking firmly to the west for the next marker, I asked, "Do you think I'm responsible for Davie's disappearance?" The trees thinned out and the rise of the hill became sharper. It was going to be a difficult climb. I could hear Evan's breathing just over my shoulder, raspy with effort.

"No. I don't."

"Why?"

"Gut instinct. Intuition. Insight and perception. All those things."

I fought a smile, determined to give him nothing. "Sounds suspiciously like St. Claire gifts."

"Yeah. I know."

"You trust them, those gifts you said you didn't have?"

"Yeah. And that really sucks."

I laughed and looked back at him. His face was rueful, green eyes soft, lips parted for the heavy breathing the hillside required. Something clenched deep inside of me, a trill of heat, like liquid fire over rocks. *Ashes and spit....* Shocked at my sudden raw need, I looked beyond him.

Over his shoulder the cat gathered himself and leaped. He landed and leaves flew. The cat settled to its meal, too hungry after the snow to play with its food first. One white ear twitched when it drew blood. Much like Evan Bartlock could devour me if I let him get any closer. If I'd been Aunt Matilda, I would have called it an omen.

I faced west and started along the property line to where the far marker should have been.

We hiked until after one, checked out two more pieces of property to no avail, then piled into the Tracker and headed back to town. We were hungry, tired, blistered by sun, wind and leather, and were ready for a break. A mile from the shop my cell phone rang. I downshifted and flipped open the phone. "Tyler."

"What's the good of being psychic if you can't tell when trouble's happening?"

"Jane?"

"You better get back here fast, Aunt Tyler. The cops are here and Aunt Matilda is getting pissed." The connection clicked off.

I closed the phone, tossed it in Evan's lap and gunned the little motor. The Tracker clawed its way up a long hill, rounded a corner and slid into a parking slot on the street. I was out and running before the engine stopped, Evan right behind me.

In Bloodstone, Jubal was helping two clients, Noe was ringing up a third, and Isaac was opening a display for a fourth. Aunt Matilda's imperious tones floated down the stairs, which I took two at a time.

"I have no idea what my nephew did for the government, Mr. Wiccam, and unless you have proof to the contrary, I suggest you cease such baseless innuendo and slanderous speculation."

I skidded to a halt at the tableau in my loft. Aunt Matilda, arms akimbo, faced down a group of three men in my kitchen. Jane stood behind her, scowling. The Tarot cards were scattered on the table to their side. Evan lifted me like a child, hands beneath my arms, and set me aside so he could see better. I showed great restraint by not cuffing him.

"Your nephew has approximately eighteen-point-two-million dollars stashed in offshore accounts," Adam Wiccam said. "Far more than he made working as a government employee. And roughly two times what was missing from special government accounts when he disappeared."

"We've had our eyes on David St. Claire and his sister for years," Harry Boone said to Wiccam, his voice self-important.

"My guess is, you've been watching Tyler with the smaller of your two brains," Aunt Matilda said.

I smothered a laugh and walked into my home. I'd never seen Aunt Matilda do battle, but I was impressed already. She had once been a buxom woman, now withered to a bundle of sticks and sinew and large wags of fatty skin. But there was something of the warrior in her, something fierce as she faced down the men, and something of the courtesan, the actress and the femme fatale in high choler. Though she must have seen me, she didn't look my way, holding their attention with fierce eyes.

"I don't trust you, young man." She focused on Harry, her head reared back. Throwing out her hands, flesh wobbling in soft bags along her arms, she said, "Your aura is a dark brown where it rests against your skin, the somber shade of a deceiver and a swindler. I sense malfeasance in your soul, a darkness that removes you from God." Her tone dropped, sonorous and deep. "Hidden sin follows you. Old cruelty."

"Aunt Matilda as gypsy queen," Evan whispered into my ear. "Ever seen her?"

I shook my head no.

"Very theatrical. I saw her go into it once when I was visiting years ago. A state tax man was giving her heck and she started telling him about this little perversion he had with his toy poodle. The guy turned and ran."

I squirmed. The description was uncomfortably close to what Jane had done to her pediatrician. My niece watched the conflict with wide eyes.

"And you, young man." Ignoring Wiccam, she turned to the third man, Detective Jack Madison. "You stand at the apex of light and dark. Death stands square in your path and at your right hand. You have much to lose or gain from your decisions today. You also have an unfortunate tendency to slovenliness and overeating, like a bovine at pasture, grazing without thought. If you are not careful, you will grow fat like your uncle. I foresee a lifelong struggle for you."

Her eyes closed a moment before her lids popped open. She speared the detective with her eyes and sniffed at the air around him. "I suggest you get that nagging issue of blood looked at. It isn't cancer yet, but it will surely develop into that dread disease should you continue to procrastinate." Madison took two quick steps toward the door, his face paling, then suffusing with what almost looked like relief.

"As for you," Aunt Matilda finally faced Wiccam. Her eyes widened and she retreated a pace, one hand on the Tarot cards scattered on the table. A subtle change came over her, a drawing in, a gathering of forces. She gripped one of the crucifixes that dangled around her neck. "You are earth and fire flowing together," she said, using the tone she employed only for readings, "darkness and burning. One who has chosen the shadow path, the path of darkness. Your life and choices are utterly divorced from reality."

The words were familiar but for an instant I couldn't place them. Then I remembered. Jane's reading. The Hagall Spread. A chill crawled down my spine on little insect feet. To Aunt Matilda's side, Jane wavered on her feet. Her eyes closed slightly, face going slack.

"You bound the Ace of Swords with lies and earthly chains. You seek the King of Cups to do him harm, but you seek in vain. The Knights battle against you and the Queen of Cups binds you."

"What does all that nutty stuff mean?" Evan whispered in my ear.

I shook my head. I had no idea. "Gibberish." But I didn't really believe that. It almost made sense at the edges of my mind. It meant something to Aunt Matilda. And I was afraid it meant something to Jane, too.

Without looking, Aunt Matilda reached out and picked up

a single card. "This is for you." She held the card out to Wiccam. It was Death on its white horse. "You do battle with the light. Blood will spill. Death will come with darkness."

"That's enough," I said, shaking the insect of fear off my shoulders. I wasn't sure why I was so disturbed, but I wanted to put this farce to bed fast. "I don't know what you guys want, but you're scaring my niece." Jane's eyes opened at that and she blinked slowly. "Say your piece and get out," I said.

Wiccam turned to me and bared his teeth in a smile. He *knew* me. Instantly. He knew my gift, the holes in it, the wall around it. He came toward me fast. I thought for a moment he might hit me. Instead he strode on out the door and down the steps. After a moment, Boone and Jack Madison followed. And they were gone.

Aunt Matilda fell into a chair at the table, her head in her hands. "Oh, merciful heaven. What awful souls." She wrenched in a deep breath and sat straight, still the melodramatic woman I remembered from my youth. She began gathering her scattered cards.

Jane moved around the table until she could see both Aunt Matilda and me. "Say something," she demanded. Aunt Matilda pressed her lips together in a tight line. "Say it. He has a wall, like Aunt Tyler's," Jane said. "He's creepy and mean." Jane looked at me. "He wants to kill you. He wants to do bad things to you and he wants to make a baby with you. And he can't decide which he wants more."

The stool beneath my backside was too hard, too circular, too flat. Whoever designed seats like this either had no concept of human anatomy or had a wide sadistic streak. Ignoring my discomfort, I switched on three tumblers, each polishing bloodstone beads for the Valentine's Day sale, and secured an unfinished, irregular-shaped bead in the drill press. Checking the position of the bit, I slowly rotated the wheel, lowering the wet drill. Even through the ear protectors, the sound of drill and tumblers created a cacophony of high-pitched, grinding, whining noise. Damp bloodstone dust blew into the air, bouncing off my eye protectors and respirator. The drill punched through the stone, and I pulled the particle-mask/air-filter off my sweaty face.

The odor of bloodstone was bitter and sharp, a distinctive scent. I often thought I could tell what stone was being drilled just by the smell, though that was surely fancy. A new shaped bead in place, I rubbed my face and reapplied the mask and ear protectors, whirling the wheel down to bore a new hole. It was mindless, numbing, backbreaking work.

For comfort's sake, I could have stood while drilling, or pulled in a chair from the front of the shop, or even sat on a pillow. But I was feeling like a failure, a useless, washed-up, has-been. Or better yet—a useless, washed-up, never-quite-was. Yeah, that was me. Never quite was a St. Claire, never quite an athlete, never quite a singer, poet, dancer, skier, artist, never quite a success at anything except cutting and shaping stone. I felt morose, self-pitying. Ill-natured, ill-humored and worthless, that was me. The drill bit punched through. I put on another. Again and again, until I had drilled enough for a half-dozen sixteen-inch necklaces.

I was sweating profusely, so intent on my work I was unaware of the world around me. When something tapped my shoulder, I jerked, whirled, and almost fell off my stool. Grabbing a mallet, I reared back and almost hit Aunt Matilda.

"Spit and decay," I cursed. I slammed down the mallet, turned off the drill press and tumblers, and yanked off my masks and ear protectors. "I could have killed you!" I shouted.

Aunt Matilda lifted her chin in a gesture that clearly said, *You could have tried.*

"What?" I demanded, hearing the sullen tone in my voice.

"You are not a failure." Her eyes spit sparks. "You are exceptional."

"What?" I threw the masks to the worktable.

"If you are going to project so loudly that every receiver for miles can hear, then at least project the truth."

"Which is?"

"You were ripped from the financial and emotional protection of the St. Claire environment when you could barely toddle. You were raised by a frightened, weak-minded woman who would rather run than face down her own demons. When she died, you were left to a coldhearted, sick man who barely allowed you space to grow up in and gave you no emotional support whatsoever, and who then passed away without seeing to your education or your future. And, you survived the transition from child to gifted without losing your mind."

"Well, whoop-de-doo. So I had a lousy childhood. This is supposed to make me feel better?" I slid from the stool to the floor and planted my feet.

"Yes. You are now a resourceful, capable young woman, a talented, though blocked, St. Claire who taught herself— by the seat of her pants—how to utilize her gifts. You are a designer of one-of-a-kind jewelry, with a successful line, a flourishing online catalogue and a financially prosperous business. You not only survived what would have stunted or destroyed most young girls, you feasted on it. You forced that barren life to give you what you wanted." Tears gathered in her eyes with the force of her pronouncements. "You grew up, made friends who will stick beside you unto death, made a place for yourself, and learned how to love." Faltering, the sparks of her anger died, drowned in her falling tears. She brushed them away and touched my cheek with a gentle finger, the flesh warm and wet against my cold skin. "I am proud of you. Deeply and intensely proud."

I stared at her, this queen in a denim skirt and chambray

tank top, and didn't know what to do. Tears prickled my own lids. I backed away a step, my progress halted by the worktable against my spine.

Aunt Matilda smiled sadly and said, "You are not perfect. You have a terrible temper, a deep and abiding fear of being abandoned, and a tendency to put yourself down. You are poor at math because it bores you, and you never bothered to learn how to play the guitar your brother gave you before he left you to the callous care of that horrid Lowe man. But you know how to love."

My tears fell, making twin tracks through the bloodstone dust.

Aunt Matilda wiped her face and took my hand, tucked it into the soft flesh of her elbow. Pulled me through the workshop to the small restroom, an unheated nook with a toilet and sink. She pushed me toward the sink. "Wash up. You look like a miner, or the Hulk after someone let all the air out of his bulk."

Meekly I turned on the hot water, let it warm, and washed bloodstone dust off my face, arms, hands and neck. Wet bloodstone dust had coated my exposed flesh, leaving pale ovals at eyes and nose, and turned me into a greenish-reddish comic-book monster. It made my skin stiff. I really needed a shower, but that would have to wait.

Cleaner, I left the bathroom and spotted Aunt Matilda standing at my workbench. Her worn, well-thumbed deck of Minchiate Tarot was placed in the dead center of the table. To its left was her Bible, a big, leather-bound book with her name embossed in gold. To the right was my mother's tin box, open, as if to display all my mother's ceremonial possessions. Mama's crucifix was draped on top.

Head lowered, Aunt Matilda stared at the items, her fingers clasped in front of her, her arms bare to the chill of the room. I had never seen Aunt Matilda wear a coat, sweater, or sleeves of any kind. In the Low Country, that was reasonable. Here in the mountains, in the cold of winter, it looked odd to see her standing thus, in the chill of the room.

Sensing my thoughts, she said, "I do not expect you to understand who I am or who the St. Claires are." Her head lifted. Through the little window above my workbench table, she stared at the brick wall of the building beyond. "Some of it you won't listen to. Some of it might frighten you. You aren't ready yet. But I can tell you that you are a wonderful, good person. That if Davie has a chance in the world of being found alive, it will be because of you." She turned sad eyes to me a moment before she gathered up the cards, the box and Bible, holding them close to her chest.

I wondered what she had intended to do with them. I had a feeling that, whatever her plan, she had changed it unexpectedly. Thoughtfully, she moved from the bench to the doorway. Like a pull toy being drawn by the string of her will, I followed her through the shop where Jubal and Noe were both helping customers. Neither looked up.

We started up the steps to the loft. "I can't sense Davie," she said finally. "I have tried to scan for him numerous times since he was taken and I get nothing. I can remember only a few times that has happened with St. Claire family members, and always when they are deeply stressed. But you, with your damaged gift and untrained mind, with your fears and trembling, you can reach him. And that is because of your love for him and his for you. I will trust this love to bring him home. And I will help as I can."

A sense of relief washed through me as she intended it to, born manipulator that she was. But I couldn't make myself add, "the old battle-ax," even if only in my thoughts. Something had changed between us. I didn't want to damage our newfound accord, or whatever it was.

"Now. As to Jane." Her voice was hollow in the echoes of

the stairwell, our feet shushing beneath us. Aunt Matilda glanced at me, lips tightening for battle. "I am willing and eager to train Jane to use and honor her gift. But I can train her only one way—the only way I know—with the Tarot as a focus and fulcrum. Not to tie her to the devil, as your mother taught you, but to open her mind, to give her young brain visuals for concepts and theories for which we have no words. If this is anathema to you, I will pack and go."

I sighed and rubbed my forehead where a headache was starting. It hammered and sang at the fringes of my brain. "I have one question." The words drilled into me as I spoke them, piercing the edges of my mind. I stopped at the top of the steps, one hand on the knob, my eyes on the dirty butterfly-strip bandages. There was bloodstone dust ground into the edges and into my cuticles. The dust was reddish, like old blood. Old wounds. "Why didn't anyone come when I came into my gift? You knew about Jane when her time came. You had to have known about me."

Aunt Matilda didn't touch me. I was grateful for that. She shifted, the sound bright in the echoing hall. "Your uncle was dying. You had met my husband, William."

I remembered a wizened older man who sat on the front porch, whittling, carving small animals out of swamp oak, cherry and hickory. He was a quiet man, engrossed in the wood. I had a lop-eared bunny somewhere carved by him and gifted to me. He had smiled when he placed it in my palm. The Goth bunny came to mind, the one I had used to test Jane. Had I taken the image from the carving? I nodded. "I remember."

"Will was diagnosed with cancer. He lived with the disease for years, taking different types of chemotherapy, trying all sorts of treatments. He ate only green, raw food, organically grown. He saw Cherokee healers and shamans and European herbalists and practitioners of Eastern medicine. He drank teas and took supplements. He lived for almost ten years. But when you were thirteen, he began to decline. He was dying when you came into your gift. And I sat by his side and held his hand. Loving him to the very end. And by that, by that dedication, that love we shared, so utter and complete, I failed you."

Suddenly I knew where the lop-eared bunny was. I could see it in Mama's trunk, in the corner, on its side in the dark. Alone. Once again, tears fell down my face, burning where they touched my weather-chapped skin. "Teach her. I don't know enough to help her and I have a feeling that Jane is a lot stronger than I would ever have been."

I opened the door to my loft. The television was on, music from *The Little Mermaid* filling the open space. Across from the door, Jane kicked and hit an imaginary opponent. It reminded me of me, kicking at things that weren't there. I took a deep breath. "Thank you for coming, Aunt Matilda. I didn't know what to do for her." I looked at my aunt, a short woman, like me, her eyes on a level with mine. And I took my fear in my hands like reins. "And while you're here, would you teach me, too?"

Happiness suffused her face, leaving her glowing. Aunt Matilda patted my cheek once and held her hand there. "I would be honored, my dear."

12

I knotted six Valentine's Day necklaces in record time, the focal stone hearts for each shaped from our dwindling supply of the most vibrant bloodstone. The beads were natural ovals from less colorful rough, silver or gold roundels crafted by Jubal, and glass beads picked out by Noe to complement her part of the design. We would need close to seventy-five necklaces, if this year's demand matched last year's, and an equal number of earring sets and bracelets—Noe's specialty. This year she was crocheting some of the bracelets, adding lots of little venetian glass beads and seed beads, and duplicating the look for the dangly earrings that she knotted into molded hearts. Very art deco.

After I scrubbed the filth off my hands and peeled off the dirty butterfly-strips, I showered and changed. The flesh was knit beneath so I smeared on a bit of antibiotic ointment and applied a Band-Aid. Downstairs, I helped with the final rush of Friday-afternoon shoppers, making myself available to help close up shop. Business was good, even with the unpredictable weather. I sold three charm bracelets to a Knoxville businessman on his way home from a convention in Atlanta, wrapped them for him and then convinced him to look at a tribal-art piece Noe and Jubal had created. He took that for his wife, and mentioned an interest in a "black stone" necklace for his anniversary. I showed him a mixture of snowflake obsidian and black onyx in extra large nugget-shaped beads, designing on the spot a fine, removable pendant I would cut from the best snowflake. He was charmed—and a lot poorer when he left the shop than upon entering.

When he walked out the door, I spotted Gail Speeler sitting in my favorite wing chair. Her face was drawn and pale, dark circles beneath her eyes, her hair piled up in a smooth chignon, the kind my curly tresses typically straggled out of in an ugly tangle. Jubal rolled his eyes over the shoulder of a client to let me know he had spotted her and couldn't get to her first.

Gail stood the moment I was free. It was clear she was waiting for me. *Goody, goody gumdrops. Is this my lucky day or what?*

She was wearing a business suit with a deep V-neck and a necklace, one of last year's lapis-and-silver-bead designs that Jubal, Noe and I had worked on together as a special creation for a local politician. The beads were made of glass, heated and embedded with delicate gold droplets, the denim lapis cab carved into a tulip and polished to a luster. The lapis pendant was in a setting of gold leaves and a delicate stem, one Jubal had taken great pride in.

The necklace marked Gail as having dated Zeddy Anderson, a county councilman. Zeddy had been married for over twenty years and still was. Zeddy had been at the council meeting where the tree huggers had booed Hornsburn. Gail Speeler really got around. All this went through my mind in a flash as she approached.

"Have you heard anything?" she asked, tears already rimming her lower lids. "The police won't tell me anything. They say I'm making a nuisance of myself, and that I have to quit calling and coming by."

It hadn't occurred to me to call or go by the police department. But then, I had my very own cop communicator in the person of Evan Bartlock, a man with one ear in the local law-enforcement center and the other in Aunt Matilda's bony fingers. Had to be painful.

"I miss him so much. Please tell me you know something." She wiped a tear and I wondered how long it had taken her to work up into a good cry. Okay, I was feeling snarky. I had been, ever since Stan left me for another woman.

"No. Nothing new." *Not that I'd tell you, you…you…* The word *tramp* came to mind but I repressed it.

"We've fallen in love. Deeply in love."

"No. I didn't know." *Or I hadn't until I heard it on television. Now, ask me if I believe it.*

"I just need to know that he's coming back. That I have something to hold on to, to hope for. So many men have asked me out now that he's gone." She blew into a tissue and dabbed her nose. "But I can't say yes, if Davie's still alive."

"Say what?" Okay, that was a weird twist. And then it hit me. I couldn't keep the incredulity, the stunned shock from my voice. "Are you trying to ask me if Davie's dead, so you can start dating? Or are you thinking that he's still alive, so you intend to hold off on dating a while longer? You know, just in case." *You little slut.*

Gail's eyes widened and dried fast.

I was pretty sure I hadn't said that last part aloud, but I was so mad I didn't stop myself from continuing my analysis. "Davie's a really good catch," I said, looking her trim form up and down. "Very stable. *Very rich.*" I focused on the necklace. "Fortunately single. One of the nicest men on the planet. But if he's gone, you don't want your dating life to be inconvenienced? That's what you mean?"

I reached out and gripped her wrist, opening myself to her. And was sucked down into a darkness. Her center was a miasma of need entwined with shame. Hope and fear. Want. Guilt and regret and craving. A whirling quicksand of light and dark, cold and heat sucking me down. A sexual compulsion so strong it staggered. Obsessive, silent, aching secrets. A memory-vision of Davie, naked, stretched out on a bed.

My gorge rose. I wanted to wash my hand, scour my soul.

I saw am image of a man, older, face suffused with passion, excitement, determination. Bending over her.

He…grandfather…

NO!

"Spit and ashes," I whispered, whipping my hand away.

Her eyes widened, face grew even paler. Even her lips were bloodless.

Davie had touched this woman? This desperate, lonely, abused woman? How had he borne it? But I had sensed Davie there somewhere in that swirling miasma of pain and need. He had cared for her. On some level, he had felt a responsibility for this broken soul.

Jubal was suddenly here, an arm around my shoulders. "We'll call you the moment we hear anything," he said. He took my hand. I was instantly bathed in his concern, a peaceful warmth that banished the heated prison of Gail Speeler's mind. "You have a call, Tyler," he said, moving me toward the workroom.

"A call?"

"Promise?" Gail asked.

"I promise," I said, looking over my shoulder.

"From Colin Hornsburn."

I looked up at him. "It was awful."

"I gathered, from the look on your face. And I know something of her history, so I'm not surprised."

"What? Her history?"

"Later. Come on, honeybunch. Buck up just one more time today. Then you can soak in a hot bath and listen to Matchbox Twenty."

"Promise?" I echoed Gail.

Jubal nodded, settling me onto a bench and putting the receiver of the land-line phone in my hand. I looked at it, then back up, and saw Evan Bartlock, a phone in his hand, as well. "Okay."

"We'll punch the button at the same time," Evan said. "On three." His finger poised over the keypad. "One, two, three."

I punched the talk button. "Tyler St. Claire."

"Tyler, Colin Hornsburn here. How are you holding up?"

I fumbled through the pleasantries. Agreed the weather was awful this winter. Heard myself asking after his health.

"I know it's too soon, with your brother not found yet, nothing finalized."

Confused, I looked at Evan. He made a circular motion with his hand, telling me to keep going. "Yes?"

"But I understand you will be executor of his estate. And I want to say, want to tell you I'll be happy to help in any way I can. I know how difficult times like these are to family members, the feeling of being lost, tossed to the four winds."

"Yes?" *Times like these? What times?* Then the confusion cleared. *This idiot is implying Davie is dead.*

"Your brother and I, while not close friends, were associates of sorts. And I know he'd want me to help you get through this painful, perplexing time, help you to provide for Jane's future."

The white mist in which I'd been wandering parted. *Associates?* Davie and this man? I raised my head, feeling the blood pound through my system. "Yes?" My voice sounded stronger. Hornsburn didn't seem to notice. Evan's lips twitched.

"Wading through settling an estate, dealing with estate taxes and such can be a frightening and overwhelming experience, especially in the midst of the grieving process."

"Really?" *You pompous imbecile.*

"I'd like to offer the services of my lawyer. He's the best moneyman in the state."

Evan made the rotating gesture again, but I had no idea what he might want me to say or ask. "Davie has a lawyer, I'm sure."

"Well, of course he does. He would. And you would want to keep using David's first choice. I fully understand. But remember my offer. I'm here to help."

"Thank you." *Sure you are. You just give and give and give. A real humanitarian.* The mental sarcasm gave me strength. Evan was laughing silently, holding my gaze.

"And while I know it's too early, I'd like to discuss with you—whenever you're ready, of course—the purchase of several pieces of property that your brother had offered to sell. I've faxed the properties we had talked about to your man of business."

Evan pointed to himself and held up a sheaf of fax papers. I nodded.

Colin Hornsburn was still talking. "I'd like to proceed with the purchase, at a handsome profit to Jane. Very handsome. Her welfare is uppermost, I assure you."

"My brother?"

"Beg pardon?"

"Davie," I deadpanned.

"Well…yes."

"My brother, Davie, the world's biggest environmentalist?"

"Ah—"

"The region's most dedicated tree hugger, in a town full of tree huggers, offered to sell property to you, a developer." I felt stronger. Crossed my legs and started tapping my foot. "A man he recently accused of raping the land, a man who puts houses on the sides of hills and destroys the habitats and makes money off of it. That brother, Davie?"

Evan had turned red, and I thought he might be biting his tongue.

"Well, now, you know, Tyler—"

"Colin?"

"Yes?"

"Go jump off a high ledge."

"Uh—"

"You are lying to me. And because of that, not counting the fact that Davie hated your guts, I wouldn't sell you the time of day. I wouldn't sell you the street corner where your mother walks."

"Uh—"

"Nothing! You dithering detrimental diphthong. You devious destructive dolt." I hung up the phone and looked at Evan, who burst out laughing. He dropped the phone on the workbench.

"You just called his mother a streetwalker."

"Yeah."

"And what is a diphthong anyway."

"A vocalized sound. An open-speech sound."

"Like 'uh'?"

"Yeah. I personally have no feelings against development, if it's done well and right and the environment isn't harmed much. But not by that man. I could feel the smell of his lies through the phone lines. He gets off on lying and getting away with it."

"I like you, Tyler St. Claire."

Quite suddenly, I felt warmed through and through, the heat banishing the specter of Gail Speeler's pain. "I like you, too. We won't tell Aunt Matilda, though."

"Oh, heck no. She'd have us married with babies before we could take another breath." Evan looked like that wouldn't be so bad a thing, however. His smile was way too soft for a cop.

I felt like squirming under his gaze. "She'd never let us live it down that she played Cupid."

"Horrors." Evan Bartlock stood and walked the short distance to me, bent and pressed his parted lips to mine. I reached up and encircled his neck, sighed into his mouth, and kissed him back. Aunt Matilda or no Aunt Matilda, Evan Bartlock could kiss.

My visits and calls by those thinking—or perhaps hoping—that Davie was dead, were not over. Only minutes before we locked the front door of the shop, Orson Wylie entered Bloodstone Inc. and sauntered up. The moneyman behind Colin Hornsburn had been in a business suit the last time I saw him. Now he sported a fedora, heavy khaki slacks with a knife-edged crease, lace-up boots and a plaid flannel shirt beneath a down vest, all brand-spanking-new, each with little logos in strategic places. Orson hadn't bought his clothes at the local Wal-Mart. He was the high-end department store, *GQ* version of a mountain man.

While he didn't have the savoir-faire of the developer, Wylie was a charismatic businessman, the kind who made eye contact with every person in the room as he entered and instantly looked at home. He nodded to Jubal and tipped his hat to Noe, who flashed him her tongue stud and grinned. I had to give him points for not reacting to that one. He pulled his hat off when he saw me. I had just finished gift wrapping a heavy amber ring for a repeat customer, the last customer in the shop, when he sauntered up and held out his hand. "Orson Wylie."

I don't know why, but his greeting just got all over me. I crossed my arms, looked at his hand, and when I spoke, my voice had icicles hanging from it. "Mr. Wylie. Tyler St. Claire. What can I do for you?"

"I'd like to steal a few minutes of your time, Ms. St. Claire."

Like you stole my brother? I felt my throat flush and knew I was getting the splotchy red welts I hated so much. My shoulders went back and I smiled. "Sure. We're open for business for a couple more minutes. What would you like to see?" I asked, pretending an obtuseness to his purpose. "We have some new items, excellent for Valentine's Day. Over here," I said, moving behind a counter, "is this year's Bloodstone heart jewelry. Perfect for the woman with the moxie to wear big, chunky-style jewelry."

"Well, I—"

"Of course, not all women like big stones." Jubal snorted softly at my choice of words. I pretended not to hear. "And in that case, Bloodstone Inc. offers some smaller stones, delicate designs created to please a woman of discriminating taste and a desire for elegant, semiprecious jewelry." I was quoting from Bloodstone's online catalogue.

He held his fedora in both hands, circling the rim. "Ms. St. Claire—"

"Now, take this little necklace right here." I held up a long strand of pale, faceted aquamarine beads with a pendant in a darker shade. The depending stone was cut into a teardrop shape, and the molded eighteen-carat gold setting appeared to snuggle around it like arms. "It is a lovely piece, and notice the setting for the pendant. It has little hands that grip the stone. Just as your loved one might grip your heart." *And squeeze till it pops.* "Very pretty."

Wylie placed the hat on the counter. "Yes, it is. Ms. St.—"

"And if she likes amethysts, we have a large selection that are sure to please that special lady on your list. Look at this one." I held up an eighteen-inch strand. "It's one of my favorites. Elegant and sophisticated, with just a touch of whimsy in the pendant. I always did love bear totems, and this one is charming. Note the garnet used to make the bear's eye. And it's only twelve hundred."

"I'm not here for that," Wylie said, frustrated. "I'd like—"

"Something more refined. I understand. Like this simply sumptuous piece of pearl and amber. The freshwater pearls are a golden shade that catch the light, and the free-form shape is stunning, isn't it?"

As I talked, Noe had locked the door and flipped the Open sign to Closed, grabbed a cup of tea and pulled one of the wing chairs around. She sat facing me, crossed her legs and settled in, as if for a good show. Jubal just sighed and started putting the more expensive items into the safe. I kept on with a practiced prattle that allowed Wylie no time to speak. I showed three other items and then came back to the pearl-and-amber necklace.

"Clearly you liked this one best, an indication of your excellent sense of style. We take all the major credit cards, and have a layaway plan that is more than fair. We do our own wrapping and shipping. And I can guarantee that your lady love will adore something from Bloodstone Inc. We design to please all tastes and styles. Don't you like the pearl and amber?"

"Ms. St.—"

"Yes or no?"

"Yes, it's fine."

"Great! Cash or credit?"

"I came to talk, not to buy."

"But this is a store, Mr. Wylie. We are here to sell, not talk."

"Ms. St. Claire, this is a beautiful shop. Do you own or rent?"

I paused at the non-sequitur. "We own."

"Glad to hear that." Wylie plopped his hat to the countertop and leaned across on his elbows, a musing expression on his face to match the one in his voice. "And do you have adequate insurance? On the building and stock, as well as on each other, your business partners?"

A cold dread skittered up my arms and down my legs at the words. "Our business arrangements are none of your concern."

"Because, as a businessman, I understand how important it is to obtain and maintain appropriate coverage. Accidents happen all the time." He smiled. The momentum of our one-sided dialogue had changed. Wylie owned the discussion now. "Fires, electrical shorts, accidental death of partners, like when a car goes off a slick mountain road at night. So sad what the loss of property or people can do to a business."

Fear made me mad. Always had. And mad made me cocky. I leaned across the counter to him, invading his space. "Are you offering advice, or a threat of some sort, Mr. Wylie?"

"Neither, Ms. St. Claire," he said, eyes wide with faux-surprise. But a threat danced in the deeps of them. "Merely the sage wisdom of my years in the business world."

I wanted to scratch his eyes out. "And what would I need to do or buy to lessen the threat of accidental injury or loss?" I could hear the sound of my breathing in the suddenly silent room. The pulse pounded in my head, starting a headache.

Wylie smiled, a paternal smile that made me wish I had a handful of heavy stone in my fist. His voice didn't drop. He didn't care who heard him. "The good wishes and good grace of good men?"

"And I do that by giving them what they want," I said flatly. I gripped the edge of the display case to keep from coming over the top at him.

"There is that. Or you could buy big policies and hope for the best. Please allow me to steer you to my insurance agent." He positioned a card on the counter exactly between us. "You have access to something we want, Ms. St. Claire. Land. Mr. Hornsburn and I are willing to pay handsomely for the land we hope to develop. I suggest you sell. Or you may find the cost is too much to bear."

A red haze closed in around me. "All I want is my brother back, Mr. Wylie. And for the people who took him to pay for it."

Wylie started. I could have sworn it was real surprise. "We don't have your brother, Ms. St. Claire. If we did, we wouldn't need you." Holding my eyes, Wylie placed the fedora on his head, shoved it down against the possible tug of wind. "Think about it." He turned his back to me and walked away.

No one else in the shop moved until Wylie reached the door, which Noe had locked. He stood there a moment silently, his back to us. Finally Noe unwound herself from the chair and walked across the shop. Her boots made clopping sounds in the silence. She jangled her keys until the *GQ*-style hoodlum moved aside. The back of his neck was red, his exit line ruined. Served him right. Noe unlocked the door and opened it. An icy gust blew in.

Just as he stepped across the threshold, Noe said, "I recognize the accent. Brooklyn, right? Yeah. I got a cousin from Brooklyn. She thinks she's tough too." Noe patted her thigh, drawing Wylie's eyes. She was holding a gun against her leg. A big gun. *Where did she get it?* Wylie looked amused as he turned to the street.

"You ever hear of survivalists, Mr. Wylie? People with bomb shelters, caches of food, and lots—*lots*—of weapons?"

I couldn't see Wylie's face but Noe smiled. It was a scary smile. Wylie's shoulders tensed.

"Around here, we look after our own. New York tough don't mean nothing. Bunch a wimps with thirty-twos and a couple cans of gasoline. So let me say this once. You come after us or Bloodstone Inc., and your cost of doing business goes up dramatically." Her smile widened. "C4 and antipersonnel mines can make a real mess out of construction sites. Water in gas tanks can bring an entire project to a halt. And houses under construction can go up in flames. You think about it. 'Cause I got friends. And so does Tyler." Noe shoved the door shut in his face, turned the lock and stood there, her back to him.

Noe's eyes were blazing, her shoulders were stiff and her hand cradled the gun against her leg like a lover. The blue streak in her hair stuck straight up, incongruous against her pose. "That was fun. He gone yet?"

"Oh, yeah," Jubal said, his tone awed. "Totally gone. Your parents—those first-generation immigrants to the hills—they like guns?"

"We do. And we really don't like being pushed around." She walked to her bag beside the wing chair and tucked the gun in. It was a floral patchwork bag with big puffy poppies on the front and a hummingbird in one corner. A granny bag, with a gun it. No. A small cannon.

"Tomorrow. I'll be wearing loose clothes so I can wear a waist holster and an ankle holster. Looks like I finally get to make use of the 'permit to carry' I got last year. And I'll get my brother to keep an eye on our cars so they can't get clever with pipe bombs. You two be sure to lock up and set the alarm system." She pulled on her coat and slung a knit scarf around her neck. She looked at us and her brows went up. Then she laughed. "What? Never seen a survivalist get ticked off?"

"If I weren't gay, I think I'd be turned on," Jubal said.

"If I *were* gay I'd be turned on," I said.

Noe walked through the shop to the workroom trailing laughter. As a dramatic exit, it beat Wylie's all to heck.

Jubal and I looked at each other from across the shop. "She left us with the close-up duties again," he said. "You mind?"

"Not me. I'll never be upset about that again. Did you know she carried a gun that big in her granny bag?"

"I didn't even know they made guns that big."

Noe's tinkling laughter trickled from the back of the shop, followed by the sound of the door closing firmly. Evan Bartlock emerged from the back. "You people are just full of surprises, aren't you?"

I started. I had forgotten he was still here.

Evan didn't stay for supper. I figured it was because Aunt Matilda was upstairs, the coward. But I'd have avoided her, too, if I could, so I didn't say anything. I saw him out the door and set the alarm system. Jubal had gone up the stairs to his loft, leaving me alone in the shop. Lights off, the room illuminated by the glow of outside lights, I wandered, touching a ceramic display, letting my fingers trail across the wood of our antique cases, avoiding the glass fronts and sides so I wouldn't have to reclean before we opened in the morning.

Orson Wylie had threatened the shop. Threatened my friends, threatened everything I loved. Yet, he had been truly surprised when I accused him of holding Davie. So, if it wasn't Hornsburn and Wylie, who had my brother? I hadn't felt his presence in so long. Was he even still alive? Did I have the guts to try another scan for him? I shivered. It would take more guts not to try. What if Davie was dead?

I roamed to the back of the shop, checking the back door, and stared into the alley. The stairs leading to the small private porch off my loft were blocked with snow that Jane and the guys had tossed off the rooftop garden. The rest of the alley, protected from the sun by the enclosing walls, was still white with the recent snowfall. It might be June before the last of it melted.

Icicles hung from the porch and from the garden, one almost four feet long. Mounds of snow that had been pristine had begun to shrink, revealing bikes, wooden skids, a pile of painter's supplies, the fender off an old car that had been there as long I could remember. The red fender was surrounded by paw prints, a clear sign that a feral cat or several had taken up residence. Someone had placed a bowl of food there, likely hoping if the cat stayed through the snowfall, it would keep the rat and possum population down.

I checked the windows, made sure all the flames were turned off on the torches and braziers, and that the kilns were cool, all the electrical cords curled and out of the way. I stacked some bottles and cans below each window and the back door to act as an additional alarm should anyone manage to bypass the security system or enter by unconventional means. Finally I opened the storeroom and stared through the darkness at the four boxes Davie had sent. Gold. Land. Protecting the environment and habitats. Money. Lots of money in offshore accounts. Money Davie had surely not been able to earn. And Orson had no idea who had taken my brother. Tucking my despondency deep down inside, I squared my shoulders and climbed the stairs to the loft and Jane and Aunt Matilda.

The smell of chicken soup permeated the apartment, a CD played softly in the background, some new-age stuff of bells and a wood xylophone and wood flute. Jane and Aunt Matilda were sitting at the kitchen table when I entered, a lit candle between them. They had their eyes closed. Aunt Matilda was praying.

I stood at the doorway, caught Dyno when she made a run for freedom and watched them, the unhappy cat in my arms. She would have scratched me if she could, her declawed paws making swipes on my T-shirt. Dyno was being ignored and it made her mad. I knew just how she felt. Closing the door, I listened to the prayer.

"…bring her the light. Protect her from the darkness. Show her the well-lit path that, though narrow, brings the greatest contentment and everlasting peace. Keep her feet firmly on the shining way. Let her take up the weapon with which you have gifted her. Let her wield the sword with wisdom and might. Protect her steed with the armor of the angelic host. And let her know we love her." They both opened their eyes and turned to me. And I realized they had been praying for me. *Me...*

I shook my head. "I don't own a sword, a horse, or armor and I have never kept to a path in my life."

"But you thought the prayer was cool. I can tell." Jane jumped from the chair and ran to me, hugging me. "You're Daddy's Knight of Swords."

I stroked her hair, so soft it could be silk. A fierce, protective craving unfolded within me, blooming like an orchid. I would protect this child. No matter what. I hugged her, transferring the cat to Jane's arms as I met my aunt's placid gaze. "Actually, I think you or Aunt Matilda have to be the Knight, pumpkin. When I was born, Aunt Matilda said the Fire card of the Minchiate Tarot was my symbol. You can't change significator cards in midlife. Right, Aunt Matilda?"

The older woman smiled and steepled her fingers before her mouth. "Jane, bring me the print that hangs on Tyler's bathroom wall. The one on the lower left that shows flames the color of her hair."

The cat jumped and ran from her grasp, standing in the center of the room tail twitching. Jane ran to the bathroom, stepped in the tub and stretched up to the print. She returned with the print and handed it to me at Aunt Matilda's gesture.

"On the back are two clips, if I remember rightly when I prepared them for Giselle. Open the clasps and remove the backing." I took the print to the table and laid it facedown. It was dusty from where it had rested against the wall and not been removed since I painted last, two years ago. When I turned the clasps, I left clean places with each fingerprint. I pulled off the backing, pseudo-velvet glued to pasteboard.

"The prints were gifts," Aunt Matilda said, "one given at each turning point in Giselle's life. Take them out."

I flipped the frame and the print slid out. Except that there were two prints, not just one. I turned them both faceup. The Fire card. And the Knight of Swords from the Renaissance Tarot.

I had never opened the framed prints before. No one had opened them recently. Aunt Matilda hadn't placed them here just today. The hidden Knight had been there all along.

The Knight of Swords from the Renaissance Tarot was a powerful, bearded warrior, gilded sword held high in his right hand, reins in his left. He wore white armor with black lines to show where the armor came together, a helmet with a golden plume, metal boots in silver stirrups. His mount was heavily muscled, pale gold, and was depicted rearing against a hilly background and open sky. The card caught the candlelight and shadow and the destrier seemed to prance in commanding motion.

"I take a reading at the birth of each St. Claire child, to see what I might learn of their talent long before that gift is born. And then I do a one-card reading of the Major Arcana, and the Court cards, which I repeat several times, to solidify what I see of that child's personality and purpose. Usually, it becomes clear who and what they are and will be, and eventually a single card stands out as their significator card. But for you, there were two cards that kept coming up over and over. And until now, I never understood why." My aunt blew out the candle and stood.

"Jane? Get the bowls down and set the table. Tyler, while I dish up the soup, pour us drinks. I'd like a glass of red wine, if you please. I brought a bottle. And then let's all turn in. It has been a long and intensely tiring day."

I fingered the print of the Knight on its heavy stock paper. It was old, the paper brittle, the ink faded, the gilding loose.

Careful of the print, which was valuable in its own right, I set them both back in the frame, this time with the Knight in the forefront. Sealing up the backing, I took it to the bathroom wall where I replaced it, straightening the frame so it hung evenly. Thoughtful, unsettled, I went to pour the drinks.

After the meal, Aunt Matilda placed an ugly green bundle on the living-room rug and pushed a button. A steady sucking sound filled the air mattress with air, and as it bloated up, she shoved it into place with her foot and tossed sheets over it, followed by blankets. From a suitcase, she pulled a pillow, shaking out the down and placing it at the head, in the center of the queen-size mattress.

"Where did you get this?" I asked, toeing the mattress, unconsciously mimicking her gesture. Realizing my action, I withdrew my foot, feeling my face flame, embarrassed and unsure why.

Ignoring my foot and my reaction, Aunt Matilda pulled pins from her steel-gray bun and let the tresses down. "From the delightful boys across the way. I didn't stop to think where I might sleep when I got here." She finger-combed and began braiding the mass of hair. "I like your friends. They are honest and honorable. Pure of heart."

"I thought, as a Catholic, you would hate them for being gay," I said, watching her nimble fingers as she twisted and turned the three tresses into one.

"I find it easier to hate lies and murder and betrayal, the abuse of children and the helpless, than to hate two people who care for each other and for you. I have never been a very good papist.

"I put my dirty towels from my shower in the corner of the bathroom. The kitchen is clean, and I'll wash clothes in the morning." She pulled off her dress and crawled into the sheets wearing a shift. "We'll have to talk while I lie down. I've spent the last several nights sleeping upright in a Greyhound bus seat. One night more than expected. The first bus broke down at the base of the foothills and left us stranded. Then the snow piled up and stranded us again. My legs hurt, my back hurts, and getting horizontal is a luxury I can't pass up. You may ask your question."

I didn't pretend confusion. "Will you tell me about my parents' gifts?"

She yawned and stretched beneath the covers, her legs flailing at the sheets. "Giselle was a strong talent, with a gift for the cards, for seeing the truth about others in the spread. Her interpretations were concise and clear and touched with compassion. But she wasn't very strong emotionally or mentally, was easily agitated, anxious and fretful, even before her gift came to her. I think that, left to her own devices, she would never have married, and not Niles St. Claire. But she was a biddable girl and her own mother was persistent. She wanted a granddaughter out of two St. Claires." Aunt Matilda looked up at me in the dim light. "She wanted you."

I had never heard this story before, and I sat slowly on the sofa. My grandmother had died not long after we had left the Low Country and Mama had never spoken of her.

"So she married Niles and their love seemed to grow. They seemed happy, happier than most, or maybe that was just what we all wanted to believe." She looked down at her hands for a long moment, a taste of failure and despair in her mind. "I never intruded on them, never forced a reading, of course. How could any of us do such a thing? And they never asked."

"And my father?"

Aunt Matilda's face seemed to attract the shadows that drowsed in the corners of the room, darkening the lines and creases in her skin, obscuring her eyes. "Niles was the strongest St. Claire in a generation. But he was a cruel man in many ways. Cold, unkind even, to everyone but your mother. To her he was always unfailingly gentle, as if he recognized her fragility. I never understood their relationship. Perhaps if I had…" She let the words and the thought trail off and almost visibly changed the subject. "Your father had a gift for prescience. And he was never wrong."

"If he could see the future, why did he disappear? How did he die?"

"Now that is a question I have asked myself often, and have never been able to answer. But he did indeed disappear. I never told your mother this, but two days after Niles left the Low Country, I felt a disturbance."

Part of me wanted to chortle at her choice of words. *I felt a disturbance in the Force, Luke Skywalker.* The rest of me shriveled at what she was saying.

"Violence. Bloodshed. Great pain. I have never caught even a trace of his presence in all the years since."

Aunt Matilda let the silence build after her words, deep and weighted. Finally she shook herself. Yawning delicately behind her hand, she rolled over, her back to me, her down pillow beneath her head. "Good night, Tyler."

I looked longingly at the tub and sighed. I wouldn't get my long, hot bath tonight. And I really needed a hot, restorative soak. "Good night, Aunt Matilda."

13

Saturday, before dawn

I woke to an unknown sound, something foreign, but heard only the ticking of the rooster clock on the kitchen wall. By the ambient light, I could see its black legs wagging back and forth, a funky pendulum. I had bought it on my honeymoon after seeing an old dance called the funky chicken on the TV at the bed-and-breakfast. Stan and I had laughed like teenagers at the goofy dance and laughed just as hard when we hung the clock on the kitchen wall. Stan was a mistake, but I still liked the clock. Funny what goes through your mind in the middle of the night.

The soft grating that woke me sounded again. Not Aunt Matilda snoring. Not the sound of someone moving about the apartment. Rolling my head, I found the soft breath sounds of Jane and Aunt Matilda.

The grating sounded again, metallic and furtive, quiet. Heat lanced through me, a sudden hot sweat of shock. I lay in the pile of silken covers, trying to place the soft noise. It wasn't coming from the bathroom or kitchen. Not from the door at the loft stairs. Rolling slowly, I focused on the back door used so seldom in winter, but the grating came from over my head, to the right.

Ashes and spit. The rooftop garden. The alarm system

didn't cover the doors there. Why should it? There was no way from the ground to the garden unless you were a superman. Or unless you came through Jubal and Isaac's. Fear chilled the sweat that lay on my skin, freezing my heart. Had someone gotten in there, killed them, and come here? I could see their kitchen in my imagination, blood splattered. Terror rose in me, an icy mist.

Where did I put the gun? The gun with which I could shoot the wrong person.... *Spit and decay.* I eased my head to the right and up. The night was dark, the moon hidden behind the banks of clouds rolling in. As I often did, I had forgotten to pull the drapes. A darker shape shifted slightly against the black of the sky, barely visible through the windows of the door.

The gun... I couldn't remember where I put it. My mind was blanked by fear. I didn't remember putting it in the trunk—I didn't remember bringing it back upstairs from the shooting range. I reached a stealthy hand to the bedside table and found the little gold cell phone, pulled it under the covers with me and dialed 911. The phone rang. Twice. Again.

"Emergency services. What is the nature of your emergency?" Prim voice. Precise.

"Someone is breaking into my loft apartment," I said, giving my address. "And the alarm is set on every window and door except the one he's using."

"Can you describe him?"

"No, I—"

The door lock clicked.

"He's inside. Get someone here fast. I'll leave the connection open." I set the phone down, ignoring the tinny voice calling to me, and rolled off the far side of the bed, hitting the floor with sock-covered feet.

He entered, a dark form silhouetted by the night sky, a shadow against shadows. He was medium height, beefy. And he was alone. I could *feel* the solitary mind.

I ducked, walking low so as not to attract his eye. In the dark, I found the bowl of polished stones, recognizing them by touch and size alone. I wrapped my left hand around the bloodstone sphere, my right hand around a slightly larger oval that glowed in the dark. White quartz. I slowly stood, positioned my feet and pulled back my arm.

I heard a faint click, an almost familiar sound, to my right. Aunt Matilda murmured and rose up on her mattress. Voice thick with sleep, she called, "Who's there?"

The man turned toward the sound and the movement and lifted his hand. I threw the quartz, grunting with the effort. Transferring the bloodstone to the right in a fast shift, I threw it, too, slightly higher. Two smacks sounded. He staggered, groaned. His hand dropped.

There was a brilliant white-red flash. Blinding. An explosion of sound. A shot. Two. Three. Close together. Overlapping blasts of sound that ripped out the night.

Pain whispered through me and was gone.

I grabbed two much-larger spheres and hefted the first like a shot-putter. It struck him as he turned. He saw me. Across the blackness of the loft, our eyes met. The brown man. Slender, made beefy by a down jacket.

Overhand, I threw the last stone sphere. It went wide. Landed with a soft thump in dark.

He came at me, moving fast, and raised his hand at me. I froze.

Sirens sounded, swift in the night.

He stopped, then raced out of the apartment and ran across the snow-free porch. Without pausing, he vaulted over the railing to the alley below. The harsh stink of cordite filled the air. My ears were ringing. *Jane.* I raced to the trundle bed and lost my balance as my foot struck something hard. I fell onto the mattress and gathered my niece in my arms. She was shaking.

"Aunt Tyler?" Her voice sounded frail, tinny through the concussive damage to my ears. Without asking or searching for blood, I knew she hadn't been hit by the rounds, though my hands felt feverishly across her.

"Aunt Matilda? Are you hurt?" I asked.

"No. I'm fine," she said, her words almost lost beneath the ringing in my ears.

"Jane isn't. Something's wrong."

Sirens gathered in the street outside, blue lights strobing. I pulled my niece onto my lap and rocked her. Aunt Matilda stood and slipped into her dress, which she had left draped over the couch. She bent over the bed and stroked Jane's face. "All will be fine, dear. We will handle everything." She dropped to the floor in a squat, then stood again and turned on a light. The sudden brightness was painful and tears gathered for a moment as I watched her. The older woman's eyes roamed the loft, taking in Jane and me huddled on the trundle bed, spotting something at the fireplace, noting the door to the garden still hanging open.

Isaac was suddenly there, bare chested, skin gleaming in the lamplight. His nut-brown body was poised in attack mode, eyes wide. He flowed into the apartment, moving with a predatory smoothness. The grace of the trained warrior, liquid death in white boxers. Jubal was behind him, dressed in a red kimono with a white bird in flight across the chest. He held a fireplace poker over his head. It gleamed golden brass in the lamplight. My avenging gladiators, armed for battle. Laughter tittered in the back of my throat.

"He's gone," I said. "Over the back wall."

Isaac and Jubal ran to the rear, out of the glow of light. Downstairs, someone was banging on the doors. The glass rattled hard enough to hear through the intervening walls and floor. I picked up the cell phone from the linens and said to the woman, still calling out to me, "The police are here. Thank you."

Watching me, Aunt Matilda stuck something in her pocket and crossed the room to the loft door. Her expression held a curious mix of emotions as she disappeared down the stairs to let in the police. Anger, frustration, curiosity, and some nonspecific warning. Warning of what? And then I remembered the sequence of shots. Something was wrong with them, out of place. But what?

I rocked Jane, hearing the approach of booted feet, rough male voices and Aunt Matilda's soothing tones. The sound of bullets replayed over and over in my mind. Three shots? Or four? They had overlapped. And Aunt Matilda had something in her pocket. What had she done?

I turned Jane over to Aunt Matilda to tend as Isaac, Evan and I dealt with the scientific types and the questions of the detective. My mind straying to the overlapped shots and what Aunt Matilda had in her pocket, I made the mistake of admitting that I thought that maybe, conceivably, the man who entered the loft was the brown man from the rock-and-gem show. Perhaps. By the way he moved. Yes. In the dark.

Stupid, stupid, stupid! I should have kept my big mouth closed. How could I have seen him, the nondescript, middle-sized brown man, on the roof in the deep of night? I couldn't have. No way. *But I had. And he had seen me.* Had there been something in his mind? Had I picked up on it? What was it? I pushed the worry to the back of my mind.

Jack Madison was not a happy man. The wattled skin of the detective's neck and jowls quivered each time I repeated that I hadn't clearly seen the attacker, but that I still felt it was the brown man. Though I couldn't say why I thought that. Madison grew a bit grayer each time I spoke, and I felt a lot more stupid. I watched as he went from actively taking notes to simply looking around. Bored. Why hadn't I kept my big flapping mouth closed? What did Aunt Matilda have in her pocket?

The cops gathered, tagged and confiscated the rock spheres I had thrown, all but the bloodstone sphere, which couldn't be found. Not that they looked very hard. They generally acted like I was making it all up, as if it were an attempt to cast suspicion away from me.

Uncharacteristically, Aunt Matilda said nothing at all, simply holding Jane, shushing her occasionally, and watching us all, that odd expression now more thoughtful, as if she were waiting for something to happen. And when the investigation moved to the rooftop garden her expression changed to one of expectation.

The situation changed for the cops when Evan, who was alert and wired at five in the morning, discovered a splatter of blood in the garden, a trail that led over the wall and down into the snow. At that point, the disinterested, perfunctory investigation evolved quickly into a full-blown workup.

Dawn came fast as a crime-scene cop dusted the door frame for fingerprints. Another found a small brass bullet casing where it had rolled under the sofa. A third tech dug a bullet out of the wall over the fireplace, where it had remained hidden in the dim light.

One casing. One bullet. Three or four shots. I was sure of it. I looked at Aunt Matilda again. The warning on her face was penetrating. This time, I kept my mouth closed.

Other cops in winter jackets, scarves and gloves followed the blood trail and tracks through the alley, from the spot the brown man had landed in the pile of snow and fought his way clear to a connecting alley and the street beyond where the trail disappeared and they lost him.

At the appearance of blood, the surly law-enforcement techs, who had been pulled out of bed before sunup, had stopped grousing continuously. Now as they worked, they made careful notes in little notebooks and palm-sized electronic devices. They found a second casing on the floor near the door, where it had rolled under the fringe of a rug. More excited, they inspected every pane of glass in the French doors to the garden, dusted the top of the wall, which was a waste of time, and the ladder leaning against the wall to the rooftop garden. They got dozens of smudged prints off the ladder, but nothing from anywhere else. Nothing they seemed very hopeful about. Especially not the ladder. It had obviously been cadged from the pile of painter's supplies exposed by the melting snow. They figured the man who entered my loft had worn gloves.

Well, duh.

Except for my brother's kidnapping, the attempt to remove Jane from the school, and my assertion that I knew the invader, it looked like an attempted crime of opportunity. Attempted burglary. Yeah, right. The cops took samples of the blood splatters to prove an ID, saying they wanted to compare it to the DNA of the men who had waited in the alley and attacked Davie. I told them it was a waste of time, but they said it was procedure. What could I do about the waste of taxpayer money. Not a thing.

And then, a tech, packing up his big orange-and-beige equipment box, knelt on something hard. I wasn't watching, but I *felt* him tighten. I stepped around Jack Madison to watch. The tech was a little scrawny fellow, the kind with mountain-climber muscles and high metabolism wrapped around an anal-retentive mind.

He moved his knee and pushed aside the rug, where it rested on the edge of a second rug. I hated cold floors. He picked up something that shone gold in the artificial light. Carefully, he placed it in a brown paper evidence bag. As he did, he paused as if thinking. Remembering. Comparing. I knew what he had found. This casing was different from the others, smaller or longer or something. He looked up, saw me watching him and schooled his expression to neutral. Giving me his back, he continued packing and stood to go. Before leaving the loft, he stopped and spoke quietly into Jack's ear. The two shifted glances at me, then away.

Madison ambled over, deceptively casual. "I understand you have a thirty-eight. Mind if I take a look at it?"

"Sure." I walked over to Mama's trunk, squatted down and opened it. Of course the gun wasn't there. I knew it wouldn't be. I rocked back on my heels, looked at Madison, and lied with a straight face. "I don't know where I put it." Well, that was only sort of a lie. I didn't remember where I had put it, but I had a good idea where it was at the moment. Anyway, Madison didn't ask me that. "I was doing some target practice down at the KO range. It might be in my Tracker. You're welcome to look. Keys are on the hook at the door." I pointed. Jack followed my finger and left, my keys in hand. After his departure, the techs took off, too, back into the cold to the LEC. Shooting me a look rife with suspicion, Evan went with them.

None the wiser, Isaac and Jubal went back to their apartment. As dawn grayed the sky, we three females were finally alone. With the loft empty, Jane instantly fell into an exhausted slumber, Aunt Matilda's hand on her shoulder.

My apartment looked like a herd of buffalo had wandered through in the night. Everything was tossed around, dirty with red fingerprint dust, smudged and messy. Of course, there was no buffalo poop. I could be happy about that.

I checked the locks on the doors and windows, walking like an automaton, watching my hands move as if they had a will of their own. Neither of us spoke.

When we were secure, I dropped my hands and met Aunt Matilda's eyes across the way, holding them. She had the grace to look abashed as she stood and straightened her wrinkled dress. As she moved, she pulled my small bloodstone sphere from a pocket and placed it on the bedside table near the clock. The sphere rolled slowly to the center where it stopped, rocking back and forth languidly.

From another pocket, she pulled my little .38 Smith & Wesson Airweight and one brass casing, and laid them on my mother's trunk. The brass casing was a dead ringer for the one taken by the tech. I sighed.

That faint click I had heard before the firing started. Three or four shots, overlapping. I hadn't injured the attacker with the rocks I'd thrown. He'd been injured by my gun. "Why didn't you just say you shot him?" I asked.

Aunt Matilda swept a tendril of hair from Jane's face, resting one hand on the sleeping girl's shoulder. When she met my eyes again, hers were fierce. "I didn't shoot him."

I looked at my niece, half-buried in the deep drifts of my linens. "Spit and decay," I whispered. *I taught her how to fire the gun.*

"Indeed."

Because it was Saturday, I dressed with special care before going down to open the shop. Staring back from my reflection in the bathroom mirror was a stranger, pale skinned, frowsy haired. The lack of a full night's sleep for days at a time was getting to me. I had dark rings beneath my eyes that makeup only pretended to hide, and my hair, always ready to curl into kinks, was rather more like a bird's nest than usual. It resisted any attempts to smooth it down, and when I tugged and twisted the locks into a tight French braid, stiff tendrils crimped out like coiled splinters. I looked like a porcupine, so I smeared gel into the sides, sweeping the loose hair back against my head. Now my head looked like a porcupine after it had crawled through an oil slick.

I dressed in a bright teal-and-coral ensemble that called attention to the multicolored, seven-strand, turquoise choker made with Arizona turquoise, Chinese turquoise, rough nugget turquoise and heishi turquoise, with tiny antique silver beads and a fabulous coral inlaid silver focal bead from Thailand. The necklace hadn't sold last year, partly because the old silver appeared drab in the display. It needed to be worn to sell, and it looked perfectly lovely on me, even with the black eye rings and a new pimple that reddened my chin. The puckered scar near my collarbone looked irritated in the morning light, as if even it suffered from lack of sleep.

My manicure was long gone, nails broken and chipped, so I removed the nail polish, filed down the tips and added a single coat of clear before clipping the choker's matching bracelet to my wrist. I slid on three rings, hoping jewelry would draw the eye away from my hair and pallor. Except for tired eyes, frizzy head and the zit that threatened to rise like Mount St. Helen's in the middle of my chin, I looked pretty good. I added my own turquoise hoops to each ear, and draped the ornate key on its thong around my neck under my shirt. I was still thinking about next year's Valentine's Day necklaces. I really liked the idea of a key as motif, and with good bloodstone becoming so hard to find, a silver key on a nugget strand might be just the thing. Key to my heart, and all that.

As satisfied as I could be under the circumstances, I bent over Aunt Matilda and touched her shoulder. My eyes firmly on my niece, I softly asked, "Have you tried again to get a scan on Davie?"

"Yes. I tried. I get nothing. And Jane is trying, too, far too hard. She wants so desperately—" she drew in a ragged breath "—so desperately to find her father."

I nodded. This couldn't go on. It just couldn't. I stood and looked at my aunt. "I'll try a scan for Davie. Tonight. Will you help me?"

Relief flooded her face. Tears gathered in her eyes. "Oh, yes. Yes, I'll help."

* * *

I was wrapping the turquoise necklace, bracelet, and the set's matching earrings in a bright pink Valentine's Day box when Harry Boone came inside. He had on his cop face, stiff and cold and unyielding. But because I once had peeked inside his mind, I felt the underlying malice of his intent and the small-minded meanness of his heart. He was here to cause me trouble. And he was going to enjoy it.

I smiled brightly and nodded the customer out of the shop. For the moment, Bloodstone Inc. was empty. Jubal put a foot on the rail behind the counter and leaned over it, resting on his elbows. Noe came from the back carrying fresh stock and stopped in the doorway, looking back and forth. I let my smile die a quick death and crossed my arms. "What?" I asked the cop. It sounded like an accusation.

"Just thought we would let you know," Boone said, his eyes boring into mine, watching, eager. When I didn't speak, he went on. "We found Quinn Baker this morning, 'bout a half hour ago."

I still didn't speak, but my heart rate shot up. I was glad my fingers were resting against my arms, because they trembled faintly.

"He's been shot."

Shock weakened my knees. *Quinn? What…?* My mind raced, drawing the obvious deductions. They thought Quinn was the one who had broken into the loft. They thought he'd either been shot by me, and I wasn't telling, or he'd been shot by my accomplices and the break-in was staged to make it look like a justified shooting. I *knew* the man in the door this morning hadn't been Quinn. My shoulders relaxed and I placed my hands on the display top. I smiled. "I'm sorry to hear that. I'll send flowers to him."

Boone's face twisted in victory and my bowels turned to water. "I'm sure his mother will be tickled pink about that,

Tyler. Have them delivered to MacDermit Funeral Home. Once the coroner releases the body."

Jubal caught me before I slid to the floor.

Pleased with his announcement and my reaction, Boone walked out the door.

Jubal made me sit and drink a mug of tea, while Noe wrapped an afghan around me. They hovered like worried mama and papa birds, until three customers came in and I shooed them back to work. Numb, I drank my tea and took my break, for once not worried that the clientele might see me sitting, doing nothing. The business of the store wound around me, passed across me, like shadows thrown by lace in the morning sun, not really touching me but dappling my thoughts, intruding in a slow wave of darkness and light.

Quinn? Dead?

A long shudder of fear I had repressed ran through me, freed by the cop's words to thrash my soul. My body felt unsubstantial, ephemeral, my limbs deadened as if anesthetized, even the cup of hot tea not warming my fingers. The sounds in the shop seemed higher-pitched than usual. Everything was just a little not-quite-right.

Jubal brought me back, pulling me out of my lethargy by bringing a customer over and using me for a mannequin as he slipped a silver chain and lovely, dangling, green-and-brown turquoise pendant around my neck. When he placed the back of his hand on my cheek for a moment, I knew my friend really just needed to touch me, to reassure himself I was all right, so I forced myself back from the shadowy place where I crouched, licking my wounds, and smiled up at them both. I let Jubal slide matching bangle bracelets over my hand, and displayed both with a practiced flip of my wrist that set them to clanking prettily, and held silver loops to my ears, next to my own turquoise ones.

The customer, a late-traveling snowbird on his way south for what was left of winter, bought the entire set. I was on a roll, selling. Too bad I wasn't having any luck with my personal life.

The customer was a talker, introducing himself as Ken Green, and telling Jubal about his grandkids, his two sons and his life before he retired. Because Jubal was a good listener, and I was a great store dummy, Mr. Green also purchased a sunset-toned coral and carnelian choker and matching bangle set and had them shipped back north. He filled us in on the two women who had set their sights on him, one in Boca and one in Maine. He was happily keeping company with both, one in summer, the other in winter. That was his term—keeping company. But, with a sly smile and a wink, he also mentioned Viagra, and we knew the company he was keeping was of an intimate sort. The salacious old coot.

While I sat and tried to decide what to do about Quinn—*Quinn? Dead?*—Noe sold an overpriced but very dramatic twelve-strand, ocean jasper nugget and bronze pearl necklace and two really nice aquamarine chokers, and managed to find time to call Evan Bartlock between customers.

Evan came in about the time my limbs were unfreezing, carrying white bags of Chinese takeout from the mom-and-pop place four doors down from Bloodstone. I stood, shakily, to meet him. He came over and put an arm around my waist. "I'm sorry I had to leave this morning," he said. "I wanted to stay, but figured there might be things to learn at the LEC. Can you get free for lunch?"

"Only if you brought enough for us when you're done," Noe said, unabashedly eavesdropping.

"I didn't know what you might like, so I got cashew chicken, sweet-and-sour shrimp and teriyaki chicken with vegetarian fried rice, steamed veggies and sides of spring rolls," he said. Looking at Noe, he added, "And yes, there's enough for everyone."

"Save me the veggies, a roll and some rice. I don't eat meat."

"Since when?" I said, surprised my voice sounded almost normal.

"Since my logger told me he's a vegan. Can you believe it? I get the best sex in my life and all I have to give up is cows and birds for it. Who knew?" She flipped back the blue streak of hair and smiled widely. The tongue stud was missing today and she was wearing shrimp-toned lipstick, not her usual dark brown. I hadn't noticed. If one didn't search too closely, she looked almost…ordinary. Just like my life seemed almost ordinary, until I peered into the dark corners.

"How long can you keep up the pretense of being a grazer and not a meat eater?" Jubal asked. "You like your steak still mooing."

"Yeah. There is that. I need my protein. I told him I still eat fish, which grossed him out. He's trying to convert me, but I'm not giving in easily, so save me some shrimp, too. God, I miss protein that had a heartbeat and hooves. There's only so many ways to eat beans and sprouts and tofu."

Leaving them talking about the relative merits of soy-based products, Evan and I went to the back of the shop where I lighted the gas logs we seldom used and pulled out two fairly comfortable chairs, while he created a makeshift table from a low workbench Jubal used when beating different colors of gold into a single solid piece. The smell of Chinese filled the room. Evan pushed me gently into a chair and dished up cashew chicken. I didn't ask how he knew what I wanted. St. Claire nutty strikes again, even if he hadn't noticed.

"Noe tells me Harry Boone came by with the latest news," he said.

"My fan and pal at the cop shop? The fair-minded, law-abiding, honorable Harry Weasel-Faced Boone? Yeah. He came by." I sounded caustic and I didn't care. "Quinn is really dead?"

"Very."

My heart did a little lurch. I guess I hadn't completely believed it, had held out hope that it was a lie, until now.

"Eat. I'll tell you about it after. Under that spiky-hair thing you've got going, you're pale as a ghost."

"Ha-ha, boo." But I ate.

Evan finished before I did and leaned back in his chair, one suited knee crossed over the other, watching me. I studiously watched each bite lift to my mouth.

"You want to tell me about the thirty-eight?"

I put down chopsticks that were halfway to my mouth and pushed away the last three hunks of cashew chicken. It didn't look so appetizing all of a sudden. Kinda greasy. I wiped my hands on a napkin, not able to meet his eyes. "Is this off the record?"

"No."

"Then I have no idea where the gun is now."

"Did you shoot Quinn?"

"No. And no, Quinn was not in the loft this morning. It really was the brown man."

"Why should I believe you?"

"Why shouldn't you?"

"Where is the gun?"

"I don't know."

Evan paused. "Well, crap." He sat forward suddenly, surprise in his voice. "Aunt Matilda shot him!"

I didn't say anything. And I still couldn't look at him. He dropped back in the chair, hands hanging over the chair arms. He had beautiful hands. The ring I had noticed on our first meeting caught the light, the beaten copper-and-silver setting glinting, the band shaped like interlocking crosses clearly etched, the small lapis stone almost black in the shadow. I really liked the ring, and wondered what significance it had for him. It wasn't often a man wore a pinkie ring these days. But I guessed that now wasn't the best time to bring that up.

"Okay. Unless someone shows up in a clinic or hospital with a wound from a thirty-eight, we can say that the casing was one Jane brought home from target practice. She thought it was cool and wanted Noelle to make a glass bead from it."

Tears gathered in my eyes. I nodded. In a small voice I asked, "Tell me about Quinn? Please?"

"He was dropped off on the side of the road near the county dump sometime before dawn. Forensic evidence suggests he was still alive when transported to the dump and dropped from the vehicle. No attempt was made to hide the body." Evan watched me. "His throat had been cut. He bled out at the scene."

My eyes flew up. "He wasn't shot?"

"Oh, yeah, he was shot, too. With a nine mil. But he died of blood loss from a knife wound."

Jane hadn't killed him. I had known it, but the reassurance was comforting. And Harry Boone should be neutered to keep from contaminating the rest of humanity with his genetic code. I shuddered a breath and held Evan's eyes. "Thank you."

"You're welcome."

"Cops suck."

He laughed and something flickered in the deep pools of his eyes. "Yeah. We do. But we're great in bed." His voice challenged and caressed all at once, and I caught an image from him of us, tangled in my sheets, all sweaty and hot and laughing. His imaginings, projected at me.

I felt myself blush—the curse of redheads. His face tightened, green eyes going hard and hot. I fought squirming in my chair, fought giving off signals I wasn't ready to follow through on, what with a house full of women upstairs and the store still open and demanding my attention. And Davie still lost to me.

To give myself space, I stared at my plate and the last three bites of greasy chicken. Without bothering to use the chopsticks, I ate them all, not tasting a thing. Finally, licking my fingers, I said, "Find my brother. Find Quinn's killer. Make sure Jane is safe. Then you can show me just how good cops—with the exception of Weasel-Face, who I refuse to envision in bed, not after that meal and on a full stomach—are in bed."

"I'm counting on it. Feel better?"

He was talking about the meal and the images both, and I knew he had done it on purpose, shared his fantasy. My blush deepened. "Yeah. Thanks."

"We have an early-morning eyewitness who saw a black SUV near the dump. That's not much help in a county where more than half the population drive SUVs, but it's something. We know that Quinn was in deep debt to the local collection boys and possibly Roman Trio for his gambling problem. And there's speculation that he was involved with money laundering to help pay off his debts."

I nodded, trying to see dumber-than-a-box-of-rocks Quinn working with money laundering.

"And because Davie has so much money perched offshore, the cops are wondering if Davie was involved. Maybe in charge."

"No way," I said instantly.

"We have to consider it."

"No."

"Tyler—"

"You waste time considering that. I know better."

"How?"

"Because Davie couldn't hide that from me. I'd know it. I'd *see* it."

"He hid years of his life from you. Why not this?"

I blinked slowly. Davie had indeed hidden years of his life from me. Years I had never bothered to ask about. Years... *Ashes and spit.* Could Davie be someone I didn't know at all?

"Orson Wylie and Colin Hornsburn are investors in a local bank. Usually federal banking laws protect banks and their investors from fraud being perpetrated by the employees or trustees. But Connersville Bank and Trust got around it by making loans to highly speculative companies and for highly speculative land deals. Your brother was an investor in that bank."

I gathered up the chopsticks and tea mugs and stood. "My brother is not involved with land speculation or money laundering. He isn't."

"The bank was buying up land, just like David was. And the bank holds the mortgage on much of the land David bought in the last few years. David was in bed with Hornsburn and Wylie, just like Hornsburn claimed."

Bending again to close up the paper containers of food for Jubal and Noe's dinner, I propped myself against the table, one hand supporting my upper body. I tilted my head to him and said very distinctly, "Then we just have to find out why. Because my brother did not do anything wrong. *He—did—not!*"

"Okay. Let's—"

"Aunt Tyler?" Jane stood in the open door, surprise on her face. "Why are you wearing Daddy's key around your neck?"

I stared at my niece and then looked down. The ornate key was swinging on its thong, back and forth on my neck. "Davie's key?"

14

With a single click of the remote, lights blazed on in Davie's house, warming the cool color scheme, the windows black with the night beyond. Jane used the remote to light the gas-log fires in each room, to turn up the heat, and to turn on her favorite bubblegum radio station. The top one hundred pop chart was on, and a boy band sang surprisingly innocent lyrics about kissing and holding hands. Jane danced and sang along as she led the way to her room.

Jane's sanctum overlooked the rushing stream, the white water caught in the outside security lights, cascading from above and plunging down only yards beyond the glass. Her suite was decorated in purple and blue, with a hand-painted mural of a *Lord of the Rings* landscape on the wall opposite the windows. A gas-log fire in the cave mouth of the mural flared up and capered along to the music. An antique canopy bed, hung with heavy drapes against the winter chill, stood in the center of the room. Jane could draw the thick, velvet, tasseled hangings closed to make a tentlike enclosure. A purple upholstered couch and matching white antique French armoires stood along the wall, framing a door that led to a closet big enough to house an elephant, and a bath right out of a fairy-tale princess daydream.

Jane went straight to her closet and stood in the doorway looking back at us, her expression urging us on. Evan and I followed through the Princess-Barbie-Doll room to find Jane on her knees in front of a box on the floor. Lifting off the top, she removed a key from a jumble of costume jewelry and offered it to me. While Jane shoved her hanging clothes back to reveal a blank wall, I compared it to the key around my neck. It was an exact match. I handed it back.

Jane stood and grinned at us, both victorious and secretive. With one hand, she pressed the wall a couple of inches to the left of the rod support. A faint click sounded and a small panel gave way to expose a keypad lock and a keyhole. Jane punched in six digits, hit a green button, then stuck her key into the keyhole and turned it. All very 007.

"Abracadabra," she said. The wall opened up to reveal a well-lit room about eight feet on each side, and only seven feet high. Shelves lined two walls, with Murphy bed–style bunk beds and emergency supplies on the other.

"Holy sh...ah, moly," Evan said.

Jane laughed, twirling on her toes with excitement. "It's my Secure Room. Only four people in the whole world know about it, you two and Daddy and me. Not even Quinn knows about it."

My heart did a painful little shuffle at the realization that I still had to tell her about her bodyguard's death.

"It's fireproof and bombproof, up to, like, nuclear, but not against the newer bunker-busting bombs," she said with that informative yet lofty tone young girls seem to manage so easily. "It has its own ventilation and air-filtering system against nuclear fallout and germs and stuff. And we got enough supplies to last three weeks—food and batteries and solar battery backup, and battery-powered TV and radio, and everything. Everything except places to pee." She rolled her eyes and took on an aggrieved tone. "Which would be really gross, but Daddy said plumbing would mean other people would know about our Secure Room. If we ever get stuck in here, we have to pee in the empty water containers."

"What all's in here?" Evan asked, his tone still dumbfounded.

"Stuff. That's my secret stuff." She pointed to the narrow shelves to the left of the entrance. "That's Daddy's." She pointed to the back wall. Davie's shelves were considerably deeper, stacked with lots of specialized electronic equipment I could only guess at, and dozens of wooden boxes.

I moved into the claustrophobic space and reached for a random box on the shelves at the back wall. The box was dovetailed wood, an antique cigar humidor with a gold crest on the top. I opened it. Inside were discs, old three-and-half-inch floppies. They were dated one for each week in April, seventeen years ago.

I closed the humidor and checked another. It, too, contained floppies, each in order by week. I estimated there were several years' worth of floppies, if each box held the same thing. They did, up until ten years ago, when the floppies changed over to CDs. I opened each box and passed it to Evan, who glanced inside and nodded, once or twice grunting with what I took to be he-man, big-bad-cop interest. It was clear he had no idea what he was looking at. When he finished inspecting each box, he slid it back in place.

The last box I carried back to the bedroom. Jane was stretched out on her big bed, watching the plasma-screen TV in an open armoire. I held up a CD. "Jane, can I try to load this onto your PC?" I asked.

Not taking her eyes off the screen, she shrugged.

I touched the mouse to bring up the screen and inserted the CD. It opened instantly, displaying a Department of Defense logo in one corner, and a Q Core logo in the other. Feeling chilled in the warm room, I scrolled down. It was a series of reports matching the date marked on the front of the disc. The first report concerned a man named Francois LaMarche, who appeared to be a banker. The report covered a mundane conversation over his office phone between the banker and a Londoner listed as M. Fitz-Howard. Fitz-Howard was footnoted and cross-referenced to another date and CD from earlier in the year.

I scrolled down. The other reports were less prosaic, most transcribed and translated into English. One group of reports concerned ten-year-old conversations between the head of Exxon and several other men, one in the Sudan, one in Libya and one in Iran. They dealt with oil deals, the kind of insider information that would have made a canny investor on Wall Street drool. And rich enough to find an appropriate medical cure for his condition. I thought about the money in Davie's offshore accounts and ejected the CD. I inserted the next.

It too contained written transcripts, translated and footnoted. All were about financial deals between men in power and who I understood to be shadowy figures in governments with which the U.S. was having problems, a decade ago and now.

After the fourth CD, I sat back in Jane's leather desk chair, swinging the chair left and right. Evan sat to my side, thoughtful. "I'm guessing that your brother was part of DOD back when DOD wasn't supposed to have much intelligence-gathering power. And he took his work home with him. Literally."

Suddenly Jane sat up. She clicked off the remote and listened. A soft beeping sounded from the intercom speaker near the door. Jane crawled to the edge and jumped from the bed, ran to the intercom and punched a button. A screen appeared with green lights. And one blinking yellow light.

"Spit and decay," she said. I started at hearing my swear words come from her mouth. "We got an intruder."

She ran to the PC and pushed the desk chair aside, with

me in it. Two keystrokes later the security system was on screen, including a layout of the house and grounds and a schematic of the alarms themselves. Jane pointed to a blinking green light that turned orange as we watched. "Someone's coming through the front gate. They forced it open." The light turned red. At the bottom of the screen words appeared.

SECURITY BREACH AT MAIN GATE ENTRANCE. VIDEO ACQUIRED.

VIEW VIDEO? YES. NO.

FOLLOW PROCESS OF INTRUDER? YES. NO.

ALERT LOCAL LAW ENFORCEMENT? YES. NO.

Jane hit yes to all three questions. Over the computer hookup, we could hear the ringing of the county cops. On the monitor, the screen split in thirds, horizontally. The security schematic remained on the top. The middle view became the detailed, recorded video from the front gate, and at the bottom was the video from the security cameras as they tracked, in real time, the progress of a monster-sized SUV speeding up the driveway.

On the center screen, a face in a black ski mask appeared for an instant, recorded before the vehicle crashed through the wrought-iron, reinforced gates. In the passenger seat, I caught a glimpse of a second figure in black.

On the bottom, the video whipped from one camera angle to the next as the SUV raced toward the house.

"Get in the Secure Room. Now!" Evan barked. He pulled his weapon with one hand, his cell phone with the other, and sprinted for the stairs.

Jane didn't move. She sat frozen, staring at the monitor.

"Emergency Services. What is the nature of your emergency?"

I jerked, adrenaline kicking in late. A computer voice from Jane's PC said, "This is SecureMountain Security Systems. We are reporting a security breach." The calm, digitized voice gave the address and went silent.

I grabbed the phone beside the PC and said, "There's a black SUV approaching the house, viewed on the security cameras. Masked men inside. An armed state police officer is on the premises and has gone to the front of the house. My niece and I are taking refuge in the lower level of the house in a—" Jane grabbed my wrist "—in a closet. We are not armed."

"I am dispatching an officer to the location," the 911 operator said.

Jolted to movement by my near gaffe, Jane punched other keys. The video on bottom settled on the front driveway. The SUV slammed to a halt. Four men poured out. They were heavily armed. Jane hit other buttons.

"*One* officer?" I said. "If you send one officer, he'll be cut down in two seconds. These guys are carrying automatic weapons." Why automatic weapons? Not to ransack a house or find some*thing*. Only to kill or kidnap.

I heard a faint hum as something happened upstairs and behind me. I turned and saw the black of the windows and the white water outside slowly vanish as massive steel plates closed in. I had once seen hurricane shutters close on a high-tech, beachfront condo. That system had nothing on this. In moments, the entire back wall was a solid bank of folding steel plates.

"What *is* that?" I demanded.

"Security and storm shutters," Jane said. Her voice was shaking and so were her hands, but she moved with certainty, a well-practiced ease.

"You've done this before," I said.

"We drill security measures every week. I can do this in my sleep." The claim seemed to steady her. "In my sleep," she repeated, stabbing another key that divided the middle screen into two smaller screens with differing views of the grounds and house.

Evan appeared in the doorway, his gun at his thigh, pointed to the floor.

"I thought I told you to get in the Secure Room."

"We have time," Jane said. "It'll be a while before they get in."

On the screen, on the bottom third, the camera angle looked down on the entryway. I could see two men bent over at the front door, which now wore a metal overcoat. I couldn't see what they were doing, but I didn't think they were leaving a calling card or a basket of fruit. On the split middle screen, I could see another man as he rounded the side of the house. He was well lit in the security light until he turned and aimed his weapon at the fixture. Jane punched another key as it went dark and the computer voice said, "Going to low-light resolution." The man now appeared as a pale greenish form against a darker greenish background.

"I'm glad your brother is on our side. He is, isn't he?" Evan asked. "On our side?"

I didn't respond to the rhetorical question. I was watching Jane. Welling pride damped down my fright. My niece was amazing.

"I lost my cell connection." He flipped his phone shut.

I handed him the house phone, which was still connected to 911. The landline was still working, which had to mean that the cell had died due to the steel plates. Maybe some EM interference, as well? I could see Davie installing something that would jam an attacker's communications. It was all one great big computer game to my brother. Wasn't it? I looked at the CD still in the computer. Maybe not…

"SBI, Special Agent Evan Bartlock. Who is this?"

"Emergency Services. Charlie Harrow."

The voices were coming through the PC speakers, making a weird distortion and a split-second time delay. The words seemed to hiss as the echoes superimposed the electronic background.

"Harrow, I was just on the line to Detective Jack Madison. He should be dispatching three armed units and calling in SWAT. Can you patch me through to him?"

"Will do."

The muted sound of gunfire came from above. Jane stabbed a key and the upper two-thirds of the screen began to darken. A soft *whomp* seemed to shake the air in the house. My ears reacted to a pressure change.

"Into the room," Evan said.

This time, I grabbed Jane by the arm and pulled her into the closet. She was finally ready to come and plucked Davie's CD from the unit as she moved. As I moved her into the Secure Room, I looked back over my shoulder. On the bottom screen, two men shoved back the security shutters and smashed through to the front door. A second *whomp* sounded, louder. The men were inside. The PC went through a fast shutdown.

In the Secure Room, Jane opened a panel on the inside wall and hit a button. A tiny screen lit up and I realized the security system and PC were linked to this screen. A miniature shelf with an even smaller keyboard slid out beneath it. Double-O-Seven for real.

On the screen, two men appeared at the top of the stairs, and the entire apartment went black.

"What the—" Evan started.

Jane had cut the lights. The green screen showed the men pulling on goggles. When they had them in place and started down the stairs, Jane hit the button again and the lights shocked the men motionless. One cursed and threw off the goggles. Jane laughed. Evan joined us in the Secure Room. Jane hit a key and the door began closing us in. "Cool," she said. "Just way freaking cool."

A computer-generation kid playing computer games with paramilitary hit men. Because that is what they were. They had come here to kill us.

Or take us.

I lowered a bunk and sat in the tight space, watching my niece. She hit a button and the men fell to the floor covering their ears. "That one was, like, this piercing scream of sound. They'll be deaf for a long time and probably can't get up anytime soon. And they probably peed themselves," she said with glee. "High-pitched sound does that."

Like they took Davie? No. Davie had been pummeled. This was something else.

I closed my eyes and reached out with my mind.

Anger. Pain. Voices that ricocheted, pulled along behind it. *We didn't expect this freaking fortress. There was supposed to be only the little girl and her expendable aunt. Pain. Have to get out of here. Get out.*

I pulled back behind my wall. They had intended to take Jane.

On the small screen, the two men made it to their feet and stumbled out the door. Jane punched a button, changing cameras. Four men raced into the SUV and it started up. It careened out through the front yard, throwing sod and bouncing across a dormant flower bed, out the front driveway into the street.

Jane sat back, pleased with her work. "Daddy will be really happy his system worked."

"Your father designed this system?" Evan asked.

"My daddy can design and build anything," Jane said proudly. "He owns the company that sells the systems to rich people and governments and businesses all over the world." She looked at me and her expression slipped a bit before it firmed with resolve. "They were after me. And they had orders to kill you."

"Let's not jump to conclusion," Evan started.

"It isn't a conclusion," I said.

"St. Claire sh—ah, stuff—again?"

I nodded, holding Jane's eyes. "What else did you get?"

"They aren't the ones who have Daddy, but they want him, too. They want him even more than they want me." On the small screen, blue lights were flashing, closing in on the drive fast. "And they really want the computer discs. They think Daddy stole them." She paused. "He didn't. Did he?"

I looked at my niece, her eyes holding the first glimmering of awareness of potential fallibility in her parent, of discernment that Davie might not be perfect. I couldn't stand to see her father crash and burn off his pedestal. "Your father more likely took them from bad men who were misusing something. If Davie did anything wrong, it was to protect what was fragile and in danger." As I said the words, they took shape in my mind and solidified. They were the truth. Jane smiled at me and I smiled back. "You and me against the world, kiddo. You and me and your daddy."

"And Aunt Matilda."

"What am I, the yardman?" Evan said.

The rest of the night was predictably torpid. That is, once the county SWAT team and the local cops got over storming the place, descending from offense mode and settling in to observe, take notes and investigate.

The hurricane-style shutters that covered the windows and doors had worked as designed, giving the household time to call for local enforcement and get into a secure location. The cops were impressed. Even old Weasel-Face, who walked around the house as if he owned the place or was about to make an offer for purchase, lock, stock and barrel. The security program was a marvel to them and they wanted particulars, which Jane happily provided, down to numbers of cameras, demonstration of a simulation exercise, discussion of the system's encryption bits, and the fact that Davie's company was working on an artificial-intelligence program that would work the system all by itself.

She downloaded the video feed from the attack onto CD and gave it to the cops, saving other copies for Evan, me, herself and her father. That one, she also uploaded to his secure site without telling anyone what she was doing. *That's my girl.*

Because the only damage was to property, all the cops wanted to do was to file a report and head back to the job. According to them, it was likely only a thousand dollars' worth of damage. Yeah, right. A thousand dollars for the steel shutter and the inside door, which was reinforced steel shaped to look like mahogany. I guessed the door alone would go for a couple thousand, but what did I know? Of course, if I knew my brother, Davie would not even report this attack to his insurance company; he would simply absorb the financial loss and upgrade again, delighted to have the excuse.

When I finally was allowed to see the damage, I was shocked into silence. The steel shutter at the entry was peeled inward as if attacked by a giant with a can opener, and the door itself had been knocked off its hinges by an explosion, possibly from some form of plastic explosives, according to the SWAT team's demolition expert.

The entire attack had been carried out with military precision. That part the cops noted with unease. But it wasn't as if they had any idea what to do about it. One uniformed officer mentioned terrorists and homeland security. I wanted to laugh. Yeah. Call the Department of Defense.

Only the SWAT officers, who might be expected to show some concern for an armed paramilitary unit operating in their county, were interested in what more could be gleaned from the crime scene. They roamed the grounds and the house, and grilled Jane about the system, walking around in black camo and—once Jane punched a button and their communication system started working again—talking into little mikes attached to their jaws. Rambo meets James Bond at his private estate. An estate that was no longer secure but open to the elements, curious wildlife, and any passing masked attacker. Evan helped the cops nail a sheet of plywood over the front door opening.

Jane preened under the attention of the SWAT team leader, a good-looking man in his thirties, with flashing blue eyes above streaks of black grease. She played the expert as she showed off the bells and whistles of the top-of-the-line system to him, all but the Secure Room, which we all agreed was off-limits to everyone, even cops. Jane acted as if the closet was the secure room. The cops believed her.

Finally, around midnight, shaken and subdued, the SWAT team leader, Sergeant Lopez, settled on the couch next to me. I watched Evan's eyes track the cop, and got the feeling that he knew the sergeant but didn't want to let the other cops know.

"Anything else you might want to tell me about tonight?" His eyes were penetrating. "Off the record, if you like."

I shook my head, feeling a flush rise with the lie, and tried to cover for it. "I'm tired, scared and seriously ticked off. Someone took my brother, and now they're trying to take my niece. Or kill us all."

"Anyplace you can go until we catch these guys? Until it calms down a bit?"

I thought about Aunt Matilda's home, a tidewater house situated in the middle of an inland marsh, surround by miles of water and swamp grass and alligators. Anyone who wanted to could drop in with a helicopter anytime. The house had minimal electricity, an ancient hot-water heater and no security system. I kicked off my shoes and pulled my chilled feet up onto the couch. "No. There's only here and my loft."

"I've seen the loft," Lopez said with a glimmer of amusement. "It's less secure than here by far. Even with the door off."

"Yeah, but the cops are only thirty seconds away there. Here, we're alone. With a front door a raccoon could get through."

"There is that."

"If we have more snow, we could get stuck out here, roads closed, no way for help to get to us fast. And bad guys, if they have money, could find a way." I was thinking helicopters again, with men in black rappelling to the ground. "I want to go back to the loft."

Lopez scratched his cheek, smearing the black greasepaint, and released a breath. "It's against my better judgment to let you abandon a house with a security system this sophisticated, but you have a point."

And I hadn't even mentioned the chopper or rappelling.

"Okay. Pack what you need and we'll escort you back to town."

Relief puddled my bones at his words. I had been trying not to think about the ride home on winding mountain streets. We loaded up the Tracker with Jane's belongings and several wood boxes that had appeared mysteriously in her closet to be carted out by Evan. Guarded by a SWAT team, we left the sanctuary of Davie's violated house.

The air outside was cold, wind blasting with ice pellets. The heater in the small Geo warmed up fast, but my heart stayed frozen in my chest for the ride back to town. We were part of a cavalcade that included a SWAT van and two police cars as escort. No chance for anyone to run us off the road in the dark, or finish us off with Uzis, AK47s, shoulder-mounted rocket launchers, or big-rigs filled with explosives. If I hadn't just left a fortified house that the bad guys had attacked with automatic weapons and plastic explosives, I'd have known I was paranoid and overly imaginative. No such luck. My imagination couldn't even begin to conceive a night like this.

We made Jane strap in to two seat belts while lying across the back seat, shielded from sight beneath blankets. I drove. Evan rode shotgun, his grip relaxed on his nine millimeter. My knuckles were white on the wheel, and I clenched them tight at every car and truck we passed, expecting a second attack. The drive was an anticlimax. Nothing happened until Evan's cell phone rang.

Opening it with his left hand, gun steady in his right, he answered. "Bartlock. Who?" After a long silence, he said, "Yeah. She was with me. Yeah. I agree, it sucks." He snapped the phone shut.

"What?"

"You won't like it."

"I don't like anything about today so far," I said, flexing my hands, trying to get them to stop cramping on the steering wheel.

"Your brown man. He's been identified."

"Why do I get the feeling that isn't good news?"

"Because he was ID'd by the coroner who was checking the wallet of a COS. He was shot in the back of the head, probably with a nine millimeter."

Shock peppered me. "What's a COS?" I asked, knowing it wasn't the right question but unable to stop my mouth.

"Cold at scene. Dead," he added, in case I was too stupid to put dead together with cold and shot in the back of the head. "His name was Willard Blythe."

When I said nothing, Evan said, "They're killing off one another."

I had figured that part out on my own. The cold of the night crawled through the floorboards and beneath my skin like tiny maggots of destruction. I shivered once, hard. "So they won't have any compunction about killing Davie, either."

"Yeah."

I briefly closed my eyes, shutting out the sight of the cop. Unable to shut out my ancient dream images of Davie, dead in the snow.

Back at my loft, the cops secured the area. That's what they said, meaning they went though the loft, the rooftop garden, the shop and workroom, and talked to my neighbors to see that Isaac and Jubal were not being held against their wills by black-bag, black-ops, bad guys. After the all clear, Evan carried Jane inside, shielding her with his body, and up the stairs. I followed. The loft was empty of attackers in black stocking caps and free of danger. But it felt hollow, open and extremely unsafe. Aunt Matilda was gone.

As if reading my mind, Evan said, "I called Isaac while you talked to Lopez. Aunt Matilda went to their loft just as the attack happened, hysterical. She saw the attack play out." He shrugged his shoulders as if they were too tight. With quick swivel motions of his head, he cracked his neck, confirming my hypothesis. "She's sedated, medicated with something Jubal had on hand. I didn't ask what it was. Don't ask, don't tell." His eyes smiled. "A good motto sometimes."

"So what now?" I didn't want to say that I was afraid to be alone in my apartment, but I was. Terrified.

"Pull out the trundle and put Jane to bed," he said, handing her the kitten. "I'll let myself out and set the alarm on the way."

"I can put myself to bed," Jane said, and yawned hugely.

I figured anyone who could hold off invading commandos single-handedly until the army arrived could indeed put herself to bed. Still in her clothes, she pulled out the trundle, folded down the covers and crawled in. She was asleep instantly. I envied her that talent, wishing I had the release of instant slumber. I was wound so tight I'd never get to sleep. Evan patted my shoulder and left as I tucked Jane in, seeing the SWAT team out.

"Great," I said to the loft. My words echoed. My reflection looked back at me, worried, from the black windows. "The one time I need to be protected, the one time I want to lean on a man's brawny shoulders, I'm on my own." I put on the kettle to warm and drew a bath. I wandered to the roof-garden windows, where I checked the locks and pulled shut the drapes on my reflection and any prying eyes.

I stripped and added bubbly, lavender-scented bath oil to the water, dropping my clothes on the floor and stepping into the rising water. I adjusted the temp to hotter and settled in. The cell rang. I knew it was Evan before I answered, and a soft smile curved my mouth. With a wet hand, I answered. "Hello."

"Want company?"

"I'm in the tub. Soaking."

"Want company?" he repeated.

I laughed.

"Seriously. I'm checking out of the hotel and I'll be at your door in twenty minutes, luggage in hand. Lopez has a roll-away bed I'm borrowing and setting up in the workroom. Assuming that meets with your approval. Of course, if you'd rather I joined you in the tub—"

"Jane's here."

He laughed. "You won't always have her as a buffer."

"Promises, promises."

"I've borrowed a few private weapons from the SWAT team, but they denied me access to smoke bombs and flash-bangs."

"Whatever that is."

"Things that go bang in the night. They have some tactical weapons. They won't share them, either."

"Selfish beasts."

"I'll let myself in."

"Who told you the alarm code?" I asked, surprised that he knew it.

"Jubal."

"Okay." I yawned wider than Jane had and slid deeper in the water.

"I'll leave my cell on. Call me if you need anything. Anything at all. Your back scrubbed. Feet massaged. Anything." I didn't answer, just flipped the phone shut. But I was still smiling.

When the water was too cold for comfort, I stepped out, greased my skin up, shaved my legs, put on night cream and pulled on a velour sweatsuit and fuzzy socks. I stared around the loft, uncertain, bored, wired still. I yawned again, but knew I'd never get to sleep. So I opened the door to the stairs and called Evan on my cell phone. I heard his simple ring through the open door as I worked the cork out of a bottle of white wine.

"Want company?" I asked. "Wine?"

He didn't bother to answer. He just clicked off the phone and I heard the soft pad of his feet on the stairs. I poured the wine, got some sliced fruit out of the fridge, added crackers and a six-inch wheel of brie to a plate.

Evan's arms came around me to take a glass. When he drank, his cheek was next to mine, his coppery beard rough on my skin. "I am a hero," he said.

"Yeah?"

He swallowed again and tightened his arms around me. "Yeah. This is good." He crunched down on a cracker. "I caught a certain cat escaping down the stairs."

"Oh, no! You *are* a hero. I forgot about her." I turned in his arms, rose up on tiptoe, pulled his face down to me and kissed him. I felt my worries melt away in a wash of warmth. I curled an ankle around his knee and pulled him closer. With my lips against his I asked, "Did you remember to close the loft door after you let her go again?"

"I did."

"Even better." I kissed him again. He kissed back. The cold of the empty loft receded.

"Even better than being a hero, I noticed that Jane managed to lift a few of the CD boxes from the Secure Room before we evacuated it. Assuming that your virus-fighting skeleton is still guarding your PC, I brought my laptop up with me."

"Smart and a hero. I like that in a man."

"Don't forget, I'm good in bed, too."

"Braggart. A gentleman would leave that judgment in the lady's hands."

"I intend to. As soon as humanly possible."

He pulled me to the sofa, sat me down with my feet up, and then went back for the wine, glasses and plates. He put a glass in my hand, tucked the down throw around me, and sat beside me, putting my feet in his lap and the laptop in my lap. All very cozy. I liked the way this man thought.

My eyes were on the laptop, my feet pleasantly warm and resting in Evan's lap, being massaged by his big hands. My belly was full of wine and fruit, cheese and crackers, and the gas-log fire popped and roared, creating a cocoon of intimacy. I was scanning through CDs, reading bits and pieces of the contents to Evan, sharing the screen with him on some.

Jane had managed to bring three wooden boxes from the Secure Room. Two contained floppies and CDs similar to the ones we had inspected on her PC. The other was less full and contained CDs with very different contents. These CDs contained personal information scanned from paper documents, comprehensive and complete. One contained medical records, another tax forms and data, documents for posterity. I skimmed the contents and something caught my total attention.

I stared at a document on a CD labeled Official Documents

in Davie's precise hand, and cold chills ran up my arms. It was a death certificate for a twenty-two-year-old woman named Jannetta Warren Lowe. Minimized on the screen was her birth certificate and a marriage license. She had married one David Lowe, in a chapel on the outskirts of Washington, D.C. Warren was a St. Claire name, part of the matrilineal line.

"I remember a Jannetta from a family reunion one year," Evan said. "She was my age, give or take. I remember the aunts and uncles gathered there for the reunion all whispering about her gift. She was supposed to be a prodigy." He looked at me. "A St. Claire prodigy, with a gift that no one had seen before. How did she meet David?"

I shook my head.

"He didn't tell you about her?"

"No. We never talked about his time away. He never seemed ready and I never pushed. Which was really stupid." But I remembered a distant cousin from my one trip to the St. Claire holdings. She had been Jannetta Claire Warren then, an older, black-haired girl, with pierced ears and huge dangling hoops. She had done cartwheels in the backyard, and had that mysterious glamour that teenaged girls a few years older often had. A hint of womanhood, a status I had longed for. That Jannetta, that worldly, winsome girl, had married my brother, born him a daughter and died, all in the space of one year. And I never knew. This was how Jane, named after her mother, carried the St. Claire gene.

"Tyler?"

"I don't know. I really don't know." I looked over at the trundle bed, at the curve of Jane's head, her dark hair tangled on the pillow, partially under the sleeping form of Dyno, who was draped over her. If I held my breath, I could hear the cat's soft purr. "The biggest question is why Washington, D.C.? Why didn't they get married on St. Claire holdings, like all the other St. Claire weddings?" It was a tradition, whenever a St. Claire married, for the event to take place at Aunt Matilda's, on the lawn if the weather was pretty, in the nearby Catholic church if not, and if hurried due to pregnancy or other extenuating circumstances, in the huge old house itself. I had broken the custom, thumbing my nose at family and getting married in a chapel in town and getting divorced soon after. But Davie…?

"And how did a marriage between two powerful St. Claires take place without Aunt Matilda getting involved? Because Aunt Matilda always sticks her nose into wedding plans," he said. "But she knew about Jane, so we have to assume that while she didn't know about the wedding, she knew about the baby."

Something in his statements made me pause. Something out of place, some niggling little inconsistency. Letting it rest in the deeps of my consciousness, I asked, "Is that cop instinct?"

"St. Claire intuition. And on that note," he said, standing, "I'm going to take my tired self downstairs to my borrowed, squeaky, lumpy, slightly musty smelling bed. Unless you want to invite me into yours? We could carry Jane downstairs and lock her in. As long as you don't howl like a chimp during hot monkey sex, we should get away with it."

I closed down the laptop and put the CD back in the box. "That's tempting, and a terribly romantic come-on, but I'll pass." I stood on tiptoe and kissed Evan good-night. Good-natured about his ousting, he left, once again foiling Dyno's escape attempt.

I was standing at the top of the landing, listening to Evan's footsteps as he passed through the shop, when I suddenly understood that niggling little thing about Davie's wedding and Aunt Matilda. Davie had told me almost nothing about his life in the years while he was away. But it seemed he had told Aunt Matilda everything. I couldn't help the flicker of envy that realization caused.

* * *

The clock ticked steadily near the door as I settled myself on the rug in front of the couch. A candle burned in front of me to focus my eyes, both spiritual and physical. The lights were off, only the gas logs flickering in time with the candle flame.

I hadn't asked God to help. Not since my first attempt to find my brother. I prayed silently now, prayed for help in using a gift I feared and scorned. Prayed to El for calm, for peace, for a clear mind. *For once in my life, I need a stronger gift.* And I threw down my wall.

Pain started in the front of my head, a needle over my right eye this time. It was my usual headache, though milder than before, a cool pressure rather than burning agony.

Calm rested on me even before I was centered, before I had my breath under proper control, a strange calm like a heavy coverlet, warm and promising and soothing. It was a peculiar calm, an outside-of-me thing, rich and deep and with a texture to it, like the buzz of bees. Or like the breath of another.

Fury rose, a violent tide. "Aunt Matilda!"

Don't raise your wall!

I halted the action even as she named it. *Spit and decay. What do you want?*

You can hear me?

Sort of. You sound like a bunch of angry bees in my mind. Get out!

I've been waiting on you. You said you would try a scan for Davie. I want to follow you in. Breathe. You're losing focus.

I breathed. Slowly. The buzz receded. The pain that had rebounded with my discovery of my nosy aunt eased. *I didn't know you could do that, follow someone into another person's mind.* Even in my head, the tone sounded surly.

You were never trained. Some of us can piggyback. Actually, you have always been near unto impossible to scan for and read, but you've been distracted. I managed to find you. That wall of yours stands firmly in the path of every beneficial thing, but we can study that later. Are you ready to scan for Davie?

I resented her presence in my mind, but I needed help. Hadn't I just prayed for help? El had a wicked sense of humor. *Yeah. Fine.*

You have something of his?

I opened my eyes and saw the ornate key and the clump of gold and the CD. *Yes. Now, be quiet.*

When I was centered, so calm my skin pulsed with life, my muscles liquid, bones soft and pliable, I took up the quartz in my left hand. It was warm, and nestled into my palm as if alive. I placed the CD in my lap. Took up the key in my right.

Davie? Davie, I'm here. Davie? I called with my mind, searching for my brother. *Davie? Where are you? Davie. Davie. Davie.* As always, the cadence of the syllables slowed, matched to my heartbeat. *Davie. Davie. Davie…*

Something there, some muzzy almost-scent, almost-sound, almost-texture against my mind. *Davie?*

Brat? Davie awakened fast, his mind instantly alert.

Aunt Matilda's here. She's piggybacked. Tell us fast. Where are you?

I don't know. I've been moved twice.

I saw a room, windowless, cramped. Empty rails over his head and shelves at the back. A walk-in closet with a mattress on the floor.

But I'm warm now and they got me some medicine. I'm on antibiotics, cephalosporin. The label's been ripped off, but the bottle belonged to a little girl. I can sense her on it. She had a kidney infection. If you find the little girl, you can find someone who is part of this.

My eyes roamed the room as we spoke. As in the first room where he was held, there was a table. On it was a lamp, a decanter, and something that glinted. Davie blinked and looked away. That was the first indication that I was seeing through his eyes. Vertigo undulated through me. I swallowed it back down and tried to remember to breathe. *Okay. What else can you—*

I've been trying to reach you. There are three parties involved now. They're in negotiations over me. It's not just about the gold anymore, but if you offer the gold, the first party may take—

Davie?

Davie?

He was gone. I made it to the bathroom, where I retched, emptying a noxious mixture of wine and brie into the toilet. I collapsed on the floor. I was going to have to get a rug for the bathroom if I kept spending so much time on my knees in here. The tile was freaking cold.

Are you still there?

It was Aunt Matilda.

I'm here.

Breathe.

Yeah. Right.

You did well. And she was gone.

It was silly. Stupid. Infantile. But a hint of pride rose up in me at her words.

I rinsed out my mouth and made it to the bed. Snuggled deeply in the down pillows, with the down comforter pulled over my head to keep out the encroaching cold, I was almost asleep when it hit me, the little inconsistency on Davie's personal CD. In all the files, so total and complete, there was no copy of Jane's birth certificate.

15

Sunday, dawn

The weather channel threatened snow for the afternoon. Dawn brought dull light, lowering clouds and a gathering wind that had begun to whine as it passed through the buildings. I was curled on the sofa working, watching the sun rise behind the clouds, lighting the overcast gray. My mind hyperalert, I had given up on pretending to sleep and had gone back to the CDs. What I found, or rather hadn't found, had stopped me in my mental tracks.

Not only was Jane's birth certificate missing, every record about Jane, until age four, was missing.

I couldn't believe it was an oversight. Not something so important. Davie was too anal to have misplaced her early records. But there was no old data on Jane at all, only recent records. I couldn't even find a Social Security number for her, which would be required for her schooling. The paper trail for Jane started when she came to Connersville, when she was already walking and talking.

After going through the records box twice, I sat and simply watched the sunrise. Jane's mother had been a prodigy. A St. Claire savant. A woman with talents beyond any I could imagine. Jannetta had apparently married Davie without family consent. Davie, who had disappeared as if from the face of the earth. Davie, who had used more than one name. I had finally thought to look at the *properties* of the CDs from the Department of Defense. They had been created, modified or copied by one David Lowe. And David Lowe was the name that Adam Wiccam had used when he asked for my brother.

I had used Bloodstone's online account and run a credit report on David Lowe and David St. Claire. I knew my Internet search was likely not as good as what the cops could do, but I had hoped I might get lucky, and if knowledge translated as luck, then I had. It seemed David Lowe and David St. Claire were two different people, born in different states, in different years, of different parents. They had lived at the same time, both paying taxes or filing taxes on time, within hours of each other. But David St. Claire had neither made nor spent a dime until David Lowe vanished. At that exact moment, David St. Claire had come into a huge amount of money, over nine million dollars, which had been invested offshore, and had moved to Connersville, NC.

I had frittered away the night for that smidgen of information, wasting the opportunity for rest and only deepening my disquiet. Where had Davie gotten nine million dollars? How had he turned it into eighteen? I counted the years and figured that a very canny investor might succeed in growing a fortune so vast. I wondered if the DOD had really lost nine million at the same time. Was my brother a crook?

To put my anxious mind at rest, I went through each and every CD a final time, this time carefully, not distracted by a man's hands on my feet. The only good thing I gained as the clock ticked toward morning was a letter. It was addressed to me on the first CD in the personal records box. The file was labeled Bloodstone and was in Word format, easy to open but not the first thing I might see amidst the contents of the CD.

The dawn sky grew brighter over my shoulder and Dyno

started to stir again as I read it. The small cat had kept me company off and on through the night, prowling and exploring, once even walking across my body as if I was just so much furniture. Now, as I read and tears obscured my vision, Dyno sprang to my lap and purred against my face as if sensing my distress. Or maybe she was just in need of salt and smelled it gathering in my eyes.

Dear Tyler,
What is it you say? Spit and decay? If you're reading this, then maybe all that is left is spit and decay—and my records. I've tried to prepare for any eventuality, and you, dear sis, are my final fallback measure. I know it must really tick you off that I've left you again, but believe me—this time it wasn't my idea. I never want to leave you and Jane.

Anyway, if you found this letter, then things have gone to hell in a handbasket. It means that Jane is in your care, you have been given your key, and you've learned about the house's last-ditch defense measures. That means I'm either dead or missing, because Jane has firm orders not to give you the personal records box, or the other boxes, until it looks like I'm not coming back.

So, I guess a history lesson is due. I told you the truth as far as it went about my life when I left home for the first time. I took off for Vegas. I was too young to make it on the professional poker circuit, so I created a new identity for myself. It was a pretty cool lifestyle for an eighteen-year-old guy, you know? Once I started working, right way I was able to make a pretty good living. Not wealthy, but I did okay for a couple years.

Then, about my twentieth birthday, when you would have been sixteen—man, I wish I had been there to see you finish growing up, wish I had been there for you. Anyway, this thought started to pop into my head at the oddest times, that Dad was still alive somewhere, in a cage, being made to do freaky things, like for the government or something. And I knew about Q Core. We all did. So I contacted them under my new identity and went to work. Since I had started the fake ID so early in life, it worked, even for the government.

But my first real day on the job? I spot Jannetta. And she spots me. That old St. Claire thing, you know? I thought I was screwed, man. But it was like electricity, like lightning, like fireworks on the Fourth of July between us. And she thought it was cool that I was searching for Dad, so she kept my secrets. Even then, her shields were better than mine and she taught me some stuff, which helped me to shield from the up-line guys without them knowing it.

What I discovered is all the stuff in the boxes. I found out about Dad within the first eight months. I guess you'll find it shortly, so I won't spend time here detailing it. Pretty weird, huh? That one of us got blindsided so fast. Makes you think about security measures and keeping alert, on your toes.

But as I dug deeper, I found out other stuff. Some really not cool stuff. Using the information gathered by the inner core—pardon the play on words—of Q Core, the bureau chief was creating a private organization with its own funding, assets shunted to accounts not part of the official oversight stuff. He had amassed five million bucks. That was pretty good pocket change, but nothing to start a war with or anything.

Q Core had started setting its own policy. I found records where they had killed people, using their gifts, as unofficial actions during official project objectives.

They were doing evil, man. And St. Claires had been forced to participate. It had, like, torn up their minds. I had plans to take it all to an oversight committee. And it was major hard to keep it all from the scans they ran on us. I kinda thought they were getting suspicious of me.

But then Jannetta and I got pregnant. And it was real clear that high-muckety-mucks were way too interested in the baby. So Jannetta and I got ready. The day the baby was born, I was ready to send reports to the Intelligence guys in Congress, bring down the whole she-bang.

That night, Jannetta started bleeding. And I lost her. I can't tell you how bad that was. It was like having my insides ripped out. I pretty much lost it.

They gave me leave and made me take it. And then, using the social services people, they came after my little girl. So I did the only thing I could at the time. I sent records to the oversight and Congressional Intelligence committees, took the money and hit the road. Nearly four years later, we had lost them well enough to show up in your store.

But if you got this, then they may have found me. And that means you and Jane are in major danger. Mostly Jane, but if you're with her, then your life is toast, too.

I have one thing to ask you. Take care of my little girl.

If Q Core has come after me, take her away. Don't wait. Your name is on the accounts under a password only you know and you can access the accounts online, removing monies on the go or depositing them as you need. Find a place where Jane can be free and safe. I love you. I know you can save my baby.

—Davie

My tears were falling in a steady stream, soft drips onto my sleep shirt. Dyno rose up on her hind legs, blocking the screen, and licked at my face, pawing me. I shuddered a laugh and pushed the cat away. She jumped to the floor and raced into the dark. I wiped my eyes and read the information beneath the letter.

Below Davie's name was a series of account numbers, phone numbers, Web sites and other numbers that were not self-explanatory. I had no idea what they were for.

"Idiot. You didn't tell me the password." And then I realized that Davie hadn't offered to give me a password. He'd merely said everything was *under a password only you know.* As in, know already. I thought about the defensive knight on my PC and went online under the store ISP account. At random, I went to one of the sites listed on the letter.

When the home page opened, it was a drab gray-and-charcoal page with no indication what it was actually for, only the initials FAOB with one link. I clicked on it and the link took me to a secure sign-in page. There were two blanks, one atop the other. Taking a guess, I typed in the account number that accompanied the Web site address on the letter. Below I typed in *Jane.* A message block came up that said, ACCOUNT NUMBER AND PASSWORD DO NOT MATCH. PLEASE TRY AGAIN. I looked at the letter from Davie. The title of the file was kinda weird. This time I typed in *Bloodstone* and hit Enter. The boxes vanished and another box appeared. There was no indication what it was for. No prompt.

I thought about it, fingers tapping on the laptop edge. Finally I went back to the letter I had minimized and studied the stuff Davie had added to the bottom of the page. On the last line, on the left, was the word *Prime,* and on the right was *Salutation.* I looked back at the salutation on the letter. It said Tyler. Davie didn't call me Tyler. Not ever. I typed in prime numbers until there were four spaces left, and added *Brat*.

I was suddenly inside the world of high finance, on a page with gilt borders, lots of options, multiple pages and heavy encryption. That had been way too easy. Either Davie had made it simple for me, or I had used St. Claire nutty. I was betting on simple.

I clicked on ACCOUNT INFORMATION, then on BALANCE. A figure appeared. 3,372,876.91 USD. "Ashes and spit," I whispered.

I closed off the site and shut down the modem.

If Q Core has come after me… But gold was in the middle of this, not the DOD. Wasn't it? And then, suddenly, it came together for me. Q Core was—could be—another of the groups in the negotiations Davie had mentioned. So how had Q Core found my brother? And why now?

After living a quiet life for over a decade, Davie had stuck his head into the stratosphere with his environmental concerns. He had attracted attention, and maybe Q Core had found him. If so, they might want more than just the money, Davie and Jane. They might want revenge, too. If Q Core had been operating outside of proper direction and channels, they might have been shut down. Might have faced legal repercussions. This could now all be personal.

Then again, I could be a paranoid nut with illusions of danger, conspiracy and evil guys in black hats. There was a reason why St. Claires were nutty-weird and it wasn't all about psychic stuff. Seeing inside people's heads could make you really demented, and some of us had nothing much in the way of shields.

But if I was right, then Jane was in major danger.

I was still sitting when Jane woke and clambered from the trundle bed, knuckling her eyes. "What're you doing?"

"Sitting here, watching the sun rise."

"There is no sun, just clouds."

Her words struck me as funny and I laughed, curling an

arm around her as she crawled on the sofa and beneath the afghans. She yawned and dropped her head against me. I stroked her hair, soft and silky, so unlike my wild and bushy tresses.

Take care of my little girl, he had said.

With my life, I thought. "Jane?"

"Mmm?" She mumbled sleepily.

"Did your daddy give you a bunch of numbers recently?"

"Whatcha mean?"

"Like his prime numbers he loves so much, but different. Like these." I handed her the heavy card with the GPS positions on it. "Did he give you anything like these?"

She opened her eyes and stretched, looking nominally more alert. "Yeah. It's in my book bag from school."

Electricity zinged through me, an erratic pattern that settled in the hairs along my arms. "Do you have it with you? Can you get it for me?"

"Sure. Can I have Cheerios for breakfast?"

"Yes," I said, watching as she stood and crossed the room to rummage in the clear plastic book bag kids had to carry nowadays for security measures at school. When she came back, she handed me a beige card, heavy stock, like one might use for invitations. It had a shiny, embossed border. I held it next to the GPS card I already had. It was an exact match.

"Did your daddy tell you to give this to me?"

Jane, still in yesterday's wrinkled clothes, was standing at the kitchen counter, pouring Cheerios into a bowl. The round O's made a shushing sound, much like the sound of the wind at the windows. "Only if you asked for it."

"Did he tell you to give me anything else if I asked for it?"

"Nope. Just the card."

"I see." I studied the card, with its single set of numbers. GPS coordinates to one specific site. "I have to leave you with

Aunt Matilda again. You'll have to stay here until I get back. Will you be all right?"

Jane shrugged, carefully pouring milk into the bowl. "Fine by me. I'll miss Sunday school, but I guess after the SWAT team came last night we can't go to church, huh?"

Church? When had Davie and Jane started going to church? "Ah, no."

"Aunt Matilda said we can practice with the cards and with projection, so that'll be fun." Dyno mewled at her feet and Jane poured a splash of milk into the cat's bowl, too.

I stood and dressed quickly, making calls on the cell phone as I moved.

Evan called in a favor and got a temporary bodyguard for Jane. The off-duty Sergeant Lopez, who turned out to be Evan's contact with local law enforcement, came to baby-sit. He and Isaac carried on a conversation in Spanish and then bumped fists, which must have been a good thing, because Isaac had no concern over leaving Jane with him, either. Free of worries about my niece, Jubal, Isaac, Evan and I climbed into Jubal's monster SUV and drove into the hills.

The GPS coordinates indicated an isolated place, and we wound deeper and up, then down and around, and up and up along unpaved country roads, and finally old logging roads that followed the course of hills through land untouched since the last clear-cutting some fifty-plus years ago. At last we parked, got out and prepared to hike. The site indicated by the GPS coordinates was more than just remote. We couldn't get near it by any road that Isaac could find on any map.

There was no trail, no evidence of an old path, old animal tracks, old anything. Only the age of the trees indicated that man or beast had been here before. Isaac read from the GPS device while I gloved and pulled a balaclava over my face.

The location seemed to be directly uphill. I passed out bottles of water, which we all slipped into pockets.

On top of layered sport clothing, we donned thin, insulated vests and coats. Isaac grabbed a length of rope in a coil, his cell phone and a belt of tools. They looked like rock-climber tools—a hammer, a chisel, other stuff I recognized from local boys out to scale the local rock. Stuff I had no intention of using. Not me. No way.

"There," Isaac said, pointing straight up.

The wind was picking up, a cold icy bluster that sent corkscrews of drafts against us. The gusts would make climbing up the nearly vertical side of the hill like walking while a giant hand swatted us back and forth. "Spit and decay," I whispered to myself.

"Yeah," Jubal said. "Just don't spit into the wind."

"Ha-ha." I sighed and started up the hill. Even with all the exercise I'd been getting, my heart rate increased instantly and my breathing deepened as I reached over my head for a tree trunk, pulling myself up two feet. It wasn't mountain climbing, but it was close. Our footing was loose on last year's leaves, still wet from melted snow, and the ground under that was broken, unstable rock over earth, as if the mountain beneath us was rotting, degenerating from granite into earth.

My feet slipped several times in the first few yards. Evan reached out to stabilize me until he realized that each time I slipped, I was holding on to a small sapling or root or vine. He fell into place behind me and began placing his hands in the nooks and crannies I found, using them to pull himself up, but sticking behind me in case I fell. It was very macho-protective of him, and the action warmed my heart. It didn't mean he could stop me if I slipped and started back down the hill at a fast rate of speed, but it did mean that I wouldn't have to slide alone.

Isaac and Jubal worked side by side a little to our right,

helping each other, with Isaac keeping an eye on me and the GPS all at once. I didn't bother to tell my guards that I could take care of myself, or that if I started sliding, I was perfectly capable of catching a tree on the way down. I thought it was cute, and we made good time working in tandem, two teams moving uphill.

Within minutes, my arms were sore at shoulders and biceps, and my thighs burned. I broke out into a hot sweat that was cooled instantly by the wind. One of my gloves tore, splitting a seam at the outer palm. This was way harder than any step machine in any gym.

We finally located a more level place to take a breather, if a grade of forty-five degrees could be considered more level. Isaac pointed to it and I nodded. We moved right for twenty yards before we neared the spot, Jubal reaching it first and pulling Isaac onto the slanted shelf.

Isaac offered a hand, hauling me into the lee of the hill. I placed my feet against the bole of a tree, turned and dropped back against the side of the mountain. I looked back at the SUV. It was a long way down. Evan slammed into the side of the hill beside me, cursing steadily under his breath. The wind howled and slapped us from the side as if trying to throw us back down. I twisted open the water bottle cap and drank half.

"Isn't this fun?" Jubal wheezed, uttering the first words in a quarter hour. He too drank and passed his water bottle to Isaac. "Are we there yet?"

"This sucks a great big egg," I gasped. "A really, really big egg. This was a stupid, stupid, *stupid* idea and you guys should have told me so."

"We did," Jubal said, his breath no better than mine. "You were coming anyway."

Isaac consulted the GPS and aligned himself with some internal map. "There, I think."

"You have got to be kidding," Jubal said. *"That?"*

That was a dome of solid rock rising up out of the mountain. Or maybe it *was* the mountain, its dead heart of dense granitic stone partially exposed, a monster stone bowl turned on its side. It was a reddish-white monolith that curved out, a buttress that would require pitons, ropes, crampons and an experienced guide. And nerves of steel and better abs than I currently possessed.

"Yeah. I'm afraid so." Isaac laughed, his breath stuttering and rough. He drank water in long gulps and his voice sounded clearer. "Think you can climb that small rise, Robin?"

"Holy rock of ruination, Batman," Jubal said, still gasping, half-laughing. "And, no. I'm not even going to try."

Isaac laughed harder and cuffed Jubal. "You shouldn't have to. I have a feeling it's at the base of the slab. See that lighter whitish smear to this side of the dome? It looks like something broke off. Let's head that way." He nodded to tell us it was time to get moving again. Just before I turned to face the hill, a flake of snow landed on my cheek and instantly melted. The snow had come early.

We moved toward the GPS coordinates, breathless, cold to the bone, sweaty and exhausted. As we neared the site, the colors of the huge slab became clear. It was reddish brown with uneven smears of white running through it, its face desiccated by exposure to the elements. The white that peeked through was ribbons of quartz, striated by aeons of rain, tannins and the wind.

At the underside of the huge reddish rock was a ledge, fairly flat, free of undergrowth, and it was instantly obvious that this was where the gold came from. A section of the rock face had broken away in a long vertical calving. The hunk that had broken free had exposed a huge white quartz slab of stone inside the protective layer of granite. Within the quartz was gold.

We pulled ourselves to the base of the rock, breathing like a quartet of bellows. The bowl of the mountain loomed over us.

Evan dropped to the ground, threw his head back and sucked air like a dying man, exposing the long column of his throat. Jubal fell beside him. Isaac turned and surveyed the view, his face troubled. It was snowing now, fitful sheets of billowing white, rolling and waving in the wind. I sat more slowly, one hand on the fresh quartz, fingers resting on a thick wire of gold that glowed in the dull light.

I found a comfortable position, cold ground beneath me, pulled off a glove and rested my forehead against the rock, closed my eyes. I breathed deeply, blowing out the built-up tension, drawing in fresh air. I could smell a trace of smoke on the breeze.

"Someone has been here," Evan said. "Tracks."

I didn't look. I couldn't. I was too tired.

"Lots of them. Two kinds of boots," Isaac said.

"They lead off that way. There's a trail," Jubal complained. "Look! We came uphill, and there's a trail from that side that curves around the hill?" When no one responded, he said again, irritated, "I said, we came *uphill* when we could have come down?"

"There is nothing on the map," Isaac said. "For that matter, this hill isn't on the map. This place is so remote there isn't a road for a mile or more. You think you could have done better?"

"An old lady with a walker could have done better."

The men started arguing. I blocked them out and expelled a deep breath, centering myself, feeling the calm of the earth fill me as I inhaled. I smelled the rich scent of dormant plants, the promise of deep snow on the air, and fine stark earth, the dust of stone. I settled into the earth, into the stone. It was as if the earth below me seeped its strength into me, rising through my bloodstream to strengthen my heart, my lungs. My heart rate slowed. Steadied. I opened my eyes. I could see pick marks where someone had widened the scar into the mountain, exposing more of the gold-filled white quartz. I lifted my bare hand and placed it on the quartz. My palm was chilled where it touched the stone and the gold in the heart of the mountain.

Davie? Davie, I'm here. Davie? I called with my mind, scanning for my brother. *Davie? Where are you? Davie. Davie. Davie...*

Brat? Davie answered. I felt a jolt as I landed in his mind, a moment of disorientation.

Yes. Using his eyes, I looked around the room. It was subtly different, and I realized there was a chair and a real bed in the closet. On the small table was a bit of gold. I concentrated on it, using my mind rather than my brother's eyes. It was a gold ring, within easy reach on the bedside table but out of focus.

I know who took me the first time. They've reached a deal with one of the parties. They came in and...warned me.

They? They who?

I don't know. I'm not sure.

I felt a shift in Davie's mind, away from the truth. Or away from a truth. He looked at the ring. The shift of emotion was there again. Suddenly I identified the feeling behind his thoughts. Shame. It was horror and shame and a trace of fear. Like the hint of smoke on the wind, they twined through him as he looked at the ring.

I concentrated on it, willing it to come clear. It was a woman's ring, a heavy circlet of beaten gold with a spray of rubies across it like a branch of orchids. It was Jubal's work, I realized suddenly. I had seen it before, on the workbench. In Jubal's hands. *Where did you get the ring?*

That strange shift again. Reluctance in his thoughts. *I found it when I woke up just now. It was tangled in the sheets.*

Who does it belong to? Who left it with you?

Davie's mind shifted again, away from the answer. But I knew the ring's owner had hurt him. Recently. She had caused this pain in my brother. *Davie? What did she do to you?*

A sound intruded and he turned to it. The door opened. A woman was silhouetted in the opening. Davie's heart rate sped up and he thrust out at me, pushing me away. Our connection was severed. I opened my eyes.

Instantly I was in another place, windswept and icy. I could smell smoke, strong on the wind. I saw a doubled scene, one of the gold-and-pure-white stone that rested against my face. *A memory. Steel bit into the stone, wounding it, sending slivers of sharp-edged quartz flying. The pickax bit deeper. Again and again. Gold. Gold. My gold.*

On top of the memory I saw a second scene. *Four people. In the crosshairs. The scope settling on the small woman. The troublemaker. My finger tightened on the trigger. I took a deep breath and began to let it out, a long sigh preparatory to shooting. I'll kill her. The one touching my gold. I'll kill them all.*

I jerked my hand away from the gold and snapped up my head. "Get down!" I threw myself against the ground and rolled. Splinters of quartz erupted, hitting my cheek and shoulder. A shot rang out. Evan fell over me, pulling his weapon. I had an instant image of him, his gun rising, a look of controlled fury taking over his face. The shot echoed like thunder through the hills.

A second shot hurled shattered rock at us on the echo of the first. A third.

The men rolled, contorted. A hand pulled me behind an outcrop. I was screaming. Over and over.

A splatter of something hot hit my cheek.

I rolled again, seeing a spurt of red arc overhead. Blood.

A haze of anger welled up in me. He had shot my friend.

I screamed again, now with rage, and placed a hand on the wound. Pale skin beneath my bluish fingers. Scarlet blood. I balled my glove into the wound and covered it with my other gloved hand. Blood welled around my fingers, fast, spurting and falling in crimson rivulets. Jubal had taken the shot high in the back of his arm, near the shoulder. A second hole, bigger than the first, was high on the front of his chest under the collarbone. I grabbed the balaclava off my head and thrust it into the second wound.

Isaac was shouting into a cell phone. Evan scanned the surrounding terrain, searching. More shots sounded, carefully spaced, echoes like a primitive drum around the hills. Rock shattered and flew.

"We have to get around the hill," Jubal said, his voice sounding calmer than the rest of us. "The shots are coming from there." He pointed with his good arm, and Evan immediately shoved us around the nearest outcrop into a place of relative safety. He returned shots in the general direction Jubal had indicated.

"Give your belt to Isaac," I said to Jubal.

One-handed, he unbuckled the belt and pulled it through the loops. I had a single second to think about AIDS or hepatitis, and then felt shame. This was my friend. "Isaac, pull off your sweater and give it to me."

Keeping his body low to the ground, Isaac stripped off coat and sweater, and two shirts. He gave them to me and I put one tee into the shoulder wound, then one over the arm wound. He talked as he stripped. "Sheriff and park service are both on the way. They can get a chopper off the ground in twenty minutes. Ten minutes after that they can be here. If we can find them a place to land. If they think they can get it all done before the storm gets too bad to fly." He looked at me, dark eyes flashing. "I didn't tell them the shooter was probably still around or about the wind."

I shook my head, teeth starting to chatter. "Loop the belt under his arm and up over the exit wound, here," I jutted my chin to show the site. "Then pull it tight. Right," I said as he followed my instructions. "Tighter. Good.

"Now take the end and loop it around his upper arm." I lifted Jubal's arm from his side and allowed the belt to slide in freely. Then as it cinched tight, I eased my hands away. The bleeding had slowed to a trickle. "How do you feel?" I asked Jubal.

"Like I'm going to pass out. All girlie."

"Very funny," I said.

"The shooting has stopped," Evan said. "I'm going around the trail uphill to see if we can get out that way. You people stay put."

"I'm not going anywhere," Jubal said. His skin was ashen, lips blue. I helped him to lie down and Isaac covered him with his jacket, seemingly unaware that he now wore only a thin V-necked undershirt and pants. I pulled off my jacket and one of my T-shirts, giving the stretchy shirt to Isaac and covering Jubal with the jacket. I was wearing a single shirt and a thin insulated vest and I started shivering instantly. The wind cut like a knife, slicing along my exposed skin. The blood on my hands froze, drying to a crust where it was thinnest.

"He's going into shock," Isaac said.

I elevated Jubal's legs, and Isaac shoved a rock under them.

"We may have to carry him out to a landing site," he said. "We can put two jackets under him, tie the sleeves together, and carry him by the sleeves."

"Let's do it."

We rearranged the clothing, trussing Jubal into them. His breathing was fast and shallow. Isaac curled around him, shielding him from falling snow, warming the exposed skin of his ears. Jubal had lost his hat. Isaac pulled off his own, exposing his bald pate to the frozen wind, smoothing the knit cap onto Jubal's head.

I looked up into the snow, felt it landing and melting on my neck and face. My shivers worsened. Long minutes later Evan reappeared. He was hard-faced, blowing clouds of breath that were quickly whipped away. His voice was cold steel. "There's a new road over the crest of the hill. Looks like it was cleared in the last week. Cut greenery is still fresh, tree limbs oozing slightly. If we can get Jubal up there, we can be close to a landing site."

"And close to where the shooter is parked?" Isaac asked.

"I don't think so. No vehicle close by." Evan scanned the surrounding area as he spoke, watching for attack. He put down the weapon and unzipped his jacket, slipped out of it and handed it to me. "Don't argue," he said when I opened my mouth. "The tracks are old. Made before the last snow melted. How is he?" He picked the gun back up, cradled it as if it was his best and only friend.

"We think he's in shock," I said. Turning my back, I yanked off my remaining T-shirt and handed it to Isaac before pulling on the oversize coat.

"What's his pulse?"

Pulse? I almost slapped myself. Then I reached under the coats and felt for Jubal's wrist, found the right spot and checked his pulse. In his uninjured wrist it was fast. I guessed about 120 beats a minute. It was erratic in the other wrist, fast a few seconds, then nothing. "One-twenty. Give or take. And his breathing is way too fast."

"Time?" Evan asked Isaac.

He checked his watch, shivering as badly as I. "Maybe ten minutes till the chopper gets here."

"Let's move. Can you two carry Jubal?"

"Yeah," Isaac said. "We'll manage. You take the phone and talk the chopper in."

I got on Jubal's right side and looked at Isaac. Our eyes met. We lifted together. Isaac was much taller than I and Jubal rolled toward me. I felt something pull in my shoulder and back. I gripped the burden with both hands and ignored the pain. Concentrated on putting one foot in front of the other, concentrated on not falling, not sliding, not dropping Jubal.

We made it around the rock outcrop and up the hill, over the crest. Just as we reached a possible landing site, I heard the sound of rotors. "Thank you. Thank you, thank you, thank you," I prayed. It was only then that I realized that I had been praying the whole time out loud, as if I really thought El might hear.

We eased Jubal to the ground. I fell beside him, Isaac to his other side. The cold air burned and tore at my throat as it went down.

The air ambulance appeared out of the clouds, white with blue markings and a slash of red. Evan burst from the rocks and directed the helicopter to a place to land. The roar and the wind were incredible. I looked at Jubal, who was far too pale. I couldn't tell if he was breathing and fear whipped through me. Then he took a breath, shuddering and rough. His eyes opened and he found my face. He smiled. It was a smile of goodbye. I started to cry. Searching the coats, I found his hand. It was scarcely warmer than mine, exposed to the frigid air.

Jubal twisted his head as if it cost all the energy he had left, and found Isaac. He mouthed Isaac's name. The big man cradled Jubal's face, bending over him a moment. I couldn't hear what he said, but his lips moved. I looked away, sobbing once in a movement that caused my chest to ache. I watched through my tears as the helicopter tried to land. It rocked side to side, tossed by the wind. The pilot had to be a maniac or an adrenaline junkie to fly in this. The chopper came to rest.

Medics burst out of the side doors, carrying a stretcher and an orange tool kit. They swarmed my friend and I stepped back, bumping Isaac. He wrapped his arms around me, his shivers so strong they were small quakes through him. I pulled off Evan's coat. Isaac put it on and pulled me inside with him. His body was cold and hard against mine. I prayed as I watched Jubal. There was so much blood.

Evan was talking into a cell phone. I closed my eyes, shutting out the sight of my friend and the jumpsuited medics, but the suspense was too much. I opened them to watch. One medic was carrying a unit of blood. They unfolded him from the coats and pulled his uninjured arm free, then wrapped on a blood-pressure cuff and started an IV. They added padding to the makeshift bandages I had applied. I wondered why they hadn't pulled off the old bandages first. They shouted over the sound of the helicopter engine, which didn't shut down. The rotors kept twisting, creating a swirling pattern in the wretched wind. Snow started to fall harder. It seemed ages as they worked on Jubal. He looked so pale.

It was only a shot to the arm. You couldn't die from a shot to the arm, could you?

Evan came over to us, pausing to speak to the medics on the way. When he reached us, he shouted, "They're ready to go, but they can't take all of us, so I told them we'd stick together. But we can't make it back down the mountain without proper clothes. I have a transport on the way, but we aren't sure where this new road comes out. Seems no one knows about it—it isn't supposed to be here. We have to reach these coordinates." He handed Isaac a scrap of paper. Isaac compared the GPS device to the scrap.

The medics lifted Jubal and carried him to the chopper. He was strapped onto a stretcher, our blood-soaked coats still beneath him, arms dangling. We all stopped and watched. Jubal lifted two fingers to wave. His fingers were covered in dried blood, crusty brown. We waved back, shivering horribly in the cold wind. A medic tossed a bundle on the ground and moments later the chopper took off, rotors swirling snow and leaves and detritus around.

The snow was suddenly a solid sheet of white falling from the heavens. Evan raced to the bundle the medic had tossed and discovered blankets. He handed Isaac one and wrapped another around himself. Though I protested, Isaac gave me Evan's coat and wrapped himself up in the blanket. "We have to get moving," Evan said. His voice was a normal tone and pitch, odd sounding after the screaming and shouting and mechanical noise. "Which way?" he asked Isaac. When Isaac pointed, he holstered his gun and said, "If you have water, drink it now. Let's go."

We drank the rest of our water and headed down the mountain, following the road, though the term applied only loosely. It was new track, piles of stumps and trees to either side, the earth a half-frozen mess beneath us. My feet slipped in wet mud, and I stumbled over a freezing bulge between two ruts. My frozen hands were in my pockets. I was shivering so hard I could barely walk, and seeing was nearly impossible through icy tears and mucus and swirling snow. Hours passed, or it seemed that way. I stopped trying to see the track ahead and concentrated on the white blanket in front of me. When it suddenly stopped, I crashed into Isaac. "What?" I asked. My voice was a croak.

"The road's stopped."

I looked around. Equipment was gathered in a clearing. Earthmovers, bulldozers, stacks of construction equipment. A flatbed truck loaded with supplies and brick. A mortar maker. And no way out.

"Over here," Evan shouted. I turned to his voice and saw him on the other side of the clearing. When we got to him, we saw an old logging road meandering through the trees. It was a well-used, muddy mess. "They came through here. Will this take us to the pickup point?"

I looked at him. His lips were blue tinged. Isaac's were gray. I pulled off the coat and held it out to Evan. "No," he said.

I tried an eye roll, but I was too cold to make it work, so I dropped the coat on the ground and ripped the blanket off him in a single motion. "Come here," I said to Isaac. I wrapped the blanket around him, then lifted the front edge and crawled into the blankets with Isaac. "We'll be slower, and we may fall, but we'll survive. And you can pull the gun if you need to. Put it in the pocket so you can get to it easier."

This time Evan didn't argue and retrieved the coat, putting it on. With snow so thick it was like a sheet surging in front of our eyes, we started down the logging road. I don't know how long it took us, but suddenly I felt something harder and smooth beneath my feet and I realized we had been walking along a real road for several minutes. In the distance, I heard a horn blowing, three beeps, then silence then three beeps, a continuous signal.

After what seemed like days, or even weeks, later, I heard Isaac grunt and looked up to see two lights ahead in the snow. Headlights. There were headlights to go with the beeping.

We picked up our pace, Isaac almost carrying me. We reached the lights. It was a van, dark green, sitting in the middle of the road. The doors opened and the air inside rolled out, a searing flash of heat. I heard voices and fell inside.

I found myself against a leather seat, so warm it was like a little piece of heaven. I closed my eyes and breathed the heat. Someone handed me a cup of something and I wrapped my frozen fingers around the warmth. It wasn't full, which was the only reason I didn't slosh the contents out with my uncontrollable shivers. I managed to get the cup to my mouth and sipped it. *Soup.* The taste was an explosion of chicken, pepper and carrots. It felt scalding hot, but it was the best thing I had ever tasted. My teeth made little cracking sounds as I drank.

Jane crawled into my lap and put an arm around me. "Don't cry, Aunt Tyler." She wiped my face with a tissue, the weave harsh on my skin, and I saw mucus and slime come away. "Don't cry."

"I'm not cryin', shweetheart." I tried to enunciate, but couldn't. I tried to focus, but could make out only a pale blur surrounded by a darker halo. Her face and hair.

She laughed once, and I heard relief in the single chuckle. "Then why are tears pouring down your face?"

"Col'. Jus' col'. Bu'de soup is good. Too hot, but good. You ha' no idea how good." My shivers suddenly worsened and I had to put down the cup. It was the top of a Thermos jar. The soup wasn't steaming, and I realized it wasn't as hot as I had thought.

I took another breath of the blessedly warm air and blinked, becoming aware. The van was moving slowly down a mountain, headlights bright against falling snow. Lopez was driving. Evan was in the seat beside him.

Aunt Matilda was in the back with Isaac and Jane and me. Lopez was speaking and I had trouble concentrating on his words as lethargy stole over me. Something about a hospital. Then I remembered. Jubal was at a hospital. "Yesh. Take us to de hospital," I said, my words a mumble. I met Lopez's eyes in the rearview mirror. As if stunned, he looked back at me before gunning the motor and adding speed to our progress.

I shuddered once and closed my eyes. We were safe.

16

The nurses at the hospital treated us for dehydration and hypothermia, which was no fun at all. I had hoped it would be a prescription of hot cocoa and heated blankets, and got heated IV fluids and blood drawn instead. Because my body mass was so small, I had a lower core temperature than the men, so I got the most attention from the needle-bearing fiends in scrub attire. Whoopee. At least they sent us home, though my body still felt cold and prickly all over, like I had hives or the first telltale sting of poison ivy.

I climbed the stairs to the loft with feet so tired they dragged. Behind me, Aunt Matilda and Evan were closing up the shop and setting the alarm system. Jane was with them. Lopez, who had stayed with us throughout the evening, drove off in the still-swirling snow, his lights raking the shop and up the stairs.

I used the extra key—mine was in the SUV on the side of a mountain—and stuck it in the lock. I turned it and pulled it out, then placed my hand on the knob.

I felt like I was being sucked through the keyhole, a feeling so strong, so vivid, it was more reality than vision. I saw the apartment from a higher plane. From the other side of the door.

I walked through the place, hugging myself. It was cold. The little redheaded tramp likes it cold. She'd better. She's getting enough of it right now. I laughed and it sounded ugly. I modulated the tone and laughed again, the sound prettier. It echoed through the cold apartment.

Only cheap people live above a store. Commoners. Shopkeepers. Trash.

I touched a candle, my nails a bright and cheerful peach that matched my toenails and my bra and underpants. I wasn't trash. I lifted a bowl and turned it over. It was an antique. A Roseville. I stifled the impulse to throw it to the floor to see it shatter. I set it carefully back on the shelf. I wasn't trash.

I wrapped my arms around myself. It had all gone wrong. All of it. What should I do? Had I done the right thing? If I had kept at him, would he have given himself to me? And what about Quinn? He wasn't supposed to die. No one was supposed to die. It was all supposed to be so easy. Get the gold, make David fall in love with me again, get married. Live happily ever after. David had been in love with me once. I know he was, I could feel it. It should have been easy to make him love me again. It should have been so easy.

I saw David, the memory of David, in the closet. I saw myself slip out of my dress. Walk toward him. He was handcuffed to the bed. He couldn't say no.

I snapped my hand away from the knob, breaking the vision. Sickness rose up in me, acid gorge, bile tasting. I stared at the knob. She had touched it twice. When she entered and when she left. And she had a key.

Opening the door, I stepped inside. She had been here. She had been in my house. David knew the security code to the house and shop. He had given it to her. What had she done to make him give her the code?

Suddenly I understood. He hadn't been able to tell me when I scanned for him. He had been…conflicted. Or afraid.

Of what? Of whom? But he had given her the code. Why had Davie given her the code? So I could figure out who she was? None of it made sense.

Behind me, Jane and Evan and Aunt Matilda climbed the stairs. I entered the loft, catching Dyno as she sprinted for freedom.

Jane lay on the sofa with Dyno stretched out on her chest, which rose and fell with sleep. Evan and I were curled up on the floor in front of the blazing fire, the gas turned up so high the flames roared and jumped with the air flow. We were huddled under blankets, while Aunt Matilda was bare armed, sitting in the rocker, as far away as she could be and still be in the loft, overheated but uncomplaining. We had just finished a second helping of yeast rolls and soup. This time the soup was actually hot, and not the room-temperature brew that had felt like it was boiling in the rescue van.

Having waited patiently while we showered and dressed and ate, Aunt Matilda now asked, "Do you remember what happened?" It was a strange question and we looked at her, confused. "The doctor warned me that hypothermia could affect your short-term memory among other things. So, do you remember much about this afternoon?"

I shivered, big horrid, earthquake shivers that rattled my teeth. When the movement abated, I shrugged. "Maybe the doctor was right. I don't remember much about today." I didn't add that I didn't want to remember.

Evan said, "I'd estimate that we walked through the snow for more than three miles after Jubal was airlifted out, and were nearly three hours without proper clothing on the mountain in a winter storm. Before that, Jubal was shot. That's about it. I admit the details are kinda muzzy." We smiled at each other as he pushed his bowl and mug away and laced his fingers through mine.

Aunt Matilda watched the gesture, and she seemed pleased. Of course, she would be. She had probably planned out our attraction from birth. I shivered again. She tossed me another blanket, though I wasn't shivering from the cold this time.

We had all been dangerously hypothermic when we piled in the SUV. Lopez had made it to the hospital in record time, even with the snow. I had no memory of the drive into town at all.

At the hospital, while being treated for exposure, we had talked to the police investigator on call, who just happened to be Jack Madison, a man not happy to be dealing with us again, and even less happy to have a gunshot on a mountain crime scene that was now under several inches of snow and wouldn't be accessible for days, if not weeks. Or maybe he was just not happy at being called back to work at the end of a quiet shift. He had questioned us for over an hour, stopping only when the ER doctor told him we needed rest. It seemed doctor's orders superceded even a cop's persistent urgency.

Now, dressed and warm, but still feeling the chill of the storm in our bones and teeth, we waited for news. Isaac was at the hospital, and had called us twice to update us on Jubal. My best friend had been to surgery for repair of the artery in his upper arm, along with tendon and muscle damage, and had been admitted to ICU in stable condition. He had lost a lot of blood and been given two units to replace some of what he had lost. There was no damage to the nerve that served the arm, but the tendons and muscles at the rotator cuff had not been so lucky. He would likely need more surgery to correct the problems there, but he was alive and expected to live, barring complications—doctor-speak for, *Don't sue me if he croaks anyway.*

Evan squeezed my hand. "Hmm?" I could tell he had asked me something and I had missed it entirely.

"How did you know about the shooter?"

I blinked. *The shooter?*

"Before he shot, you yelled, 'Get down.' You dove to the ground before the shot."

I flicked a glance at Aunt Matilda, who was rocking and watching us with something like blissful self-satisfaction. I pulled my hand away from Evan's and laced my fingers in my lap. My nails were ragged, broken. I didn't remember tearing them on the mountain. "I, uh...I was in the head of the shooter. I touched the quartz to try to get Davie. I did, and it was weird. But then I saw this scene, sort of superimposed on the first one. I saw four people in the crosshairs of a rifle scope. The scope settled on a short woman with her bare hand on a rock. It was me."

Aunt Matilda had the gaze of a hungry hawk looking at its next meal. She was no longer rocking, but sitting completely still. "I heard—no, *heard* is the wrong word. I just sort of knew what he was thinking. *'The troublemaker.'* I was inside his head." I peeled off a broken nail, stroking the ragged edge with my thumb, remembering. "My finger tightened on the trigger, and I took a deep breath and let it out. Long-range shooters do that to steady their bodies for a shot?" I looked the question at Evan who was watching me with a penetrating green gaze, his face intent.

"The man thought, 'I'll kill her. The one who's touching my gold. I'll kill them all.' And I screamed out to get down, and I fell."

It hit me then. Just as always, the gift had failed me. I had warning and Jubal had still been shot, because I wasn't good enough. The gift wasn't good enough. *Ashes and spit.*

"And before that, when you scanned for Davie? What about then?" Aunt Matilda asked.

"I found him." Exhaustion pulled at my shoulders and bowed my spine. I had the remnants of a headache that

Tylenol hadn't helped. I rubbed my forehead, then dropped my hand back to my lap. "A woman came into the room. I think she was one of the first people who kidnapped Davie and she was giving him up to another group of people. And I sensed, I knew, that she had hurt him but he wouldn't let me see how. I couldn't tell what she had done to him. He was—" I searched for a word but couldn't find the right one and so settled on "—ashamed. Embarrassed. So it must have been pretty awful, what she did.

"She had left a ring on his bedside table. I recognized it. Jubal made the ring several years ago. A gold band with rubies. I remember it was a specialty piece, a commissioned work. But I didn't get the chance to ask him about it before the shooting started." The skin on my hands was dry. I needed more cream. "All I remember is that the client provided the rubies from a damaged family heirloom and Jubal worked them into the design. I could swear that I've seen it recently, but I can't remember where. If I can't ask Jubal about it tomorrow, I'll start a search in Bloodstone's records. Maybe I'll find who commissioned the ring. But even if I do, I'll know who took Davie, but I won't know who has him now."

Aunt Matilda walked over and handed me a nail file and I smoothed the broken nail as I talked. "There was a negotiation. That's what Davie called it. Like a bargain struck. Someone else was about to take Davie. I got the feeling that they already tried to take him once and things broke down. And I don't know why or who. I don't know anything."

"But you do know gold is at the heart of this problem, whatever it is." Aunt Matilda bent over us, gathering the bowls and tableware. "You know it's important enough for someone to try to kill you for it. And you're still alive, though he had you in the crosshairs of a rifle scope. It seems your gift was useful after all. I'm turning in. You young people don't stay up too late. And drink plenty of water to combat the dehydration."

* * *

Again I couldn't sleep. There were too many people in and around my loft—Aunt Matilda and Jane bedded down only feet or inches away, Evan asleep in the workroom of the shop—and too many people missing: Jubal and Isaac at the hospital, Davie gone. Nothing was right. Nothing was where or as it should be. Wide awake, jittery, apprehensive and exhausted, I used the laptop and went online. It had been days since I had checked my e-mail and emptied my spam filters, which I did quickly. When I saw three files with attachments on investment folios I almost deleted them, until I remembered wanting to look into the companies who had offered for Davie's land—ComPack, HFM, Inc., and Julian Rakes Mining. I had forgotten that Isaac was going to get the investment broker to take a look.

Because none of the companies had asked for rights to the exact area where we found the gold, I didn't know which one to concentrate on, so I downloaded the files and opened the first at random. I quickly scanned all the info on ComPack, and looked over their list of board members and chief investors. It was amazing what you could learn if you pretended to be a potential investor. Nothing I saw looked suspicious.

The Henderson Family Mines was wholly family owned and the broker had had little luck with them. That left Julian Rakes.

Within minutes, I hit paydirt. I stared at the list of company employees, focusing on the name of the president's executive assistant. The hair on my arms stood up and cold chills raced across my flesh. I remembered seeing her face at the county council meeting. Another memory assaulted me. She had been wearing the ring I saw on Davie's bedside, the globed gold and ruby spray. *Eloise Carter.* Was she another nutcase who had once thought she was going to marry my brother? Had she been in my apartment?

Further down, on a list of board of directors, was Jack Madison, detective with the local cops. I remembered the cheap haircut, the off-the-rack clothes, and the cop's total lack of style. How did a cop get enough money, power or leverage to sit on the board of a mining company that was big enough to be traded on the U.S. stock exchange?

"Are you sure you want to do this?" Evan asked. "Yesterday left you pretty frazzled."

"Thanks a lot. Every girl wants to know she looks shredded," I said, as I allowed Lopez to wire me up with a hidden microphone. His hands came up under my shirt, over my boobs and clipped the mike to my bra. I was shocked at the familiarity but kept my mouth closed. Evan was far too amused at my expression as it was. I was just glad I'd worn a new bra with both lace and shaping and not a ratty one with pilled fabric and webby elastic. I had also shaved my legs and washed my hair, piling it up in a loose bun on the crown of my head with a butterfly hair clasp inlaid with faux ivory and faux turquoise. I looked good and I knew it, and I was only halfway sure Lopez had be so familiar.

The shop phone rang and Evan handed it to me. I answered the call while Lopez tested the mike and then started on the hidden camera in the lapel button of my best power suit, an ocean-green silk with tight-fitting jacket and short skirt. Thankfully, the camera went on top of my clothes and around into the lining of the jacket. "Bloodstone Inc., Tyler St. Claire," I said into the phone.

"Tyler!"

I could tell from Isaac's voice that he had good news, and relief flooded through me. "How's Jubal?"

"Coming home tomorrow. Crabby. Liking the morphine way too much. Did I say coming home tomorrow?"

Sudden tears flooded my eyes as his words assuaged my

deeper fears. "You did," I said, wiping the tears carefully. "Is he awake enough for me to talk to him?"

"Sure, hold on."

The next voice was Jubal's, slurred by drugs and very happy for a man in pain. "Tyler, baby. Howsh my mind-reading, redheaded, gypsy queen?"

Through laughter I said, "Holy medical miracles, Batman. It's alive, I tell you, alive!"

"You're mishing up your movie genres, honeybunch, but ish no matter. Ish uh thought that counts. Are you coming to take me home tomorrow? They're coming to take me away ho-ho, he-he, ha-ha, they're coming to take me away!"

"You're stoned out of your gourd, aren't you?"

"Totally. Thish ish really good stuff."

"Yes. I'll be there. And I'll bring flowers tonight."

"Skip the flowers, honeybunch. Bring me shom decent food. They got me drinking my meals, and I'm decades away from finding broth and melted Jell-O a tasty meal. Not while I shtill got my own teeth."

We chatted a few more minutes and I said, "Okay, Jubal, focus. Business question. Do you remember making a gold-and-ruby ring a few years ago?" I described the delicate circlet and what I could remember about it, while Lopez went back to work on my bra. I slapped at him twice but had the feeling that he found me amusing, rather than someone who might kick him where it hurt if he got fresh again.

"Yesh, I remember that one. Isaac, don't flirt with the doctor. Hesh old enough to be your uncle." Drugged laughter. "Some cop commissioned it. Had the rubies from his mother's engagement ring. Ugly thing from the fifties. No class at all, that ring. The one from the fifties, not mine. It was exquisite."

"Do you remember who it was? Maybe Jack Madison?"

"Yeah, yeah! Guy with a neck like a turkey? Yeah, thash him."

I nodded to Evan and Lopez, said my goodbye to Jubal and hung up. "Jack Madison."

"Well. I reckon that makes this an official unofficial investigation. Don't it?" Lopez said. "Nice bra, ma'am. I really like the black lace."

Evan looked interested. I blushed. "Stuff it, Lopez. Let's get this on the road. Does this surveillance stuff work okay?"

"Yep," Evan said. "Loud and clear. Lopez and I'll be in the van parked just down the road. Do you remember the panic word?"

"Lucky."

"Good. You say 'lucky,' and I'll be there in an instant."

"If you get anything we can use, I'll take it to my boss and then to a judge," Lopez said. "With any luck, we'll have a warrant by two."

"Wait a minute," I said. "We don't have a warrant?"

Lopez didn't look up, too busy with a round disc and the front of my jacket. "You're not a law-enforcement officer. You're a private citizen who decided to tape her interview."

I didn't like the way that sounded. "This isn't legal, is it?"

"It isn't exactly *illegal*," Lopez said.

"Not exactly," Evan parroted.

"Ashes and spit," I said.

"That picked up nicely," Lopez said. "Let's try it again."

My appointment with Julian Rakes Mining had been hurriedly set up just after the company opened for business, worked into the president's lunchtime schedule between corporate meetings. I was getting in by a ruse and a lie. I had suggested that I was Davie's executor, which I was, and that I was ready to negotiate a buyout or a deal on mineral rights, which I wasn't. But I did have a list of questions suggested by Evan and Lopez, and I had the letters of offering found in Davie's box of papers.

Keenly aware that everything I did was to be recorded and

viewed, I went to the bathroom just before leaving Blood-stone. If there was anything worse than having Lopez comment on my underwear, it would be for the men to see me in the bathroom. I'd have made a pathetic undercover cop.

Totally entertained by the cops-and-robbers stuff, Noe offered to run the shop alone all day in exchange for an extra Saturday off in April. Traditionally, Monday was slow this time of year, and Noe was getting the better part of the bargain, but I was in no position to haggle. She even came in early to open the shop and help me accessorize.

What did a jewelry designer wear when going undercover? According to Noe, it required minimalist, traditional and pricey. She picked out three items in our current stock—an estate ring with a large, square, blue emerald stone surrounded by tiny sapphires we had gotten cheap, a gold bracelet with faceted aquamarine and emerald stones, and a necklace made of interlocking red-gold leaves, all of which complemented the shade of green in the silk suit. Maybe Noe had a point. Good underwear, expensive fabrics and pricey jewelry did make me feel confident, even with only four hours of sleep. And no woman wearing Manolo Blahnik shoes could ever feel insecure.

What didn't add to my sense of assurance was the sight of Aunt Matilda and Jane at the shop front door when I was ready to leave. Aunt Matilda had a look of pique, and Jane was filled with excitement. I had tried to keep my thoughts shielded from them as we planned today's little adventure. Clearly I had failed. The sight of them brought back the understanding that I was going after Davie. And that if I didn't find him, he might never be found. Ever.

Jane rushed to me, throwing her arms around me and burying her face in my stomach. "You save my daddy. He's in trouble and you can save him. I know it." I wrapped my arms around her, keeping my eyes on Aunt Matilda.

"We were trying a simple read of the Major Arcana and the court cards in a primary Celtic Cross spread," the older woman said. "Jane pulled the Knight of Swords, the Tower, the High Priestess, the Ace of Swords, Justice reversed." She stopped as she saw something in my eyes or in my mind. I wanted to push past her into the street, but I blocked the impulse.

"Go on," I said, fighting to get the words out. I hugged Jane to me, keeping my wall in place with a fierce effort.

"The King of Cups. And the World. This means something to you, doesn't it?"

A feeling settled on me, a feeling that I knew something but didn't know what, as if it was there on the tip of my tongue or hiding in the shadows of my brain. "Yes. Sort of. It's weird, but yes." When she just waited, I asked, "What did Jane get?"

"I don't know. She jumped up and ran down here. I followed." But Aunt Matilda was troubled and not bothering to hide it.

My niece pulled away, a euphoric smile lighting her face. "You're my Knight of Swords. Bad stuff is happening right now, but you're going into battle, ready to use your gifts and fight. Someone from the past is involved. I don't know who, but you do. At first it's going to go against you, but you're a fighter. You'll find Daddy and bring him home. I *know* it."

I touched her head, almost in blessing. "I'll do my best."

"We shall pray for you," Aunt Matilda said, the tone formal. I nodded and went through the door and into the morning, Evan and Lopez behind me.

The trip to the Asheville office of Julian Rakes Mining took up the rest of the morning and I was glad to let Evan drive my Tracker while Lopez followed in a van. The snow was still falling, but snowplows were clearing the primary roads and rock salt and sand had been put on bridges to provide traction. Recognizing my state of mind, Evan put on a classical station and didn't offer conversation. I put my head back, closed my eyes and tried to rehearse my lines, but Jane's reading kept intruding. Especially the one phrase: *Someone from the past is involved. I don't know who, but you do.*

17

Feeling like the fraud I was, I entered Julian Rakes Mining with an assumed saunter. The building was the East Coast office of a company that had national and international interests, and the decor showed it. It boasted a stone-and-concrete exterior with arches, huge paned windows and exceptional landscaping. Inside, it was all leather seating, soft-charcoal-and-taupe marble flooring. Display cases in the antechamber—it was too fancy to be called a waiting room—exhibited one of the finest private mineral collections I had ever seen. The seating was scattered throughout the room, positioned to allow visitors who were forced to wait to view the success of the company. A well-dressed receptionist provided me with a cup of decent tea as I wandered through the cases.

The collection revealed finished amethysts and sapphires, an uncut emerald the size of my fist and carvings of charoite and jade, some that looked ancient. There were both uncut, unpolished stone and shaped specimens of moonstone and wonderstone, lapis and hauynite, chalcedony, quartz in all the colors of the rainbow, jasper and agate and beautiful specimens of opals. It took my breath away. But it was the gold that drew my attention.

They had raw gold in wonderful varieties, from nuggets

the size of my thumb to an artist's three-dimensional rendition of gold dust caught in creek-bottom sand. There was one specimen that looked like a fountain of gold spouting up from a quartz base. There were several samples of gold wire, similar to those Davie had sent us, but with cards for each indicating where and when they had been discovered. If the company wanted to impress and intimidate a visitor with the exhibit, they were successful. I was properly cowed.

After a fifteen-minute wait, and only ten minutes after our scheduled meeting time, I was escorted by the underling through three hallways into a subdued and tasteful office. Eloise Carter rose and came around her desk to meet me, right hand outstretched. On her left ring finger was the gold-and-ruby ring Jubal had created.

"Tyler St. Claire. So good to see you again," she said with a professional smile. "You may not remember me, but I once dated your brother."

"Eloise." I smiled back, thinking about pulling her hair out but instead opening myself for a really good read. If I got lucky, I might pluck Davie's whereabouts from her. I took her hand. It was cool, the grip firm and practiced. From her thoughts I got a sense of frustration beneath a swirl of images—her computer keyboard, a clipboard, the phone and the scent of jasmine that collided unpleasantly with her perfume. "I remember. You must be the reason I was able to get an appointment so quickly." As I released her hand, a wisp of something brushed across the wall in my mind. It was familiar, this feeling, with a trace of darkness at its core. I set the notion aside to be considered at a later time.

"Actually, you're lucky to have called today. Mr. Rakes, the CEO, just happens to be in town for a series of meetings before taking the company jet to Colorado. He was delighted when I brought your name to him, as he's been interested in acquiring rights to land your brother owned. He and Davie had spoken several times. I was the one who introduced them," she said modestly.

The admission threw me. I suddenly knew that Davie had asked Eloise to arrange the meeting. Davie had pursued Eloise for just that purpose.

"Mr. Rakes is with someone but it should only be a moment. Have a seat." She indicated one of two upholstered chairs in front of her desk and I took one. Though she was smiling as she sat beside me, there was a shadow beneath her words, and when she spoke, her eyes slid away, not meeting mine. Hiding something. Hiding Davie?

I took a shot. "I remember you dating Davie. You made a good-looking couple." It was an inane comment, but it had the desired results. That shadow cracked a bit and the emotion beneath crawled out. Her hatred clambered along my skin and I had to resist the urge to shake it off my flesh.

"I had hopes we were going somewhere, until my sister got her claws into him."

That threw me. "Sister?"

"Gail." The hate twisted her face for an instant before it smoothed out. "Davie and I were getting on so great until she stepped into the picture. But then, Gail always did go after any man I wanted." She laughed, attempting to sound airy but succeeding only in sounding wounded.

My mind reeled. "Gail Speeler? She's your sister?"

"Can you believe it?" she said, stilted. "Different as night and day. Same mother, different fathers. Typical dysfunctional family. She was really peeved that I was seeing you today."

From a door behind me, several men and a woman filed out, talking about lunch. I didn't even turn around. Gail Speeler and Eloise Carter?

"If you'll give me a moment, I'll get the lunches." She stood and smoothed her dress as she went to the far side of her desk and bent out of sight. I heard a swish of escaping air that I identified as the sound a small refrigerator made when opened. When Eloise stood, she was holding four plastic delivery boxes. "I hope chicken salad from Diamonte's is okay." I nodded. "You'll be dining with Mr. Rakes, a visitor from Washington, and a local businessman in the small conference room."

The intercom buzzed softly and she bent away, balancing the plastic containers with one hand as she punched a button. The voice on the intercom said, "I'll be a moment, Eloise. Please see that our visitors are comfortable and allow them to start lunch if they wish."

"Yes, sir." She removed her hand and offered me the practiced smile from earlier. "Let me get the luncheon set up and I'll be right back."

"Sure," I said, not really thinking. Alone, I struggled to put it together. Gail and Eloise were sisters. Rivals. Both dating Davie. Gold. Tree huggers. Land and developing. Davie wanting to see the CEO of a mining company. The Roman Trio and money laundering. It was all coming together, but it left odd patches of reasoning where nothing seemed to fit. Something still wasn't right. "Gail Speeler and Eloise are sisters. Can you believe that?" I asked the mike softly, knowing there wouldn't be an answer. There hadn't been time to rig two-way communication with Evan and Lopez.

I heard a muted thump from outside the room, followed by a soft clatter that I felt through the soles of my feet rather than heard. Phones were ringing. Several doors opened and closed, all sounds that had been there, just below my conscious awareness, for several minutes.

I was alone long enough to get fidgety. When I checked my watch, I saw I had been inside for nearly forty-five minutes. I stood and wandered the office, going behind the desk to spy a credenza with the doors ajar. It was like an invitation to peek, so I nudged the doors open, exposing a microwave, a small fridge, a wet bar and a computer printer. The doors above were closed and I didn't dare. In the trash can under her desk was a plastic container with the remains of salad and a smudge of dressing smeared on the top.

I moved back to the guest side of the desk and looked out the door Eloise had taken to the hall. It was empty and I was about to turn away when I saw Eloise, her face covered with her hands, rush out of a room, cross the hallway in a flash and enter another door. From her mind I caught a hint of panic, falling colors in melting sunset hues, hysteria. Surprised, not quite sure what I had seen or felt, uncertain why I was getting colors and scents from Eloise instead of images, I almost followed.

"Ms. St. Claire. What a pleasure."

I whirled to see a man coming from the doorway behind Eloise's desk. He was trim, tanned, with Donald Trump style and smile, a far better haircut, and a suit that screamed Italy.

"Julian Rakes," he said, as he took my hand in a two-handed grip meant to charm and establish control all at once. "I was working a deal with your brother. Pity about his disappearance. Eloise had been so certain he would be found right away. It's been hard on her, so I know it must be devastating for you and his daughter."

His thoughts didn't swarm around me like most people's, overlapping with other thoughts, observations or needs. They body-slammed me, hard and forceful and utterly directed. He had a game plan for today, and he didn't intend to allow me to get away without seeing it to fruition. For him, nothing else in the world mattered except his current goal.

I pulled my hand away, wanting to wipe it on my skirt. This was a man totally without conscience, a man who would destroy a competitor in an instant with no hint of compassion or remorse and had done so repeatedly, with no shame or guilt. He was looking at me oddly, the flashy smile shrinking.

"I'm sorry," I said, struggling to remember what he had said, trying to cover. "Yes. It's been hard. Eloise has been kind. And I…" My mind grappled for polite phrases drilled into me as child. "I thank you for seeing me on such short notice."

It must have been the right line because the smile was instantly cured. Mr. Friendly, Mr. Just-Want-You-To-Be-Happy had completely hidden Mr. Stab-You-In-The-Back-Without-A-Second-Thought. "My pleasure. Let's go to lunch, shall we?"

I managed a nod and he guided me down the hall Eloise had taken, his hand at the small of my back. With a mental crash, I shut my wall against his touch and mind.

Sociopath. The word rose in my mind. *He's a sociopath. Use great care.*

It was Aunt Matilda, whispering admonitions. For once, I didn't order her to get away. It did occur to me to wonder how I was hearing her and not the thoughts of the man beside me, but there wasn't time for that now.

I nodded and let Rakes guide me down the hall. Two thoughts leaked past my barriers. To Julian Rakes I was an easy mark, an emotional little woman with big issues he could use against me. And he was concealing a strong sense of expectation. I straightened my back and stood aside as he opened the door to the conference room. I had an instant to wonder if it was Davie behind door number one, but knew that was too much to ask. I wouldn't get that lucky. The door swung open and Rakes stepped back, gesturing me ahead without glancing at the room.

Bracing myself, I walked in. A man sat at the far end of a long, oval table set with lunch for four. It took a moment for me to assemble a coherent picture of what was really before me. I gasped, a shadow gasp in my mind echoed the reaction.

He was leaning back in his chair, mouth open. Blood covered the right side of his face. A round neat hole marked the other side. He'd been shot.

Steady, Aunt Matilda whispered, sending strength through me.

Without a single thought, I turned and gripped Rake's arm, opening my mind to him. He was smiling, looking down at me expectantly. He had thought to surprise me with this man as part of a ploy to unnerve me, to make me feel off balance. I knew instantly he hadn't shot him. He expected Colin Hornsburn to be alive.

Yanking on his suit coat, I pulled him into the doorway and watched his expression as it fell. *Dismay* clouded his mind, followed by several odd thoughts at once. *I'll have to postpone the trip to Colorado—what a hassle. There will be police involved. Where the hell is Eloise? Lunch is ruined. There's blood on my conference chair. Shame about Colin.*

"Yeah. Not his lucky day, is it," I said. And then the shock set in and I sat down fast.

Evan was in the room more quickly than I thought possible, or time had done one of those weird dilation things again. *Einstein, beware.* A crazy-woman laugh tittered at the back of my throat. Evan had his gun out, his ID and badge in the other hand. Lopez appeared right behind him. Feeling lightheaded, I remained in the chair closest to the door and swiveled away from the gruesome sight at the far end of the room. I put my head between my knees and concentrated on not passing out. Bits of dialogue swirled around me.

"—don't know. We just opened the door and found him."

"How many exits to the room? Whose—"

"Three. The larger conference—"

"Who was joining you for lunch?"

"Hornsburn, myself, Eloise, my secretary—"

"Where—"

"I don't know where she is. I haven't seen her in—"

I raised my head, feeling sick to my stomach. Using both hands to lever myself upright, I stood on wobbly knees and made my way to the doorway where I leaned, trying to find my balance.

Evan took my hand in his and moved it away from the doorjamb. "Don't touch. Crime Scene is on the way."

"Oh, goody. More red fingerprint dust over everything." I giggled, the sound high-pitched, half-mad. Below my cackles, I could hear the sound of sirens growing closer. Someone had killed Colin Hornsburn. Which pretty much eliminated him as a suspect, didn't it? And I still didn't have Davie. I still didn't have my brother. "I'm going to be sick," I said, feeling my gorge rise.

"Across the hall," Rakes said.

Evan half carried me, pushing open the door to expose a room done in pale pink marble, a color calculated to make any grown woman hurl on sight.

A soft moan sounded, bright and sharp against the stone walls. Sunset colors, with a darker, deeper center, caught my attention. *Anguish.* "Eloise?"

Evan, about to let me go, drew his weapon and pushed me aside. "Where?"

I pointed to the stalls at the end of the wall to my right. "The middle one, I think."

Evan moved cautiously down the room passing a backless chaise in shades of gold and rose, a velvet throw at its foot. A long, framed mirror above gave back his reflection. He holstered his gun and tapped on the stall door. "Ms. Carter? Open the door. We'll get you some help."

"I didn't do it. I just found him like that." Her words were slurred.

I followed down the row of stalls and sat on the chaise. I

was feeling better, which was odd. But the colors I now associated with Eloise were changing rapidly, growing duller at the center, paler at the edges. Her breathing was fast and uneven, an echoing rasp in the room. I could see her crumpled form on the floor of the stall. She appeared to be draped over the toilet.

"I didn't...do it. I can't take it anymore." Her voice was rough with tears. "I can't."

"Do you know who shot him?" Evan asked, his voice suddenly gentle. When she didn't answer, he said, "If you think you know who shot him, you have to tell me, Ms. Carter. I can help."

"I can't." She crumpled farther, now lying on the floor. "But—"

"Evan!" I interrupted and pointed. A thin spray of red, like the colors in Eloise's mind splattered across the floor. An instant later another followed. *Blood.*

"Get an ambulance!" he shouted. I raced to the door and yelled for help, then rushed back. Evan was on his knees, trying to get his shoulders under the door to Eloise.

I shoved him out of the way and lay down on the pink marble, slid my much smaller body under the door. She hadn't cut the wrist, but across the middle of the elbow. I gripped her upper arm to stop the pumping. Even in the pink light, she was whiter than death. A knife, bloody and wicked sharp, was on her dress.

"She did both arms," Evan said from over my head in the next stall. "I'm coming in."

I looked at her other arm, and it was cut as well, but not as deeply. Evan's new hiking shoes landed on the toilet seat, and he leaned over and unlatched the stall door. Jumping over me, he pulled us both into the center of the ladies' room, leaving a swash of blood across the slick marble. He took her other arm and applied pressure. Blood was everywhere.

In the stall, the water in the toilet was stained red, and the back wall over it was sprayed with crimson, as if she had waved her cut arms in the air. I saw an image of Eloise trying to cut the second arm while the first pumped wildly. I looked at her, her face and hair splattered with sticky gore. Evan reached behind him and grabbed the velvet throw, covering her with it.

Could I have stopped it? Should I have known? I recalled the sunset colors, the stunning dark red of a dying sun. Or the color of blood. How did one know the difference? Shouldn't I have seen darkness, instead of blood? The darkness of depression, of self-immolation?

The outer door burst open and emergency workers entered, carrying a huge tool kit and a stretcher folded on its side. Chaos ensued and I was pushed to the wall, out of the way. I looked down at my hands. Blood was caked in the ridges and nails. I wondered if this whole awful scene had been taped in the van outside.

I watched in a state of suspended animation as the two workers in dark blue emergency uniforms stabilized Eloise, binding her elbows, taking her blood pressure, starting IVs, sticking wires to her chest to check her heartbeat, putting her on the stretcher. Once again, the conversation flowed around me, speculation, questions, answers, bits and pieces of the truth. I let them pass by like water around a boulder in a stream. Only one comment made me react.

Lopez and Evan were talking in undertones as Eloise was taken out the door on the stretcher. The room emptied, leaving us three inside alone. Evan said, "The four were going to eat lunch, a business meeting."

Four? I remembered the lunch container in the trash at Eloise's desk, and something Rakes had said. "We're being joined at luncheon by a local businessman and a visitor from Washington."

"Which four?" I asked as I roused myself from a slump. "Who was going to eat lunch?" They turned and looked at me, propped against the wall, smeared with blood. I spared a glance at my reflection in the mirror. Yep. Pretty yucky. The crazy laugh tickled again, but I forced it away. "Who did Rakes say was eating lunch?" I repeated when neither responded.

Evan said, "You, the secretary, the victim and Rakes."

"Eloise had already eaten. Her lunch container was in the trash. You probably have it on tape from when I went behind her desk. Rakes told me we were eating with a businessman, who I can presume to be Hornsburn, and a person from Washington."

The two cops looked at one another and grinned. One said, "Oh, yeah." The other said, "Gotcha," a harmony of meaning. They disappeared from the room at a run. I looked at myself in the mirror again. My green silk suit was ruined. Instantly, I repented the thought. Colin Hornsburn had lost his life today. Eloise had nearly lost hers. The last thing I should be worried about was my clothes.

I should be worrying about who killed Hornsburn. If it wasn't an employee, then someone had gotten inside. I hoped JRM's security cameras were as good as Davie's.

Tiredly, I pushed away from the wall and went to the sinks to begin the process of getting clean enough to drive myself home. I turned on the gold-plated faucet, the spigot in the shape of a rose, and put my hands under the warm water. Blood swirled into the basin and down the drain, the spiral a brutal shade, darker than the delicate pink marble sink.

A pile of wires and listening devices on the car seat beside me, I was maneuvering my Tracker over rutted snow around a mountain curve when my cell phone rang. I flipped it open. "Tyler."

"Tyler, where are you?" Evan said.

"I'm trying to get home through a blinding snowstorm while you play cops and robbers."

"Cute. We're on the way back, too, via a different route Lopez says is faster. We'll see. Yeah, yeah, just drive," he said to someone else. Mouth back at the phone, he said, "Just thought you might want to know, we got Eloise to talk. She claims she saw someone running through the hallway and out through an employee door. She thinks she can identify him. We're betting she saw Rakes and just won't say so until her lawyer gets here." I could sense the repressed glee in Evan's voice. "And she says she knows where David is."

Electric heat ricocheted through me. My heart sped up and I blew out a breath that went from the top of my head to the bottoms of my feet. Tears prickled in my eyes and my throat spasmed. I couldn't reply to Evan.

"You there?"

"Yes," I managed. "I'm here."

"She's using him as a bargaining chip to get a deal. Of course, Rakes says he doesn't know where David is. He's insulted that we think he would do anything so stupid as kidnap anyone. Not so illegal or immoral, mind you, just not so stupid. We have him in an interview room cooling his heels while a crew tears apart his offices and his lawyers call on state senators and judges he knows to pull strings for him. So far, no one is being too helpful. Julian Rakes is suddenly persona non grata. He's not a happy man."

"He's a sociopath," I said, as I steered the Geo around a tree lying across the road. "Be careful. He'll lie and you'll never know it."

"And you know that, how?"

"Aunt Matilda."

"Ah."

A second tree lay just beyond the first. The snow thickened

for a moment, creating instant whiteout. "On that enigmatic statement, I'm hanging up. The visibility and the road are awful."

"I'd have driven you home if you had waited around for me."

"Come to supper. Bring Davie with you, if you can."

Evan laughed, true delight in the tone. "I'll do my best. If I bring him tonight, let's see if we can put Aunt Matilda up in a hotel. I can personally attest to the merits of one just around the corner from Bloodstone."

I smiled into the driving snow. "And Jane?"

"She goes home with her dad."

"And you?" I asked, knowing what was coming, and ready for it. Wanting it.

His voice lowered. "I take down that mass of red-gold hair and check out those green silk sheets on your bed."

The heat that had kindled with his first words spread through me, moving like honey across my flesh. "Oh."

He laughed again, the tone entirely masculine and sensual. My hands started to perspire inside my gloves on the steering wheel. "Drive safe," he said, and hung up.

The feeling of warmth radiated out through me. Davie would be home soon. I *knew* it.

The light was starting to fail as I crunched my way into Connersville, the Tracker sliding and digging its way up the last hill. My shoulders were so tight they ached, and my hands had been gripping the steering wheel so long they were paralyzed in a circle and flexing them hurt. When I pulled into the alley and parked, my relief was so strong I dropped back my head and shuddered.

A one-and-a-half-hour trip had taken all afternoon, and required a detour devised by the devil himself when I came upon a huge boulder blocking the road and road crews working to clear the way. The directions given me by the flag man had been specific but, in the blinding snow, had proved useless. If you can't see the road you're supposed to take, you can't get where you're going. I was hungry, cold, and on the dregs of my energy. Everything I wanted was inside my loft: food, an update on Davie and a hot bath. And the back of the alley was blocked with fresh snow and a five-foot pile made by a city snowplow, so I'd have to go around.

Crawling from the Tracker, I smelled smoke, food and home. I made my way around front to the shoveled walk and stopped at the Chinese place just down from Bloodstone. They were closing early, and I got a good deal on cashew chicken, sweet-and-sour pork, teriyaki steak with vegetarian fried rice and a dozen spring rolls, two of which I devoured as I waited. Packages in hand, I made my way to the shop, opened the door and went inside.

Bloodstone Inc. was empty. I stopped just inside the door, reaching out with my mind, aware once again that I was using St. Claire gifts with impunity. And without a headache. We routinely closed the shop during bad storms. There didn't need to be anyone here at all. But the room felt wrong.

I eased the take-out boxes to the floor. "Noe?" I called softly.

Again I smelled smoke. I looked up. Black haze drifted around the tin ceiling in lazy swirls, coming through the vent in the back of the room that tied it to the workshop.

I wanted to rush upstairs and check on Jane, but I knew instantly that she and Aunt Matilda were not up there. Fear raced along my nerves with a sizzling flash. *Aunt Matilda?*

We're stuck in the snow, waiting for a pickup to pull us free. The words were solace easing my fear. *Where?*

Just down the hill from you. We needed milk and supper fixin's. Oh! What's happening? Jane smells smoke.

I didn't need to ask how Jane smelled smoke. *Stay away.*

Don't come home just yet. Take her to get a movie or something.

What—?

Not now, Aunt Matilda. I shut her away from me, my wall slamming with an almost audible clank. The smoke at the ceiling thickened. Where the heck was my gun when I needed it? Quietly I moved toward the back of the shop and through the door, down the short hallway. The smoke was thicker here and a cold breeze blew through, fanning the smoke.

Movement ahead, the sound of a torch blowing, flame turned up too high to cone. The room came clear as I rounded the doorjamb. I took in the entire room in a single instant. Our three acetylene torches were lit, their flames billowing, each in a corner of the room, each aimed at a pile of rags. The rags were burning. I smelled kerosene.

Isaac was prone on the floor, blood running from his temple. Evan was beside him, shackled to the heavy workbench with handcuffs. He covered his lips with an index finger and pointed to the storeroom. The light in the room was on and I heard the sound of boxes moving. Silent, I ran across the room, turning torches away from the rags as I moved, dumping one set of burning rags into the nearby sink and flinging on the water. Grabbing the fire extinguisher, I turned it to the second pile of rags, then the remaining pile, burying them beneath the stream of white. The flames went out. Smoke left an acrid taste in the back of my throat. Running back to each torch, I turned the knobs, the flames popping to silence. I was shaking, more with anger than fear.

Glancing toward the storeroom, I knelt beside Evan. The handcuff chain was wrapped around the table leg, holding Evan close to the floor. "So much for romance and sex," I said.

Evan laughed silently, as if my comment made him feel better somehow. "I thought Isaac had fallen or had a heart attack or something. I bent over him and found a gun in my ear.

I can't get turned so I can lift the table and get the cuffs off
the leg. Can you…?"

I swiveled underneath, my back against the underside of
the table. Bending my legs like a power lifter, I straightened
my knees. The table was heavy as heck, built to withstand
hammer and anvil, brazier and metalworking tools. I strained.
Nothing happened. The table didn't budge. I released the
load and stepped over Evan, straddling him, and braced my
back against the table near the corner for greater leverage. I
shoved up with my body. The table leg wobbled, grated once
and lifted. Evan was laughing as he slid the handcuffs out and
rolled to his knees. He was free, but his wrists were still
cuffed together in front of him. "Promise me you'll do that
again when all this is over," he whispered.

"Ha-ha," I said, half crawling out to stand beside him. I
glanced once at the storeroom door, hearing loud bumps and
thumps. Somebody was a busy little beaver.

"Your gun is beside the cash register. Get it. Have you
called 911?"

I shook my head as I ran to the front. I hadn't even thought
about it. I wasn't sure how the gun got to be in the shop, but
it was wedged under the counter, beside a roll of paper towels and a bottle of Windex.

I ran back, handing the little .38 to Evan. He took it in his
cuffed hands, broke open the cylinder and checked the bullets. Snapping the chamber back in place, he jogged toward
the storeroom, gun slightly to the side and pointed down to
the floor. Just as Evan moved, a man walked in from the
storeroom, loaded down with boxes. Davie's boxes. I had
seen the man. Somewhere. He saw Evan just as he raised the
gun.

"Stop. Police. Put down the boxes."

The man's eyes whipped around the room, taking in the
torches. He dropped the boxes with a huge crash and whirled

toward the back door and the alley. Evan shouted and followed, now at a dead run. I grabbed the nearest thing as a weapon and followed. Only after I was out in the alley did I hear what Evan had shouted. "Call 911!"

Evan was ahead about twenty feet, moving fast, gun in front of him. The other man pulled a gun and fired. Evan ducked behind the Dumpster. I ducked back into the shop.

Floyd Feaster. That was his name. He had worked for Colin Hornsburn, who was now dead. Floyd Feaster was a geologist. More shots were fired in the alley. And somehow I knew there was a third person there. Raising a gun. "Look out!" I screamed, and fell into Evan's mind.

I felt the thump as the bullet hit me. Knew I was hit. Heard the sound of the shot after. I turned and saw a woman, moving from the snow-blocked alley end. She had a gun. I heard Feaster get away, footsteps sliding and crunching on the ice and snow. She was crying. I tried to raise the gun and fire. Pain shot through my chest. I slid down the Dumpster, letting my knees take the .38 up into position.

I jerked my awareness back to me, blasted my wall tight against Evan. Fury whipped through me, a roaring fire. The woman walked past the doorway, the gun in front of her. I *knew* she was going to fire the gun. My rage flamed. I lifted my weapon over my head and raced at her. Hit her hard with the fire extinguisher. The gun went off, flying from her hands. She went down. I hit her again. Again. Pounding the heavy extinguisher into her neck, her shoulder, her back.

Suddenly Evan was there, jerking the extinguisher from me, setting it in the snow at my feet. "It's okay. It's okay, Tyler."

My hands formed claws. The woman was splayed on the snow, bleeding. Drops of crimson on a layer of pure white. No. The blood was Evan's. I took a single step back, watching as he found her gun against the alley wall, checked it and tucked it into his pocket.

I looked back at Gail Speeler, lying in the snow, crying. *It's all ruined. All of it. Unless...* She looked up at me, and I *knew*. She had Davie.

Evan checked the end of the alley. Feaster had gotten away. I wiped my face. I didn't know when I had started crying, but my nose was leaking in the icy air. Snow was falling still, a heavy swirl in the gusting wind. Flakes landed in Gail's black hair, like snowflake obsidian. Hatred flared in her eyes, and victory.

How could she feel victorious? Evan appeared beside me, his hiking boots at the edge of my field of vision. "Did you call 911?" His voice was strangely breathless, but I didn't look up.

"No. And I'm not going to." I could feel his eyes on me. "She knows where Davie is. And she's going to tell me."

Gail laughed, derision in the tone.

My rage, a fire banked beneath the ashes of fear and worry and confusion, leaped free at the sound. I reached down and lifted her to her feet, my fists in her lapels. Something in my face must have warned her because the laughter stuttered into silence and her mouth opened as if to speak. Fury gave me strength not normally mine, the energy of wrath exploding.

I threw her toward the shop door. She actually left the ground, stumbling when her feet touched the snow. Falling against the door, she hit her head. Her eyes rolled.

"Tyler—" Evan's tone held warning and something else.

"Shut up." I reached Gail and twisted my hands in her jacket again, hauling her to the shop, and I threw her inside the short hallway toward the workroom. This time, she fell when she landed. Blood welled up on her knees beneath torn stockings. Her hands were bleeding. I was on her before she could move. I lifted her and half carried her into the shop, past the ruined storeroom. Isaac was on the floor, a hand to his head. He looked up, blinking, his eyes unfocused. The sight of the blood at his temple brought the anger to a peak in me, a coned flame of fury, bright, blue-hot.

I slammed Gail into a chair and picked up Jubal's duct tape. With hard, jerky motions, I ripped away a length of tape and bound her body to the chair back. Another strip bound her wrists to the chair arms. With a third I lashed her legs together and then to the chair leg. Then I started over, taping her again to hold her in place. Only when she was secured did I look at Evan. He was slumped on the floor, hands still cuffed in front of him, blood-smeared khakis bunched at one knee, wrinkled at hips and waist. Some of the blood was dried brown. Eloise's blood. Some was fresh. His own. His shirt was open, exposing the gunshot wound. It looked like a long scrape. Evan was more angry than injured. Isaac had crawled to him and was holding a clean rag over a wound high on Evan's chest.

I looked at Evan. His eyes roved over Gail, as if surprised at the tape that bound her to the chair. They lifted to mine. Something swam in the green deeps, something dark and malevolent. "As a cop," he said, his voice strained and gasping, "I have to tell you this is illegal."

I laughed, the sound brusque. Brutal. Not me. It wasn't. I picked up a pointed pick, one with a fine, delicate tip I used to clean the grooves of shaped stone. It was a nicely balanced tool. Solid steel, with a hatch-work handle to keep a user's grip steady. "Has Lopez found Davie yet?"

Almost unwillingly, as if the words were dragged from him, he said, "Eloise lawyered up. They want complete immunity. No one's going for it. They're at a stalemate."

"And meanwhile, Davie is still suffering." I laughed again, breathing hard, the sound a rasp in the quiet room. "You can arrest me after I find my brother." I looked from Evan to Isaac.

His dark eyes met mine, still slightly unfocused. "While you're at it," he said, his Texan drawl slightly slurred, "see if you can find out who shot Jubal."

I nodded. I turned to Gail. Her eyes had cleared while we talked. Anger churned in them. She jerked away from me, the chair legs skidding in the suddenly silent room. I studied her, sitting there, her jacket and blouse open where they had come unbuttoned in our skirmish. I remembered the muddled wash of emotions when I had touched her last, the shame and guilt that clung to me afterward like hot tar.

I leaned into her and delicately pushed back the silk blouse lapel. I met her eyes, saw her anger falter at whatever she saw in mine. Her pupils widened in the beginnings of fear. I smiled softly and placed the pick against her collarbone, poised. Gently I pressed. She jerked away, a high-pitched squeal coming from her throat, followed by words that spewed hatred and begging, like her mind spewed lies, dark images of hate. I gripped a handful of her hair and straddled her legs with mine. Repositioned the pick just so. Gave a single sharp stab that pierced her flesh. She gasped hard. I opened myself to her. And fell inside.

The wash of emotions rose over me in a dark, roaring wave. This time I let them come, let them spill over me, even as I held myself aloof from them. I spiraled down through the depths of her, a precipitous, sheer drop, a dizzying whirl of images like flashes of light. I fell into her darkness. Her hidden place.

I saw the man who stood in the heart of her secrets, a redheaded, blue-eyed man. A beautiful man. *I want. I hate.* Images swelled over me and passed on, a tsunami of childhood misery and shame. I understood the horrible abuse. Felt it, *knew* it. A child in the dark, with no one to help.

Above that darkness, floating over the place of secrets like an oily film, was the woman grown and her determination to never be used again. Never be a pawn, never a thing with value only as a body. *Never.*

A desire to strike back rested in a jumbled layer above the determination, its roots sinking into the deeps like tendrils of scarlet into a black ooze. So much misery.

I realized I had sunk to her darkest heart and was rising through, toward her conscious mind. I had no idea how I was doing this or how she would react, but I pushed on, letting the images flow through me now. Images of people who had hurt her and had been hurt back. Insult on insult, pain on pain. Visions of men she had slept with, hating them. *Hating them, yet wanting. Always wanting.* Her heart beat above the pain, a fast, uneven rhythm of lifelong anguish.

Davie, I said into the images. *Davie.*

I saw my brother, a gentle man, short but muscular, wiry and athletic, blond. Dark eyes. *Not blue. Thank God, not blue.* Davie was smiling as if he understood the pain. As if he could take it all away. *I want him, but he won't touch me. Why won't he touch me? I'm not good enough… He knows! How did he find out? Eloise told him! She told him everything!*

I saw Davie, bound and gagged. Handcuffed to the bed. In the memory, I saw Eloise kneeling over him, naked. *She touched him! No!*

I held on to that image. It was in the small closet where they had kept him last. *Where?* I asked. *Where is he?*

In her mind, she turned and saw me. *How had she seen me? How did she know I was there?* I started, wanting to pull away. Instead I forced into the vision of Davie in the small room. *Where is he?*

"No! *No!*" She shouted, spittle landing on me, both in our minds and on my face. I ground the pick into her flesh. She screamed. Dimly I heard Isaac calling to me. His dark-skinned hand was over mine, pulling at the pick.

Savage, I bit the wrist. It moved away, jarring my teeth. I

gripped the back of her neck in my left hand, bruising, and ground down with the right, twisting the pick deep. I glared into her eyes, filled with pain and terror. And saw images of myself, of Jubal and Isaac, a glimpse of Noe. I bypassed them all, all the images except the one I wanted. She screamed. I closed my eyes again. *"Where? Where is my brother?"*

I caught a fleeting image. A house on the outskirts of town. I had driven by it on the way home. My eyes flew open, meeting her blue ones. Gail laughed at me, baring her teeth. "Not there. Not there anymore. I sold him. They took him this afternoon. The gold is mine. And I'll never have to let him touch me again. *Never!*"

Gail had sold him? Sold my brother? To whom? I pushed again with my mind. *"Davie!"* I saw a man. Adam Wiccam. He turned and looked at me. A syringe was in his hand. Davie was slumped on a bed beside him, eyes half-lidded.

And I realized Wiccam was looking at me. He saw me looking at him. He reached toward me with his free hand, flexed his fingers out and in, like gripping a ball, or pulling on a rope. Something jerked at me. At my mind.

I wrenched back, away from the image. *I was suddenly outside the house. A blizzard swirled around me. I saw the house. It was the house in Gail's memory. Davie was still there.* And I knew where he was.

I rose from Gail, pulling out the sender pick. It came free of her flesh with a soft sucking sound and she gasped, a wounded moan. I looked at her, at the woman who had taken my brother. I knew the entire plan now, almost all that she knew. I threw the pick across the room, heard it clatter in the silence. Shaking, I turned for the loft and saw Isaac and Evan.

They were gaping at me. Revulsion and abhorrence were present in both pair of eyes. Yet, atop the disgust rode something else, something purely masculine, primitive and earthy—bloodlust or wonder. Excitement. I didn't have time to parse their reactions and really didn't care what they thought anyway. All I wanted was Davie. "I didn't hurt her," I rasped. "Much." I wiped my hand down my skirt, which had bunched at my waist. It left a fresh blood smear. Something rose up in me, something large and ugly that I hadn't looked at in years. It was familiar, this shadowy thing that hulked in my mind. I could look at it later. If I could face seeing it again. "She doesn't know who shot Jubal," I said.

I turned and fled the bizarre, condemning, hungry stares, rushing through the short hallway and the shop, up the stairs to the loft. I smelled Chinese food and old smoke, burned oily rags, and the scent of my rage, like bitter wormwood, the things of insanity. In the apartment, I ripped off my bloody clothes, hearing seams tear, seeing the dried blood that had soaked through to my skin. Eloise's blood. I ducked into the shower, not waiting for the water to heat, letting the icy flow burn its way over my skin, and then, for just a moment, hot water, too hot to bear. It scalded me, boiling away the expressions on the faces of my friends.

I dried off hurriedly, dressed in warm clothes, long underpants, jeans, a flannel shirt, two pair of socks, heavy boots, a down coat. I gathered the afghan off the sofa, a second coat, a pair of sweatpants and sweatshirt. When I turned, Jane stood in the doorway, Dyno in her arms. Her eyes were huge, fingers tangled in the cat's short fur.

"I don't care what you did." Her eyes were dry and hot, her face merciless. "Just bring my daddy back."

I couldn't stop the rush of tears that sprang to my eyes. I hugged her once, fiercely, and I ran from the room and down the stairs, pocketing the keys. I picked up the box of spring rolls and ran from the shop into the ice and snow that blew a raging blizzard. I was outside before I registered the sight of Isaac and Evan, standing in the shop. Gail was sitting in the wing chair I favored, a wad of gauze at her shoulder. Outside, I heard sirens approaching.

* * *

I was heading for the Geo when a horn tooted. Whirling, I saw Aunt Matilda, sitting in the front of a large SUV—Jubal's vehicle, towed back from the side of a mountain where we had left it so long ago. The driver's window came down and Aunt Matilda stuck her head into the blowing snow. "I've already been pulled out of one drift today. Why don't you drive to this house where my nephew is being held and let me ride shotgun?"

"I don't have a shotgun," I said, walking to the big vehicle. "I don't have a weapon at all. No way to force him to give Davie to me."

The older woman, dressed for the weather in a smock, thick sweater and socks beneath sandals, slid over to the passenger seat, leaving the driver's seat empty. "I was speaking metaphorically. We are St. Claires. We need no weapons except our minds. After your recent experience with the Speeler woman, haven't you learned that yet?"

The cold of the storm seemed to coalesce inside me. Behind me, two cop cars came to sliding halts. An ambulance climbed the hill at a crawl. The falling snow obscured me from the cops and they ran inside Bloodstone Inc.

I threw my supplies into the open window, except for the food, and opened the SUV door, climbing inside. Raising the window, I adjusted the seat forward. In order for my feet to reach the pedals, the steering wheel nearly touched my chest. Stupid American car makers. I put on the seat belt and stared at the front window, already blanketed with a layer of snow. I turned on the wipers. Finally, with nothing left to do to occupy my body and mind, I turned to her, a taste of acid on my tongue. "You were there? With me? When I... tortured Gail?"

"Of course." Aunt Matilda's face was calm, composed. "And when you raped her mind to find out where Davie is."

I flinched, knowing that was what I had done. I looked away, swallowed back the rising horror. Then I put the SUV in gear and eased down the road, past the cop cars with their flashing blue lights and the ambulance with its flashing red lights, down the hill beyond Main Street. I took a left and headed out of town. Ravenous, I ate spring rolls as I drove, sharing with Aunt Matilda, who seemed hungry, too. For a long space of time, in which I fought wind and snow and tried to compose myself, we said nothing at all.

"Tell me what you know of this Adam Wiccam," she said at last.

"He claims to work for the government, for the Treasury Department. But Davie thought he worked for Q Core, a—"

"I'm perfectly familiar with Q Core."

I glanced at her, surprised. "Then maybe you can enlighten me," I said politely, wondering if she knew more about the group than I had learned from Davie's letter.

"Q Core was a small division of the Department of Defense back in the sixties and seventies, a secret agency-within-an-agency dedicated to investigating whether paranormal activity, psychic gifts such as those possessed by the St. Claires, could be used in intelligence gathering."

"And?"

"Unlike its counterpart in the CIA, Q Core was successful." She pointed across the cab to something at my side, and I spotted deer cantering across the snow, a doe leading two large fawns. I slowed to a stop and the animals raced in front of the SUV, prancing, pawing, running for sheer joy, blowing clouds of breath with wide nostrils. When they were out of sight, I eased back into motion and she went on. "So successful were they that their budget was tripled, and they turned from mere observation to trying to change events. They planted ideas in the minds of foreign heads of state, nudged paranoia in others, suggested new or different ways of thought."

"And you know this, how?"

"They started recruiting psychics from all over. The St.

Claires were already known as a family of gifted individuals, and so they came to us. Several of our people joined them, worked with them, until Q Core changed its tactics and its original purpose yet again. The new presidential administration brought new people into Q Core. People who tried to turn the talents into weapons."

I remembered the feel of the pick inside Gail's flesh. My mind piercing her mind, a weapon, cutting and hungry and utterly without conscience. Oh, yeah. That I understood. I forced down the images. *Not now. Not yet. Not until I find Davie.*

"In the mideighties, they experimented with key members of the then Soviet Union, causing accidents. And they taught the St. Claires, working with them, on how to kill. Your uncle was one of them."

"Uncle William? He was a gifted St. Claire?" When she nodded, I said, "I always thought he was head-blind."

Her face was pensive in the failing light. "He was the second Q Core talent to make a kill. He went into the mind of a KGB colonel, driving drunk along a dark road after a party. He planted an image of a sea serpent rising out of the dark waters beside the road and striking the vehicle. The colonel swerved hard in the other direction and crashed into a tree. William was still in his mind when he died, in terror and pain. Will never got over it. He lost the use of his gift. Started drinking. They booted him out of Q Core, which was what he wanted. He came home to me and I did what I could to heal him."

"My father was recruited by Q Core," I said, remembering the information Davie had learned while working for the government as David Lowe.

"We think so, though we never learned if he made it to them or not. Unlike the others, who went to Washington, D.C., your father went to New York. And he seemed to simply disappear. Which was why Davie went to the agency when he reached his majority and joined them under an assumed name. He wanted to look for your father."

I glanced at her. I hadn't known about his search until I found the letter in the personal records box from the Secure Room, hadn't known about his need to find our father. It seemed Aunt Matilda had. "And?"

She shrugged. "I don't know. Davie won't talk about those years."

I thought about that, downshifting to make the last hill. "Yeah. He never talked about them with me, either." Why hadn't he told me?

"According to all the St. Claires who worked for them, Q Core was disbanded nearly a decade ago after some scandal was brought to light. Most likely the scandal David exposed when he left the DOD. Adam Wiccam is all that's left of the unit. It's possible he came to punish David for stealing the money that Q Core had amassed in private accounts not part of the government budgetary and audit process. It's possible that he holds David responsible for the loss of his dreams and power."

I understood, putting one of the odd-shaped pieces into the puzzle. "Davie caused all his problems? So now it's personal?"

She smiled again, a slight tightening of her lips. "Yes, that's what I think. So now we pay the price of Davie doing both the right thing—turning Q Core in to the proper authority—and the wrong thing: stealing. Though it was illicit money that Q Core had gained by use of their gifts, it wasn't money that Davie himself owned." She looked out the side window, away from me. "So you see, I am fully aware that our gifts can be used for evil as well as the good we try to do. And when we misuse them, we always pay a price."

"I'd do it again," I said, my tone fierce, my hands tight on the wheel, knowing she was referring to Gail Speeler.

"I know. And that is indeed the sad part of it all. The end always seems to justify the means. And absolute power does tend to corrupt absolutely."

I turned away from her, back to the storm that offered a physical fight with a tangible opponent, but I fought down shame. If I let it, I knew regret would cripple me, and I couldn't let that happen, not right now. I slowed and turned into a driveway, gently easing the big vehicle over the fresh snow, hoping I didn't slide into a ditch. "We're here."

Aunt Matilda inspected the small house bracketed by tall cedars and a row of bare-branched trees. She closed her eyes. "David is no longer here."

No. I gripped the wheel hard, staring at the house through the falling flakes.

"A car was parked there." She opened her eyes and pointed to a place near the small house where dark ground showed through the snow. Tracks left the spot, making a U-turn and heading out the back of the property. "Only recently gone."

I started to follow, but Aunt Matilda placed a hand on my arm. "Violence has been done here, but one is still alive. Inside."

"But—"

"No buts. We *will* offer aid." She opened her door, unclipped the seat belt in a single motion and slid down to the ground. I shut off the big engine and followed her through the shadows. It was dusk now, darkness hunched beneath the trees and bushes, waiting to pounce. The back door was open, hanging half off its hinges. The lock was gone, replaced by a basketball-sized hole. Splintered wood lay all around. I could faintly smell cordite from the blast.

Inside, Aunt Matilda paused only a moment before plunging down a long hallway, her smock skirt surging behind her. I followed more slowly. Blood had splattered the wall to my right, tiny droplets in an intermittent arc. *I saw a man, bleed-*

ing. Both hands worked a shotgun, breaking open the chamber, inserting two large rounds, slapping it shut, the motion throwing blood up and away. He stalked down the hallway Aunt Matilda had taken. I couldn't see his face, but I knew the scent of the man. I followed them both. *He raised the gun, his heart and mind cold, as he rounded the corner into the room.*

Aunt Matilda was bent over a man's body. I knew he was dead. In my mind, I saw the man with the gun. *Adam Wiccam pumped two rounds into the cowering form on the floor.* Now, Floyd Feaster was a broken mass. His face was missing, and part of one arm. He had been followed back from his attempt to steal the gold and burn Bloodstone Inc. Had he purchased Davie from Gail Speeler? Convinced her to share him, perhaps? Found a way to make Davie tell him where the gold was? Had she joined forces with him? But she had said they had sold Davie. To whom? Feaster? Or Wiccam?

And then another puzzle piece slid to the right and into place with a soft clink. They had what they wanted out of Davie. And they sold him to Wiccam after.

I reached for my cell phone to call police. It wasn't clipped to my jeans. I had remembered the spring rolls but not the phone. Stupid. Stupid, stupid, stupid.

Aunt Matilda stood. "In here." Moving into a room across the hall, she knelt beside a second body and said, "It's all right. We're here to help." The light was dimmer moment by moment, and I was losing my chance to follow the tire tracks in the snow. I had to leave. Now. But the sight of Harry Boone on the floor, propped against a chest of drawers, stopped the words in my mouth. The cop looked up at me, barely conscious, his body in a pool of blood that had stopped spreading. I turned on the light switch, throwing the room into sudden detail and vivid color. I had seen so much blood today. Too much.

"Find a phone," I said as I grabbed the spread and a pillow off the bed. "Call 911. Tell them a cop's been shot." I knelt beside Harry and pressed the pillow into his abdomen, into the hole there. He was still breathing, but shallowly, and so fast I couldn't count the breaths. Biting into the edge of the spread, I tore it into long strips and tied the pillow into place on Harry, talking to myself as I moved. "There is no egg in the world big enough to be the egg this sucks."

I heard Harry's breathing change. He was laughing silently, the sound abruptly cut off as pain claimed him. His faced wrenched, smoothed, and he fell unconscious again.

Aunt Matilda came back. "They're on their way. I didn't know the address, but they're coming to the address on the phone. They'll be here as fast as they can."

Harry's eyes fluttered. He was out cold, only the almost imperceptible rise and fall of his chest revealing that he still lived. I stood and looked at the bed. It was the bed in my vision of Wiccam, the one where Davie was given a dose of drugs. I looked out the window into the darkness. I had lost my chance to save Davie.

With a violence I hadn't known I possessed, I hit the wall with my fist.

18

The shop was empty when Aunt Matilda and I finally got back. In a panic, I raced upstairs to check the messages and discovered that Jane had gone with Isaac and Evan to the hospital. Of course. The men needed medical help. I remembered the blood at Isaac's temple when I saw him prone on the workshop floor, and the wound in Evan's upper chest where Gail had shot him, the bullet grazing his flesh.

And of course, Gail herself needed her knees cleaned and bandaged, and the neat hole in her shoulder needed tending. The memory of the pick digging into the flesh near her collarbone rushed over me, a torrent of sensation. The smell of blood and sweat and fear. Silent, Aunt Matilda came into the loft behind me, carrying the Chinese food, which had been left at the shop door.

I called Noe and left word on her answering machine that we were safe, but ignored the other messages.

I stripped again, adding more clothes to the bloody pile I had started earlier. Naked, I climbed into the shower and let the scalding water run over me, taking with it the blood and my failure. Once again I had used my gift and gotten nothing for it. Not even Harry Boone's life, which had seeped away long minutes before the ambulance and police got to us.

They had been led by Lieutenant Jason Reasoner, Harry's boss, the man furious with questions and mordant suspicion, and equally furious with my inadequate answers. It took hours and I still didn't know why he let me go. He had wanted me to be guilty of killing his officer. He wanted *someone* to be guilty.

All that, and I still didn't have Davie.

Standing in the scalding shower, I washed Harry Boone's blood off me. Leaning into the shower stall wall, I cried, huge tears, racking sobs, misery that flooded out and yet seemed to back up deep inside me, a dam of blood and corruption clotted together in my soul. So much blood. *What had I done? What kind of beast was I?*

When I was clean, when no more blood ran from my body, I dried off and smeared cream into my cracked and chapped skin. I dressed in a velour jogging suit and fuzzy bed socks, but even after the hot shower, I couldn't get warm. I was cold as death. Aunt Matilda had the Chinese food reheating on the stove, and she passed by me with the admonition to keep an eye on it for her. She too dropped her bloody clothes and stepped into the shower.

Left to my own devices, the voices in my own mind, I watched the food simmer and sizzle, and drank three Blue Moon Blondes in quick succession, wanting to cloud my mind. Wanting to get away from the pictures, the images, the visions of the day. Wanting to block the remembrance of what I had done to Gail Speeler.

Moments after Aunt Matilda was dressed in a fresh skirt and blouse, they all came in, Evan and Isaac and Jane, trudging and thundering up the stairs to the loft. They turned on the lights and it was only then that I realized I had showered and dressed in the dark.

Jane rushed across the loft to me and buried her head in my waist. She hadn't cried till now. But I felt the loosening of the tension in her back and shoulders, the punch of the first sob. I didn't have to tell her that her father wasn't with us. She just knew. She was St. Claire nutty-weird. She pulled away and looked up at me once. "It's okay, Aunt Tyler. It's okay." But it didn't take a St. Claire to know she was lying through her teeth. Remorse roared down on me, an avalanche of guilt.

Gently I pushed her away from me and left them, and went to stare out at the roof garden, now beneath eleven inches of fresh snowfall. I leaned my head against the glass. I fancied it was scarcely cooler than my own cold flesh. I finished off the third beer, seeing the bottle rise and fall in the window reflection, feeling the alcohol dull my system.

"We got home just in time," Isaac said behind me, breaking the silence. "On the way, the snowfall got so hard and heavy that we could barely see. The streets are impassable."

"Uncle Evan can drive as good as my daddy, though," Jane said. "Not bad for a city boy." In the reflection of the window, I saw him ruffle her hair.

"What smells so good? I can eat a horse," Evan said. Trying, trying so hard to be normal. What was normal? What did that mean anymore?

"Tyler brought home Chinese earlier. I heated it up," Aunt Matilda said. All cheery. Jocular. As if nothing had happened. As if I hadn't tortured a woman, raped her mind, and then thrown away all I had gained when I lost Davie.

If I hadn't stopped to change from the blood-soaked suit, if I hadn't showered, would those few minutes have made the difference? Would Wiccam have still been in the house? Could I have saved my brother? Or would he have shot Aunt Matilda with the shotgun? Killed her and me and still taken Davie?

"Table's set," she said. "Go wash and we can eat right away."

They milled around, washing hands, getting chairs from

the rack on the wall, pouring drinks. Then they sat. I stayed away. My hair was hanging down my back in snarls I hadn't bothered to comb out, obscuring my face. Raggedy Ann. That was me.

They ate, glancing my way occasionally, their expressions guarded as if they knew I watched their reflections in the window. Aunt Matilda filled them in on Floyd Feaster and Harry Boone. Evan told about the investigation into Gail Speeler's wild accusations. It seemed I was in the clear, as far as torturing her went. I shuddered at the callous words—the truthful words—Evan used. Since neither Evan nor Isaac had backed up Gail's claims and offered a different version of events, their story was accepted. She had been fighting with Isaac when they slipped and fell, Isaac hitting his head, Gail falling on the sharp tool with which she had threatened them. When Evan said this, no one looked my way. I didn't look back at them. They had lied to protect me. I stared out into the dark at the frozen, falling snow.

Moments later, the power went out, dropping us all into darkness. In the distance we heard a muted explosion, a transformer blowing somewhere nearby. Saying nothing, I moved through the dark, found a match and lit a tall taper. I carried it around the loft, lighting candles.

"I don't guess the heat works when the power's out?" Evan asked. "I have gas logs downstairs in the workroom, but it's going to be mighty cold tonight."

I remembered our earlier lighthearted plans. Was that today? Evan was going to bring Davie home, we were going to celebrate. Then he was going to let down my hair and try out my silk sheets. The memory resounded deep inside, touching only emptiness, the hollow place where my soul had once lived.

"You can stay in the guest room at our place," Isaac said. "It has a gas fireplace with a passive blower. You'll be warmer there. And no one will be out in this storm. You won't be abandoning the women folks." I felt them all look at me. I didn't exactly need protection, did I? I was a torturer of desperate and mentally ill women. *Ashes and spit. Spit and decay. What was I?*

I was lying in the dark, alone, in the big bed, wide-awake. I hadn't been able to close my eyes, though I had slept only a few hours a night for days. Tonight, I kept seeing the steel pick, light glinting off it as it pierced pale flesh. Blood welling up around the circular wound. I felt the grate of the pick when it hit bone once. I hadn't noticed that at the time, I was so intent on her mind, but I had ground the steel into bone. The memory, buried in my own flesh, brought it back to me. And each time, I flinched on the mattress, jarring myself back to full awareness, one hand on the old scar on my shoulder, the scar that had given me the idea to torture Gail.

The power was still off, the house still dark, a darkness so dense and heavy it seemed to have a texture, a presence. I could hear the tick of the rooster clock, which ran on batteries, and the steady, deep breathing of Aunt Matilda, the lighter puffs of Jane's breath as she dreamed.

Dyno raised her head. I felt it at the same time. Someone was in the loft with us. I opened my mind, reaching out—and encountered only empty space. Dyno twisted and hurtled to the floor, racing to the bathroom, her feet delicate pads, nearly silent.

From only feet away came a rasp of sound. Cloth on cloth. *Tyler?*
I'm here.
There's someone here, in the loft. Aunt Matilda's voice whispered in my mind. *But I can't find him.*
You get an emptiness, like a wide-open space.
Yes.

A smell touched me in the dark, chemical, almost sweet. I had no gun. No sphere of bloodstone to throw. Nothing but my mind. Slowly I turned my head. A shadow within the shadows loomed over the trundle bed. Touching Jane.

Fury welled up in me so fast it took possession of my bones and viscera, my deepest being. I had learned today that I could use my mind as a weapon. That sometimes there seemed no choice but to lose myself in violence. Tears of rage gathered in my eyes, salty, acrid, bitter. The man rose up, lifting Jane, her mind dark and silent, filled with the smell of the chemical he had forced her to breathe.

Lying in the dark, I coiled my mind into a fist. In it I shaped a tool, a pick, long and lethal with a razor point. I felt Aunt Matilda there, steadying the image.

Are you sure? I asked her.

I'm sure.

Rearing back the weapon of my mind, I thrust out. Hard. Swift. And Aunt Matilda thrust with me, a violent, devastating blow.

He dropped Jane. She fell, bonelessly, to the trundle, landing in a heap. The cloth over her mouth fell away.

I sat up in bed, in the cold air, and pulled back the weapon. Struck again. Something howled, the sound grating down my nerves, a screech of fury and pain.

I pulled back the image and struck again.

A snake rose up beside me on the bed, hissing, a cobra, its hood open, tongue flicking. The image of my fist wavered. The snake struck. Its fangs sank deep into my shoulder, near the ancient, puckered scar. Acid spread, burning, into my bloodstream, poison, reaching for my heart. Aunt Matilda stabilized the fist-and-pick image and I struck again. But this time the image bounced off with a strident sound, like metal on stone. And the snake wrapped itself around me, coils slithering.

I knew it wasn't real. I *knew* it. Yet my breath faltered. Pressure tightened around my ribs, forcing the air from my lungs. *Aunt Matilda!*

"Tyler!" she gasped.

I realized he had both of us. And he was winning.

In front of me, Jane moved. Rising slowly, drunkenly, she knelt on the foam mattress, supporting her weight with her hands. Wavering, a slow-motion specter, she stood, and held out her hand. "Daddy?" she whispered. "Daddy…" Blue fire blazed, crackled. Lightning shot from her fingers. Hit Adam Wiccam midbody. He fell. Clutching his chest. Gasping.

The pressure on my ribs vanished. I caught myself with one hand on a mound of pillows. Aunt Matilda sucked in a hoarse breath. Another.

Jane wavered, feet buried in the mattress to her ankles. "Daddy!" she screamed. She stumbled from the trundle and fell over the man at her feet, found her footing and reeled to the door. A flame lit, with the stink of sulfur and the rasp of match-head to box.

"Daddy!" She beat at the door, scrabbling for the knob and lock.

I caught her. "Jane, no. No baby."

"Daddy! Daddy!" She fought me, scratching weals down my arm.

"Let her go," Aunt Matilda commanded.

"But—"

"Let her go."

I dropped my arms and Jane wrenched open the lock and the door. Cold air rushed up the stairs like an icy shroud, covering us. Jane scrambled against the flow, down the stairs to the shop.

The power came on in a disorienting flash. Jane was standing at the shop's front door, her bare feet on the frozen floor. Her eyes were wild, her hair standing on end, electrified. "Let me out," she said. "Let me go to Daddy!"

"You'll freeze. You need shoes."

"Here," Aunt Matilda offered the boots Noe often left at the door. Jane slipped the oversize boots on and accepted the throw handed her from the chairs. I opened the door and followed my underdressed niece into the storm.

The streetlights were back on, little blobs of brightness illuminating white mounds and swirling snow, and Jane's dark hair, black in the night, bobbing before me. Cold like needles and red-hot pokers burned into me. My sock-covered feet froze instantly, an agony. My lungs ached with each breath, the cold so severe it ripped away my defenses. I saw Jane ahead of me. She was at a car, a little all-wheel-drive Camry parked in the middle of the street, its lights making twin halos of brightness on the falling snow. Its engine was running, a constant thunder of sound.

Jane raced to the back, banging her fists on the trunk, screaming, "Daddy, Daddy!"

Aunt Matilda appeared at my side. "Here are the keys," she said, "from his pockets."

I ran to Jane's side, fingers so cold I feared dropping the key ring. If I did, I would never find them again. Not in the dark, not with hands that had lost all feeling. Shivers caught me.

I tried the first key, then the second and third, my fingers like wood, ungiving, unyielding. On the fourth try, the key slid in and I fumbled the lock open. The lid rose and the light inside came on. Davie was curled in the trunk, naked but for a dirty blanket. Behind him was the body of Detective Jack Madison, a bullet hole in the center of his forehead.

"Daddy, Daddy, Daddy!" Jane screamed, the sound oddly dead, absorbed by the snow.

"Davie!" Was he dead? I touched his face, so cold it was like stone. *I'm too late.*

A faint scrabbling at my mind, dreamlike. *"Brat?"* Something shattered its way through me, cracking, breaking, falling away. "Davie!" I reached inside the trunk, tried to get my arms around him. He didn't move. He was asleep, or drugged, unable to help.

Isaac appeared from the darkness and carefully pushed Jane and me aside. He braced himself against the back fender and bent forward, lifted my brother out, holding him like a child. Davie woke, flailing wildly. An elbow caught Isaac in the nose, and Davie tumbled free, into a drift. Blood splattered the snow, crimson on white, melting and freezing at once. Blood from Isaac's nose. Blood from Davie's hand, unbandaged and bleeding.

My dream… I stopped. The thunder of the engine filled the street. I looked down at my hands, snow falling and melting on the flesh. Though they weren't bound, they had been useless to help my brother. And Davie, lying in bloody snow. Jane… Her face was white as death in the cold light. This wasn't my dream, yet it was.

"It's okay, man. It's just me. Isaac." The big man knelt and again lifted Davie, carrying him through the snow to the front door of the shop. Isaac mumbled in Texan tones as he plowed through deep drifts of snow. Something like, "Damn psychics won't let a man get a decent night's sleep. Bust my nose open. Ain't fair, a man just tryin' to do the right thing." I thought I heard Davie laugh, a weak chuckle. Yelping with joy, Jane followed. I trailed behind her.

Inside the shop, Evan closed the door behind us and led us up the stairs to my loft. He was talking on the cell phone to the cops, once again calling for assistance. How many times in one day? Oh, wait. It was tomorrow already. I caught Jane at the top of the stairs as she wobbled and nearly fell, and steered her inside. With my other hand, I caught the escaping Dyno and tossed the cat across the room to the trundle bed.

In the loft, which felt like a furnace after the cold of the street outside, Isaac set Davie on my bed and covered him. I found the electric blanket and plugged it in. "Jane, get dressed," I said. "Warm socks. Layers."

"But—"

"*Now.* Then you can help me with your daddy."

"Okay." She stumbled again and Aunt Matilda caught her by a shoulder. She helped the girl to the closet and clothes that would warm her. Davie's shivers were so bad they were shaking the entire bed. I gathered the top sheet around him, and then covered him with the electric blanket, which I tucked under him. Lastly, I threw the down coverlet over him.

Isaac and Evan were standing, watching me. "You want the cops to get here and see you like that?" I asked.

They each looked down at their exposed skin, Isaac in white long john bottoms and no shirt, and Evan in ancient gray jogging pants and a V-necked, short-sleeved T-shirt with rips at the underarms, his chest bandage visible through the thin fabric. Both wore socks and no shoes. They turned to the roof garden and disappeared.

"Guess not," I said. I went to the kitchen and put the kettle on. I could *feel* his thirst as I got Davie a glass of water, tossed in a straw and crawled onto the bed. Cradling his head, I placed the straw against his mouth. He was so cold he could barely pucker his lips. He sucked air with the water, but the moisture filled his mouth. *Nothing ever tasted so good. Nothing.* He drained the glass with little slurping sounds. I put his head back to the pillow. I could smell him, a rank stench. I caught images of him, tied. Beaten again. He had been kept hungry, thirsty, not given access to a toilet. Not since he had been moved from the closet room long, long hours ago. He had soiled himself.

"Sorry 'bout the sheets, Brat," he croaked.

I kissed the top of his head. "Shut up."

Warmth filled me, so light, so fragile, so delicate it was almost ethereal, almost the touch of God's hand. Almost the presence of El, in all his glory. Almost. I touched Davie's head, brushed back his slick hair, assuring myself he was real. I had him back. Against any odds, I had my brother back.

Jane raced over, wearing a running suit with a pair of my mint-green long johns hanging out beneath. She crawled up the bed and snuggled down with her father, kissing his face.

"I heard you. I heard you breathing," she said.

He sighed, the sound of escaping terror. Uncertain disbelief. Sleep pulled at him, drugged and sluggish. He closed his eyes.

Jane and I clutched hands across Davie, fingers digging tightly. Holding each other, Davie between us, his shivers threatening to dislodge us both. Sirens sounded far off, moving slowly closer. Davie jerked suddenly. Panic, blinding fear.

Brat? Baby?

We're here.

You're safe.

My brother was safe.

Sirens came closer, climbing the hill until they sounded from out front. Blue-and-red emergency lights flickered in the windows, brightening the tin ceiling. I hugged Davie and Jane tightly one final time, and met Jane's bright eyes over his shoulder. Her happiness blazed out, filling me with her joy.

Hard boots pounded up the stairs. Ready to meet the cops, I stood and surveyed the room. And only then did I realize Adam Wiccam was no longer here.

19

Aunt Matilda and I sat in the empty waiting room, down the hall from the room where nurses were changing Davie's dressings and doing all sorts of things to him that I didn't want Jane to know about. Exhausted, she had fallen asleep, her head in my lap, her breathing soft, cyclical puffs of sound. We had turned off the lights to let her sleep and the room was dim, with a startling brightness flooding in through the open door. It was quiet at last, and I knew Aunt Matilda and I would have to talk.

"Well?" I said. I could hear the challenge in my tone and the resulting amusement in her mind. I cleared my voice and tried again. "Well?"

"Well what?"

"Aren't you going to say anything about the St. Claire gifts and how I need training so I don't go off like a loose cannon and beat people up with my gift and do evil deeds?"

"Do I need to say that?"

No. She didn't. "*Ashes and spit!* It's not fair."

"To be given gifts and then have the responsibility to use them wisely?"

"Rot and decay, Aunt Matilda!"

"I don't have the power to make you do anything. You

know what you need to do—it's all your choice. You *know* that. In the way of our people, you *know* it."

"I can't use the cards. I just can't." That sounded stupid even as it came out of my mouth, but it was the truth. My mother had ground it into me. Evil could come of the Tarot, and if it came, I couldn't control it. It would control me. "I just can't. I'm sorry."

The older woman blew out a breath, the sound tired, the kind of soul-deep tired that comes from years, not merely physical exhaustion. She was wearing a sweater in the cold, sterile hospital, and she picked at it now, pulling at a loose length of yarn. It looked odd not to see her arms bare. "I've been thinking about the cards. We didn't always use them, you know."

I watched her face in the too-bright light. She kept it turned away, her focus on the frayed thread. "There are records, older records, that detail other training methods. One that uses a scrying bowl, much as Daniel the prophet used, or Nostradamus. One method uses painting, brush and paper and watercolors to focus the images. One uses dreams." She smiled, the motion scarcely a tightening of her eyes. "I think you may respond well to that method. But I think there is also one that uses stone."

I sat up straight in the uncomfortable chair. Jane's head lolled in my lap and her breathing caught. I steadied her and relaxed back into the seat. "Stone?"

"I'm not familiar with that method, but I've heard of it, from the old people talking when I was growing up. There may be ways to focus on stone, on its crystalline matrix, its natural order and chaos, to open the mind to its gifts." She glanced at Jane and then at me. "I am willing to do some research in the older tomes of family lore. If you would be willing to try." Her voice was half-pleading. "I want the chance to make up to you, if only in some small way, for abandoning you when you came into your gift. Alone."

"I…" I remembered Mama, her gentle face by the light of a candle, telling me the cards were evil. But she hadn't said the gift itself was evil. One could use anything for harmful purposes—take any gift and use it for evil. Or for good. "I'll think about it."

Aunt Matilda smiled and turned her face back to the hallway light. "But you'll have to leave that dreadful cell phone at home. I'll not have it in my house. It gives me hives."

"Yes, ma'am," I said, careful to screen my amusement from her. But I had a feeling I didn't do a good job of that. Her lips twitched.

Saturday, 1 p.m.

I turned from the sink to find Davie's eyes on me. He was sitting on my sofa, wearing his own clothes, his feet on the ottoman he had insisted be brought from his home when Isaac made the trip to pick up his personal items. He was still weak but the fever had gone down. His hand was bandaged where his finger had been sliced off with a boning knife. His bruises were fading. He was breathing easier, though I could still hear the pneumonia that had clogged his lungs for a time after we found him. We had nearly lost him to fever and infection. But this morning he had shaved and showered all by himself and the hospital had released him to my care. He was still gaunt, eyes full of shadows, but he was alive.

"Yes. I am."

We shared a smile. Since finding him in the middle of a blizzard, I had found it impossible to raise my wall against his thoughts. In fact, I couldn't wall out any St. Claire. None of them. For the first time, we inhabited each other's minds like all St. Claires did. It took a little getting used to, especially when there were more than two of us together. Then it was a jumble of hopes, impressions, scents, memories, fears. Too much for me to handle for an extended time.

I had learned how to shield a little, which was a mental exercise very different from my wall, but I was a novice. I had a lot to learn about being a St. Claire. After the spring line was finished, I was going to stay with Aunt Matilda for a while. Jane and me together, to learn about our gifts and how to be real St. Claires. And I was going to explore the old ways of teaching the St. Claires, with an emphasis on using stone to focus my gifts and learn how to build a shield that would give me privacy.

One little, two little, three little St. Claires, sang in my mind. *Four little, five little, six little St. Claires...* Davie grinned at me. *Seven little, eight little, nine little St. Claires...*

Ten little St. Claire psychics. I finished the song for him. *So, how many St. Claires would it take to rule the world?*

One, if you could find one in his right mind. But there are no psychics in their right minds. They're too busy sitting in other people's minds.

Ergo, no St. Claire will ever rule the world. Old joke. "You were telling me about Daddy," I prompted him.

"Sorry. I have these moments..." He looked around the loft, amazed to be here, alive.

"Me, too. A lot of these moments."

Davie rubbed his stump beneath the bandage, a mound where his finger used to be. It itched. I could feel the sensation in my own hand.

"Dad was enticed to New York City by a man who offered him a job, one with a big salary that would allow him to move us all away from the St. Claires. He didn't know it was Q Core, I don't think, though I'm not sure. He wanted a real life, I guess, away from the family, a private, normal life. At least, that's what I've always surmised," Davie said, to my unspoken questions.

"At the time I got to Q Core, Adam Wiccam was second-in-command of the department, but when Dad disappeared, Wiccam was the new head of acquisitions. That's what they called the people who went out and found and recruited new talented people to Q Core. So he was responsible for getting Dad, if he could be brought to work for them."

The cat jumped to the couch and walked across Davie, stopping to sniff the bandage. She sneezed at the smell and pawed it once, curious. Davie stroked along her head and down her back and she arched for him, purring. Liking the sensation, she settled in his lap.

"I learned that Wiccam had intended to lure Dad to New York, kidnap him, and bring him to Q Core in D.C. They had already used that method to force people to work for them, and figured they could do it again, though I never understood exactly how they did it. Dad was strongly gifted. They shouldn't have been able to convince him to leave home, shouldn't have been able to fool him, but somehow they were. They must have used someone who truly believed what they were telling him, to convince him the job offer in New York was real.

"Who knows, maybe they set up an office there and hired real people, head-blind people, to run it. His first day in New York, before Wiccam could even get to him, Dad was killed by a mugger." Davie's face was expressionless, immobile as old rock, yet I tasted his emotions, the futility, the chaos of chance. "I never did understand how someone got to him. Maybe they were stoned and he couldn't sense them clearly or Dad was distracted."

He smiled crookedly. "Then again, I got mugged, so I guess it can happen. I found records of Wiccam claiming the body, taking it to D.C." He scratched the stump again. The itching was driving me crazy, and I tried to shield myself from it. The cat rolled over and swatted at the bandage, playing.

Davie swatted back, his actions gentle, as if the cat paws didn't cause him pain when they bumped his stump.

"They autopsied him."

I turned away, refusing to see the pictures that Davie had seen. Pictures of the autopsy. I didn't remember my father and I didn't want to remember him like that. "What did they find?"

"Nothing. They never did, in any PM they ever performed on a psychic. Nothing about the physical brain of the gifted is any different from the nongifted. At least not in a post mortem."

"But?"

"With the development of MRIs and PET scans, positron-emission tomography, they discovered that when a psychic is sending or receiving images, there is increased frontal-lobe activity. A lot of activity. It looks like a lightning storm in there. Our brains are normal, but we can access them in different ways. We use them differently."

"Better? Like Superman?"

He chuckled, as I had intended him to. "No. Just different."

"And Adam Wiccam. What about him?"

Davie's smile faltered. "Jane didn't kill him. She *didn't*," he insisted when the doubt formed in my mind. "He froze to death."

"Yeah. After he ran out onto the rooftop garden and fell into the alley. After he was blitzed with something that shot from Jane's fingers. Something like lightning. Something that left a burn mark in the center of his chest, but not on his clothes." I remembered the feel of the pick buried in Gail's flesh, the sense of power as I forced her to recall specific memories.

"Stop. You did what you had to. We'll train Jane to use her gift responsibly. Train you to use yours with a bit more restraint," he said with a tender smile.

"It's a useless gift. It brings more headaches than help."

He sent me an image of the inside of a trunk. "Sometimes it helps."

"Like it helped you to know you were about to be attacked in the alley?" I said, unable to stop playing devil's advocate. "That's what started all this, the fact that the amazing, spectacular St. Claire gift didn't warn you in time."

Davie's smile widened and he rocked his head against the sofa. His lids slit with amusement. "Shall I tell you what had my attention so absorbed that I didn't sense them?"

"Let me guess," I said, unable to rein in the sarcasm that laced my words. "You met a new woman."

The sensual smile stretched Davie's mouth. "She's really something. I want you to meet her. I invited her and her aunt to dinner tomorrow night. Hope you don't mind cooking for two extra people."

I caught the humor behind his words—me, cooking—and an image of two women. One was Abby Marshall, the older woman I had heard speak at the county council meeting. The other was a younger, softer version of the tough-as-leather woman.

"Her great-niece, Naomi. I think you'll like her. And better than that, I think Jane will like her."

From within his mind, I studied the image of the young woman. She had a pretty face and a winsome smile. I had glimpsed her at the county council meeting. *Ashes and spit. You're in love again.* Suddenly I knew that the girl didn't know him yet. They hadn't even spoken. He had seen her across the room and fallen headlong in love with her. Just like he had fallen for Jannetta. I stopped my scathing retort before it could begin.

This was the first time Davie had ever brought a girl to meet me or Jane. And he was bringing her great-aunt, too? It must be serious. Very serious. Not willing to let the beginning of the argument go yet, I crossed my arms over my chest and said, "And the gold?"

Davie looked innocent, splaying his hands out in a shrug. "What gold?"

I laughed. "Right. I forgot. There never was any gold. All four boxes are missing, never to be seen again. Therefore, the gold never existed."

"Right. I have a habitat to protect, and a plan for the environment to put before the governor. There is no gold in them thar hills. None at all."

"And we may never know who shot Jubal. Isaac finds that difficult to accept," I said. "He still needs closure. He needs someone to beat up."

"Don't we all. It had to have been Madison or Boone, or maybe Feaster. All of them hunted. All had rifles. Unfortunately, all of them are dead. If the cops figure out which gun fired the shots at the scene, maybe they'll tell us. Someday. Especially as we seem to have personal access to the local cops. Is he taking the job?"

"I don't know." I could feel Evan climbing the stairs, transporting something heavy, his steps lagging behind Jane. The usual warmth flooded my limbs, settling deep inside me.

My brother grinned. "When are you going to act on those urges? You're running out of excuses. Aunt Matilda is gone, Jane and I will be heading home soon. You won't have an excuse at all then. It'll be poop or get off the pot."

"Now that is a truly disgusting image."

His grin widened. Dyno rolled to her feet, clambered over him and jumped to the floor. She sprinted to the door to meet Jane, tail upright, tip waving. The door opened. Because she didn't rush down the stairs, the cat got a treat, a morsel of salmon, which Jane bent and gave her from a Ziplock pouch kept in the cold hallway. Already the cat had learned the value of sticking around the top of the stairs.

Dyno fed, Jane sped to the sofa and fell on her father, who gathered her up in his arms and kissed her head. Bliss spread across her face and through her soul. But a hint of darkness welled up in my own mind. What must it feel like to know one was loved so utterly and completely? How safe a childhood St. Claires must have to know that kind of love. Davie and I had never had that, as St. Claires raised among the ungifted.

Jane placed a hand on her father's cheek and said, "You're not cold as 'lasses or hot as a pancake, either. Better and better." Swiveling, she kissed his cheek beside her hand.

Evan appeared in the doorway and stopped, his eyes seeking mine first. A slow grin stretched his lips. His green eyes danced like spring leaves in a torpid breeze. I felt myself grow warm and busied my hands at the sink. *Not in front of Jane.*

Why not? she wondered. *Not what in front of me?* She looked back and forth between us, curious.

"Go to Isaac and Jubal's and practice some moves," Davie said.

"More grown-up stuff," she groused. "What's the use of being able to read minds if you keep getting sent away to play when the good stuff starts?"

"Go."

"Okay. But I want to know when Aunt Tyler is going to do the big dirty and jump Uncle Evan's bones, too." Evan and Davie howled with laughter. I blushed hotly. Satisfied with our reactions, Jane ran outside and crossed the sunlit rooftop garden, banging on the door to her best friends' house.

The tenor of Davie's thoughts changed. A pliant dread whispered through him. I stepped away from the sink and looked at Evan. He was standing at the door watching us. At his feet was a wooden crate. A box just like four others that once had rested in the storeroom downstairs. It had been opened. Evan looked down at the box, his cop face on. He bent and lifted the crate. Davie's fear slithered its way into my brain and coiled there. We watched Evan as he crossed the room and set the box on the floor at Davie's feet.

"The fifth box?" Davie asked. When Evan nodded, he asked, "Where did you find it?"

He looked at me, expression sober. "In Noelle's car."

The viper of fear lifted its head, watching my soul with unblinking obsidian eyes. I shook my head in denial. "Not Noe." But the final puzzle piece fell into place.

"Your regular postman has been on vacation. Ten days in the Bahamas. This box came a day before the other four. He remembered it specifically because he pulled his back when he dropped it off and it put a damper on his trip. Noe accepted the box from him."

Tears gathered in my eyes. I turned away and took the kettle, turned on the water, hearing the echoing rattle of water on copper. The lop-eared bunny stared at me from the high window ledge. I had rescued Uncle Will's carving from the corner of the trunk and placed it here, where I could remember the man who whittled it for me. I touched the satiny smooth wood.

Evan placed the box on the ottoman at Davie's feet. "So far as we know, Hornsburn didn't plan, or even know about David's kidnapping. He had been after David to sell his land and call off his plan for the animal refuge. David had been talking to Julian Rakes Mining to see if there was any way to safely remove the gold without harming the environment."

"There isn't," Davie said. "No way."

"Roman Trio, its underworld leaders and its money-laundering plans were never involved with David or his kidnapping. They were after Hornsburn, who owed them money and hadn't paid, and they finally caught up with him inside Rakes's headquarters."

Evan watched me, wisely not coming near. Giving me

time to process the betrayal that was coming at me, flying at me, a hammer of broken faith. "Noe knew about the gold before you did. She must have opened all the boxes and seen the gold, read the papers. Enough to know she couldn't find it on her own. So she called in her girlhood friends, Eloise and Gail. And she knew Harry Boone would do anything to get back at you. She kept one box for herself. Set up the kidnapping. She ran it all from the shop."

And I never knew.... I turned off the water, put the kettle on the burner, and turned on the flame, my movements slow, deliberate and oh, so careful. The kettle sizzled, a soothing sound. I braced myself against the cabinet top, the sharp edge digging into my palms. "Where is she?"

"She's being processed now, charged along with Eloise and Gail, probably with conspiracy, kidnapping. Murder, if the evidence in Blythe's or Quinn's death warrants it."

I turned to him. At my puzzled look he said, "Blythe. Your brown man. Though it's possible that all the deaths point to Roman Trio, not your friend."

My friend.

"Noe will be housed here in town until bail is set." He paused. "I don't recommend that you visit her."

Feeling as if I had been punched in the gut, I went to the far door and looked out at the rooftop garden where Jane was sparring with Isaac, both of them bundled against the cold, laughing like maniacs.

So much for the St. Claire family gift. Psychics-R-Us fails me again. As usual, being a receptor for the mental and emotional feedback of others hadn't saved me from danger or prevented bad things from happening. It hadn't let me see the evil in the heart of my friend because I hadn't known to look. Hadn't let me save my brother before he was tortured because I hadn't suspected Noelle. My St. Claire gift hadn't let me do much of anything useful.

You got me back. Alive.

I smiled without turning around.

And Jane is safe. That's enough for me, Brat.

Evan came around behind me and slid his arms through mine, pulling me close. I felt his warmth, his solid goodness. I rested my head back against him. Carefully I opened myself to him. His mind met mine with a soft tone of joy, the color of a rising sun, golden and full of hope.

On the rooftop garden, Jubal emerged, balancing a tray with one hand, carrying a pitcher, six glasses and a plate of cookies. He looked up and nodded his head from me to the table in the sunshine. Suddenly I remembered my wistful thought, when I saw Jane with Davie, basking in his love—it would be wonderful to know I was loved like that, so completely.

I hadn't realized it, but I was.

A Dr. Morgan Snow novel

M. J. ROSE

The Scarlet Society is a secret club of twelve powerful and sexually adventurous women. But when a photograph of the body of one of the men they've recruited to dominate—strapped to a gurney, the number 1 inked on the sole of his foot—is sent to the *New York Times*, they are shocked and frightened. Unable to cope with the tragedy, the women turn to Dr. Morgan Snow. But what starts out as grief counseling quickly becomes a murder investigation, with any one of the twelve women a potential suspect.

THE DELILAH COMPLEX

New York Times **bestselling author**

JENNIFER BLAKE

Lisette Moisant is a widow, courtesy of the swordsmanship of
Caid O'Neill. He bested her loathsome husband in a duel, but
now she is a target for schemers who wish to steal her fortune and
see her dead. It is Caid to whom she turns for protection, and
guilt leaves him no recourse but to agree to Lisette's request.

But soon New Orleans is flooded with rumors, suggesting the
two plotted to kill Lisette's husband all along. In a society where
reputation is everything, the scandal threatens Lisette and Caid
with ruin…and the person responsible will stop at nothing until
they have paid with their lives.

Dawn Encounter

"The first in
Blake's new series
evokes everything alluring
about New Orleans."
—*Romantic Times BOOKclub* on *Challenge to Honor*

Available the first week of January 2006 wherever paperbacks are sold!

A SALLY HARRINGTON NOVEL

MR. MURDER

LAURA VAN WORMER

Sally Harrington may be growing up, but she isn't settling down.

Sally Harrington starts her new job anchoring a newscast created just for her: DBS News America This Morning. For most people that would be enough excitement. But not for Sally. She has to be the last person to talk to a jet-setting millionaire who turns up dead shortly after their interview.

While Sally is trying to sort out her feelings for two men, an old acquaintance is found barely alive in her home in Connecticut. Then this attempted murder is connected to the death of Sally's infamous millionaire. And by the time anyone realizes that Sally herself might be the primary target, it may be too late to stop a killer from achieving his ultimate goal.

> **"Laura Van Wormer specializes in creating smart heroines with glamorous jobs and a knack for solving complicated murder mysteries."**—*New York Times Book Review*

Available the first week of January 2006 wherever hardcover books are sold!